MISS McGHEE

BY

BETT NORRIS

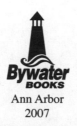

Bywater BOOKS

Ann Arbor
2007

Bywater Books, Inc.
PO Box 3671
Ann Arbor MI 48106-3671

First Bywater Books Edition: May 2007

Cover designer: Bonnie Liss (Phoenix Graphics)

10-digit ISBN 1-932859-33-0
13-digit ISBN 978-1-932859-33-1

All people, places, and events (other than actual historical persons and events) are products of the author's admittedly somewhat warped imagination. I can move mountains, roads, and rivers, so I did. If you think you recognize yourself in these pages, you are so wrong. You're all much nicer in real life.

Acknowledgments

I grew up in Alabama, just down the road a piece from where Miss Lee still lives. It calls me, and I return as often as I can.

There are many people who contributed to this effort and to the story. First, there are friends and family, all of whom listened to me talk endlessly about this, who read and gave invaluable feedback, including Angie, Lori, Shellie, Terry, Robert, Pat, Amanda, Sue (and her son John, who gave me Miss McGhee's name), Helen, Marge, and Julie.

Then there are many professional people without whose support and encouragement this book would not be what it is: first, Cynn Chadwick, a writer of extraordinary ability, whose "get off your ass and do it" is still the best advice I ever got; Val McDermid, whose generous contribution is much appreciated, Connie Conway, a writer's editor who taught me so much, and whose encouragement and enthusiasm taught me to love the editing process; Katherine V. Forrest, whose work inspired me and whose advice and support for an unknown writer meant everything; and Kelly Smith and Marianne K. Martin of Bywater Books, whose ability to see what I was trying to say, and whose patience and skill brought this novel into being. Also to Mandy Woods, a copy editor who goes above and beyond.

Finally, I'd like to thank Sandy Moore, my partner and an artist of great insight and whose understanding of the creative process and whose encouragement and unfailing support and faith made this book possible. Her contribution cannot be measured.

This book is dedicated to all those strong ladies who never married and who somehow made their own way in the world in a time when it was not easy to do so.

Part One

Chapter One

REPORT TO THE GRAND DRAGON: I thank you for coming down and helping us form our Klavern. We never had any trouble here, but it's good to be organized and ready.

Monday, April 5, 1948

FEAR GOD.

Mary McGhee had seen the hand-painted sign nailed to a fence post along the highway on her bus ride from Mobile to Myrtlewood. She couldn't get it out of her head. It haunted her as she found a place to live and unpacked, getting ready to start her new job. That ominous warning was chilling, as though it marked a border between the real world and this new alien place. She rode in a bus that smelled of diesel exhaust, watching the appealing countryside go by her window, the cows munching placidly on the grass, already green and growing, with buttercups and wild daisies and black-eyed Susans waving on the shoulders of US Highway 43, and then that sign, black lettering on a whitewashed board, that rang with a kind of cautionary reproach.

Mary felt alien herself as she walked along the cracked sidewalk, and admitted that she was dressed inappropriately for the south Alabama weather. It was hot for so early in spring. Oh, well. She wanted to present a certain image, at least at first. She pushed open the door of the Early Bird Diner and surveyed the establishment. Sitting alone at a table or a booth didn't appeal to her, so she took a seat at the counter. The waitress, a very young girl with pale skin and freckles, seemed self-appointed to glean information.

"You're the new secretary for the lumber mill. Stayin' at Miss Louise's, I heard. She driving you crazy yet?" The girl fairly leaned over the counter studying Mary's face. "What can I get for you?"

"Just coffee, I think." Mary stared at the girl, but any hope she had of embarrassing her into silence was dashed. *I must be losing my touch.*

A heavy white ceramic mug appeared in front of her, with a chip in the rim and a grainy crack running down its side. To her displeasure, the girl lingered after supplying a napkin and spoon.

"Guess you met Mr. Tommie already?"

"No, I haven't."

"You'll sure have to watch him. I heard he's showing up at the mill every day, like his daddy, poor fella. He must think he's the boss now. That wife of his, now that's another story I could tell you about. Can I get you some cream with that?"

"No, thank you. Black is fine."

"Well, you just let me know if you want anything. I'm Gloria, by the way. The pie's fresh today. You might be wantin' some—Miss Louise ain't much of a cook."

Mary sipped the coffee rather more quickly than she had intended, and gave up any thought she might have had about taking her meals there. Gloria of the freckled face moved off, but still stared without embarrassment at Mary, who suppressed a sigh. Her landlady, who insisted on being called "Miss Louise," was the same way. In fact, every stranger Mary met was quick to ask personal questions, as well as to share all they had heard about her. People would soon get used to her, she hoped. She stared at herself in the mirror behind the counter and saw an attractive young woman of twenty-eight with a sort of prim beauty a possessive father would approve of and told herself to bring a book or a newspaper if she came again.

Gloria occupied herself at the cash register at the far end of the counter, not even trying to hide her curiosity. The door opened with a jangle from the bell, and she greeted the new customer. "Hey, Mr. Wilson, Miz Wilson throw you out already this morning? Set yourself down, then." Mary observed what must have been a ritual as Gloria plopped coffee in front of the wizened man who joined her at the counter, and watched in horror as he proceeded to fill his cup to over-flowing with milk, then spoon some of it into a saucer from which he slurped while the coffee in the cup cooled. She would have thrown the man out of the house too, if he did that every morning.

Looking around the diner with the help of the mirror, Mary realized

4

she was the only woman in the place, save the waitress. Gloria busied herself with the coffee pot, walking around and refilling everyone's cup, standing for a moment at a table of sleepy men with her hand on the shoulder of one. "That there's your new boss, Clyde. Best finish up and get to work on time today." Clyde, a hulking individual, shrugged off her friendly pat and stated, "Vince is the boss. And long as he's settin' right here, I don't see no need to hurry."

Another jangle as two women entered and took up a booth, looking somewhat ill at ease, Mary thought, as they checked the table for cleanliness, settled their purses on the seat beside them and pulled menus from behind the condiment tray, glancing through them with interest. They weren't regular customers. The way Gloria hurried over to provide silverware and place mats and actually took her order pad out of her pocket confirmed that this was an unusual event. Mary resisted the urge to smooth her skirt and tug on her jacket. She just sat up straighter and kept her eyes on her coffee.

"Yes'm, that's her. What can I get for ya'll today?" Gloria stood and waited.

"You have any doughnuts left?" a tall, thin woman inquired, wearing what Mary thought of as a Sunday hat. Did one wear a hat to eat breakfast in a diner? "I feel positively sinful, but I guess if it's all right for half the men in town to lounge around here every morning, I suppose we can indulge ourselves for once."

The waitress hustled off to the kitchen. After a few seconds of nudging from her companion, the thin woman got up and approached Mary. "How do you do? You must be Miss McGhee. We'd heard they were getting someone new to work in the office at the mill. I'm Melissa Carpenter."

Mary stared at the gloved hand offered to her, and shook it briefly. "Hello. Nice to meet you."

"Well. We just thought to say hello, welcome you to Myrtlewood, you know. I can't imagine Miss Louise has been very conscientious about introducing you. She stays at home, mostly. You know." The woman hesitated. "Well, anyway, I'm at the town hall. If you need anything, be sure to drop by."

Unable to imagine what on earth she'd ever require of the town hall, Mary said, "Thank you, I will." She picked up her cup as a signal

5

to end the woman's hesitance. With a slight nod, Melissa Carpenter, town hall employee and apparent purveyor of official welcomes, returned to her booth. Mary heard whispering immediately.

"Well, just what would you have said? I didn't see you jumping in."

The second member of the gloved and hatted league spoke somewhat louder. "At least we know how to dress when we come to town. She looks like she's wearing a uniform, like those WACs or something. The war's been over for three years. My word, nobody wears suits like that any more."

Mary stopped herself from glancing down at her suit, one of her best. True, it was a little worn, a navy blue gabardine that had seen better days. The jacket had been made over from a man's suit, in accordance with wartime directives and a Butterick pattern, with darts converting it into a fitted look that emphasized the shoulder pads she didn't need. Her figure unfortunately lent itself to the style, with wide shoulders, narrow waist and hips. She wished she had the same curves as Maureen O'Hara, to whom she had been compared more than once, though she knew the comparison had less to do with physical resemblance and more with the temper she never much bothered to conceal. She sneaked a look at the two women and their attire. Loose, A-line skirts gathered with wide belts, blouses with wide collars and lace. And heels of more than the suggested one inch during the years of rationing and making do. Mary herself still adhered to those wartime standards, but apparently the women in Myrtlewood had wasted no time reverting back to an extravagance of hem length and material. She was proud of her efforts to economize and contribute to the war effort. The day before had been spent unpacking her professional clothes, shaking them out, getting ready for Monday and her first day at a new job.

Gloria came back with their orders and nodded in Mary's direction. "Ya'll make friends yet?"

"Hush, Gloria, my word, the whole world can hear you."

Mary finished her coffee and left two dimes, the second one as a tip. She stood, taking her time, and slowly withdrew gloves from her purse and pulled them on. Settling her purse in the crook of her arm, she turned, nodded at the ladies, and walked out. The tight feeling between her shoulder blades didn't ease until she turned the corner.

"How you doing, Miss McGhee? You settling in all right down at Miss Skinner's? Don't you let that old lady talk your ear off now. You give an inch, she'll have you doing her yard work for her. She outright lies about her rheumatism. She's healthy as a horse," said Mr. Howard Butler at the drugstore, where Mary had stopped to buy some aspirin. When she offered no response, he went on, though in a more quiet and kindly manner than she had just endured at the diner.

"Wait till you meet Mr. Tommie. He's something, I tell you. Spitting image of his daddy, finer man never lived, Mr. Dubose I mean. He was awful proud of his boy. Took him everywhere." Refusing to respond to the man's speculative, though benevolent, expression, Mary paid for her aspirin and left with only a nod. Why was everyone so eager for her to meet her new employer?

A brief meeting with the bank president, Gerald Buchanan, had left her feeling uneasy as well. He was apparently the executor of Dubose's estate and the meeting had left Mary with the firm belief that she wouldn't trust the man with a nickel, much less an estate.

"I 'spect you'll find everything in a mess over there," he had said. "Think you can get everything cleaned up and organized?"

"I'm sure I can. I imagine Mr. Dubose is anxious to get everything in order."

Mr. Buchanan gave a snort of derision. "Oh, Tommie, he'll be in and out. I wouldn't expect too much help from him though."

Why not? Surely the man was concerned about getting his business running smoothly again? She held her silence while Buchanan stared at her rudely, as though estimating whether she was up to the task. His eyes were too bold, his demeanor too condescending.

"Seems a little strange to me that you'd take a job so far away. You come highly recommended by Sam Stewart, but nobody 'round here's ever heard of the man, except Mrs. Dubose, I guess. The name don't mean anything to me. Just so you know, Mrs. Dubose has nothing to do with the mill. I been tryin' to help her out. But this man from Texas calls her, and the next thing you know, we got us a secretary here for the office. We'll see how it goes, all right?"

Mary left the interview feeling vaguely insulted and somewhat confused about just who was in charge. She didn't like the man. He had looked at her as if she were something in a specimen jar, barely disguising his disgust. And there was something else in his eyes that she didn't like: he seemed secretly amused, but maybe he smirked that way at everything.

When she stopped to buy two red apples from a man selling fresh produce off the back of his truck on the corner, she recognized the man as Mr. Wilson from the diner. The farmer, a small, bent little man, launched into his own narrative that apparently required little encouragement from her.

"Name's Wilson. Saw you down to the diner, didn't want to bother you. You looked like you had something on your mind, kind of preoccupied, you know? I don't like to intrude on a person's thoughts. You doin' all right today?" He thrust out a gnarled, arthritic hand with swollen knuckles. Mary tried not to stare, but there was no way she was going to shake that hand. Instead she simply touched it briefly with her fingers. This pleased the little man no end, as though she had met some sort of challenge. "You're that secretary from out in Texas, that right? Them people out there, they still raise them longhorn cattle, don't they? Ever come across some real cowboys out there?"

Mary wanted to push the old man off the tailgate of his rusted-out Ford, but instead reminded herself that she had chosen to accept this job in a small town where everyone was curious, albeit some obsessively. Ignoring the sharp pain as she recalled the only real "cowboy" she had ever met, she said, "No, Mr. Wilson, I worked in an office, in a city. I was told that some ranchers still keep longhorns though, mostly for tradition."

The grizzled man again seemed pleased that she had responded. Mary gathered that most people probably tried to avoid starting conversations with him. He shot a hand into the air, thumb up. "See, what'd I say? Just 'cause you see them longhorns in the movies don't mean that's what they raise out there."

Five minutes later, she had managed to extricate herself from a conversation the contentious Mr. Wilson conducted without her input about the verisimilitude of Hollywood movies. She headed home to Miss Louise's, gratefully closing the door against the gauntlet of inquisition, only to find she could not escape until she had satisfied the old lady's curiosity about a number of things.

"Did they start repaving the road downtown? City council said they would, but I don't recall seeing the trucks go by."

Mary shook her head. Miss Louise, oblivious to Mary's disinterest and impatience, prattled on. The living room, with ancient, worn furniture covered in hand-stitched doilies and family photographs on every available surface, was dusty and smelled. It seemed that nothing would succeed except endurance.

"Seems like everybody's still using the war shortages as an excuse not to get back to work, if you ask me. Dr. Morgan told me those potholes nearly tore up his car, and him on his way to see about somebody sick."

Mary agreed that the streets should be kept in repair, that the city council was remiss in its duties, that it was a shame some people couldn't seem to realize that the war was over, and of course the Depression had certainly affected everyone, but things were different now. She excused herself and left Miss Louise to her radio.

On Monday morning Mary arrived at seven thirty to find the door to the office locked. She hadn't thought to ask the banker about keys. While she was standing there, wondering what she should do, one of the men in the sawmill yard broke away from the group and approached her.

"Mornin'," he said, nodding as he dug in his pocket and came up with a set of keys. He found the right one and unlocked the door for her. "I'm Vince Dunn, the mill foreman."

She offered her hand to him and said, "Mary McGhee. How do you do?"

The man just looked at her hand, and then raised his eyes to meet hers. "I do just fine. I heard you met with Buchanan down at the bank."

"Yes, I did." She couldn't figure out if the man was resentful or just naturally gruff. He was frowning at her.

"Well, that man don't know how to pour piss out of a boot. I hope you know something about shuffling papers around. We ain't been paid regular in months."

Mary opened her mouth in surprise, matching the man's frown with one of her own. How on earth could anyone let a business go downhill like this? Why hadn't Tommie Dubose seen to it? Why hadn't the banker taken care of it? "Mr. Dunn, I'll look into the payroll, first thing. I know all about shuffling papers."

After staring deeply into her eyes for a few more seconds, he reluctantly handed her the keys and nodded. Touching his cap, he said, "We'll see, won't we? Things couldn't get much worse, anyhow."

Mary watched him walk away before releasing the breath she had held, and opened the door. Along one wall was a row of wooden file cabinets, while another held huge, floor-to-ceiling windows overlooking the work yard of the sawmill where she could already hear men coughing and talking in early morning voices, the southern accents still new but appealing to her. The outer office showed a film of dust on every surface, confirming that nothing had been touched in quite a while. Though the secretary's desk appeared to sag under the weight of tall stacks of papers, Mary glimpsed the clean surface on the desk in the inner office. She found a typewriter and an adding machine on a second desk and her hands revealed no nervousness as she smoothed the green leather blotter inlaid on the fine oak desk.

Tommie Dubose burst through the front door of the Dubose Lumber & Supply office, startling her. He was a handsome man, about thirty years of age, but dressed somewhat sloppily in a business suit, his light brown hair still wet from its early morning combing, with his tie slightly askew, his belt buckle off center. To Mary, he looked as though he had dressed hurriedly. The yellow shirt and flowered pattern of the tie did not match each other or the double-breasted blue suit that appeared a bit too large for him. His handsome face was split by a huge grin. Mary was struck by the impression of a schoolboy on the first day of school. His shoes were shined, she noted. He greeted her with an overly loud, overly cheerful, rehearsed tone that struck her as odd.

"You're bright and early for the first day! Have you found everything you need? I can show you where everything is, supply room, bathroom, all that. I'll just get myself a cup of coffee and we'll get started. Things are in a mess since Miss Jones left. She worked for my daddy. He's gone too."

His voice trailed off as Mary handed him a cup of coffee. He stared at it as though she had conjured it from the air. He seemed as nervous as she felt about him. She was struck by the childish quality of his speech and demeanor. When she spoke, he jumped and almost spilled his coffee.

"I've already made coffee, and I found the supply room on my own. I'm ready to begin when you are. I assume your correspondence is behind. Should we start with that?"

Mary stood with her pen and pad, hoping to steer the man toward the inner office. She ached to organize the leaning stacks of papers and mail that completely covered the secretary's desk, but Dubose appeared to be somewhat anxious about being in close proximity to this disorder. Perhaps, she thought, he was afraid she would quit at the sight of it. He might, she thought, be more comfortable in his own office, where the massive desk was suspiciously clean. But he seemed reluctant to get down to work, as though dreading it. She hoped it was only because of the backlog, and not because of disinterest. Mary could not tolerate laziness or inefficiency. She moved into his office and stepped closer to his desk, refusing to sit in the chair opposite his and give up the small advantage her height gave her. She found that erect posture and high heels were sometimes a great equalizer, deflating male arrogance as well as deflecting male attention.

"Where do we start? Let's see now ..." his voice trailed off. Mary decided it was not embarrassment at the clutter. The man really did not know what to do. She knew he had taken over the business from his late father. Beginning to be irritated, Mary returned to the secretary's desk, peeled the top layer off each stack and began sorting.

"Let's start with these," she said. Dubose stood in the same spot with the coffee cup in his hand.

Mary mentally kicked him as she waited. "Maybe you'd prefer to give me a couple of hours to get things in order? Then we can sort through the most urgent things. I suppose you need to be down in the lumber yard getting the men started."

She continued to briskly sort files and envelopes. Dubose pulled on his tie as if it were strangling him. His eyes darted around the room, refusing to look directly at Mary. He smoothed his hair, and accepted her offer to leave with obvious relief.

"That's a good idea. I need to get to the mill and watch the log trucks go out. Daddy kept things neat. I'll be back later, okay? I'll help, I really will. Annie says I could be a big help to you." The man looked as though he had been called into the principal's office and could not wait to get out.

"Thank you. This way I'll have some time to settle in."

Mary turned away from him, unable to watch his faltering for a minute longer. Any moment now, he was going to break out in perspiration. He was like a schoolboy, she decided, worried about his homework. With a cursory nod, she turned her attention to the stacks of files. Here was a bigger challenge than she had supposed on accepting the job. Things were in complete disarray. Some minutes passed, with Mary so absorbed as she dug through the paper wreckage of the business that she barely noticed Dubose leaving. Her uneasiness about his strangely childlike behavior was pushed aside.

She sorted and read through unpaid invoices, unanswered letters, and dunning letters from creditors. It appeared that nothing had been done in several months. Soon she found a footing and made a plan. She discovered the company checkbook but resisted the impulse to start making out checks until she could get a good look at the books. Then she drafted letters to all the creditors, a sort of generic announcement that the company was under new management and all accounts would be brought current.

She had everything ready for Dubose's signature when he returned shortly before noon and stood staring at her now clean and organized desk. Mary walked over to him, taking him by the arm.

"I have everything neat and ready for you now. Just like your daddy liked it." She led him into the inner office where her letters lay awaiting approval and signature. "You sit here, all right? I have some papers for you to sign." She pulled out the chair for him and gave him the ornamental pen from the brass penholder on the desk.

"Just sign your name where I put the red X. That's right. And here and here."

Dubose seemed delighted with the signing process, and made no effort to read anything at all. He nodded and signed as she explained

12

what each document was, but soon she dispensed with descriptions and just indicated where to place his signature. He took some care, forming each letter in a scrawled cursive that looked like a third grader's best effort. This time she paid scant attention to his strange behavior. Entirely absorbed by her work, she no longer cared to solve the mystery of Tommie Dubose. He was now simply someone she had to help function, as she needed to get her job done.

"Thank you very much, Mr. Dubose. I have a lot of work to do this afternoon. Perhaps you could come in tomorrow morning and help me again?"

He nodded eagerly and left. Mary turned to the company books now, eyeing the file cabinets. She shuddered to think what she might find there.

And yet she reveled in the sad state of affairs at this business where she had taken a job. The not-inconsiderable skills of one Mary McGhee were desperately needed here. She would be very busy. The business would be put to rights. Her employer might not be a help, but neither would he be a hindrance. Soon she would have the place functioning as an office should.

That night after work, Mary allowed herself to be waylaid by Miss Louise. Diverted from her plan of a long, hot bath and a quick sandwich, she found herself cooking a meal for both of them, accompanied by the constant chatter of the little landlady who seemed genuinely lonely. There was something a bit sad about Miss Louise, her odd manner of dress just one indication of her lack of interaction with the other ladies of the town: her white hair was haphazardly pulled back into a bun, hastily pinned up each morning in her eagerness to get outside to her station on the front porch. She was attired in a shapeless, faded house dress that had seen better days, over which she wore, despite the increasing warmth these days of spring were bringing, a sweater full of holes, its pockets sagging with things she kept stuffed in there—Mary had seen her pull handkerchiefs and keys from those pockets, and a tin of snuff. Even bits of leaves and roots emerged, found, the old lady explained, on her strolls through the yard. Her fingernails had dirt under them and were yellowing with age, and on her feet were house slippers with the heels worn away.

The thick, flesh-colored stockings she wore rolled down to just below her knees were the same Mary's grandmother had worn. The wrinkled face had bright eyes that shone with interest in Mary's every move as she set about preparing their dinner, which Mary had learned was called supper in the South, and which she had persuaded Miss Louise to let her cook.

Miss Louise sat at the kitchen table, as Mary moved around the unfamiliar kitchen. "I reckon you know by now about Mr. Tommie. The way his daddy babied him is the biggest part of what's wrong with him. Like a poor little rich boy. He could do a lot more, if you ask me. Being coddled like he was his whole life is what retarded him."

Mary did not want to discuss Tommie Dubose. "Miss Louise, where do you keep your skillet?" She'd cook something quick: a couple of pork chops and a salad would do.

"The cabinet next to the sink. That man is not as slow as people around here make out, especially that Buchanan at the bank. He's always been jealous of the Duboses, Tommie especially. Them two was in school together, before Tommie's daddy took him out and kept him at home, when he was about twelve or fourteen, I reckon it was."

Mary tore the iceberg lettuce, chopped some garden tomatoes and peppers, swiftly mixed a dressing, then turned the chops and prepared a plate. "I'm just here to do a job. Past history and imagined slights don't really concern me."

"Sweetie, just fix yourself something. I couldn't eat a bite. Been out in the yard all day. I believe I got too hot."

Forcibly restraining her tone, Mary said, "You might want some tea, then, and some of this salad."

Mary put a pork chop on Miss Louise's plate just the same, and took a couple of bites of her meal, but the headache she'd fought all day had returned and her appetite couldn't compete. She got up to run water in the sink, soaking the skillet. Miss Louise managed to finish her plate in record time, despite her testimony as to the heat and its effect on her appetite. She went to hand it to Mary at the sink, but instead, without even a show of embarrassment, slid Mary's leftovers onto her plate and finished them off too. Mary washed up, hung the dishtowel on the oven door, and began rolling down her sleeves.

"Child, you look as tired as I feel. Why don't you go on to your rooms now? No point in you cleaning up after a day's work. I used to fix supper for my daddy, after my mama got too feeble in her mind. I 'spect I could do the same for you, since you're a working woman. You go on now." She smiled, but seemed to be reflecting on old memories. "I 'magine looking after Mr. Tommie will be as tiresome as feeding and bathing my mama was. Reckon you see by now what you're up against."

Mary certainly did see. She left the kitchen with the old woman still ruminating. She closed her door and loosened her clothing, lighting her first cigarette of the day. Opening the window, she sat on the sill in the darkness. The fragrance of the wisteria and gardenias that grew wildly in Miss Louise's side yard did not seem so cloying as it had her first night here. Now it was soothing. She inhaled deeply, and the cooling night air refreshed her. She had been shut inside the Dubose office, with its distinct smell of old paper, ink, and dust, all day. It had the stuffiness and feel of a room that had been closed for a long time. Tomorrow she would work on getting the floor-to-ceiling windows opened to let in some air. The heat would be stifling in the upstairs rooms, she thought, anticipating the long summer ahead. She breathed in and exhaled slowly, letting go of her irritation with Miss Louise and her annoyance with the stares of the people she had passed on her walk to and from work.

She didn't know if she could tolerate the undisguised curiosity and the sense of wait-and-see much longer. She longed for the anonymity of a large city. She'd grown up in a small town, and understood how they worked, the initial distrust of strangers, the gradual acceptance. But she didn't really want acceptance. She wanted to be left alone, not taken in and granted membership in this closed society that had nothing to offer her.

There was an eagerness that bordered on anxiety about the casual greetings and nods she had encountered. She already knew after one day's research that the mill was in a bad state. But it was the largest business in the area, so maybe there was concern about it being put in the hands of an outsider, and a woman. Well, it wouldn't be the first time she'd had to deal with that.

She thought about the silent Negroes she had seen in town, none of whom had spoken a word to her. The men, most in overalls with long-sleeved shirts buttoned at the throat and wrist, would step off the sidewalk and touch their hats as she passed them on the street. The women never met her eyes, but they moved aside as she passed and silently crossed their arms. She hadn't seen any Negro children at all out enjoying the spring weather like the white children she had encountered, and this she found particularly odd.

One little redheaded girl clung to the fence at the corner of Mary's street every evening. The girl was very thin, freckled, and dirty. One of the numerous Jackson children, Miss Louise had said with a sniff of disdain. The name meant nothing to Mary, of course, though to her landlady it seemed to carry the mark of the devil. The small sentinel with her ragged dress hadn't spoken until today after work.

"Miss McGhee, how you doin'?" The little girl had said, her voice piping out and startling Mary enough to slow her down. "My mama says you got a big mess to straighten out, but she don't see what one woman alone can do. She says there ain't a chance in a hunnerd a woman can set that lumber yard back to rights. It's a man's job. They ought to have hired a man, my mama says. Like my daddy, he could do it. His sister owns the whole thing anyway, and she ought to have got one of her brothers to look after it for her, that's what my mama said." By the time Mary was well past the child, she could still hear her spouting what was surely a learned speech.

Mary put out her cigarette, closed the window and decided to forego the hot bath. She undressed and got into bed. In the dark, her mind returned to the job. There certainly was plenty of work, enough to take home nights and weekends and keep her from thinking about the past. She had solved the problem of picking over wounds that had not yet healed. She was too exhausted for that. This job had given her the luxury of gaining perspective, the prospect of taking an unsentimental survey when she was ready to confront the past.

But now was too soon. Looking back now would only lead to self-pity and self-doubt, tears and sleepless nights. Mary had no patience for that, however real or recent her pain, believing that indulgence only increased one's capacity for it. She had indulged in enough tears and anguish, and her hard-won discipline would not allow for more. This job was perfect.

Chapter Two

REPORT TO THE GRAND DRAGON: We initiated two new Ghouls. That makes a total of four. I appointed one as our Klabee. We're getting ready for our first gathering tonight.

Sunday, April 18, 1948

Lila Dubose paused in the hallway, holding her gloves in one hand, wondering if she should check her hair one more time. Though Annie did her best with it, inevitably, what began as stylish and sleek deteriorated into frizzy and uncontrolled by the time she reached church, only just across the street. It was the humidity, unusual in mid-spring, and the recalcitrant nature of her black curls reacted to the slightest change in atmosphere by stubbornly returning to their unruly state. She wished hairstyles would change to something she could approximate herself. She would be late if she tried to force her hair into obedience, and she wouldn't have Tommie as an excuse.

She smoothed a hand down the material of her dress. Lila admired the clothes her late father-in-law had insisted on ordering for her from Atlanta. They were expensive, conservative, and by far the most elegant things she had ever owned, but she always felt like she was playing dress-up when she wore them. Now that Mr. Dubose was gone, she missed his companionship and advice and the validation that his presence lent her. He had been more of a real father to her than her own had ever been. He'd always been kind, considerate of her feelings, especially devoted to Tommie and, like Lila, he had enjoyed church. She wondered if it would be easier to attend the Baptist church across town, where her own family made infrequent visits. But that wouldn't look quite right. She was a member of the Methodist church now. The Duboses had belonged to it since before the Civil War, and now she was the only Dubose left to continue the

17

tradition, as Tommie had once again simply refused to go, as he did more and more often these days.

She made one last inspection in the hall mirror, and suppressed a sneer at her reflection: she still saw a poor, barefoot country girl with gray eyes, made up to convince folks she fit the part as the wife of the most prominent man in town. Lila saw an over-powdered face, mascara applied too thickly, lipstick of a shade she did not like, and hair threatening to spring back into its natural wild state if she didn't hurry. Four years ago, dressed like a princess in a fairy tale, she'd been marched down the aisle of the church she now attended alone by a momentarily sober and shaved father whose hand on her arm had shaken with the need for a drink, and everything had changed. How had she convinced herself she could play such a part in this farce of a marriage? She could not remember. Whatever it was she sought, it would not be found here, in her own reflection. She picked up her purse and went downstairs.

She settled into her usual pew just as the service began, but could not settle her mind to listen. This town sometimes reminded her of a fiefdom. Right now, for instance, just when she longed for some uninterrupted time to think, the woman sitting next to her was dipping her wide-brimmed hat in Lila's direction, as if Lila were some kind of royalty, getting Lila's and everyone else's attention.

"How're you today, Miz Dubose?" whispered Nancy Dunn, whose husband Vince was the foreman at the Dubose mill. Vince and his father and grandfather had been loyal employees since the mill was started, right after the Civil War. Their families had sat next to the Duboses in church for as long as Dubose Lumber had been in existence. Lila wondered what would happen if she walked in some Sunday and sat somewhere else; she couldn't imagine the consternation it would cause. No chance at all for her to sit next to someone new, or slip in and sit in the back. It simply wasn't done.

"How's your little Katie?" Lila whispered back to Nancy. She knew as well as everyone that a bout of measles had run through the school children.

"She's almost well now. Thank the Lord, she can go back to school tomorrow. I love my children, but staying shut up in the house with all of 'em sick is trying. I'm sure you'll be finding that out for yourself someday." Nancy, whose tight permanent made Lila's head ache, beamed with parental fortitude.

Lila flushed, and quickly turned her head toward the podium, where Bill Sullivan, his high, shining forehead gleaming, waited for the congregation to settle its focus on him. What on earth was the woman thinking? Surely no one in town believed that she and Tommie would ever—the whole town knew and understood what Tommie was. They couldn't think she would ... Or maybe they did. Maybe they even *expected* it.

Lila tried to focus on the sermon. She liked the new pastor, though she knew many of the others had not yet warmed to him. Pastor Sullivan was young, a war veteran, tall and distinguished, and subtle about sneaking humor into his sermons. He actually smiled sometimes while preaching, and this unsettled more than a few: the congregation was used to stern and serious declamations.

Smoothing a wrinkle from her dress, Lila imagined that people were beginning to believe she was as simple-minded as Tommie, but without the benevolent attitude toward him that they all copied from his father. She was sure they talked about her constantly. There was nothing else for them to do, except speculate that she was either a scheming, money-hungry predator, or too slow to understand and take advantage of her situation now that Mr. Dubose was gone. She knew perfectly well that when she had first come to live as Tommie's wife, rumors had flown that it was actually the elder Dubose who was her lover and that it was Annie who had, through her extensive network of friends, other maids, storekeepers, and the Negro community as a whole, put that salacious story to rest. It was true that she had spent very little of the fortune at her disposal, and that was probably evidence enough for some to judge her stupid, if not retarded herself.

The one smart thing she had done was agree to hire someone to manage the mill. She recalled the strange conversation she had had with a friend of Mr. Dubose from Houston. Sam Stewart had called one day, just to find out how things were going, he said. His excessively hearty voice had boomed in her ear through the phone line.

"Honey, if I had the time, I'd be glad to come down there myself and give you a hand. I guess sellin' the whole thing's out of the question. Tell you what I can do for you though. What you need is an organizer, someone who knows all about getting your office running right, gets the money coming in and going out like it should, somebody who's a whiz with that sort of thing. I can send my girl, Miss McGhee. Don't know what I would have done without her during the war."

Lila knew about the war effort and how it had affected the Dubose mill. Her father-in-law had nearly worked himself to death during the war, trying to keep up with the impact of huge government contracts. So she had accepted Sam Stewart's offer, though she was still somewhat surprised that he had thought to call a confused young woman who had found herself in the position of guarding something of an empire. She was certain the new secretary would find the Dubose holdings small potatoes after working for Big Sam's oil business.

Lila had yet to meet this Miss McGhee, though Annie had tried to get her to attend the interview. Gerald Buchanan, the banker who oversaw their accounts, had urged her to be there with him, but he seemed too eager or something. After all, the interview was just a formality. Big Sam had already arranged it. Lila wondered what sort of inducement or loyalty could have motivated Mary McGhee to accept a job sight unseen.

After the first day of dressing up, trying to sit still in the office while Miss McGhee had no doubt worked around him, Tommie had come home in a quite agitated state. "She's tall!" he had exclaimed. Lila interpreted this to mean intimidating. Still, Miss McGhee had somehow managed to ease Tommie's fears enough to get him to go back each morning to sit at his father's desk and "sign things." But shouldn't someone keep an eye on what Miss McGhee had Tommie signing? Maybe she should invite Miss McGhee to the house for dinner, welcome her to Myrtlewood, and explain more about Tommie. No, she would wait and ask Annie about it. Annie would know what to do.

To Lila's surprise, the sermon ended. Nancy Dunn and Melissa Carpenter smiled their goodbyes, and Lila marveled at how deference and condescension could be conveyed at the same time. As she walked down the center aisle, she saw a new face, and assumed this was Mary McGhee. She was tall and angular, stern, with a

20

cool, detached air. Lila stopped to allow her out of the pew. Miss McGhee preceded her down the aisle, sparing Lila an awkward self-introduction. She watched the woman, dressed in a dark, tailored suit with a matching cloche hat, pause briefly to speak to the pastor, shaking his hand firmly. Lila caught a glimpse of fine auburn hair slipping from its knot at the nape of the neck as the woman descended the steps and was gone. Lila in turn gave her hand to the Reverend Sullivan, but her eyes followed Mary McGhee's brisk walk down the street. She seemed utterly foreign as she hurried by other church-goers who chatted among themselves and nodded knowingly after her. There was no reason to hurry in Myrtlewood; but of course this Miss McGhee was not yet of this town. She'd learn soon enough. Lila brought her attention back to Bill Sullivan, aware that he was speaking to her.

"I said, how did you like the sermon today?" There was a twinkle of amusement in his eyes.

"I'm afraid I wasn't paying as much attention as I should, Pastor."

"I could tell. Usually you're frowning, writing notes, nodding in agreement. What's on your mind?"

"Have you met Miss McGhee?"

"Only just now. I noticed you two didn't speak. Haven't you met her yet?"

Lila looked away. "I don't quite know how to go about it."

"Mrs. Dubose, surely you could just see her in the office? She does work for you, you know. Or you could join us for supper Thursday night. We've invited her."

Lila hesitated. Dinner invitations were rare. She knew she should accept. She should have already invited the Sullivans to her house for a meal. They were new in town, and that was what one did. The reverend and his wife were really very kind to think of her, apparently unaffected by, or perhaps unaware as yet of, the gossip about her.

"Well, no, I can't. Thank you though. I'll have to think how to go about arranging something with Miss McGhee, I suppose. I'd better go. Tommie is waiting for his dinner. He likes to listen to the ball game on the radio after he eats. If we're late, he'll want to listen to it during the meal. Annie and I can't stand it."

21

She hurried away. Then, annoyed to find herself imitating Mary McGhee's fast pace, she deliberately slowed down. The reverend was right; it was a simple thing, really. Why couldn't she just introduce herself to the woman? After all, she owed her some sort of explanation about Tommie. Miss McGhee probably wondered just what she had got herself into.

Still, she had stayed the week. Lila had heard from Mr. McFarland, the mailman, that the office was in much better shape already. Could she just drop in? Would Miss McGhee feel she was interfering, or checking up on her? Deep in thought, running a variety of opening sentences through her head, Lila found that she had walked past her own house, and had gone three blocks further down, to Louise Skinner's place. She could not avoid the old woman, who was sitting on her porch swing waiting to snare anyone who happened by into conversation. Lila stayed on the sidewalk, racking her brain for an excuse to be standing there.

"Hey, Miss Louise. It's awful hot for this early in the spring, isn't it? Your yard is a picture. I declare, I don't know how you do it all by yourself."

"Well, I've got that office lady of yours staying with me now. She got out here the other evening and helped me do the weedin'."

Just then, Mary McGhee herself came outside, a stack of files in her arms, apparently headed to the office. She had dispensed with her hat and gloves after church, but had not changed her dress. Lila waited until she came down the walk, hoping Miss Louise would not overhear. She pushed her hair back and touched her brow to check for perspiration. Then the woman with admirably smooth hair was standing stock-still in front of Lila, looking at her as though she were a perfect stranger. Lila belatedly realized that she *was* a stranger to Miss McGhee.

"Hello. I'm, um, I'm Lila Dubose. I've been wanting to, that is, I've been wanting to meet you, actually."

"Yes, of course. Nice to meet you, Mrs. Dubose." Miss McGhee shifted her files to one arm and extended her free hand. Lila shook it, feeling her own palm moist and limp in Miss McGhee's larger and firmer hand.

"I wanted to explain about Tommie. I'm sure you've noticed that

22

he's—special. But I really believe he is capable of much more than we ask of him."

Miss McGhee seemed to soften a little. "Mrs. Dubose, that may very well be true. But I was hired to run your business, which, I'm sorry to say, is near collapse." She hesitated. "Perhaps you should come to the office and see the state of affairs for yourself."

"But I couldn't, that is, I don't even know ..."

Lila found herself staring into cool blue eyes that gave no hint of either pity or arrogance. For a moment, while silence hung between them, she wondered how any woman with such natural beauty, beginning with vivid blue eyes that mesmerized, flawless skin, and red-brown hair that shone with health in the sun—how any such woman could appear so rigid, stern, almost cold. Lila could not think of anything at all to say.

"Well, then," Miss McGhee said, with one eyebrow raised. "I'd better get to the office. It was nice to meet you, Mrs. Dubose. Good day."

She turned and walked away, leaving Lila to stare at her perfectly straight posture as she receded. Even Louise Skinner, who clearly had heard the entire exchange, was speechless. They both watched Mary until she turned the corner.

Lila reached the heavy mahogany front door of the Dubose house and gratefully pulled it closed behind her, shutting out the heat and the confusion that once again assailed her. She stood in the wide entry hall for a minute, absorbing the cool and the quiet. Then she sighed and went up the staircase whose curved banister had been hand fashioned at the Dubose mill. She should change and get Tommie ready for Sunday dinner. Annie would be back from her own church by now and have the table set. She hoped Tommie had not got into tinkering with the car that had sat unused since his father passed away. He was fascinated with tools and machines, and since neither she nor Annie could drive, they were grateful when Tommie confined his repairs to the car; he had at various times dismantled the ancient washing machine and other household appliances to their unending aggravation. He somehow always managed to get all the pieces and parts of the automobile back together, though Lila had no way of knowing

23

whether it was in functioning order or not. She slipped into a loose cotton dress and padded barefoot down to the kitchen. Annie was already there.

"Child, you look overheated. Sit down and have some tea. Mr. Tommie is washing up."

Lila sank into a chair and accepted the glass of sweet tea. Annie moved about efficiently, heating up their meal, setting out place mats. Working around Lila, she placed a bowl of peas, a plate of cornbread, and some sliced tomatoes on the table. Usually they worked side by side, but today Lila felt tired of the routine, tired of everything.

"I saw Miss McGhee in church today. I spoke to her at Miss Louise's, but I didn't really know what to say."

Annie looked at Lila. She shook her head. "So you practically ran home to hide. Girl, what am I goan do with you? Why didn't you just bring her back here to eat with you and Tommie?"

"Oh, Annie, I don't know. She was on her way back to work. On a Sunday! She says it's in really bad shape, the business, I mean. But we must be doing okay. Mr. Buchanan would tell us if it was really bad, wouldn't he? The war contracts—"

"War contracts is ancient history, child. The war's been over for three years. You know that. I expect the lady did find quite a mess to deal with."

"Yes, I know. Then I tried to explain about Tommie."

"She's been here a week, so I reckon she knows about him. There's no use being so shy you can't even speak up for yourself. I spoke to Mr. Dunn yesterday. He said that Miss McGhee is a wonder. She's already learned how to handle Mr. Tommie." Annie paused. She eyed Lila darkly. "Mr. Tommie ain't the real reason you acting so scared. You got to stop using him as an excuse for staying home. Get on out and be more a part of things, Miss Lila. You need to show some back-bone."

Lila made a sound somewhere between a whimper and a groan. "Annie, you know I get talked about if I don't go out, and talked about if I do."

It was true. She had rarely ventured further than church since Mr. Dubose had died. When Lila had first come to live in the big house, Annie, a tall, dark-skinned Negro of imposing stature who commanded great respect in town, had taken the girl under her wing, forming an affection for the shy, terrified eighteen-year-old she had been. Understanding perhaps better than Lila had that Mr. Dubose intended to groom her to take over as the responsible adult for the Dubose family, Annie had mothered her, and developed a fiercely protective attitude. Just as the elder Dubose had served as a father to Lila, so had the imposing Negro woman served as the maternal buttress she'd never really had. She'd adamantly defended Lila to anyone brave enough to criticize her, just as she had Tommie. But Lila knew that sometimes her diffidence frustrated Annie to the point of erupting.

"I've worked for the Duboses since before Mr. Tommie was born. I know what folks say. I know this town. They're not as bad as you think. They're for sure not anything to be afraid of."

Lila sighed. Annie was right. Annie was usually right. "I just worry about Tommie. I know he misses his daddy."

The truth was that the two women missed the elder Dubose just as much as his son did. A man possessed of great dignity and hard common sense, he had been both gentle and firm with his son. Just as he had anchored the town, Mr. Dubose had been the very center of Tommie's world after his mother's death when the boy was only six. And now that anchor was gone. Since his death, Tommie's normally sweet nature had sometimes been disrupted by petulance or outright contrariness. It took all Annie and Lila's combined patience to help him through his grief. Lila was grateful that Tommie seemed to think of her more as a substitute mother than a wife, someone provided by his father to take care of him—a natural conclusion on his part—since that was exactly what his father had intended.

"Are ya'll talking about me?"

Tommie came in, stopping in front of his chair. He looked at the ceiling and recited his usual report, hoping to hurry up and eat, "I washed my hands and face. I combed my hair. I changed from my working-on-the-car clothes. Can we eat now? The game starts soon."

His hands were clean, though Lila spied grease under his nails. She should trim them for him. His canvas high tops were laced and tied, and his khaki pants were rumpled but clean, though he hadn't managed to tuck in his shirt. She smiled. "Yes, we can eat. We already have the radio set, so don't go fiddling with it. Eat slow, sweetie. You have plenty of time. And look—Annie made a chocolate cake."

Tommie collapsed into his chair with the gracelessness of a twelve-year-old. This week had been hard for him, Lila thought, dressing up every day in a suit, going in to see the "tall lady" who turned out to be not so scary after all. His head was tilted slightly to the table radio on the kitchen counter. He knew when the Star Spangled Banner played that the game was about to start. He'd learned the words and sang along. He probably realized that Lila and Annie only pretended to listen to the game, not like his daddy, who had really listened and explained it to him. After their dinner, while Annie ate, Lila would sit on the sofa with him, and soon enough, Tommie would fall asleep to the drone of the announcer's voice without his father's explanations to hold his interest. Lila was only beginning to realize just how long a run she had signed up for.

Chapter Three

REPORT TO THE GRAND DRAGON: The boys from across the river was all impressed with our Klonvocation. Had a big bonfire, fried some catfish, did a little drinking. Might get some new recruits. I told 'em it's a great way to get away from the wife for a while, and she can't complain about it, since it's for a good cause.

Monday, April 19, 1948

Monday afternoon, precisely one week after starting her new job, Mary McGhee sat in Gerald Buchanan's office studying the man while he shuffled papers, trying to look officious. She understood the tactic of making her wait and sat patiently. He was about her own age, too young to be running a bank, already balding, with hands soft as a child's. Mary could tell he had not served in the war. He didn't have the attitude of the soldiers who had returned. She wondered about his qualifications. Was he a simple man trying to do a job, or was he ambitious enough to realize that control of the Dubose finances meant real power in this small town?

After five minutes, he looked up. Folding his hands together, he finally spoke.

"Now then, I know you've met Mr. Tommie, and you see the problem we have on our hands. I feel bad I didn't get over there to see you last week, but frankly, I thought it was best to wait and see if you wanted to stay on after seeing the state of things for yourself."

He paused, perhaps waiting for Mary to admit the job was beyond her capabilities. She stared into his eyes. Finally she spoke softly.

"Given the state of things, it would seem to be to everyone's advantage if Mrs. Dubose were involved a little more. It hardly seems prudent to have Mr. Tommie—"

"Yes, well, Mr. Tommie now, he's slow, that's true. Not quite right

27

in the head. It was his daddy that arranged the marriage to Lila Jackson, she was, just to have someone to take care of the boy someday." He waited, but Mary withheld comment. "Marriage might be extreme, but Thomas Barrett Dubose liked solid deals, and that girl had to get some assurances herself, I imagine. He didn't want to hire a nursemaid for his son. I suppose he just didn't like the way that would look. He wanted his son to have a wife, make it look like he was just like everybody else, I reckon." He paused again, and took a deep breath, as though preparing to reveal dark secrets, Mary thought. *Just get on with it*, she silently prompted.

Clearing his throat, the banker continued. "Miss Lila, now, she knows what her job is, her place. There's no other direct heirs. I talked to him about setting up a trust, with the bank as trustee, so that if something happened to him, Tommie and the mill would be taken care of." Mary's interest perked at the mention of a trust, and she noted how carefully the man had avoided stating that there was one and that he was in fact the trustee. "Course, half the town is related in some way to the Duboses. I believe I'm related in some distant way myself. You'd have to ask my mama to get all that straight."

She rather doubted that Mr. Dubose would have chosen a man who had once picked on his son to act as his protector now. "Yes. Well, all that aside, I think Mr. Tommie needs to be put on a salary. He seems to have no personal checking account. Just where do all the profits from the business go?"

"His daddy had a personal account. That money is Tommie's, of course, but we don't want him running around writing checks against it, do we?"

Mary's expression didn't change. Shrugging, she said, "If I may speak frankly, I couldn't care less if he and his wife spend all the money in this bank, which I believe belongs to them. But I think it's in the interest of the town and the bank to get this mill back on its feet. I need to put Mr. Tommie on a salary and open a personal account for him so he stops taking money out of the cash till at the office. I really can't balance the books unless we do this."

Now Mary waited. She had subtly accused Buchanan of mishandling the Dubose fortune. She would give him some time to formulate a reply. The man cleared his throat, preparatory to launching a defense, she was certain. She said softly, "You know as well as I do that this is the right thing to do. In fact, we might want to call in the state auditors to look at the books, just to assure everyone that things are being done properly."

Again she waited. He could deduce that her next step might be to ask the state people or maybe even the feds to look at the bank's books as well. She was used to this sort of hesitation while he gathered himself, the same sort of pause she had endured from men who inevitably would end up having to agree with her. Usually she found a way to help them save face, making it appear that she was appealing to them for help, allowing them to believe her proposal was their idea. But this time, for a moment, she contemplated not letting Buchanan off the hook and wondered just how fierce an enemy he could become. Gerald Buchanan, despite his exaggerated corn-pone delivery, did not strike her as any sort of redneck country farmer, though he did put on something of a good-old-boy air. For now, at least, he appeared resigned to the idea that she would insist on a workable solution for both of them, and for the business.

"Yes. Well. I could do that, I suppose. Let me think about it. Now, I understand you've found a way to get Tommie to sign things. You shouldn't be doing that without oversight." He paused for a moment. "You was hired to do typing and paperwork, not to run the place."

Mary found herself amused at his lapses in grammar as he became agitated. She decided to push him a little further while he was off balance. "We really need to make that a joint account, don't we? Mrs. Dubose should have access to funds to pay household bills. I understand those have been allowed to accumulate since Mr. Dubose passed away. The merchants in town need to be paid." She saw from the man's reaction that she had guessed correctly.

"Now wait a minute here. I've been looking out for Lila. They ain't gone hungry. You wouldn't want to give that woman a chance to get above herself. She's got her place, got a job to do, just like you, and that's all. She don't need no checking account."

"I think she does." Mary sat back. She was now convinced that Buchanan had been playing both Tommie and Lila Dubose for fools. "I think it would help us both to have her name on the accounts if an independent audit of the books should occur."

Buchanan's hands clenched together. Mary thought she heard his teeth grinding. "I see what you mean. Yes, well. I could set that up. Transfer his daddy's account to Tommie and Mrs. Dubose. I'll have to have a talk with her of course, and explain that she is only to use it to pay for the household expenses."

"Mr. Buchanan, how has her staff been paid? I understand there's a cook and a gardener. How have her groceries been paid for until now? I've looked over the books, and while the business has of course suffered since the war contracts ended, there was still enough money coming in to take care of those things, but I see no evidence that they've been paid. Think of the town, Mr. Buchanan. That money must have been sitting in this bank while other businesses suffered, waiting for payments. It will help everyone concerned, sir, if you and I agree together to do this, and to keep an eye on things."

Buchanan's face had gone a crisp pink color that reminded her of the scalded hide of a pig. He stood up, more than ready to conclude the meeting, Mary judged. "I see what you mean. Yes, you and I could oversee things, couldn't we?"

"I think that would be best, don't you agree? I propose, with your advice and guidance of course, a quarterly review of the books. Apparently no effort has been made since the end of the war to replace the government contracts with private ones. This business has kept going simply because it has no competition. It won't take someone long to realize that, and if we don't make these moves, competition will surely move in. But—with your oversight—we can get this put to rights, and the mill will thrive. Dubose Lumber is the single largest employer in the county, after all. It will help everyone, the bank included, for us to ensure its survival." Mary gave him a slight nod, conveying fealty and collusion, she hoped. "You need have no fear of me overstepping the limits."

Mr. Buchanan regained his composure. "Good. So I'll come by, let's say once a week, and take a look at the books. Before the checks are made out, the payroll, that sort of thing."

Good, she thought. She preferred to let him underestimate her. The more she pretended to defer to him, the freer she would be to do what she wanted. Mary rose abruptly and extended her hand. Buchanan drew back, clearly startled.

"Thank you, Mr. Buchanan. You get that account set up, and I'll have a talk with Mrs. Dubose for you. It might embarrass her less coming from me, rather than from the president of the bank, don't you think?"

After staring at her for a long moment, he finally took her hand and shook on the deal. Mary felt his eyes on her as she turned and left. She had no doubt that he would indeed look at the books. He might even be moved to call Sam Stewart in Texas and make inquiries about her. Let him. Big Sam would not dare to undermine her here, though he might tell just enough of the truth to make Buchanan more wary of her. It was his idea to banish her to this backwater town in the first place. Now she knew everything she needed to know about Gerald Buchanan. He struggled to convey the image of a southern "gentleman" who would never admit that women should or could work, that a woman could have as much sense for business as a man. He was not afraid of underhand dealings and he had probably been skimming off some cash since Mr. Dubose died. Mary was certain of it. But it was clear he respected money above all, and therefore admired those who knew how to make it, save, and invest it—especially if they carried him along on their coattails, as she suspected the late Mr. Dubose had done. Even if the coattails were a woman's, Buchanan would grudgingly respect smart business moves, couched in the sneaky terms he was apparently accustomed to using.

But she was angry at his heavy-handed attempt to force Lila Dubose to depend on him. The woman must be blind if she hadn't yet realized it, Mary thought. She remembered Mrs. Dubose's claim that Tommie was not as slow as some seemed to believe, and hoped for her sake that she was right. Mary could see the young woman's unusual gray eyes, the way their clarity was shadowed as she stared up at Mary during their first encounter. She had been abrupt, blunt. *Great going*, she told herself. *I've managed to make Tommie's wife afraid of me too.* She thought that both Lila and Tommie were peculiarly unsuited for the life they had inherited.

All week, Mary had been stared at by the mill hands, in some sort of silent treatment she felt certain was a concerted act. Vince Dunn grudgingly answered her queries about the business, avoided her when possible, and encouraged the men in their attitude toward her, she was sure. After burying herself in the books, working long after the mill whistle blew each day, she dreaded having to disrupt her schedule to have dinner with Reverend Sullivan and his wife, but commitments must be honored. Bill turned out to be a surprisingly relaxing companion and Mary easily fell into conversation with him while Barbara cleaned up.

"Mary, everyone has commented on the wonderful transformation we've all noticed in Tommie since you took over at the mill. He has calmed down, and is much less given to fits of temper now, I hear. I think he really believed it was his duty to carry on for his daddy. I'm sure Lila especially appreciates the change." Bill Sullivan's quick, broad smile underlined the point he was making.

"I need to talk with Mrs. Dubose about the business soon. I keep meaning to, but I've been so busy," Mary said, knowing it was a poor excuse. She shifted in her chair.

"She is a bit of a mystery, but a sweet person, really," Bill said. "I think she's genuinely fond of Tommie; she certainly seems to know how to manage him." After a moment, he said, "You could just pick up the phone, you know."

"I've been looking through the accounts and Clyde Moseley can't seem to ever pay his bill in full. He's always short." Mary changed the subject abruptly, hoping it didn't cause Bill to speculate about her reluctance to face Lila Dubose.

"His wife goes to our church, you know. He gambles and drinks." Bill shook his head. "Lots of men were affected in different ways by the war, as I'm sure you know. He was a Marine. Served in the Pacific, like I did." He fell silent for a moment and Mary wondered what effect the war had had on Bill himself. He seemed to effuse good health and a placid benevolence that sometimes irked.

"He always buys the cheapest grade of lumber."

"He cuts corners, I suppose. His oldest son will start college in the fall, the first of their family to go. He works a shift at the mill, and does contracting on the side. That deserves some consideration, I think."

Mary sipped her whiskey. "All the same, character cuts more corners in the long run, getting the job done right. Soon people will refuse to hire him."

"Mary, I agree! But it is difficult to maintain character when your oldest boy has a chance to achieve more than you ever did." An odd comment coming from a minister, she thought. Probably just evidence of the strong sense of loyalty she had witnessed among all the men who had served in the war, whether they knew each other or not. The nice thing was how she and Bill seemed to be able to debate things and remain friendly. But the pastor still seemed too forgiving at times.

"The end doesn't always justify the means. Once the son is grown he will eventually look his father in the eye and question why he didn't trust more and worry less about making his own ends and means."

She took another sip of her drink. Was it her imagination, or was he probing for clues to her own character in this conversation? She could tell he enjoyed the pragmatic discussion they were having about the town and the people they were beginning to know, but she also wanted Bill to know that she would cut no corners for herself. She told him about her meeting with Gerald Buchanan, and Bill was frank about his distrust of the man.

Barbara was standing in the doorway with a dishtowel in her hands. "Let me guess," she said to the pair of them, "you two talked about the lumber business all night," Bill answered, "Yes, we did. I'm very impressed with the breadth of knowledge Mary here has acquired since her arrival. She's doing a great job over there. Everyone says so."

Mary smiled, but did not reply. When she looked up, she caught Barbara staring at her quizzically. She refused to acknowledge the curious glance.

"I don't know why I didn't think of this before. Why don't we invite Mrs. Dubose to join us next week? The two of you should get to know each other better," Bill said.

Mary knew both of them were watching her response, but she only nodded vaguely. Soon after, she took her leave, waving a hand on her way out.

Mary inspected the office in an effort to defuse her nervousness. Although she refused to think of Buchanan as her boss, or to admit that he even had any right to go over her work and look at the books, she was allowing this to happen. She still was uncertain just why she had arranged things this way. A nagging suspicion, based on nothing more than her instant dislike of the man and his own obvious dislike of her, ensured that this would be uncomfortable and pointless. The books were in good order. She'd made sure of it.

"Looks nice in here. I see you've done some straightening up." Buchanan nodded at her as he stood before her desk.

"Yes. Should we get to the books?" She stood.

"Might anxious, aren't you? All right, let's see what you've done." He strode ahead of her and sat behind the big desk in the inner office, like a patron at a restaurant, waiting for her to serve him. Pulling the ledger from a drawer, she placed it beside the checkbook and sat on the other side of the desk. She'd be damned if she would stand by his shoulder. She wanted to know that he knew how to read double entries. Remaining silent, she waited for him to ask questions.

Apparently, he was comfortable with the ledger entries, as he put on a pair of half glasses and began comparing the check stub entries with the line items, one finger moving down the column to keep his place. The last checks were still in the checkbook, payroll all made out, awaiting Tommie's signature. Finally Buchanan closed both books and looked up at her with a slight grin that somehow conveyed both approval and resentment.

"Everything looks in order. Neat job. Most of the men will prefer to be paid in cash, you know."

Mary said, "I wasn't aware of that. I should just have them endorse their paychecks on the back and I'll need to have cash on hand to pay them, then."

Buchanan said, "I'll send someone over with a locked bank bag. I notice there's not a check made out to yourself here."

"That's one thing we hadn't discussed yet. My salary." She met his gaze.

"How does a dollar fifty an hour sound?" Buchanan waited. She stared at him.

"I'd prefer a salary, not an hourly wage. But I'll discuss that with the Duboses."

He gave a snort. "To be blunt, neither one of them would have any idea how much a secretary should draw. Miss Jones made a dollar an hour, and that's a good wage for a single lady."

Mary said evenly, "I'm sure it is. As I said, I'll discuss it with Mrs.

Dubose." Miss Jones had worked for Mr. Dubose, who undoubtedly had run the mill and only needed someone for typing. Buchanan knew as well as she that Mary was doing much more than that. And she simply did not want to grant him the authority to assign her salary. The business belonged to the Duboses. True, there was debt, loans held by the bank. She wasn't going to budge on this issue though.

"You can talk all you want to Lila, but she don't have a clue about the business. I told you that already. She wouldn't have any idea how much you should be paid." He paused. "The books look in fine shape. You did a good job. I don't know why you want to be salaried instead of hourly, but that's up to you. I'll give Lila a call, talk to her about the range she should consider." Then he eyed Mary up and down. "See, one way or the other, I'll be the one deciding how much you get paid. I tried to tell you that Tommie and Lila don't know anything about the business."

Mary kept her tone neutral. "No, you deliberately left me in the dark about Tommie. I resent the way this entire town withheld that information, like a practical joke, waiting to see how I'd react. Not very welcoming." When Buchanan only grinned, she continued, "I ran a company ten times this size. I know what I'm doing."

"I can see that. I just don't think you should be doing it without close supervision. The bank has an interest in seeing this business pay its debts and meet its obligations."

"That's why you're here, looking over the books. If you'll send the payroll cash over this afternoon, I'll sign for it, and deposit the endorsed checks tomorrow afternoon." She stood, wanting to root Buchanan out of Mr. Dubose's chair, where he looked far too comfortable.

Buchanan heaved himself up. "Okay then. You've done wonders in your first week. Now that you've got everything in order, maybe I should talk to Lila about hiring a manager to run the mill."

The tension in her neck and shoulders increased. "And I'll talk to Mrs. Dubose as well."

"Do what you want. When I explain the mill's dependence on the bank, she'll listen to my advice."

Mary couldn't wait to get him out of what she already considered her office. "I'm sure Mrs. Dubose will appreciate any information she gets. She's been sadly lacking in help and advice up till now." This time Buchanan wasn't so quick to meet her gaze, and his skin turned slightly pink.

"I'll drop by next week before payroll. I'll be keeping an eye on things, you can bet."

Mary wanted to lock the door behind him. She sank down into the chair Buchanan had vacated and drew a deep breath. She couldn't get a handle on her reaction to him. And she was surprised at her attachment to the job. She looked around. She had an entire business in her hands, and she enjoyed working alone. She decided she needed to know much more about the sawmill and the lumber business, so she went searching for Vince Dunn.

The next Sunday, Bill managed to catch the attention of both women after church. "Mrs. Dubose, wait one moment, would you? Barbara and I would like to invite Miss McGhee and you to supper and perhaps a game of bridge this Thursday night. Won't you come?" He held Mary's arm as he called out to Lila Dubose, several steps ahead of them.

"How kind of you," Mary said, but she shot Bill a look that said the exact opposite. Bill merely grinned as he kept his eyes on Lila Dubose. He really was much too boyish to be a preacher, Mary thought.

Lila, demure and subdued in a soft pink dress that fit her slender waist snugly but flared out from there, stopped and turned. Mary's breath caught in her throat.

"Thank you," replied Lila. "How thoughtful of you. I'll come, though I'm afraid I don't know how to play bridge." Mary watched her skin flush to virtually the same shade as her dress. Lila had an expression of eagerness mixed with apprehension. Mary suddenly realized the young woman was beautiful.

"So, will you be there?" Bill asked as he and Mary watched Lila walk away. He caught Mary's piercing, grim look. "Come on. It won't be that bad. You said you needed an opportunity to talk to her."

"All right. But you just put me on the spot in front of my employer." She left him standing alone and walked off.

"Mr. Dunn says we need more men," Tommie said as he entered the office. Mary looked up, surprised that Tommie had got by her to go to the sawmill. "When my daddy was alive we had lots more men working here. Mr. Dunn says we could use more help now."

"Okay then. I'll talk to Mr. Dunn. Did he send you up here?"

"Yes ma'am. He said you had some more papers for me to sign or something."

"I do, but you sign papers on Thursdays, not Wednesdays, remember. You know, if we are short-handed, the men will be working twice as hard. Maybe you better stick to checking on them just on Thursday afternoons, like we talked about."

"Okay. I know you have to stay out of the way when they're really busy. They don't have time to show me stuff."

Tommie soon left. Mary sighed. Her opinion of Tommie had not developed into scorn or exasperation. She had simply adjusted to him, just as the town apparently had. She would run the business for him and refused to acknowledge any similarity to her former situation in Houston, which had ended badly. After all, she had no reason to assume the same would happen here in Myrtlewood.

Vince Dunn, the mill foreman, had been the first to thank her when she went down to the sawmill yard on Monday to tell the men personally that they would be receiving regular pay from now on, without fail. She saw the relief on all their faces when she announced, "And Mr. Tommie will be coming to see you only on Thursdays."

"That's a good thing you done, gettin' Mr. Tommie in hand," Vince told her. "We all been worried sick he's going to get an arm cut off poking around the saws. His daddy worried about it too, but he kept a close watch on him. Tommie's interested in how things work, he just forgets between times. You're doing all right, so far."

On Thursday evening Mary arrived at the Sullivans' house to find Lila there already, deep in conversation with Barbara. After they'd greeted each other, she hesitated to insert herself into the conversation, preferring to listen to the women chatting.

Lila was saying, "I grew up in a large family, and so all my cooking is geared for ten or twelve people. Annie says I waste food that way, since it's only Tommie and her and myself. I can't seem to get the knack of making smaller portions."

37

Barbara smiled. "I don't have any brothers or sisters myself. What was it like?"

"Well, I have eight brothers and sisters. The Jacksons have always produced large broods. There are four younger ones still at home with Mama, and four older ones married with children of their own, so it makes quite a large group when they all get together. We, I mean they, live on the old Dubose farm place at the edge of town, that house that looks like it's about to fall down. It has seen better days. Before the Civil War, the Duboses grew cotton out there. My family farmed for them after the war, until the mill was started. I guess Jacksons have always worked for Duboses one way or another."

"Oh, yes, the Jacksons. Now I know. That house was the original Dubose home? It really should be preserved, don't you think?"

"It's pretty run down," Lila said, looking away. "I doubt any of my family have an appreciation of its historical value." She gave a short, embarrassed laugh. "But if anyone could explain how it might make money for them, they'd jump at the idea, I'm sure."

"It must have been difficult for you, moving into the house in town, taking on new duties."

"You can't imagine. I feel the eyes of everyone in town on me every time I step out the door. That's why I don't go out very much. It was easier when Mr. Dubose was alive. I miss that kind old man."

"I'm sure you do," Barbara agreed, looking at Mary for support. "Shall we eat now?"

"It seems to me that you and Lila share a common objective," Bill was saying. "Have you had that talk with her about the business yet?" Lila and Barbara were in the kitchen, washing and drying the dishes. Mary was helping Bill set up the card table and move chairs.

Mary shook her head, and Bill went on. "Don't you see the advantage of having her become more involved? Having Tommie sign things approved by you and Gerald Buchanan could prove dangerous. Think about it. If any creditors, or, indeed, the bank, decided to call things into question, it could be bad. And there's Lila's relatives to consider, too. A lazy bunch, all of them—and practically destitute. They talk about Lila all over town. They resent her success and think they have a right to share in it. And what about you, Mary? If something goes wrong, who do you think people will blame? Do you honestly think Gerald Buchanan will protect you?"

Mary smiled at the thought. "I'm quite certain he wouldn't. He would be more than pleased to supply all the information anyone would need to blame things on me. I set it up that way, unfortunately." She thought for a moment. "It could be that you are right. Maybe Mrs. Dubose should learn at least a little about the business. Do you think she could?"

"Well, she's certainly shy, and easily frightened. Maybe she simply doesn't realize what is at stake. But you do. Teach her enough to be a help to you."

"I suppose I could. But I don't need or want help. If Gerald Buchanan gets his hands on the business, then I'll simply move on."

"That's my point. You are free to do so. You have nothing really at stake here, but Lila does, and she doesn't have the option of moving on to the next job."

"You're right, of course." She could not explain to Bill her reluctance to have anything to do with Lila Dubose. She did not need an ally, as he was suggesting, because she would refuse to go to war with Gerald. But Lila might have to, and she would need some skills, especially if Mary decided to leave, move on. Involving herself with training Lila would hasten that decision, she was certain. It seemed unavoidable. And nothing lasted forever, after all. That was how it had always been for her. Why should this time be any different?

Soon they arranged themselves around the bridge table. Bill explained the basics of the game, while Mary sat longing for a cigarette. Laughter broke out as mock hands were played, and finally Mary was paired with Lila. She watched Lila lose some of her shyness; and the high pink color came into her cheeks, just as it had last Sunday, as she made one wrong move after the other.

She seems so young, Mary thought. How old could she be?

Mary knew how to play bridge, but did not offer her partner any help, as Bill and Barbara proceeded to confuse Lila with the finer points and to trump her best cards and collect tricks. Finally Bill got up to offer everyone an after-dinner drink, and Mary accepted the wine gratefully. She would be paired with Barbara now, and Bill with Lila, so she did not have to look directly into those disturbing gray eyes during the game. When she did look up once or twice, she caught Barbara Sullivan studying her. The bold, almost amused look in the woman's eyes seemed odd for a pastor's wife, Mary thought. They seemed to convey a hint of challenge, as if Barbara were daring her to engage with Lila.

The evening ended, but then—against Mary's will and her better judgment—they agreed to play again next Thursday night. She and Lila began walking home in the same direction, the silence between them awkward, until Lila spoke. "That was fun, wasn't it? I don't know if I'll ever figure out all the rules about bridge, though."

"Sure you will." The woman's insecurity irritated Mary and also tugged at her. They stopped on the corner where they would part ways. Mary finally spoke directly to Lila, forcing herself to look at her.

"Mrs. Dubose, I have some things regarding the business that I am afraid we really need to discuss. Could you come by the office tomorrow morning? It won't take long."

Lila turned toward her, and there were those eyes again, with the same appeal that Mary remembered. "Of course. Tommie isn't pestering you too much, is he?"

"Not at all. It's just that there are some things you need to be aware of, some things I have neglected to tell you about, that's all. Come about ten. I should have my desk cleared by then."

Mary walked home slowly, bracing herself for the onslaught of questions from Miss Louise.

"Well, how was it? I heard the pastor's wife is quite a cook."

Mary couldn't recall exactly what she had just eaten. All she remembered was a dry mouth and something sticking in her throat as she had forced herself to swallow. "Yes, she is," she said.

"Did you get anything out of that Mrs. Dubose? They say she's quite above herself since she married. She's just one of those Jacksons, you know. All they're good for is producing more Jacksons."

Louise Skinner could be irritatingly rude at times, and Mary's store of polite responses had been seriously depleted by her dinner engagement. She sighed. The old woman was her landlady, after all, and seemed to have no friends or family.

"I believe she is simply shy. She's in an impossible situation, you know."

"Seems to me she's got it made. Married into the richest family in three counties, husband not capable, she can do just about anything she likes with all that money, with no one to stop her."

Mary looked at her, making her eyes deliberately hard. "But she has done nothing with all that money yet, has she?"

The old lady faltered for a response. "I stayed up too late, waiting for you to get back. I should go to bed. You'll lock up the house for me, won't you, dear?"

Mary sighed again. It was like kicking a cripple. Why had she responded so sharply? The old woman intended no malice, she knew. She was just curious. To Miss Louise, Lila Dubose was simply a story-book fantasy of someone going from rags to riches, like in a Hollywood movie.

But Mary could not even rid herself of a burning need to know more about this person who was barely more than a girl, really, so how could she scold Miss Louise? To begin, why had Lila Dubose accepted the unusual proposal made by old Mr. Dubose, denying herself the chance at a real marriage and children and all the things women were supposed to want?

Once in her room, she opened a window and lit a cigarette, enjoying being alone. She had always enjoyed working alone too, and the freedom it gave her. She could teach Lila about the business and then move on. It was what she had always done. She should think about New Orleans or Atlanta as options.

She grew restless as she thought of inquisitive gray eyes staring at her. She commanded her mind to refuse images of small, soft hands, the determined chin and unfashionable, almost wild curls. Instead she redirected her thoughts to the want ads in the *Atlanta Constitution* and to her trunk, stored in Miss Louise's attic. She should check train schedules, just in case.

Then she thought again about the young woman with the creamy skin that so easily blushed pink, and she saw again those calm gray eyes looking at her, watching her. Late that night, lying in bed, her list of options ran out, and she moaned softly, and whispered aloud into the dark, "No."

Chapter Four

REPORT TO THE GRAND DRAGON: We sure have been holding regular meetings. The four us had a good time last Friday night, shot off our guns when some niggers was walkin' by, scared 'em into the next county.

Friday, April 30, 1948

Lila discussed things with Annie over her last cup of coffee before she got herself ready for her meeting with Miss McGhee. She had worried all night about what she should wear, what Miss McGhee could possibly want to talk about, how she should handle herself. For the tenth time, she posed this question to Annie, whose patience was wearing thin.

"What on earth do you suppose she wants to see me about, if it's not Tommie?"

Annie shrugged. "The lady probably just wants to report to you what she's been doin' the past few weeks. God knows, Mr. Tommie's not much of a boss."

"Well, should I just wear what I've got on? Or dress like I'm going to town, do you think?"

"Honey child, no matter what you wear, Miss McGhee knows who that mill belongs to, and she works for you. Why don't you just get up and go? Then you'll find out what she wants."

"I better change. Maybe she wants to quit. Annie, if that's it, I don't know what to do. I don't want her to quit. I imagine it's difficult to work in an office with no one directing you."

Annie snorted her skepticism. "I've seen and heard enough about Mary McGhee to doubt that. Strikes me she knows what she's doing. You better hurry yourself, or you'll be late. I've got the floors to do. Why don't you get from underfoot? Go on now."

Lila went upstairs to dress, wondering why was she so intimidated by Miss McGhee. She admitted to herself that she admired her, a single, working woman, free to do as she pleased. She was curious about her, that was all. Mary McGhee always looked just right in her business suits, with her perfect hair, her straight posture and imposing height, exaggerated by her slim figure. Lila's own figure was more given to curves. She dressed, looked at the time, and silently wailed about her hair. She could not ask Annie to interrupt her work to help her subdue it. She'd have to let it go as it was. She grabbed her purse and ran down the stairs.

Mary waited for Lila as she tried to calm her own thinking. She recalled yet again the unusual eyes that sent a silent plea for help, or was that simply her own imagination? She sat at her desk and tried to anticipate her discussion with Lila, who must be on her way now. Mary would keep everything strictly informative. Formal, but definitely not looking at her either.

Her plan in place, she looked up as Lila walked through the door, and forgot everything. Lila was simply lovely to look at. Mary's mouth was dry, her palms moist. She had not felt like this since seventh grade.

Lila stopped just inside the door, looking around curiously. She stared as if she had never been in the office before. If she'd heard tales of the disastrous state it was in, and had imagined huge piles of papers to the ceiling, dust and cobwebs, Mary hoped she was pleased by the clean, orderly room. Mary's desk with the green blotter was clear. The wall of oak file cabinets shone after she had polished them with wood oil. The brass ceiling fan churned slowly. Mary watched Lila's eyes take in all the changes that had been made, and then her attention finally devolved to the woman who sat rigidly behind the desk. Mary resisted the impulse to sit straighter, and tried to look businesslike, not rushed or harried as she knew she appeared on the street, going to and from work each day, walking past Lila's house. She wanted Lila to see her in her element here. She was wearing her newest, most formal gray suit, with a silk blouse, belted jacket, and her black pumps polished last night in the kitchen as Miss Louise watched, peppering her with questions about the upcoming meeting, laced with dire warnings about letting the Jacksons get their hands on money that didn't belong to them.

Lila returned Mary's stare, and then relaxed into a smile.

"I hope I'm not late."

"No, not at all. Please, sit down."

Lila sat on the opposite side of the desk, and waited. Her expression struck Mary as eager but mixed with trepidation.

"Mrs. Dubose, I've been here a few weeks now. It's time I brought you up to date on some things."

Lila interrupted. "You've done wonders with the office. Everything just gleams."

"I've done more than house cleaning." Mary frowned, and regretted the clipped tone of her voice. Lila looked stricken.

"I didn't mean to trivialize your work, not at all. And please call me Lila, like when we were playing bridge."

Mary stared at Lila for a moment, watching her discomfort grow. She knew no way to make this sound less intrusive and embarrassing.

"All right, Lila. I'm afraid I must ask you—how do you buy your groceries? Who pays for them?"

"What? Annie does the shopping. Mr. Dubose always paid the bills before he died. Since then, I just assumed the bank took care of it."

Meaning Gerald Buchanan, Mary thought. "And you walk around with no money of your own?"

"Money?"

"Cash, Mrs.—Lila. Surely you must keep some around for incidental needs?"

"Sometimes, that is, Tommie sometimes has cash in his pockets, and when we do the laundry, Annie and I, we find the money and keep it in the kitchen, just in case." Now Lila was looking at Mary with horrified embarrassment, as if she had done something wrong. "I don't need much in the way of cash. Mr. Dubose took care of everything from the groceries to my wardrobe. I can assure you I would never spend anything as much on my own clothes like he did for me."

Mary wished there were some other way. Why did this woman have to be so young and innocent? She should be outraged at Mary poking into her private finances, not ashamed!

"I'm sorry. I should be able to answer these questions, but I can't.

You must think I am pretty naive." Mary saw her chin come up. "I promise I will find out for you. I will. I could talk to Mr. Buchanan. Is it very important to you, to your job here, to settle the household accounts? I should be able to tell you more—"

"Please, Mrs. Dubose, Lila, don't worry. It's just that I'm afraid the bank, Mr. Buchanan, has been rather late in taking care of things. I spoke to him about rectifying the situation. I hope you don't mind. It's not really within the purview of running the business."

Lila looked shocked. "You mean that nothing has been paid since Mr. Dubose died? That's almost four months now. Oh, my God. Why would Mr. Buchanan allow things to go unpaid? What must everyone in town be thinking of me?"

Mary thought that the town did a great deal of thinking, most of it perpetuated by Lila's refusal to get out of the house and dispute some of the more lurid rumors. The woman's lack of confidence began to irritate Mary.

"What people think is no concern of yours or mine. Doing what needs to be done is. I've set up a bank account for you. Here is the checkbook. I'll teach you how to use it. I put Tommie on a salary that will be deposited each week. The past due accounts have been paid, and the balance you see there is for future expenses. Let me go over this with you."

"How long have you known about all this? Why didn't you tell me sooner?"

That's a good question, Mary thought wryly. "I apologize. I had a lot of work to do. I had to go through the books, and have a talk with Gerald Buchanan. A talk, I might add, that he himself should have had with you after Mr. Dubose's death."

Mary's lips pressed together in anger. Buchanan was her problem, for now. There was no need to prejudice Lila against the man, not yet.

"Please don't feel embarrassed," she went on. "Just listen to me now, and I'll explain things to you. Every bill has been paid in full, and the storeowners are extremely grateful. No one is mad at you. I paid them all personally from the company account, and talked to them. It's going to be okay, really."

Mary resisted the impulse to reach across and take Lila's hand. She moved to the other side of the desk, pulling her chair with her. Opening the checkbook, she began to talk to Lila about the bills.

"If you want Annie to continue doing the shopping for you, you can just give her a signed check to take with her, and then write down the amount in the check register when she gets back. I would advise you to go yourself, at least the first time, and pay in person, get to know the owners—"

"But I do know every one of them! This is humiliating."

"Don't feel that way about it. Just reassure them that they will be paid at the time of purchase from now on. I've already spoken to them."

"I see. Are there other things you've undertaken in my behalf, Miss McGhee?" Lila's voice had suddenly lost the edge of desperation and anxiety it had taken on. It was a soft, quiet voice, low in tone but feminine. It had a melodic pitch, and Mary wondered how Lila's voice would sound singing. She cursed herself and forced her attention back to the situation at present.

"Lila, you do realize that Tommie's family founded that bank, and that he practically owns it? His father sat on the board of directors. That seat is vacant, and by rights should be Tommie's. This means that without a Dubose on the board, Mr. Buchanan has had a free hand in making decisions that affect the town, and certainly affect the Dubose holdings, all without the input of a Dubose."

"Are you implying that I should go? I couldn't. I wouldn't even understand what they were talking about."

"They'll talk about whatever you tell them to talk about. You're married to Tommie. Either you or he needs to be there. Or, if you request it, I could go as your secretary and take notes, then report back to you."

"Are you certain you could explain it all in terms I could understand?" Mary caught a glint of amusement in Lila's eyes. She returned the smile. At least the girl wasn't beyond making fun of herself. She might be innocent, but she certainly was not stupid.

"I'm sure it's not beyond you. It's very simple really. The bank makes loans. The money they lend out is mostly Dubose money. You should have some say in how and when that money is distributed. Most of the stores in town have mortgages or loans held by the bank and many of them are behind on their payments now, due to the irregularity of the payroll from the mill and, consequently, people's accounts in those stores being past due. The most logical step would be for the bank to call in some of those notes and to take over the businesses and I'm not so sure Buchanan wasn't planning just such a move. Half the merchants in this town are in fear of that happening. I assured them, when I contacted them to bring your personal accounts up to date, that you have no interest in the bank foreclosing on them, none at all."

Lila laughed. "It seems that there's a lot you need to teach me, Miss McGhee. Sam Stewart was right about what an extraordinary woman you are. Where should we begin?"

After Lila left two hours later, with the new checkbook in her purse, and somewhat bemused at all there was to absorb, Mary sat alone and recalled the dimples, the spark in Lila's eyes, even her scent that brought to mind the flavor of the whole South with its sweet, indolent charm. The girl's softly sibilant accent had cast some sort of spell in the room, Mary thought. Now she was gone, and yet the spell seemed to linger with her scent. So much for extricating herself from this job. It seemed she'd just contracted for a longer stay and gone from dreading Thursday night to looking forward to it.

Mary was beginning to settle into a routine, and settle into a certain image in Myrtlewood. The role of spinster-bookkeeper did not offend her, and it accelerated her acceptance by the town if they could label her this way. She felt a growing affection for the place and for her job and its real importance to the town. She even felt affection for Miss Louise. But weekends were difficult. Now that the mill accounts were up to date she no longer needed to work on Saturday or Sunday. Mary had too much free time so she bought a car in order to drive to the Gulf coast, only two hours away.

"I'll be gone for the weekend," she told Miss Louise one Saturday. "There's leftovers in the icebox. I'm going to the beach." She had rented a fisherman's cabin on the eastern shore of Mobile Bay in Baldwin County.

"Whatever for? There's nothing to do down there." The old woman looked stunned, clearly disappointed that she wouldn't have Mary's company.

"I'll be back Sunday night," Mary spoke firmly.

"But you'll miss church." Louise looked like she might cry. Mary didn't deign to respond.

Stopping at Riser's Service Station, Mary sat in the car while Bobby Riser hurried over to her open window. No older than twenty but looking even younger, with an amazingly clean appearance for a gas station attendant, Bobby had a freshly barbered crew cut of sandy hair and pale blue eyes that stared out of a thin face with a pointed jaw. His name was carefully stenciled over his pocket, and the greasy red rag hanging out of his back pocket was the only detriment to a cultivated professional presence, right down to his black dress shoes with white socks. His uniform was starched and pressed.

"Fill her up for you?"

"Yes, please. I'm going out of town."

Bobby unscrewed the gas cap and began pumping. "Where you headed?"

"I thought I'd drive down to the Gulf."

His eyes widened a little, as if she'd said Mars or the moon. "You'll want to hit Highway 43 then, straight shot into Mobile. I got a map in the station."

Before she could say anything, the young man shot into the office, grabbed a map, and hurried back.

"Just let me check under the hood real quick." He pulled the oil stick, stared at it gravely, wiped it off, inserted it, inspected it again, and seemed satisfied. Then he put the rag over the radiator cap and eased it loose with the delicacy of a surgeon. "I'll just add a little water here," Bobby mumbled to himself. The hood was then slammed firmly shut, and he hustled around to wash her windows. Mary sighed. Apparently there was no shortchanging the full-service treatment. She got out of the car and watched. Bobby pulled a tire gauge from his front pocket and set about checking the pressure in all four tires.

"Ma'am, you got a tire going bald." He swallowed nervously. "I mean, you'll be all right for your trip, but you probly need to get a new one soon. The others look fine, lots of tread still. That one somebody put on to replace a flat, I bet. Maybe it's your spare. Didya check for a spare when you bought her?"

Mary shook her head. "No, I didn't even think about it."

"Lemme just look in the trunk." Taking the keys from Mary he opened the trunk of the car. "Just like I thought. You ain't got no jack, and that bald 'un's the spare, all right. This tire here is flat. I ain't minding your business, but if I was you I wouldn't be goin' off 'thout a spare and a jack."

Damn it all, Mary thought. "I really wanted to get on the road today."

Bobby looked alarmed, as though the delay might be blamed on him personally. "We'll get you fixed up. It's no problem. I can slap a new tire on for you quick as anything. And we got a jack, if I can find the stand and the handle for it. I'll just throw that in your trunk, you'll be good to go."

Impressed, Mary said, "Thank you." She leaned in the open window and grabbed her purse. Standing in the shade, she watched Bobby, painfully thin but evidently strong as steel cable, ease her car into an empty bay, loosen the lug nuts, jack it up, replace the tire that didn't meet his standards for road safety and then also replace the flat tire he had found in the trunk. She smoked two cigarettes, and by the time she had finished, he was backing her car out and pulling it up to the pumps again. Then he proceeded to wipe the whole thing down as if he had just washed and waxed it. When he could find nothing more that didn't meet his approval, he took the map out of his back pocket and unfolded it on the hood.

"See here," he pointed with a finger, tracing a road on the map until it turned onto the one than ran to Mobile, "You just stay on this road right here till you get to 43. Hang you a right and off you go." Then Bobby subsided into silence, having exhausted his checklist for preparing her for what he apparently believed to be a great journey. Amused, she offered her hand to him.

"Thank you so much. I can't think when anyone has been so thorough. You might have saved me from being stranded with a flat."

He blushed with earnest embarrassment. "My daddy'd have my hide if I let a woman drive off alone on that tire." His Adam's apple bobbed up and down. "You come on back after your trip, I'll change the oil for you."

"I'll do that." She got back into the car and cranked the engine. "Thanks again."

He nodded. "Take it easy. Come on back now."

Mary pulled into the street. She had been entertained by Bobby's conscientious efforts, and properly rebuked for not checking the car more thoroughly when she bought it. She smiled as she hit the highway.

The "fisherman's cabin" turned out to be little more than an old shack but it was perfect for Mary. She walked the beach, and sat and stared at the waves. She wondered more and more how a young innocent like Lila had accepted the strange arrangement as the Dubose consort, and found herself growing increasingly curious about what kind of person the lovely Mrs. Dubose really was.

That night, Mary sat on the beach, smoking, staring out to sea, and recalled a past she had tried so hard to forget, and not allow to shape her life.

At first, there had been the physical pain to dull her mind. The pain was everything. It hurt to breathe. She'd used all her concentration on preparing for each breath, for judging how much air she could draw in before the pain caught up to it and took it away. Her broken ribs dictated everything. She had tried to clean her face, using a mirror from her purse, but she needed water and soap and that would require negotiating with the pain of breathing and standing up straight and walking. She kept her head down and pretended to sleep, until the train pulled into the terminal and stopped. By then, both eyes were black, the left one swollen shut. Mary tied a scarf around her head, drew as deep a breath as possible, and stood, with the weight of her suitcase pulling her back down. She managed to get down the steps of the train by concentrating on each jarring step, each attempt to suck in the air to make the next step. When she made it and stood on the ground, she slowly straightened her shoulders and stood erect, relinquishing the hunched-over accommodation to the pain. After that, it was a matter of focusing on each step. Short quick breaths seemed to work best, though it was so much like panting that Mary felt light-headed. She had made it. She was away.

It was the sounds that made her nauseous, the sound of the fist meeting flesh, the crunch of the bone in her nose, the animal whimpers she emitted, the sound of her father's boots shuffling in the hay-strewn floor, trying to gain purchase to invest his weight behind each blow. It was the sound of his voice, not even raised in anger, speaking in a conversational tone, repeating the words, "My own flesh and blood," that he used to punctuate each blow. She remembered being on her hands and knees, watching each drop of blood as it fell to the floor while she waited for him to return, remembered being grateful that he had thought to bring her purse, grateful that she had been wearing shoes, because she had done a lot of walking after the train. She remembered each step of that walk with great clarity, learning how not to wince, because wincing caused her broken nose to hurt. And later, the reactions of the nuns who took her in. Some of them had revealed true kindness and sympathy, others had been disapproving and stern. But they had let her stay, even after they discovered she wasn't pregnant, as they had first assumed.

Since then, Mary had always concentrated on the step before her, and refused to look behind. She rarely thought about her father. She had spent some time, in the beginning, wondering if her mother had ever searched for her, missed her, forgiven her. She remembered the satisfaction her father had seemed to take in beating her, as if he had been waiting for the opportunity her good behavior had denied him, as though he had suspected for all her sixteen years that she was bad and had been unsurprised to finally catch her. She wondered if he had in fact sensed something in her that she had not known herself, not really, until her experiences in the barn with Elizabeth. Maybe parents could sense this in their children, and so withheld love, approval, so that they could sacrifice them without too much guilt or grief. Maybe her mother had never looked for her or missed her enough to question her father about what had happened.

When she remembered the beating in the barn, it was slowed, and without sound. Mary rarely allowed herself to remember these things, because they prevented her from going on, going forward, just as she did not allow herself to recall the details of her break up with Samantha, Big Sam's daughter. If she wanted, she could recall with minute detail the look on Big Sam's face when he burst through the door and stood, his hand still on the knob, staring at them in bed, sitting up in surprise at his entrance, Sammie naked and defiant, smiling at him, almost triumphant, but unable to hide the fear her

51

pride tried to mask. Mary imagined her own face as a perfect blank, as she absorbed the realization that Sammie had engineered this scene, that she had used Mary to embarrass or enrage or trump her father. She remembered getting up and pulling on her robe and leaving the room, tuning out the words father and daughter hurled at each other, sitting in the darkened living room with a drink until Big Sam left. He stopped on his way out and stared at her in disbelief. "Mary McGhee, you'll regret this." He shook his head and closed the door.

Mary understood that she had been a pawn in this game between father and daughter. She received a milder punishment in the end, another train ticket, a large amount of cash to ensure her silence, and a job in a backwater, forgotten town, working for an imbecile. Usually, she wasted little time on the past. It was a discipline of long standing she imposed. This time she deliberately called it up, in an effort to derail the path she was speeding down.

The next Thursday night, Lila called to say that Tommie was sick and she couldn't come to the bridge game at the Sullivans'. Mary wondered if this were true or if she was too embarrassed about their meeting in the office, but refused to dwell on it. She was far more comfortable without the disturbing presence of Mrs. Dubose distracting her. Instead, Mary thoroughly enjoyed the meal this time, and afterward she and Bill shared a fine bourbon. The pastor's wife didn't drink, but seemed not to mind that her husband enjoyed an occasional glass. She appeared to take no interest in the conversation that followed, but Mary wondered if she weren't surreptitiously taking in every word.

Mary dealt the cards for another round of gin rummy, trying with little success to ignore Bill's smug satisfaction.

"You know I planned this, the two of you becoming friends," Bill said to her.

"We're not friends. She's my employer's wife." *Why must they end-lessly discuss Lila Dubose?*

"She's still not getting out enough though." This from Barbara, who sat reading while Mary and Bill played. Mary tried to concentrate on her cards.

"We'll get her out of her shell, or you will. Just takes some time."

"Stop talking and play your hand." And damn both of you, Mary added silently.

Mary walked home, thinking that this entire town devoted far too much time and interest speculating about the Duboses. She found herself wanting to protect Lila. Mary had suffered from more practiced hands than the idle gossips in this small place. Here, people were judged over coffee, over back fences while clothes were hung out to dry along with the reputations of their neighbors, and just as casually. But like Miss Louise's mindless chatter, Mary found no harmful intent in the slander. She resigned herself for another grilling from her landlady as she opened the front door. Taking the back way was a coward's way out.

"You're back early. Did ya'll have a good time?"

Mary sank into a chair. "Yes, I did. Mrs. Sullivan made up a plate for you. You can heat it up in the oven."

Miss Louise pounced on the food. "No need to go to all that trouble." She removed the wax paper that covered the dish and began eating leftover meatloaf with her fingers.

"Mrs. Dubose wasn't there. Tommie is sick."

"Seems it's always something with Mr. Tommie. I heard downtown that Mrs. Dubose finally started spending some of his money. Wonder what took her so long?" Louise Skinner had not been downtown. She meant she had accosted someone on their way home from town and gleaned the latest news.

"She's just paying bills, like everybody else. That's all."

"That ain't all, either. I heard she gave a huge donation to the church yesterday."

"The church needs a new roof, Miss Louise. You know that." Mary watched with a sick fascination as Miss Louise used a piece of bread to scoop mashed potatoes into her mouth. Crumbs fell into her lap completely unnoticed as the old woman plowed her way through the congealing food. She picked up butter beans with her fingers and shoveled them in.

"We've been taking up a special offering each week. She didn't have to pay for the whole thing." Miss Louise did not attend church, but she sent her offering faithfully each week through Bill, who visited her. The woman acted as though she was personally affronted by the

Dubose generosity. And yet they had all been criticizing Lila for not doing more for the town. Was there no end to the mystery of the smalltown mind? "Mary, honey, could you get me a glass of milk?"

Mary rose and accomplished this task, supplying a fork as well, while continuing her defense of Lila. "What I understand, Miss Louise, is that the Duboses have been doing things like that for generations."

"That may be, but there ain't no Duboses left, except Mr. Tommie. You reckon he understands she's spending all of his daddy's money?"

"The balance needed for a new roof is hardly all of their money. And Lila is a Dubose too. She is only continuing the tradition of Dubose philanthropy this town has become far too dependent on, in my opinion. I'm going to bed. Good night."

Once again, Mary scolded herself for being too harsh with the woman. It was not up to her to defend Lila's reputation. When would Lila start defending herself? Mary slid into bed with a huge sigh. She was sure her every word would be repeated by Miss Louise first thing in the morning. She wasn't helping her cause or Lila's by adding to the litany.

Dialing the Dubose number, Mary didn't even try to justify what she was about to do. "Hello, Lila? If you're not busy, I wonder if you could come down to the office this morning?"

"Sure. I'll be right there."

Ten minutes later, Mary looked into Lila's face, freshly scrubbed, without makeup, and cursed herself for a fool. Lila sat down and said, "What did you want?"

Very good question, Mary thought. "I wondered if you could come into the office a few mornings each week and help out. I could teach you how the business works like we discussed and you could really be a help. You need to understand what goes on here. And I need to know I have the approval of the owners for some of the decisions that need to be made."

Lila gave a nervous laugh. "I'm not sure how much help I would be. I don't even know how to type."

"I'll teach you. What if you came in for a couple of hours on Monday, Wednesday, and Friday? Oh, and Thursday afternoons, that's when we need to get the payroll ready."

"Okay. Where should we start?"

Taking a deep breath, Mary said silently, we shouldn't start at all. Aloud, she said, "This is the P and L for last week. I'm sorry, the profit and loss statement. I'll explain everything to you and then you can initial it. And don't worry. Just ask me about anything you don't understand. Let's get started right now."

Chapter Five

REPORT TO THE GRAND DRAGON: Full attendance for our Fourth of July Klonvocation. Some visitors. Hadn't seen fireworks like that since Bastogne.
Wednesday, July 7, 1948

Lila and Annie sat at the kitchen table shelling butter beans. The box fan they had put in the open window simply blew in more hot air. The garden had exploded with produce, with everything ripening at once in an abundance that would waste on the vine if they did not keep up. Every day in the early morning dew, Thad, the gardener, and Tommie picked the peas, butter beans, corn, tomatoes, okra, snap beans, squash and cucumbers, peppers and onions. Tommie was on the back porch now, having fallen asleep. He had toiled all morning, and had eaten an enormous lunch. Afterwards, he and Thad had shucked corn, which Thad had taken home in a bushel basket for his wife to cut off the cob and can for them. Even with Lila helping, the two women could barely shell, pick through, wash and can the rest of each day's produce. The rows of Mason jars in the pantry gave her a sense of pride. They really didn't need such a bountiful garden just for themselves, but Lila gave away nearly half of everything. Her family was always in need of food, and Annie knew several colored families who welcomed the supplement to their own gardens. It pleased Lila to be able to do this, but it was a lot of work. Peas and beans had to be shelled before they spoiled. Lila was good at it, but Annie shelled faster than she could, her hands calloused from years of carrying out such tasks. Lila felt distracted and irritable. Her unruly hair was pulled back from her face with barrettes, ineffectively restraining her curls, and without make up, she thought she probably looked like the barefoot girl she had been before her life had changed. She sighed, again, and finally Annie spoke.

"What's on your mind? You look like the world's coming to an end."

Lila expelled another breath, pushing all the air from her lungs. "I don't know, Annie. I feel so restless and out of sorts. Maybe it's the heat. I wish it would rain."

"It's always hot. You been so quiet I wouldn't know you was in the house. What's bothering you?" Annie's hands continued to shell as she spoke amiably.

"Nothing, really. Miss McGhee said she loves the heat."

Annie looked at Lila. "Miss McGhee says. You sit around in the office heaving those deep sighs, Miss McGhee would probably throw you out."

"I don't know just what it is. I want something, but I can't seem to figure out what. I ran into my mother the other day."

"Yes, and what did Miz Jackson have to say?" Annie's tone became more reserved. She didn't much care for Lila's mother.

"The usual complaints: her health, her heart, the heat, she needs money."

"And you gave her some, didn't you, now?"

"Yes, and she suddenly felt a lot better, and I felt worse. Am I a terrible daughter? I can't take all those hints about her moving in here. If she did, the next thing, the whole bunch of them would be tramping in and out of here. What would people think about that? Besides, it doesn't seem like I have the right to have them here. This isn't really my place, you know? And it would upset Tommie."

"Honey, this is as much your home as it is Tommie's. You have the right to have anyone you want in here."

"I know, but it doesn't really feel like that to me. It feels like I'm just tending, care taking. Like any minute the sheriff will come in and say, 'Okay, it's time to go. Back where you came from, girl.' Maybe it would feel different if Tommie were different, if this was a real marriage. I'm not a wife, I'm his playmate, his nursemaid. My god, I have to make sure he brushes his teeth!" She also helped Tommie with shaving, a skill she had acquired by shaving her father on the mornings when he was so hung over his hands were too unsteady to hold a razor.

"Child, you knew that from the start. You wish you had a real husband, some children running around?"

Lila got up and emptied the box of bean hulls into a big crocus sack, packing them down. She got them both some fresh tea and sank back into her chair. "No, not really. It's funny, I never sat around dreaming about getting married, like I suppose most girls do. When I thought about it, I always imagined I would be married, but I dreaded it. I felt like, that's what I'm supposed to do, so I'll just do it, but I never was eager about it." She ran a hand through her bowl of shelled beans, letting them spill through her fingers. "What else is there for women to do, anyway? We get married and have families. Isn't there some other choice, some other way to live? Look at Miss McGhee. Is there some kind of law that says this is what women have to do, and that's it?"

"See there, some ladies have serious jobs. No reason you can't do that too. You're learning about the business."

Lila got up to wash her butter beans in the sink. Maybe I am getting tired of pretending to be Tommie's wife, she thought; maybe I do want out of the situation, but doesn't everyone at some point feel that way? Lila did not know. She considered Annie for a moment. Annie had always been comfortable in her own skin. An impressively tall Negro woman, Lila imagined Annie descended from the Masai warriors she'd heard the missionaries talk about in church. Lila couldn't remember imagining anything for herself when she was a child.

"Annie, did you get along with your mother?"

"My mama taught me to read and write, and speak properly. She told me, honey, don't you ever be ashamed of your height. I used to pretend I was a princess from an African tribe, and Mama said for all we know, maybe you was. Arthur Parnell was the only boy who didn't make fun of how tall and skinny I was and treated me like I really was royalty." She smiled. Annie rarely mentioned her husband, who had died after five short years of marriage, leaving her with two small children. Annie had lived in two rooms at the Dubose house and raised both her children and Tommie.

Lila tried to recall anything that her own parents had taught her. At least she had not acquired any of the greedy, grasping qualities that caused Lila to avoid her mother. Her father was just a mean drunk who had disappeared when she was young, and whose sons seemed in haste to follow his example. His rare appearances were

58

usually precipitated by a short jail stay that dried him out and left him momentarily guilty about the family he had deserted. They really are a worthless bunch, Lila thought wryly. Well, at least none of them would ever go hungry, as long as she and Annie could keep up with the garden, anyway. It would be easier to just take them the produce and let them shell and put it up, but she knew most of it would go to waste if she did that. Sunday afternoon, she would take most of what they had canned this week and deliver it to her mother's house, where she would force herself to sit for a while on the porch of the once grand farmhouse and listen yet again to a list of varied complaints. She shook her head to clear it of such thoughts. Annie rose to take over from her at the sink.

"I'll finish up here. Why don't you go lay down for a while? I'll get supper ready."

"No, I think I'll go down to the office. Maybe I can help Miss McGhee with the typing."

"Hi. I didn't expect you today." Mary looked up from her work. Lila dropped her purse on the desk nearest the door and stood watching Mary.

"I know, but it's so hot I had to get out of the kitchen. How do you always look so cool?"

Mary did not answer. Instead she inspected Lila, and suddenly, Lila found the heat and Mary's apparent ability to withstand it irritating. Why was she staring at her? Her lack of response annoyed Lila further.

Mary finally spoke. "You need something to do. Sit down. Feel like typing?"

Lila sat. "I suppose so. I know you could do it in half the time. You're just giving me something to play with while you do the real work. I think I slow you down instead of helping." Lila could not control the petulant tone. She knew she sounded childish and whiny.

"I type faster because I've done more of it. You'll get better at it. It takes practice. Those letters really do need to go out today. I have the payroll to do."

"Why don't we just hire a girl for the office, somebody who already knows how to type?"

"Because you are perfectly capable of helping."

59

"Yes, but I—"

"And because you like having something useful to do."

Lila looked down, studying the narrow little pumps she had chosen because they made her ankles look nice. They hurt her feet. Mary, she noted, wore more sensible shoes. "You're right."

"You need to learn how the office and the business works."

Mary kept working the adding machine as she talked, her eyes on what she was doing. Lila stared at her. She sighed again. It was so hot. It was not fair that Mary seemed impervious to the heat. She marveled at the self control of this woman, who seemingly willed herself not to perspire. Mary's hair remained in place, while Lila's always sprang back into its natural curl in such humidity. If only it would rain and clear the air.

Lila sat at the desk opposite Mary's and rolled two pages with a carbon sandwiched between them into the Underwood. She pecked at the keys, hitting them with more force than was really necessary. Mary seemed to ignore her. They sat across from each other as an hour ticked by, and Lila slowly made progress on the stack of handwritten letters, as she silently cursed the man who had invented typewriters. She took a break to watch Mary work, the slight frown between her brows making her face seem drawn tight. Miss McGhee was attractive, but most women would not think so. She had an interesting, intelligent face, rather than being conventionally pretty. Lila realized she was staring, focusing on Mary's face. She came out of this reverie to find Mary watching her.

"What is it?"

"How often do you use your car?" Mary asked.

"Never. I don't know how to drive it, and neither does Annie. It just sits in the car shed since Mr. Dubose passed away. Tommie takes apart the motor and puts it back together all the time."

"Want to learn? That is, if Tommie has put the motor back together correctly."

"Really? Tommie's pretty good at reassembling it. Bobby Riser at the service station taught him. He cranks it each time after he 'fixes' it." Lila hesitated. "Could we?"

Mary leaned back. "Wait now. Call Bobby first. Ask him to go and check the battery and oil and tires. If it will start, he can take it down and go over it. Then this evening, I'll pick it up from him and take you out on a back road."

"I know just the place. This will be fun. Oh, but it's Wednesday, I have church tonight."

"Well, get Bobby to look at it anyway. We'll do it some other time. We wouldn't want you to miss church for something fun." Mary smiled up at her, her eyes revealing something Lila would have thought was teasing, if it wasn't Miss McGhee.

"I will. I'll call him right now. Thank you. I'm sorry I didn't get much done. It's the heat. It has been wearing me down."

"That's all right. Why don't you leave now and go home and rest?"

"No, I feel better now. I'll stay and get these letters done."

Mary got up and opened a window to let in the breeze. Lila watched her. Maybe Miss McGhee wasn't as reserved as everybody supposed. Somehow, she had sensed Lila's restless mood, and offered a distraction. The barest hint of a breeze did not relieve the heat at all. The air was muggy with the threat of rain. Lila felt strangled with each breath she drew in. She refused to look at Mary when she sat down again and took up her work. She had no idea why she was avoiding Mary's eyes.

"Keep it slow and easy, now. Watch the curve coming up." Mary kept her voice even and steady, consciously refraining from gripping the dash. They'd had several driving lessons over the past two months, and really, Lila was doing quite well. It was her own nerves that were shaky.

Lila was grinning widely. "This is so much fun! When we get around the curve, can't I go faster? It's nice and straight after that." Mary wrenched her gaze from the road to glance at Lila. Her cheeks were rosy, her eyes sparkled, her hair flew with the air blowing in through the open windows, and a look of pure delight was plastered on her face. She held her chin up, peering over the dash, the steering wheel held much too loosely to suit Mary's stomach flutters. Mary took in the line of her throat, the white blouse that flapped with the rushing air, the neat belt that secured her skirt, and let her eyes move downward to assess the curves of calves and ankles. With effort she returned to the road which was passing alarmingly quickly.

61

"Take it easy for now, apply the brake just a little—" Mary braced herself against the back of the seat, her right foot pushing against the floorboard. As they made the curve, she relaxed. "That's good, you're doing fine."

Lila increased the speed just a bit. Mary kept her eyes on the road. It was straight, clear of other vehicles. She looked around. This road led to Bladon Springs, and they hadn't met another car for quite a while. The leaves on the trees which she had learned were called sweet gum were beginning to turn from green to yellow and deep red. They reminded Mary of maples. Behind them were towering pines stretching as far as the eye could reach toward a smoky horizon, hazy with heat and dust, ridge after ridge offering a glimpse of foothills that would rise into mountains. Lila was grasping the concept of applying more gas when climbing up those undulating ridges to maintain speed, then slacking off on the downhill side. She was becoming a good driver. Mary put her arm on the windowsill of the car, adjusted the side-view mirror, and smiled. Lila's hair was freeing itself from the scarf that had served very ineffectively to hold it back, and her obvious pleasure was infectious. She breathed deeply, and for a moment imagined a scent of burning wood, reminiscent of fall. They were just on the cusp of summer turning into autumn, but the heat and humidity lingered.

"Have you ever been to the springs?" Lila's question interrupted her daydreaming.

"No, I haven't."

"Then we should stop. You know, this used to be a vacation spot. I think there was even a hotel here. People would come to enjoy the springs. I guess they thought the water had medicinal or therapeutic properties."

"Really? Maybe we can cool off then."

Lila laughed. "You can stick your toes in the water if you want. But the water is sulphuric. I don't think you'll want to drink it. It stinks."

Lila expertly pulled in, turning off the paved road onto a dirt one covered in pine needles, and it was instantly cooler under the trees. Mary got out and stretched. There was a wooden pavilion that she supposed housed the springs. She moved closer cautiously while Lila stayed by the car. The odor reached her before she entered the area.

The smell of sulphur was very strong. Abandoning her idea of cool, bubbling springs with water fresh enough to drink, Mary returned to the car, leaning against the fender while she lit a cigarette, hoping it would diffuse the smell that now seemed to permeate the air they breathed. It was quiet and still under the trees. She imagined people dressed in white linen arriving in horse-drawn wagons to avail themselves of the curative powers of the water. She recalled Roosevelt returning again and again to the springs in Georgia.

"Have you ever been to Warm Springs, where the president went to swim for his health?"

Lila was startled out of her silence. "No, I haven't. I've never been out of Alabama at all, in fact."

Mary opened the car door to put out her cigarette in the ashtray, afraid to drop it on the ground. The lack of rain made everything as dry as tinder. She envisioned the pine trees going up like candles from the cigarette butt.

"Where can we get some cold drinks around here?"

Lila moved to get behind the wheel again. "There's got to be a store or a service station around somewhere. We're not that far from Coffeeville and the river."

Mary closed her door with a satisfying thud. "Let's go. I'll treat you to a Nehi."

"Make mine an RC Cola."

"All right."

"Why do you suppose the colored folks like to drink those flavored sodas like orange and grape Nehis?" Mary had no answer for this, but wondered if Lila thought drinking them would be uncouth.

Lila backed up carefully, then put the car into drive and pulled back onto the still empty highway. She drove cautiously on Highway 84, and stopped at a country store. They got out for drinks, pulling the cold bottles from the cooler, popping the tops off at the built-in bottle opener on the side, then going inside through a screen door that scraped across a sandy floor to pay, standing under the fan for the first delicious, soothing sips. Lila bought herself something in a cellophane wrapper called a Stage Plank, which Mary discovered was a soft ginger cookie coated with purple icing. There were two in the pack, so Lila shared.

Mary took the wheel for the rest of their trip. She still didn't like Lila to drive when there could be log trucks and traffic on the busier roads. She turned north on Highway 69, back to Myrtlewood, back to work, back to the present. Mary left behind her daydream of another era where people moved more slowly, carried parasols, and took the treatment at the springs to escape the effects of a long summer of heat and dust. Lila held her hand out the open car window, letting the rushing air dry the sweat and offer some relief from the heat, still grinning like a child with the thrill of the whole adventure. Mary resolutely turned her thoughts to work. She kept the image of Lila's enjoyment like a copper penny, shined and saved for another time.

Lila had learned to drive quickly, as she had learned everything that Mary had taught her. After months of vacillation, frustration, and occasional tears, Mary felt she had achieved a certain balance in her relationship with Mrs. Dubose. She was her teacher, and her employee. That was all their relationship would ever be.

Chapter Six

REPORT TO THE GRAND DRAGON: It's hot as hell. We haven't held a meeting since the 4th, just too damn hot, and men got fields to work. It's a damn shame about Truman's integrating the armed forces. We the ones did the fightin' and dyin' the last time, and we'll do it again if called.

Monday, August 30, 1948

When Lila arrived at the office at ten, Mary was on the phone with Gerald Buchanan.

"I can bring the books over to you if you like. It gets pretty hot down here in the office and your suit will get ruined with sawdust." Mary nodded at Lila as she listened for a minute. Lila knew it was a losing battle. Buchanan rather enjoyed coming down to the office and lording it over Mary.

"All right then. Wednesday at noon. I'll order some lunch from the diner." Mary hung up, looking exasperated.

While she studied Mary's face, Lila thought about it for a moment. "Mary, why don't we have lunch at my house Wednesday? I could talk to him then about your changes instead of setting up a special meeting." Why not move the meeting to a place where Buchanan would feel more comfortable?

After staring at her for a moment, Mary smiled. She called Buchanan back and extended the invitation. After some hesitation, he agreed. Then they settled in their usual places on either side of the desk they shared, Mary poring over the ledgers while Lila sorted invoices. They worked in silence in the gathering heat of the stuffy room until noon. Then Lila stood and stretched.

"It's too hot to walk home for dinner. Let's eat in the office today. This afternoon I have some letters to type. Will that disturb you?"

"No. Do you need me to see them first?"

"I think I have it in hand. Should we send the mill-boy down to the diner for something to eat?"

"I'm not hungry, just tired. I may take a nap on the sofa in the office."

"You do look tired. Won't your suit get rumpled?"

"I don't have to see anyone this afternoon anyway. You can deal with whoever comes in. I can be rumpled."

Lila had never seen Mary with so much as a hair out of place. "All right. Lock the door so you won't be disturbed. I'll go home for lunch then. I'll see you at one thirty."

Walking up to her front porch, Lila was greeted by Henry, whose father was Thad, the Dubose gardener. He was trimming the hedges around the front of the yard.

"These azaleas just went crazy this year, didn't they, Miss Lila? We should cut 'em way back after they get done blooming every year."

"You shouldn't be working today, Henry. It's a school day."

"I know, ma'am, but I got to help my daddy. The harvest starts next week and your place needs to be done before then."

"Thank you, Henry, but your daddy would get to it eventually. It's getting hot. You finish up and go on home."

Mary arrived early for her lunch with Lila and Buchanan. It was her first time inside the Dubose house. She looked around while Lila acted like a tour guide in a museum. It was a huge, two-story Victorian mansion with porches around both floors. From the outside it looked big enough to be a hotel. Inside was a central hallway leading to the back of the house. Lila rattled off the functions of the rooms as they passed them, sounding for all the world like she'd memorized a script.

"That's the front parlor. Here's the living room. That's Mr. Dubose's study. This is the dining room. And here's Annie."

An imposing Negro woman with hair that was beginning to gray turned from the sink as they entered a kitchen that certainly was big enough to serve a hotel. The apron and the gingham dress did nothing to undermine the dignity and authority this striking woman exuded. She dried large, capable hands on a towel and Mary found herself pierced by a hard stare that she didn't dare refuse to meet. She had never been so closely studied: the wide-set, probing dark eyes took in her face and—it seemed to Mary—her whole soul with one intense glance. She understood that this was a test, and so she held the taller woman's gaze as her measure was taken. After a few seconds, they began to smile at each other. Mary sensed kindness that masked a shrewd depth she found comforting rather than challenging. *I think I've been approved,* she thought. Mary relaxed, wholly at ease for having passed inspection. She liked this impressive woman. Intelligence shone back at her from Annie's eyes; she found that she did not mind the scrutiny at all. Annie gave a nod, put down her towel, and spoke.

"Well now, Miss McGhee. I been trying to get Miss Lila to invite you here for dinner I don't know how long. Mr. Tommie's on the back porch. You could speak to him if you want, but he's not wearing his suit today, you know. Says he'll do no such thing unless he has to go down to the office."

Mary took this to mean Tommie was being himself, and that her presence outside the office might upset him a bit, make him feel as though he had to play host. She nodded her understanding. She gave Annie her hand, surprising her. A second passed, initially an awkward moment; maybe one didn't shake hands with cooks and housekeepers. But Annie took Mary's hand in both of hers and held it.

"You've been a pure blessing to this house, Miss McGhee. Ya'll go on now, I've got things to do before Mr. Buchanan gets here. Miss Lila, show your guest to the living room like you're s'posed to."

Annie turned back to her work, and Lila guided Mary out of the kitchen. Lila smiled and showed her into the living room that was comfortably furnished with pieces from the 1880s—a high-backed sofa with a flowered pattern and claw-foot legs, matching wingback chairs, all facing a huge fireplace, which must be useful in the winters, Mary judged, looking at the twelve-foot ceilings. She sat down, Lila across from her, and let some of her nervousness out with a breath.

Lila leaned toward her, grinning a bit foolishly, Mary thought. "I'll be okay, Mary. Don't worry so. I know what to do. I could recite things in my sleep. Just tell me again how long I'm supposed to wait before letting him have it."

"Who?" Mary had been watching Lila's dimples. The sheer size and the unapproachable air of the Dubose house seemingly provided a buffer from the world and had a frightening effect on Mary's inhibitions. She could begin to understand why Lila had stayed locked away here for so long.

"Buchanan. Tell me again exactly when I begin to stand up to him?"

Mary wrenched her mind back to the task before them. "You'll know. It won't take long. Just play hostess, feed him, talk to him."

The bell sounded, and Lila gave Mary a wink before she left the room to open the front door. Mary took the time to inspect the parlor more closely. Windows flanked either side of the fireplace, the heavy drapes pulled back to reveal sheer curtains that stirred slightly from a breeze. The wallpaper was a pale stripe, while the wainscoting appeared to be mahogany. She guessed that this room wasn't used much, though one of the chairs looked more sat in. That one must have been Mr. Dubose's. A goose-necked pole lamp stood behind it, with a dinner plate–sized ashtray on the end table beside it. A huge, ornate, beveled mirror rose above the mantel of the fireplace, reflecting the crystal chandelier. The enormous pocket doors, which were also mahogany, slid open to reveal the dining room.

Mary gathered her thoughts, as she tried to overhear the talk between Lila and Buchanan in the front hall. She anticipated the meeting, eager for her pupil to show off her recently acquired grasp of the Dubose financial situation. She knew that Lila had not quite the same eagerness—in fact, she was probably anxious, worried that she would disappoint Mary. Mary hoped it wasn't a mistake to involve Lila in the power struggle growing between herself and Buchanan.

"Mr. Buchanan, come on in and join us in the living room. Won't you sit down? Miss McGhee has the books ready in Mr. Dubose's study. I thought we'd eat first. Is that all right with you?"

Gerald Buchanan was looking around. Mary tried to smile congenially at him, but she disapproved of him standing just inside the door, surveying the house with a proprietary air as though appraising it for sale, or as if seeing it for the first time, when he must have visited his employer's house many times. That was it, she thought. Before, he must have come as a supplicant to Mr. Dubose with his proposals, but this time he felt like he was in charge. *We'll see about that*, Mary said to herself. Buchanan was in for a surprise, if Lila didn't fold.

Buchanan apparently decided charm was the way to handle two ladies in over their heads with business matters. "Lila, you're pretty as a picture today. My mouth's been waterin' all day just thinking about Annie's cooking. By all means, let's eat first." He took Lila's arm and escorted her to the dining room, leaving Mary to trail behind. He held Lila's chair for her and sat himself at the head of the table. Mary seated herself. Folding her napkin in her lap, she was disturbed by Buchanan's pin-striped suit, with a gold watch chain winking as it dangled from a vest pocket. He was dressed much more formally than usual, she thought. He must view this meeting as the capitulation he had been waiting for, anticipating, for some time. He seemed jovial and eager.

"Where did you get this pork roast? It's so tender it just falls apart. Does your family still raise hogs like they used to? I remember my daddy taking me with him to see your daddy every fall to get him to slaughter one for us. That man sure could cure hams."

This was Lila's first test. Mary almost smiled at Gerald's blatant attempt to remind Lila of her background. She watched and waited, refusing to help. If awkward jabs like this threw Lila off balance, then she would be no help when the real sparring began.

"My daddy has been gone for years, Mr. Buchanan. We got this roast from the Piggly Wiggly in town. These butter beans came from the garden. Would you like some fried okra?"

Mary had not yet grown accustomed to the lavish, heavy meals Southerners seemed inclined to serve at lunchtime. Fried green tomatoes were served along with the fried okra, a bowl of fresh sliced tomatoes, cucumbers and onions, as well as both sweet and hot green peppers, peppery mustard leaves, gravy, and the sweet iced tea she was beginning to like. Even the desserts were served hot, the banana pudding or berry pies and cakes. She sampled her food sparingly as she watched Buchanan load his plate.

"I sure would. Just pass me that bowl of mashed potatoes. How's your garden doing this year? And I'll have to have some more of that cornbread. My wife has yet to get the hang of making good cornbread. She grew up in Birmingham."

Mary thought his last remark was a bit cryptic, but Lila nodded in sympathy, as though being from Birmingham explained everything. Maybe Buchanan was trying to compliment the hostess and at the same time, disparage her sophistication. She didn't think he was that subtle.

Lila said, "I heard that she's not from around here. You just help yourself."

Annie came in with the tea pitcher and refilled glasses. She glanced at Mary and they shared a quick grin. Buchanan was already finishing his second plate of food. He seemed to be eating in a hurry.

"Where's Mr. Tommie?" he asked, then took a huge gulp of tea and sat back.

Ah, thought Mary. Buchanan did not want to eat with Tommie at the table. Annie had been right to have Tommie eat earlier. Mary thought that she might have enjoyed watching Buchanan's discomfort in Tommie's presence. Anything that distracted him and kept him minding his manners would work to their advantage. Her disgust for the man increased. She was going to enjoy making him squirm.

"Tommie already ate. He's in the back with Thad. Miss McGhee, would you relay the same summary to Mr. Buchanan that you gave me earlier?"

"Certainly." Mary turned to face Buchanan, who was belching discreetly behind his napkin. "I expect you already know that deposits for the quarter are up ten percent. We've also let out some bids to lease timber rights. *And* we just got a contract with Scotch Lumber to supply them with pulp for their paper mill."

Buchanan nearly swallowed the ice cube he had been noisily crunching between his teeth. He had been leaning back in his chair, stretching in the way men did as if it aided digestion. He sat forward, placing his napkin beside his plate. He cleared his throat of all obstruction and grumbled disapprovingly.

"I don't know about taking on Scotch Lumber right now. You'd have to hire more men, more loggers, more trucks. That will surely wipe out any profit."

Lila answered for Mary. "I think the idea is to run two shifts at the mill. As for the loggers, Miss McGhee seems to think it's best to pay them per load, not by the hour. They become independent contractors that way, isn't that the term you used?" She nodded at Mary, who nodded back.

"Yes, that's right. They don't need to be on the payroll. They can work at their own speed and earn as much as they want, or choose to stay on at the sawmill and pull overtime. They buy back the trucks from Dubose with every load they deliver. In a couple of years, we could be out of the logging business."

Buchanan shot a suspicious look at Mary, then turned to Lila. "The Duboses have been in the logging business since 1880. They are the single largest landowners around this part of the state. You're talking about a major change in the way the company does business. Let's not jump ahead of ourselves here."

"That's right, the landowning thing. Miss McGhee explained that to me too. She proposes buying the timber rights instead of outright purchase of the land." Lila interjected this sweetly, in the same tone she used to ask Buchanan if he wanted more tea. Mary had to press her lips together to stop a smile from forming. She hoped Lila hadn't sprung the trap too soon.

"She does, does she?" His tone of voice had changed from charming to almost snarling. "Maybe that's how they do things in the oil business out in Texas. That's not how we do things here."

Mary interrupted. "This is a sound practice that will save Dubose Lumber a lot of money. We don't need the land. We need the timber. I've researched how other mills operate. It means we decrease our debt and increase our production. Anyone can sell us their timber, and we'll come cut it for them, and they still keep the land. We won't have to wait for a new stand of pines to mature on our own holdings before we can harvest it."

"Two shifts at the mill means we can pay off our notes on the timber land that much quicker, doesn't it?" Lila seemed intent on posing this pointed question with all the innocence she could muster, which, for her, was a lot. Mary was enjoying watching Buchanan's head swivel from one to the other. Seating himself at the head of the table was not as smart a move as he had assumed.

"Men with families like a regular paycheck. I doubt you'll find many that want to work for themselves."

"I've already got five who have accepted the chance to own their

71

own log trucks and work for themselves. We'll see how it goes." Mary sipped her tea, waiting for the moment when he would begin to perspire.

"You see, well, I've already signed the agreement with Scotch. Mary brought me the papers yesterday," Lila spoke up brightly, as though she had solved a great problem for him.

Now Buchanan's head whipped around so fast his jowls shook. He stared at Lila for a long moment. "Mrs. Dubose, you shouldn't be signing things like that without having me look at them first."

"My goodness. I hope I haven't done something wrong. I probably should have consulted you, but Miss McGhee said it was urgent. They were waiting for an answer, and we would have lost the deal to White's lumber mill in Thomasville. I believe you lent them their startup capital last year, isn't that right? So now we have some competition." She paused while Buchanan glared first at her, then at Mary. "You know I really depend on your advice. But there just wasn't time. But Miss McGhee explained it all so thoroughly, I thought I understood that a new source of cash coming in would help pay down the obligations at the bank. Mr. Dubose wouldn't want to be so burdened by debt, I believe. I try to think what he would want me to do."

"Well, we'll have to see how this works out, won't we? Of course the bank will always be there to help out, if this doesn't pay as much as you've been led to think it will." He turned a furious gaze to Mary. "Let's go look at those books now, Miss McGhee. I don't think we need Mrs. Dubose to sit there with us, do you? You tell Annie how much I appreciated her cooking. I'll wash up and meet you in the study."

They sat silently until the bathroom door closed, then Mary relaxed and grinned at Lila. Cutting short their moment of shared triumph, she excused herself to wash her hands in the kitchen so Buchanan could continue his polite, silly compliments before dismissing Lila in her own home. She was hoping that the heavy meal meant he would soon just nod and frown at the figures she would rattle off as soon as he joined her in the study. The man just radiated resentment at the ideas they had proposed. He would certainly be more wary from now on. Meantime, their first meeting with Lila present had been a complete success. Mary longed for a private moment to tell her so. Instead, she shared her glee in a whispered update to Annie in the kitchen.

In the study, Buchanan's barely restrained anger exploded. He lit into her even as she was closing the door. "Just who the hell do you think you are? It's not your place to go proposing business deals to Miss Lila, or to Scotch, or anybody else, do you understand me?"

Mary shrugged. "I understand that you encouraged first Mr. Dubose and then Lila to incur mortgages for land they didn't need to buy."

Buchanan stared at her, his mouth open in slack-jawed surprise. "I thought you and me had an agreement. You'd run the office and I'd take care of the business."

"I agreed to let you look at the books and to keep you informed, since Dubose has loans at the bank. When those are paid off there will be no need for you to assure yourself that the bank's investment is secure."

Now he studied her as though she were a three-toed sloth, or some other exotic creature. "You think you got Lila under your thumb, don't you, now?"

"On the contrary, I've simply got her out from under your control."

If the man's face turned any redder, Mary thought he'd burst. "I told you Lila was to have nothing to do with the business."

"That's not for you to decide. In fact, it seems that Lila is quite smart and capable when it comes to making her own decisions."

"Her own decisions, huh? She's just a trained parrot, repeating what you've taught her to say."

"Dubose Lumber will pay off all the notes on the timber land."

"We'll see about that. This scheme of yours may not work out like you think it will. You've doubled your payroll on the speculation that you can keep up with the demand from Scotch and still make those payments."

"Or we could offer to sell our holdings to Scotch; I'm sure a big company like that would jump at the offer."

"If you default, I might just foreclose and offer them the deeds myself."

When hell freezes over, thought Mary angrily. "Like you said, we'll see how it goes. I don't think that will happen."

"You've over-extended. And you, Miss McGhee, are over-reaching yourself. You're a goddam secretary!"

"Maybe, but Lila is Mrs. Thomas Dubose, and she has the right to do anything she likes with the Dubose mill and its holdings."

"She would never have thought this up on her own, a little girl from that Jackson crowd, a bunch of lazy bootleggers and drunks. I'm gonna be keepin' my eye on you. You just watch your step, Miss High and Mighty."

Name calling! Buchanan was on the ropes, she thought, as she watched him gather himself and stomp out in a huff.

"What was that noise?" The sound of children yelling came through the open window. Lila jumped up to look through the screen and saw two little kids on top of her car.

Mary ran through the house and flew down the back steps. "Hey, what do you think you're doing? Get down off of there." A small Negro boy, maybe eight or ten years old, stood on top of the Buick, screaming and pointing. The other one slid down and ran away.

"You heard her, get down right now. And get out of this yard before I call Sheriff Dunagan." Lila had followed her outside. She was livid with anger. "This is private property. Ya'll don't ever come into this yard again, you hear me?"

The boy was obviously terrified of something. "There was a dog after me, a big dog. I got up here so he wouldn't bite me."

Mary grabbed him by the shoulder when he tried to run away, and looked up and down the block for a dog. She didn't see one. Tears had washed two clean tracks down a dirty face. Big, scared eyes stared up at her; the little boy's chest was heaving.

"I don't care what's after you, you stay off my property, do you hear me? I'll call the law. Who's your folks?"

The boy grew still and his eyes got even bigger. His lower lip protruded and trembled. Mary could smell his fear; it radiated off his little body as sweat dampened his shirt.

"Hush, Lila. He didn't hurt the car." Mary kept her hand on the child's shoulder but loosened her grip. "Where do you live?"

He looked at the ground and mumbled, "Under the hill."

"Go back in the house, Lila. I'm going to take him home."

"They know better than to come up here. Coming right into the yard like that."

"Hush Lila, it's all right. He's just a little boy." Mary was amazed that Lila couldn't seem to calm down. She seemed almost hysterical about the breach of unspoken law. Finally she backed up a step.

"You shouldn't go down there now, it's almost dark. And you tell his mama to keep her younguns under the hill where they belong."

Mary ignored her and opened the front passenger door for the boy. After some hesitation, he climbed in. His little shoulders still shook with silent tears. She glanced at him. The boy's knees were dirty, as was his ragged, striped T-shirt. His short pants had holes and his feet were bare and dusty. He kept his head down and she was grateful. She didn't think she could bear to look into those eyes again. His hair had a reddish tinge, as though it had been burned by the sun. How could a child cry so silently? She looked again at his feet which stuck straight out from the seat; his legs were too short to hang down. He could have sat in the footwell of the car and had enough room to play a game of marbles.

She drove slowly down the steep and curving road that ran down the side of a gully of red clay. She stared at the shacks of corrugated tin and tar paper perched precariously on the slopes, most in deep washes cut by rains, which turned the red clay into a slippery mud that no car would be able to navigate. It was better suited for sliding; in fact, she observed several children with pieces of cardboard or tin perched on the steep slopes for just that purpose, she supposed. The boy merely pointed when she asked for directions, and she negotiated turns on the unpaved dirt road carefully. It was so deeply rutted that she was afraid she would get stuck. She came to a stop at a cabin sided with rusted, beaten tin and roof shingles. Smoke rose from a stove pipe chimney. She saw a faded curtain move. The boy opened the door and took off at a run. Mary had parked on a sharply graded yard. The car leaned and made opening her door on the uphill side difficult. She climbed out of the car and waited. After she had been standing stock still a few minutes and waiting beside the car, a colored woman with a rag tied on her head emerged from the house. She stood on the porch with her arms folded, which Mary had learned was a sign of respect.

"Good afternoon. Did you see that little boy that just ran around the corner of the house? Is he yours?"

The woman shrugged noncommitally. Mary tried again. "He was about this tall," she held her hand about waist high, "and he had kind of bushy, almost reddish hair? And some freckles under his eyes." The woman remained silent and Mary realized that she must be afraid her son was in serious trouble to have brought a white woman alone under the hill.

"Look, ma'am, he said a dog got after him, and he came onto Mrs. Dubose's property and jumped on top of her car, this car I'm driving. I'm Mary McGhee. I work for the Duboses, you know. I just wanted to make sure he made it home safely, that's all."

Finally reassured, the woman opened her mouth and called, "Mark Anthony, you get out here right now, you hear me?"

Mary was certain the entire settlement had heard. The boy in question soon enough came slowly around the corner of the house.

"What you mean, jumpin' on this woman's car? You apologize right now, and you stay away from uptown from now on. You got no business up there."

"He's all right. I just want him to know that if a dog, or anything, anybody else, is ever after him, he can come into the yard and knock on the door, and someone will let him inside, and he'll be safe, okay? Miss Lila didn't mean what she said, she didn't understand that something was after you. If I'm not there, she'll let you in, or Miss Annie will. You know her, don't you?"

Answered by silence from parent and child, Mary continued. "Miss Lila's not mad at you, not really. She didn't know a dog was after you. She thought you were just playing, jumping up and down on the car like that."

With that, she received a nod from the mother on the porch, and Mary got back in the car and drove back to Lila's. She walked in the back door to find Annie in a snit of silent huffiness and Lila sitting at the table looking both contrite and defiant. She joined Lila at the table.

"Why on earth were you threatening that poor little boy? He couldn't have hurt the car."

"He doesn't belong up here, coming into people's yards like that! He should know better than that."

"Well, my word, what would you do if a dog was chasing you?"

"I never saw any dog."

"So you think an eight-year-old just took leave of his senses and decided to cause damage to your vehicle? That child could not lift the hood on that car and you know it. And he didn't weigh enough to cause a dent if he jumped on it all day."

Annie snorted. Mary supposed that was agreement. "Lila, you scared that poor boy to death."

"Well, he shouldn't be up here anyway. They ought to stay where they belong."

"You know as well as I do that Mr. Howard Butler's dog gets after any Negro that walks past his property. He chases Thad every time he comes to work."

"I didn't see any dog. If people are going to come into my yard like that, then maybe we should put up a fence."

"And get a dog, and teach it to snarl and bite colored people?"

Annie turned and walked out of the kitchen, her lips pressed together in anger. Mary watched her leave, then turned back to Lila. "Do you realize what you sound like?"

Lila looked at her. "I can't help the way things are. That's just how it is. They have their place to live, and they should keep their children at home where they can watch them."

"You sound just like Gerald Buchanan. Thad went in to the bank the other day to ask for a loan for a used tractor. I was there making a deposit." She tried to imitate Buchanan's nasty, sneering tone of derision. "He said 'I wouldn't loan two cents for that piece of land and that run-down shack you live in. Go on home and get back behind the plow, nigger.' I stood and watched him humiliate Thad."

Mary sat back in her chair and remembered the money sitting in a Mobile bank. Buchanan was right about one thing. Thad's land and house probably weren't worth much. She wouldn't make him use it as collateral, unless his pride insisted on it. Most of the Negro farmers were losing their farms, in just such desperate deals like the one Buchanan had denied Thad. Belatedly, she saw that Lila was still sitting there, looking offended and defensive. The pink color in her cheeks gave away her embarrassment.

"Never mind about all this right now. I want to talk to Annie for a minute."

"I think she went to the garden to pull tomatoes. Don't you apologize to her on my behalf. Annie knows what I'm talking about."

"It's not that. And I wouldn't dream of denying you the chance to apologize yourself."

Mary scooted out the back door before Lila could respond. She went down the steps and spotted Annie half way down a row of tomatoes and joined her. Annie was using a stick to scrape big, fat green worms off the tomato leaves they were destroying and squishing them.

"We ain't goan have no tomatoes left if we don't get rid of these things," she said as she mashed another one. Mary began searching for them on the leaves, pulling them off and stomping them with her foot.

"Annie, how much land does Thad have?"

"He's got about a hundred and sixty acres, I reckon, a quarter section out along the river. Some of it floods when we get too much rain, so he loses those fields most years. Probably only farms about half of it."

The worm killing was making her nauseous. She gave it up in favor of swatting mosquitoes and gnats away from her face. "Do you think he'd accept a loan from me for that tractor?"

Annie stood up straight, forcing Mary to look up at her. "Why would you do something like that?"

"Just because Buchanan wouldn't, I suppose. Because of what Lila said about them remembering their place. I don't know."

She endured Annie's sharp-eyed stare. "You know Thad's worked the Dubose garden and kept up their yard for longer than I been workin' for 'em?"

Mary realized that the man must be older than she thought.

"How many children does Thad have?"

Annie considered. "Now, he's been married before. Had five with his first wife, she died after birthing the last one. Four with his second one. Most of the first ones is grown and gone."

"Where did they go?"

"What do you mean?"

"You said the first bunch is gone now."

"Oh. Well, seems like his oldest girl, she's still here in Myrtlewood. Teaches at Harper High School, that's our colored school. The others, boys, they moved over toward Enterprise, I think, share cropping on one of them big peanut farms."

"And there's four younger children still at home?'

"That's right. What's got you so interested in Thad?"

"I don't really know. Maybe I'll talk to Thad the next time he comes by the lumber yard."

"This ain't something you'd be wantin' Miss Lila to know about, is it?"

"Well, maybe we should keep it between us."

The two of them stood there, up to their hips in tomato vines and bugs, with the smell of the rich earth and the mosquitoes buzzing around them, the sun now gone and dusk falling so that though they stared at each other, features and expressions were indistinct and unreadable. Mary wasn't sure she wanted to see Annie's face right then, and she was certain that she didn't want Annie reading what she was thinking. Suppressing the urge to shake her hand, Mary simply nodded and turned to go.

As she walked home, Mary wondered why she was getting involved. It made no difference to her that Buchanan was mean and rude and he did have sound financial reasons for refusing the loan to Thad. Had he extended the loan, he most certainly would have foreclosed at the first opportunity.

On the other hand, Mary didn't want or need the money that sat unused in the bank. She had spent some of it to buy a car, but otherwise she had not touched it. She didn't care if she loaned it out and never got it back, didn't care if it earned interest for her. It made her feel degraded. Big Sam's way of ensuring her silence about his daughter, she had kidded herself that it also ensured his silence about herself. The fact that she had taken it still left her with an uneasy conscience. She had colluded in her own guilt. It was better to get rid of the money. It might not salve her pride, but at least it wouldn't be there as a reminder.

She was startled out of her musings by Dr. Morgan, who stopped her as she gained the steps of Miss Louise's house. He was just emerging from the living room, his hat in one hand, black doctor's bag in the other.

"Hey, Miss McGhee, how're you this evening?"

She sat down on the porch swing, still distracted by the recent events in Lila's yard and her conversation with Annie. "I'm fine. It's awful hot, isn't it?"

He perched on a chair and fanned himself with his hat. "That it is. I've just been visiting with Miss Louise. Hope she isn't getting out too much in this heat."

"Is she all right?"

"Oh, she's fine. Just refuses to recognize that at her age she shouldn't be sitting out here all day long, every day, like she does."

"Dr. Morgan, you know everybody around here pretty well, don't you? You've known Lila all her life."

"I delivered her. Well, she delivered herself before I got there, but I was the one washed her and wrapped her in a blanket and handed her to her mama."

Mary was silent for a moment. She had never seen Lila so upset. "What is it about this place that makes some people go stark raving mad on the subject of colored people?"

The doctor put his hat down and fumbled for his glasses. He put them on and peered at Mary. "You two have a disagreement on that topic?"

"Yes. Lila is the most generous, kind-hearted person I know. She seems to have a blind spot when it comes to Negroes, though. Why is that? They're just people, trying to live, like everybody else."

"Did something happen?"

"A little boy came into the yard and jumped on the car. He said a dog was after him. Then Lila went after him, wailing like a banshee that he wasn't allowed in the yard, that he wasn't 'supposed' to be in town, to get off her property and back where he belonged. She threatened to call the law. I drove him home, down under the hill."

"I see. You'd never been down there before?"

"It was like another world. Look around here. Trees lining the streets. Neatly mowed green yards. Trimmed hedges. The houses all freshly painted white, cars in all the driveways, sidewalks, streets paved ..."

"And down there, red mud and dust and outhouses and tin shacks. Poverty, disease, misery. I'm the only doctor in town, you know. I treat those people, I've been in their homes."

Mary turned puzzled eyes to him. "How do they pay you?"

He laughed. "Better than some of the people in these neat houses up here. I get a sack of hickory nuts or black walnuts, a mess of greens, or sometimes somebody comes to till my garden for me. They know I don't have time, really. My peas get picked and shelled. Firewood gets split and stacked. I get paid pretty well, most of the time." He paused to pull a thin cigar out of his pocket. "White people wouldn't dream of paying in kind like that. No offense intended to Miss Lila, but I delivered every single one of the Jacksons, her brothers' children that is, and not one of them would think of offering anything in the way of payment other than cash, which they don't have. It's beneath them to think of working off a debt like that."

"Lila's family owes you money?"

"No more than anybody else around here."

Mary was appalled. The Depression was over. How could people live like they did here, completely ignoring an entire segment of the population, effectively confining them in a camp as though they were prisoners of war? And how could Lila accept this dichotomy?

Chapter 7

REPORT TO THE GRAND DRAGON: *Held a meeting of the Klavern as ordered. Six attended.*

Friday, September 10, 1948

"Dubose Lumber and Supply."

"Mary? It's Sammie." Samantha Stewart hadn't needed to identify herself. Mary would never forget that voice, nor its effect on her.

"Sammie." Thinking she sounded too hesitant and cold, Mary repeated, "Sammie?"

"Yes, it's me. Had a hell of a time finding you. I'm out, I'm on the loose. Tell me how to get to where you are."

"You're not in school?"

"Hell, no. One year of that's enough. It'll be Thanksgiving before Big Sam even realizes I'm not there. I've been driving around for a month, having myself a fine time. Tell me how to find you in that backwater town where he stashed you. I'm coming to get you."

To Mary's ear, Sammie sounded drunk with the success of her month-long freedom and wild to follow through on her latest impulsive idea. Even after all these months, Mary still felt a familiar tension at the sound of this reckless, raspy, low-throated young woman. She had been involved in too many of Sammie's wild escapades—which usually included far too much alcohol—not to be nervous.

"Coming here is not such a good idea. There's a beach on Mobile Bay not too far from here. Can you meet me there tonight?"

"Honey, I can meet you anywhere. I'm free. Actually, I'm a couple of hundred miles from you, but I can be there by midnight. Where at the beach?"

"There's a little cottage I rent there. I'm sure you won't have any trouble finding it." Mary tried to disguise the caution in her voice.

"And you can lose that tone. I haven't murdered anyone, much as

82

I'd like to, except for that other person they keep trying to turn me into. Sweet, obedient Samantha is no more."

Mary ignored the last remark and concentrated on giving directions to the beach cottage. She hid her reluctance. She was ashamed of it. She had forgotten her distaste for Sammie's drinking and reckless-ness, but she knew Sammie was still a lost child, really. After she hung up the phone, Mary sat and thought about her resolution to re-evaluate her past in light of her present situation. Maybe having her past reappear in the flesh could provide just the jolt she needed to keep her from starting down the same road with Lila.

Lila. She was supposed to give her a driving lesson. How could she have forgotten? She stood and paced back and forth. Composing her excuse, she finally picked up the receiver and dialed the Dubose number.

"Hello." Tommie answered. Mary smothered a curse of impatience.

"Tommie, could you—"

"It's Miss McGhee! Are you at work?"

"Yes, I'm just about finished for the day. Could I speak to Miss Lila, please?"

"She's in the kitchen with Annie, fixing supper. I'm hungry."

"Could I talk to her for a minute?"

The phone clattered. Tommie must have dropped it. Mary waited. After a moment, Lila came on the line.

"Hello."

"I'm afraid I have to cancel our driving lesson this afternoon, Lila. Something has come up and I have to be out of town for the week-end."

She hoped Lila would not ask her for any details. Somehow, she was reluctant to tell her she was meeting someone.

"Mary, I can drive by myself now. I don't really need any more instruction. It's just more fun to practice with you right there. I've enjoyed every minute of our lessons."

Lila's soft laugh came through the phone line, and it affected Mary deeply, in a way she was trying to ignore. Why did she enjoy being teased by Lila? Why did she wish Lila would ask her where she was going? Suddenly, she regretted agreeing to meet Sammie.

"Don't let our plans stop you from doing something else. I make too many demands on your time as it is."

"You don't," Mary interrupted, speaking much more sharply than she had intended.

As she waited for Sammie at the cottage that night, Mary paced and smoked. She dreaded Sammie's arrival. She kept thinking of Lila, imagining how it could be different with her, tormenting herself with the fantasies and images she had fought and denied for the past few months. Finally a car pulled up, and headlights momentarily blinding her. She put out her cigarette and held open the screen door as Sammie burst in, struggling under the weight of a suitcase and an overnight bag. These she dropped on the floor, and then she wrapped Mary into a bone-crushing embrace, complete with pounding on the back.

"Oh my God, you look the same. So cool and detached and uninvolved. You even smell the same. That's my Mary. How have you been?"

Mary returned the hug. In fact, contrary to how she had expected to feel, she clung to Sammie. The familiar scent of the perfume she wore, mixed with the smell of alcohol and cigarette smoke—it all brought back memories she had until now willfully blocked. The feel of Sammie's body against her awakened nerve endings and increased a hunger along her skin she had thought was under control. The feel of Sammie's hands made her realize how long it had been since any-one had touched her. Maybe that was a part of her growing attraction to Lila, simply a hunger for physical contact that she missed. Maybe she had elevated a physical desire into something it was not. She closed her eyes and let Sammie's hands move over her with rough affection and eagerness. Mary breathed in her scent again. She held Sammie's face in her hands, and Sammie needed no other encourage-ment to kiss her. Now Mary had the taste and the smell and the feel of how it had been, and her body responded as it always had.

Mary pulled back momentarily from the kiss and shook her head. That was all. She looked into Sammie's face, at her closed eyes, her full lips. She drew closer and kissed Sammie again, unable to resist the familiar tug, the burn, as her body betrayed her once again. Then she grew angry at her inability to control herself and jerked away. She went to the window, snatching up her cigarettes as she crossed the room to stare out at the night. Her hands were trembling. She tore the cellophane wrapping off the red pack of Pall Malls and shook out a cigarette.

"Same old Mary. What's eating at you this time? Can't be me, I've only been here five minutes. Where did I put that bottle?" Sammie dug through her suitcase and came up with a bottle of whiskey. She held it up to the light triumphantly to measure its contents. "Half a pint. Want a drink?"

Mary shook her head. She inhaled deeply and refused to turn around, staring out at the darkness instead. She shook her head again and turned to face this girl who had come back from her past to haunt her, to remind her of what lay in store if she started something with Lila.

"Are you enjoying your exile?"

"Exile?"

"Yes, how do you like the little town Daddy banished you to?"

"It's okay. The job is interesting. I've been all right."

"What does that mean? You obviously haven't been pining for me. You look as though you'd rather I hadn't come."

Mary sat down on the edge of the bed that was pushed against a wall of the one-room cottage and watched Sammie carefully pour a drink. "It's not that. I've just been doing a lot of thinking. Seeing you again, when I thought I never would, makes me realize how isolated I've been." She paused, hoping she sounded more welcoming than she felt. "How have you been?"

"Look at me: all properly and respectably attired. Doesn't that tell you how I've been? Obedient and miserable. I'm through, though, that's it. I'm done being Daddy's good little girl. I'm not following orders any more. I'm done searching for a husband to take home. I'm not doing anything anyone tells me to do."

"When did you ever?"

"You disapprove. You want me to make the best of a bad situation, like you've done? You want me to be busy, active, engaged in some useful work like yourself? I could never be like you. I just don't give a damn any more. I've been in every road house and tavern between

85

here and Austin in the last month, and I've had fun. He doesn't even know I'm gone. And I'm not going back. Not this time." She leaned toward Mary, speaking the words slowly and deliberately. "Don't worry, I'm not here to ask you to take me in again. I just wanted to see you, to make sure you are all right."

"Sammie, that's not it. Or not all of it. What have you done?"

Sammie dropped into a chair. "He can't touch me if he can't find me." Mary knew better. Big Sam could find anyone if he wanted to. The man had connections all over the country—even Nowheresville, Alabama.

Mary smoked while Sammie talked. She believed Sammie was sincere about wanting to see her, but probably not just for the reasons she had given Mary. It had nothing to do with love, or nostalgia for the closeness they once shared. Sam wanted an audience for her latest adventure, someone who would chuckle at her dangerous shenanigans, who would appreciate her daring. Mary kept a slight frown on her face, displaying disapproval, but she admired Sammie for her willingness to meet life head-on.

So she let her talk and only half listened. She knew the plot, knew Sammie's style, and while the specific details may have changed, Mary knew how the story would end, with Sammie in a drunken, defiant rage against her father. She paid attention instead to Sammie's voice, and gave her appearance a closer inspection. Her blond, shoulder-length hair was stiff with hair spray and mashed flat on one side, as if she had slept on it. Her green eyes were bloodshot, her mascara smeared. The dove-gray traveling suit she wore was rumpled, and the matching pumps were scuffed. One stocking had a run in it. The expensive cut of her clothes could not overcome the effect of a month of living out of a suitcase. She had a pallor that cosmetics and a lifetime of living outdoors could not hide. Sam had grown older, and it showed. She was more careless of herself. Her gestures were all broader, exuding confidence or loss of control, Mary couldn't tell which. There was a jaded, weary aspect behind it all, something dull inside her eyes, as if she didn't expect much of herself or anyone else.

"… and that's what I've been doing. Hitting every bar being built along the highways to accommodate all the oil workers and cowboys. They all look the same, and smell the same, like sawdust and new lumber, mixed with sweat and beer and oil and cowshit. They bring their women along on Friday nights. I used to be one of those women, you know, all dolled up, hanging on every word they said, sitting patiently while they ignore us and talk about the good stuff. Real work. The women talk about nylons and makeup and babies. Christ."

Mary laughed, but didn't say what she was thinking—that Sammie had more in common with the cowboys and the oil workers than with the women, including a sexual interest in the bored but patient girls who already understood their duty was tolerance and waiting in attendance on their men.

Sammie frowned at the laugh, but continued her story. "I go to bed with most of them, the girls, I mean, but sometimes with the boys too. You know how it is."

"No, I really don't."

"I remember now, you pretend you don't like men, and you ignore your attraction to women whenever possible."

Sammie rambled on as she drank. She'd found herself attracted to the "boys" who were really men, the ones who fought in the war and came home to dig wells and herd cows. The ones who had scars but never mentioned them, who ignored their women to talk among themselves about the bull that had turned on them that day, or the well that was a bitch to cap, or the horse that threw them, the truck that broke down at the farthest possible point from the ranch. Mary listened, caught up in her story now, seeing a different Sammie. Apparently this was her world now, among men who drank happily, talked loudly, leaned heavy shoulders forward, and only occasionally remembered the women sitting beside them. She spoke of them fondly, these men who often disagreed to the point of throwing punches, then bought each other beers and grinned, as if nothing could be more pleasing than to smash a best friend in the face and then help him to his feet, brush the sawdust off him, and buy him a drink.

Mary realized with growing alarm and disappointment that Sammie was describing Big Sam's world. She seemed much colder and harder, and intent on a path of personal abuse while she waited for her father to die. Mary tried to hide her dismay as Sammie sprawled in her chair and conveyed with attitude and posture the slumped image of a drunken cowboy.

"So what about you?" Sammie asked abruptly, halting the recitation of her exploits.

Mary thought for a moment before replying.

"You've caught me at a funny time. I've been thinking about things. Rummaging through the past like a box of old pictures. Some of it's not so flattering."

"Same old Mary. Still holding yourself to a higher standard. I've missed you, your careful, proper, well-considered self. It's a wonder you ever let yourself feel anything. I can see something is bothering you. Tell me. I know it's not me. I could tell that when we kissed, and if it's not me, it must be someone new. Is that it?"

"No."

"Liar. Come on, tell me."

Sammie was quiet for a change, allowing Mary to collect herself. She lit another cigarette. "Why does this keep happening to me? What does it mean, always being attracted to the wrong person at the wrong time? I just torture myself this way."

"You mean why is it always a woman? That still pisses you off, doesn't it?"

"Yes, it does." Mary flicked ashes into the ashtray beside the bed. She was annoyed that she had said this much to Sammie, and suddenly it seemed that she could not control her anger at all, the tight hold she had maintained on her emotions for the past months snapping.

"Doesn't it bother you too? Look what your attraction to women has cost you."

Sammie's face hardened. "It'll cost dear old Daddy a lot more, someday."

"Don't you ever wonder if our lives would have been easier if we could ignore this and live like normal women?"

"We are normal, you idiot. We just like what we like, that's all."

"I wonder if my life would have been different if I could have let go of my attraction for my best friend Elizabeth when I was sixteen. But I was so young, so fascinated with my own desires, and ignorant of the cost. I actually believed that my parents would find a way to love me in spite of my peculiar predilection for girls. God. I was too wrapped up in my own exploration of this new, exciting love to see the world as it was. I was a fool."

Mary paused, and Sammie remained silent, apparently unwilling to break the mood that Mary was in. She sat holding her glass of whiskey with her eyes half closed, but Mary knew she was only feigning disinterest.

"You must be taking great pleasure in finally seeing me lose control," Mary said. Already disgusted with herself, she ran her hands through her hair. She crushed her cigarette and immediately lit another, frowning at it. The smoke she inhaled was not providing the usual calming, comforting effect. After a moment she went on.

"I didn't really understand the depth of my foolishness, not then. Not even when I got involved with you. It seems like I still don't understand it. Here I am, caught once again by emotions and desires it would be foolish to indulge. I feel trapped, Sammie, because I crave what is not acceptable. Exiled to the back of beyond, isolated, and yet it happens again. I don't understand. Am I supposed to keep moving, never stay anywhere too long, so this doesn't happen?"

Mary knew her voice rang with self-pity. Any other woman might also have been crying, but her eyes were dry. While her tone may have weighed heavily with sarcasm, its pitch was as steady as her hands. Mary felt out of control, as though she were the one drinking whiskey instead of Sam, who sat calmly sipping, clearly captivated by the real emotion and indecision Mary was revealing, even as she fought to regain some composure.

Sammie shifted in her chair. "You sure are stirred up tonight. Did you ever think back about what happened to us? It was just like what happened to you and your little girlfriend Elizabeth, wasn't it? Only this time it was my daddy walking in and finding you instead of yours. And nobody's nose got broken."

Mary flinched, remembering for a moment. The sounds and smells always came back with that memory. She could see her own blood dripping, spattering the straw on the barn floor, hear the horses shifting in unease, hear her father's expressionless voice again. Mary lifted her gaze from the floor to Sammie's face.

"Were you disappointed? I know what happened, Sammie. You

called your father and told him, or had someone tell him. You had someone give him a key. You wanted him to find us in the most blatant, unambiguous circumstance possible."

Sammie was staring back at her, but not without warmth. Mary realized she'd been angling to get the conversation to this subject.

"Were you hoping he would drop dead of a heart attack on the spot? Then all the money would have been yours," Mary said. "When was the first time you caught him with a woman, anyway? As much as you say you despise him, you can never stop trying to become just like him."

Mary said it without malice or bitterness and Lila flashed into her mind again. Mary couldn't stop thinking about how similar her present situation was to the one with Sam.

"You know, Mary," Sammie said, "there's some people who might call you a bitch. Not me. You knew all along, didn't you? I had a lot of fun with you, you know. You'll never admit that you enjoyed me too, but I know you did. Besides, I never would have let Big Sam hurt you. I saw to it that you got a lot of money out of him."

"Yes, thank you, I was paid off like a whore," Mary said bitterly. "Why do the rich always assume that money solves everything? You only think you're as tough as he is. You're lucky he didn't shoot us both." Then Mary smiled. She could look back at this part of her life now and admit to herself that she had enjoyed Sammie. But she still remembered the look on Sammie's face as she had stared at her father from the bed. All defiance and triumph, Sammie couldn't hide completely the thrill of fear she'd experienced, watching her father's reaction.

"Come on, let's go sit on the beach." Sammie put down her drink and pulled off her clothes, then searched through her suitcase for a pair of jeans and a shirt. She snatched the bottle from the table. To Mary, she looked better, more familiar, in her own clothes: young, bleary-eyed, glowing. Her blond hair, which at some point had been carefully arranged, was now hopelessly mussed, and her lipstick all but blotted away. She stood there, slim, tall, looking exactly like herself, with her worn jeans, bare feet with chipped red polish on her nails, tangled hair, one hand gripping the neck of the whiskey bottle like the handle of a gun, waiting for Mary, who paused for a moment to capture this image of the girl she remembered. Suddenly Mary knew there had been more to their relationship than convenience and need. Sam was gorgeous in her hunger and her lack of despair. She was simply born too late for the way she was made. A hundred years earlier, and a different sex, and she would have been all she yearned to be: a rancher on the open range, fighting with the land; she would have been with Sam Houston at San Jacinto, with Taylor in Mexico. She would have been her own grandfather. Mary grinned, seeing Sammie as a grand old Texas gentleman. She followed her out the door and down to the water.

They built a fire big enough to signal ships at sea. Sammie waded out into the waves in her jeans and got soaked. She laughed when she came back to the fire and fell to the sand. Mary watched her lying there, drinking from the bottle, then grinning and winking.

"The only reason you allowed anything at all between us was because you assumed it was all a ploy on my part, a scheme to get to my daddy."

Mary shrugged. "Wasn't that what it was for you?"

Sam laughed. "Maybe. You give me too much credit. It began because I just didn't give a damn what anybody thought. I wanted you, with your icy exterior, so cool and collected, so very proper. Except for that gleam in your eye when I caught you looking at me. Maybe it was you who gave me the idea of using it to rile him. I don't know. Maybe I was tired of not being able to break through that facade of yours. At the time I wasn't sure there was anything else behind it at all. But okay, I'll admit to mixed motives. I wanted our relationship to be a slap in his face, but I also hoped it would wake you up too."

"You're not seriously trying to use me as an excuse?" Mary raised an eyebrow.

"No, really. I used to imagine that if the Japanese had dropped an A bomb on Houston, you would apply your makeup, put on your hat and gloves, and walk through the rubble and the dead bodies and go to work. I thought nothing could get through to you."

Mary turned her gaze back to the water.

Sammie laughed again, still lying in the sand. "You never said you knew at the time. Though there was damn little time for discussion afterward. I knew he would exile me. That's what he always does when I misbehave. I swear I never figured he'd do the same to you, though. Why did you let him? My God, I've seen you stare down colonels from the Pentagon. Besides, sooner rather than later, one of his so-called buddies would have hired you to try to learn his business secrets from you."

Mary snorted. "Not likely, after Sam caught us. He would have told everyone about me. No one would have hired me in Houston."

"Why did you let him get rid of you—guilt? Because you'd ruined his little girl? I know you didn't care enough about me to hang around, but the Mary I knew would not have left town like a dog that's been kicked too many times. You were stronger than that."

"Don't tell me you were disappointed when I left. My part was over. I had no role to play in your next round with Big Sam. Has it taken you this long to come up with your next move? Don't you think finding me again is a bit repetitive?"

Sammie sat up. "Mary, looking you up was not a strategy. I did it just for the hell of it, to see how you are. He doesn't even know where I am."

Mary turned toward her and focused on Sammie's face. "I believe you may have been concerned about me, but you always have mixed motives, don't you Sam?"

There was enough suggestiveness in Mary's tone to make Sam grin, though blushing was beyond her. "All right, I admit that too. I missed you. You're quite something, you know that? You're the only woman who could take control of me, something I always despise when men try it. You matched me perfectly in bed. I miss that. Most women expect me to take the lead. But you—you're all fire and ice."

Sam stopped abruptly. Her voice had grown husky.

"It's okay, Sammie. I know."

But she made no move to touch Sammie. After a minute Sammie shrugged. Mary threw another piece of wood on the fire. Smoke and sparks made their eyes water. They sat for a while without speaking, the fire between them flaring up as the new log began to burn. Mary sat leaning back on her hands, watching waves lazily slapping at the shore. Sam lay back, propped on her elbows, her long legs sprawled out, her head turned toward Mary. Her image seemed to burn in the flames between them.

"So talk. Tell me what it is. I know there's a woman, one you haven't even tried to approach. You're so full of that noble, self-denial crap. Tell me about her. Is she beautiful? Young? Married?"

Mary allowed herself a long sigh. "All those. Married, young, and rich. My boss's wife."

Sam whooped and fell over laughing. "You do like to repeat yourself. You really stick to a pattern, don't you? First the boss's daughter, now the boss's wife. And you tell me I'm stuck repeating my daddy's mistakes. Whose path are you following?"

"I don't know. I just know it's back, that horrible feeling of wanting something I can't have, something forbidden, out of reach, impossible. Just like when I was sixteen and yearning for Elizabeth. But I'm not sixteen any more, and I thought I could handle this, control it, like a toothache but not a bad one, just a dull ache that will go away if I leave it alone."

"And now that I've showed up?"

"Seeing you made me realize I'm lying to myself. Age and experience don't help. Maybe they make it worse. I no longer have the energy to endure all this. I'm older and tired of fighting my feelings, but I can't afford to indulge them. I have a job I really enjoy. I like the town. It reminds me of the one where I grew up."

"But?"

"But I can't get this woman out of my head. She really is remarkable, beautiful, innocent, eager. She has no idea how she tortures me, invades my dreams, takes my breath away when she walks in the room. I hate it when I fuck with myself this way."

Mary had never said that word out loud before, but there it was. She was saying things to Sammie that she hadn't even admitted to herself. She looked up at the night sky, wondering if the distant and uninterested God she imagined was the same one Lila so obviously believed in. She doubted it. The dispassionate God Mary often railed against would remain unmoved by this rambling, pathetic disclosure of need. Mary briefly envied Sammie's freedom. Sammie had never been so consumed or so passionate about anything except herself, and certainly, Mary had never felt this way about her. Mary turned and looked at her former lover, who had been waiting patiently in silence.

"Aren't you tired?"

Sammie rested her chin on her arms. "No. I'm just waiting for you to go on about your new woman."

"There's nothing else to say. I've been teaching her how to drive a car. She comes to the office to help me out." Mary took a deep breath. "But her husband—"

"Right. Now we get to the good part. What about him? You're crazy about his wife right under his eyes and he hasn't even noticed?"

Mary laughed weakly. "You have a way of getting right to the heart of things, don't you?"

"Well? Has he noticed or not?"

"No. Lila hasn't even noticed how I feel. My God, I feel like I'm possessed. I think about her all the time, I even dream about her. There is no escape. I keep having the same dream about her, over and over. In the dream, she feels so small and fragile in my arms. We're sitting in a car in the rain, and we're soaking wet, like we just ran through a downpour. Lila is lying across the seat with her head in my lap. I brush wet hair from her face, tenderly, carelessly, like I'd done it a hundred times before. God damn it all."

Mary paused and glanced over at Sammie, who smiled back encouragingly but did not speak. Completely absorbed in her own dilemma now, Mary's voice was low as she continued.

"I love her. I know how stupid that sounds, but I wish just once I could see that slow smile on her face that says she knows and feels it too. That it's all right. I wish the dream were real."

Mary paused again. She was trembling. Sammie looked away. It must be hard for her to listen to all this, Mary thought. After all, she bore some of the responsibility for Mary's banishment to that godforsaken town. Mary was humiliated, angry at using Sammie as a listening post, angry at everything, even Lila, for being so oblivious to the effect she had on her.

"Who am I kidding? I must have wanted this. I must be enjoying it, the pain, the frustration, the unfulfilled desire, the struggle to deny it, the whole game. It lets me think about the past, you and Elizabeth, how sweet and torturous it all was. I get to feel sorry for myself. Maybe that's all I really want."

"That's bullshit." Sammie moved around the fire and reached out a hand to Mary, who took it and squeezed, then let go. "You're just

94

mad at yourself because you haven't got the nerve yet to speak to her."

"Why do I prefer women? Things would be so much simpler if I didn't, or if I could resist this urge. I envy the ease of passage through the conventions of life that this 'preference' denies me. I would prefer to live alone, not to have this need. Wouldn't you?"

Sammie laughed. "Not for a minute. And neither would you. This innocent girl has got you tied into knots. You need to loosen up." Kneeling behind her in the sand, Sammie massaged Mary's neck and shoulders.

The fire had died down. Mary was so engrossed that she didn't notice the chill. Sammie shivered and took another swallow from the bottle. Then she put her arms around Mary.

"It's funny. I never felt so drawn to you as I do now, listening to you talk about how much you want someone else. Even when we lived together, slept together—God that was magnificent, wasn't it? Even then, I mostly thought about myself. I never thought about how using you to needle my daddy would affect you." She hugged Mary closer to her and with her lips next to her ear, whispered, "I'm sorry."

Mary smiled in the dark. "It's okay. I'm sorry I spilled all this out. None of this is your doing, Sammie."

"Don't you get tired of denying yourself the chance to see if what you want is possible? The truth is—"

Mary interrupted, real anger sharpening her voice, contrasting with the almost dreamy tone she had used before. "I hate it when someone begins a sentence with 'the truth is' … I'm telling the story of my life; I don't have time to be bothered with the truth of it. I can relive the story of my life with you, and leave out the betrayal. I can remember the story of my father finding me in the barn with Elizabeth, and leave out the part where he breaks my nose, the part where I never see my mother again." She drew a ragged breath, trying vainly to calm down. "What I can't do is go through this again with Lila. If I have to endure this embarrassing rebellion of my body, then I want something in return. I don't want her concern or her pity. You know what I do want from Lila, and we both know that is not possible."

"Who says so?"

"Stop it. Even if she could return the feeling, it's who she is, the

95

situation she's in, that makes it impossible. It's nothing but trouble for her. I feel such a victim of this uncontrollable need. The past has apparently taught me nothing."

Mary stood abruptly, disgusted with her sorry tale. Sam stood up too, and reached out a hand to her. Mary took it and smiled.

"I apologize for going on like that. It can't have been very pleasant to sit through."

Sam hugged her. "You don't have to be so damned stoic all the time. In fact, I'm relieved to find you have feelings like the rest of the world. I just wish you would let go a little more, stop punishing yourself. You must be exhausted by now. Come inside and go to bed."

They walked back to the cottage. Sammie was right, Mary was exhausted, and she went to bed at once. Sam peeled off her wet clothes and crept into bed beside her, holding onto Mary and falling asleep immediately. Mary lay awake for a long time in the dark, wondering why she couldn't accept Sammie's offer of comfort.

When Mary woke, the sun was high and the heat in the room was stifling. She sat up slowly and smelled the freshly brewed coffee. She got dressed and, taking a cup of coffee with her, went outside to keep an eye on her guest. Sammie was lying on a blanket in the sand, sound asleep, and Mary sat down beside her, watching the horizon as she performed the tricky maneuver of lighting a cigarette in the Gulf wind. A returning soldier had given her his Zippo lighter as they sat together in a Houston hotel bar sharing a drink. It was the only one of his varied offers she had accepted. It was peaceful in the early morning. She poked the sleeping figure beside her.

"Wake up. Have you had coffee or breakfast yet?"

Sammie rolled over and squinted at Mary, one hand shading her eyes.

"Not enough. Gimme yours." Mary gave her the coffee. Sammie did not speak as she sipped it like a dose of medicine she must take or die. Mary lit another cigarette and handed it to her. Sammie nodded her thanks silently. She had always wakened slowly, taking several minutes to become fully alert. It was some time before she spoke.

"How'd you find this place?"

"Just driving around one weekend. There was a note on the door to call the owner about renting. She's a very old lady whose husband built it to use as a fishing shack. After he died, it was left to fall apart. I've fixed it up some for her, so she only rents it to me. I come down here most weekends now."

Fully awake, Sammie obviously decided that it wasn't too early to begin poking and prodding at this new, uncertain Mary.

"And why is that? Too hard to stay in town with your girl without marching over there and proclaiming your intentions?"

Mary didn't really mind Sammie's prying. "Something like that. Sammie, I made a place for myself when I took the job. The business needs me."

"You think the woman has any interest in you at all, that way?"

"No, I don't."

"And you're scared that giving her some sign of your interest might ruin everything, and you'll have to move on. But what's wrong with moving back to a real city, somewhere closer to where I am maybe, so we could see each other and you wouldn't be so lonely?"

"So the same thing could happen again, in the next place? And the next? Is that all there is for people like us, Sammie?"

"We get to have a life, too, you know. For me, there's the ranch. I'll get it back someday. For you, it could be your own business, maybe. And am I so bad as an alternative until the next sweet young thing comes along?"

"You're not nearly as bad as you pretend to be. Stop daring me to rush in and be impulsive like you. And please, stop offering yourself to me. You don't really mean it."

Sammie grinned. "I'm going to sleep in the bed. You sit here and stew."

Mary walked along the beach, getting sand in her shoes, listening to the wash of the waves and letting herself imagine that it was Lila waiting for her back in the little shack. She imagined them sharing weekends together here, away from that town where everyone knew what everyone else was doing. She looked out at the calm seas, the swells barely discernible as they sluggishly rolled in. It was still hurricane season. Tomorrow or the next day, this sea could be churning and boiling with the high drama of a storm. Mary irrationally longed for just such a dramatic change in her own life, and dreaded the unpredictability that getting what she wanted would bring.

97

That evening, she and Sammie sat on the small porch sipping beer. They had taken a drive and Mary had shown Sammie around the bay, stopping for a meal in a diner where Sammie tried to shock Mary by flirting with the waitress, who was unimpressed or simply unaware. Now they sat watching the light fade over the water, and Mary thought again how much the little shack and the water and the beach and the sea air calmed and soothed her. The breeze ruffled her shirt collar above the sweater she wore, and ruffled Sammie's hair, shampooed and brushed free of hair spray, and she watched as strands of it whipped across her face. Sammie looked refreshed and rested, clear-eyed, and beautiful in soft leather boots and wool slacks, a cashmere turtleneck framing her attractiveness.

"So, how's the lumber business?" Sammie asked.

"It's going okay. The place was a wreck. Tommie Dubose is a little slow, but it gives me a free hand to do what I want to straighten things out. Mrs. Dubose has learned quite a bit."

"What do you mean, 'slow'?"

Mary shifted nervously. How could she explain? "It's hard to understand. I think Tommie is retarded. He has the capacity of a twelve-year-old boy."

"You're kidding. Your little girlfriend is married to a retard?"

"Sammie, please. That's cruel and insulting. Everyone in town loves Tommie. Lila's in an impossible situation. I've set up an antagonistic relationship with the president of the bank, who wants to get his hands on the Dubose holdings. He thought the time was just about right with Tommie's father dead, when I showed up and put a stop to it. Now I've gone and educated the wife so that he can't simply take everything without her being aware. She's married to the town mascot. She is *married*. That says it all, doesn't it?"

"Why on earth would she want to marry a man like that? It could only be the money. But you wouldn't be attracted to her if she was a scheming little conniver, would you?"

"She's not like that." Mary spoke sharply.

"Not like me, you mean. It's all right. I am a schemer, I admit it. I intend to get back everything my dear old daddy took away. By rights it's mine, anyway." Sammie's tone hardened as she went on.

"You're certainly going about it in the right way, drinking your way across the country, hiding out from him."

"I'm just celebrating my freedom. Soon enough I'll be getting what I want. At the moment, we're discussing how you seem to have lost your mind. She's young, beautiful, rich, and her marriage is by no means a real one. What the hell's stopping you?"

"She is young. She's also innocent. She's probably never heard of the kind of women you and I are."

"Would you stop saying that? We aren't a 'kind' of anything."

"You know what I mean. And she depends on me to run the business and keep the banker from encroaching. I don't know if she could stand up to him on her own."

"She doesn't have to, she's got you. You've busted more balls than a wild horse. You're her hero, her rescuer."

"Oh shut up. You think she should be so grateful that she'll give in to an indecent proposal?"

"I think she's ripe for the picking. You could use a little charm and subtlety. Take me back with you and I'll show you how."

"No." Mary stood up and went inside to get them another beer. Why must Sammie always be so crude, always challenge her to act on her feelings? She didn't know anything about Lila. Sammie drank too much. Mary wished there was enough alcohol in the world to make her lose her sense of honor and responsibility and just approach Lila. "Look, I'm sorry," she said to Sammie when she returned with the beers. "I know this is not what you expected when you came here. I can't seem to stop being consumed by her. This isn't any fun. Let's talk about something else."

Sammie accepted her beer, and dutifully changed the subject, while Mary really tried to pay attention. "Red Duke broke his leg, I heard. I wonder who's running things at the ranch right now."

Red was the foreman of her father's ranch. "This could be an opportunity for you, if you'd play nice. Why don't you go home and help out until he gets back on his feet? Without trying to blackmail your father. Red's always liked you, when you weren't trying to take his job away from him. Maybe he'll talk to Big Sam for you if you show him you just want to keep the ranch running, not take it away from him."

Sammie snorted. "That's not likely to happen. Big Sam won't be happy until he sees me married and tied down with kids."

"You went too far by exposing yourself to him like you did. How was that supposed to work in your favor?"

"Oh, hell, I don't know. I just got tired of pretending. Don't you?"

"Yes, I do. So I wonder how I could ever ask Lila to join me in a lifetime of pretense?"

"Back to Lila again?" Sammie grinned. "Anyway, that's part of the price we pay. Would it be any different than her pretending to be in a marriage that can't be any more than a sham?"

"Never mind. You really don't understand."

"Okay, then. Maybe I could help you with some of that loneliness, make it a little easier for you to go back and be around her, for a while."

Mary looked over at Sammie, realized that she had probably had enough to drink, and said, "Come on. Let's get some sleep."

"I thought that's what I just proposed."

Mary helped Sammie stand up, and they went to bed. Mary rubbed Sammie's back and held her while she fell asleep, but she refused to take advantage of the offer that lay between them. She would not assuage her desire by using Sammie as a substitute. Instead, she lay awake most of the night again, dozing off to dream that it was Lila in bed beside her, whispering words to her, touching her. Startling awake to the sound of Sammie snoring peacefully, she drifted off again to dream about Sammie handling her roughly but competently, arousing a need that burned like a fever in the dream. Then she awakened again, her body still in its fever. She rose quietly and went outside to sit on the sand for a while, smoking, trying to calm the desire that raged and caused her hands to shake. She finally crawled back into bed and fell deeply asleep.

When she woke up, the sun was high and Sammie was gone. There was a note on the table by the window.

Dear Mary,
Talk to Lila. Give yourself a chance. Sometimes, you
get what you want, if you go after it. It is not as

100

impossible as you think to find love. I know, because I
had a chance to have it with you once.
Take care,
Sammie

The rest of the day Mary spent walking, chain smoking, and cursing the fates or whatever forces had put her in Myrtlewood, that had caused her to be the way she was. The sun went down, and still she sat on the beach and debated, unable to get herself to move, to go home. She had to get back, but she sat there most of the night, refusing sleep, refusing to make a decision, refusing her own will. Finally she packed and drove home at three a.m.

Instead of going to bed, she took a hot bath and dressed carefully for work. Looking at herself in the mirror, she decided that none of the tension and lack of sleep showed, but when she closed her front door behind her, she had no idea where she was going. She was as unsettled and indecisive as she had ever felt in her life. She could walk to the train station, and put this place and Lila far behind her. Or she could simply go to work and hope that she could force herself to concentrate on getting through the day.

Mary walked, unseeing, as these possibilities chased each other through her head. Without wanting to, without really knowing where her feet were taking her, she headed for Lila's house.

Chapter Eight

REPORT TO THE GRAND DRAGON: That's a fine thing ya'll did, walkin' out of the convention and forming our own party. I really like the name Dixiecrats. Strom Thurmond's a good one, he speaks our language. Attendance was 5.

Monday, September 13, 1948

Mary stood for a moment on the back steps of the imposing house; she had no idea what she was going to say. Through the window, she saw Lila at the sink. Despite her inspection in the mirror before she left, Mary felt a moment of insecurity that Lila would see how worn and tense she was. She would be sure to think something terrible had happened. Mary wasn't entirely certain of what she felt, as she watched Lila hurriedly dry her hands and come out onto the back porch, still cool in the very early morning. The two women looked at each other for a moment, Lila's eyes dark and questioning. Mary was afraid to begin. As they stared at each other, the younger woman's eyes filled with tears.

"You haven't come to say you're leaving, have you?"

"I—"

"Please say no." Lila reached a hand toward Mary, then drew it back.

Mary cleared her throat. "I know this is not the time or place to have this conversation, but I just spent all weekend thinking, and honestly, there is no proper time or place. What I want to talk about is not proper. But I thought it out, and it came to this: not speaking my mind might cause as much hurt in the long run, to me anyway, as telling you how I feel may cause you. I don't want to hurt either of us, Lila. But if I don't speak, then how will we ever know whether there is a chance for what I want? Will you hear me out?"

Mary searched the dark gray eyes staring up at her, seeing in them a measure of relief that she did not understand, and a certain amount of resolve that meant she would be heard. Again, her heart lurched for this young woman, who seemed far younger than her twenty-three years, who intrigued Mary with her mixture of innocence and determination.

"Sit down, please. We can talk here on the porch. Annie's upstairs and Tommie's still asleep. Whatever it is, I'll listen. You've helped me so much—"

"Don't be grateful. Not until you hear everything. I don't know where to start." Mary shrugged her shoulders. Exhausted from a weekend of revelations and self-examination, she now felt a numbed distance from herself, as though she watched a Mary she didn't know do something completely out of character. She felt a curious kind of courage, as though it didn't matter any more what she said or did right now, as though the cards had been dealt and she was simply playing out a hand without really caring if she won or lost.

"Just talk, Mary." Lila nodded toward two rattan chairs, and they sat down. She took Mary's hand and squeezed it. Mary sighed, and then began talking.

"My father threw me out of the house when I was sixteen. First he beat me, then he packed my clothes, gave me money, and drove me to the next town to catch a train. He didn't want anyone in our home town to see me leave or see my injuries. He broke my nose and a couple of ribs. I don't know what he told my mother or anyone else, probably that I ran away, maybe that I was pregnant. I got off the train in St. Louis. I finished school while I stayed at a mission run by the Catholics. The nuns were nice to me. I learned how to type and take dictation. Then I got a job in a newspaper office. The editor there was a good man. He helped me find a place to live. Anyway, I wound up in Houston at the start of the war."

"You're going too fast. Why did your father—"

Mary held up a hand. "Let me get this all out, please." She closed her eyes for a moment. What in God's name was she doing?

"All right. Go on."

Mary opened her eyes. "Anyway, I was twenty-one by then and I got a job in the typing pool for an oil company. Some of those oil men got rich so quick they had no idea how to run a business or what to do with their money. They just sucked it up out of the ground and spent it, some of them before they actually had it to spend. This one man, Sam Stewart, everyone called him 'Big Sam,' took an interest in me. He hired me as his personal secretary, although he had only a vague concept of what a secretary should do. He seemed to think my job was to provide companionship for him, and he spent some time chasing me around the office. We worked all that out after I slapped him a couple of times. Then he straightened up and concentrated on business. He wanted to go off and fight in the war of course, but the government wanted him to drill wells and pump out oil."

Mary paused. Lila had stopped looking at her with that shocked, worried expression. Mary thought for a moment, wanting to tell the story in the right way. Maybe she should have first explained exactly who she was and what she wanted from Lila. She shook her head. It was too late now. For now she would go on with her tale, her eyes fixed on a point over Lila's shoulder. She could not look directly at Lila while she spoke, but she didn't hide her own face from Lila's view, didn't try to control her expression. Let her see whatever there was to see.

"Big Sam had a daughter. She was uncontrollable and spoiled. She wanted to join the WACS, fly a bomber, something romantic and dangerous. She was a tomboy who never grew out of it. She was still living at home on the ranch, riding out with the hands, the ones who didn't get drafted, doing as much work as any of them. She had no respect for her father, who wasn't an easy man to respect in any case, but she looked for reasons to show contempt for him. She was named Samantha after him, but everyone called her Sammie. She wanted to run the ranch, and after Big Sam struck oil, she pretty much got to do it because he ignored the cattle business after that. Big Sam couldn't stop her from doing anything. He was too busy, in Houston all the time. The ranch hands couldn't stop her because she was the boss's daughter. She worked with them, came stomping home at night with her boots covered with cow manure and dust and grease. She was happy then, maybe for the only time in her life."

Mary could tell that Lila was beginning to wonder how she knew so much about her boss's daughter. She was muddling this up, but there was nothing she could do except continue.

"Then the oil crew boss called her father one day, when she argued with him about a new well he wanted to drill on the ranch. Big Sam hit the roof when he found out Sammie was interfering with his oil business. He went and got her, stuck her in the office with me, so he would know where she was and what she was doing. He thought I could teach her how to be a lady. He assumed I was one because I had slapped his face, I guess."

Lila shifted in her chair. She reached out a hand to Mary's arm, smiling to encourage her to continue. Maybe Lila was recalling the rumors and speculation about embezzlement or love affairs when she had first arrived. Mary looked down at the hand on her arm and wanted to cover it with her own, but she did not.

"Sammie and I became friends. I taught her to type and to walk in pumps, which she said was not so different from her cowboy boots, just more uncomfortable. I guess I taught her other things too, like how to manipulate her father's money without his knowing. He was ridiculously easy to fool. The sight of Sammie in a dress, sitting demurely behind a desk, was enough to convince him that the transformation from tomboy to young lady was accomplished. In typical male fashion, he assumed this cosmetic change was real and permanent."

Mary took a deep breath and sat back in her chair. "Nothing could have been more wrong. Sam was simply biding her time, or serving her sentence, as she put it. Her father continued to grant her every wish, except the one she most wanted—to return to the ranch. She stayed with me in my apartment on Montrose. Her father liked to drink and bring women home to his place in town, and since I was such a fine example of moral womanhood, she was left in my charge. It was a joke. She was young, and hell bent for leather, as they say in Texas."

Lila smiled at this. She wouldn't be smiling at the next part, Mary thought, grimly determined now to finish what she had started and leave nothing out.

"I really liked Sammie. She had fire and determination. She was wild, and she had never been denied anything, had never been taught the proper deference to men, had never found anything to admire about them except their freedom. I taught her more than she wanted to know about her father's oil business, since her interest was in finding ways to divert cash back into the ranch, investing in improvements, things that had been neglected since Big Sam got distracted by oil. He had never made much money ranching, but he didn't realize there was money to be made from the beef industry through government contracts. Anybody who couldn't make money during the war was lazy or incompetent, and Big Sam was both, although he did become rich enough to be powerful, in spite of himself.

"I imagine you helped with that, didn't you? You've demonstrated your skill at getting others to understand their potential."

Mary shook her head, rejecting the compliment. "He never knew or didn't care that we were playing with his money, and he'd never have refused Sammie even if she had asked permission to do what we were doing. But she enjoyed tricking him out of it, a sort of revenge for his exiling her from the ranch. Sam liked being sneaky and making a fool of her father, which, as I said, was easy to do. And she had a lifetime of practice at it. She was locked into some kind of battle with him, determined to win and prove herself the better man, so to speak. It was best for the business, best for the family, so I went along."

"That's not so different from what you've been helping me to do here, is it?" Lila smiled again, tentatively.

Mary did not smile back. Committed now, she continued, grimly determined to reach the end. "It was more difficult to keep Sammie from humiliating him in other ways. She enjoyed being secretive even when there was no need, but it was hard to get her to keep some secrets that were for her own protection. She saw nothing wrong in what we were doing. Sammie had to keep pushing things. I guess she did that with me too. When Big Sam discovered the nature of our relationship and just how far my influence and example extended, I was fired. She was shipped off to school. The difference is that this time I did not get beaten—in fact, I was compensated with this job here for Dubose Lumber. I suppose Big Sam considered this a punishment of sorts. He must have known about Tommie."

Mary took a deep breath and looked directly into Lila's eyes for the first time. Lila merely waited silently. She couldn't tell whether Lila had guessed what was coming next.

"So this is it." Mary looked away, feeling inexplicably calm, not at all how she had expected to feel. "My father caught me in the barn with my best friend Elizabeth. We were kissing. Sammie's father came into my apartment and found her asleep in my arms, in my bed. We were naked."

Lila did not look away, nor did she flinch. She grasped Mary's hand. She had a question in her eyes, but she didn't speak. *She must be shocked*, Mary thought. *She has to be. When she recovers herself, I'll be fired.* It was useless to expect anything other than disappointment from Lila. Mary stood up and moved to the porch railing. After a while, she turned to face Lila and continued, still strangely removed from what was happening.

"Now I find myself in love with the wife of my new employer. It seems I haven't learned this lesson yet. I keep repeating the same mistake, falling into the same trap. I am appalled that this is happening to me again, appalled that I couldn't resist telling you about it. But if I can find the strength to leave here before I do more than that, then I want you to know why. I love you, Lila. I can't imagine any good coming from my confessing this, even if you could return the feeling. You are married, the wife of the town's adopted son. But I wanted you to know."

Mary's voice did not falter. She would not beg, and to entice or seduce was not in her nature. Her strength of will, which had weakened enough for her to speak of her desire, would not allow the further humiliation of pleading her case. If she could maintain her distance, if she could sustain the pretense and continue with the conventions to which she adhered but did not believe in, she would stay, if Lila would let her. She would go if anything caused Lila worry or harm.

After looking at Mary for a long time, Lila turned her gaze to some middle distance between them, not focusing on Mary at all. Her expression did not look sad or angry or shocked. She seemed to be thinking about something else, but how could she after Mary's confession? It seemed like an hour before Lila replied.

"I'm twenty-three years old. I am married to the simple son of the richest and most respected man in this town. My family bartered me away like a prize heifer. Until you came, I had no idea of what I should do, what my function was, or who I was supposed to be. Until you, I never had anyone to talk to. Because of you, if you go, I can probably continue on this course you set for me. But there wouldn't be anyone to share it with, no one to talk to about it." She took a deep breath, and smiled shakily. "You set a high standard for honesty, and I'm trying to meet it."

Mary found her own breathing had gone shallow. Lila was at least remaining calm, her hands steady as she smoothed her skirt over her knees. Her tone, dreamy and bemused, was also gentle, so soft that Mary had to lean closer to hear her.

"I never knew there could be more to our friendship. Can you teach me that too?"

"I'm not sure you know what you're saying," Mary choked out past her surprise. "Did you understand what I told you about me?"

Lila's hand returned to grasp her sleeve and shook her arm gently. "I heard your story, every word of it. I'm a good listener and I'm not stupid. You're afraid that I'm shocked, or that I'll think less of you. We've been talking for months about the roles this town expects us to play, and you've been showing me how to satisfy their expectations and achieve my own ends at the same time. You just gave me another, better reason to do that."

Lila paused to gather her thoughts, but she did not let go of Mary. Mary was fascinated to watch her gray eyes change as Lila apparently decided on her next pitch, puzzled by the shy smile and the look of awe on the young woman's face.

"The town dictated your role as a young spinster," said Lila, "the level-headed savior of the Dubose business, willing to accept and protect the delusion that the Dubose heir is normal. They accept me as his consort. They figure I'm so grateful for my elevation in status that I would never do anything to jeopardize the fiction the town maintains about the Duboses. And I'm not so sure that correcting this illusion would be helpful to anyone."

Mary looked into Lila's eyes for a moment longer, then turned away. She could drown in those eyes and still not know what Lila was really thinking. She couldn't quite believe that Lila was fully aware of all she was saying.

"Have I helped or made it harder for you? I wanted to ease your mind. I'm no one's victim, Mary, not the town's, not yours. You can't hurt me, unless you want to be noble and deny us both for the sake of my reputation. But I am trapped here. I can't run after you if you go."

"Deny us both? What does that mean?" From a great distance away, she felt unable to comprehend this part of the movie she seemed to be both watching and enacting.

"You know what it means."

But Mary still wasn't sure that Lila knew. "I'm not going anywhere, not yet. Not until you've had time to think, and I've had time to rest. Consider this carefully, Lila. Even if you could truly love me, you don't know yet what it means and all it entails. Consider the strain of always hiding, never having enough time together, pretending a casual interest. Consider the prospect of cheating a man who is incapable of understanding what we do to him. Imagine the outrage of this town on his behalf if rumors begin. I'm not like Sammie. I won't say the hell with anyone but myself. And there is no place we could go where it would be any different. We fight it out along this line, or we choose not to fight at all."

Mary turned and went down the back steps, the sound of her voice paraphrasing General Grant's historic words ringing in her ears and sounding fine, but hollow. She was exhausted, but not too tired to realize the only battle they would ever fight would be a secret one, between themselves. She was also too tired to wonder why Lila's not saying no had not cheered her at all.

Mary walked across town to work, feeling some of her tension ease as she walked. She knew Lila would appear at the office later, as usual. Good, she thought. Lila would receive her first lesson in pretending that their conversation that morning had never taken place, her first taste of what it would be like to proceed as though their roles had not altered, an exercise in duplicity that would be the basis of their lives from now on. With each step Mary grew more angry and weary. Let her see now what it would be like, how frustrating, lonely, and draining. But then they were both good at pretending.

Mary felt desperately foolish, accusing herself of duping not only herself but Lila into believing they could make this work. She wondered again if this intense hunger for Lila was only a product of her loneliness and isolation. Why had she been unable to keep this to herself? Why must she continue risking rejection and scorn? Was she, at bottom, like Sammie, a thrill-seeker?

Already a part of Mary's mind sought ways they could be alone. She tried to imagine years ahead, years of cheating a mentally deficient man, years of lying, years of accumulated guilt. Still, no matter the outcome, Mary felt better for having spoken the truth. Maybe she could come to trust Lila's strength and not have to be so strong herself. She remembered Lila's hand clutching her sleeve, Lila's eyes, sharper than she had ever seen them, with a depth of understanding she had not guessed. She allowed herself one sharp flash of desire as she unlocked the office and forcefully turned her mind to the day's work.

Lila opened the outer office door quietly and sat down at Mary's desk for a few minutes. She stared unseeing at her hands folded together on the green leather blotter. She had to prove to Mary that her feelings were genuine, not just born of gratitude or friendship. She couldn't decide whether the tingling she felt along her nerves was from anticipation of what she was about to do, or simply fear. She stood and crossed the room. She opened the inner office door quietly. Mary was sitting behind Mr. Dubose's huge desk, smoking a cigarette. Lila stood in the doorway.

"I've never seen you smoke in the office." Lila took a step into the room.

"There's a lot you don't know about me."

"It was very difficult for you to decide to tell me everything, wasn't it? I hope you know that you can trust me."

Lila came into the room and sat across from Mary and studied her face. Her perfectly applied makeup could not conceal the lines of worry and exhaustion that two days of turmoil had put there.

"I'm sorry that I made you a party to my dilemma. That wasn't necessary, except to preserve my sanity. It was self-indulgent of me. But—"

"But?"

"I was hoping that telling you how I feel would be enough. It's not."

They sat regarding one another in silence. The mixture of emotions Lila had felt now coalesced into one single impulse: she wanted to touch this woman who sat before her like a judge. She studied the fine chestnut hair pulled back into a twist. The light blue eyes staring back at her glittered as if there were a fire behind them. Lila's skin tingled and her hands itched to reach out and hold that angular face between them. Her eyes dropped to Mary's lips, moved lower and watched her hands, one holding a cigarette, the other lying on the desk, the short nails shining with clear polish. Lila looked up to see color rising in Mary's cheeks. Her own face felt hot, and she was short of breath. She watched Mary's chest rise and fall, and knew she was breathing rapidly too. She had no experience in seduction.

"Which one of us goes around this desk, you or me?" Lila tried a smile as she waited for an answer.

"Excuse me?" Mary's eyebrows rose. Lila felt like time had slowed, and she noticed the elegantly shaped brows, and felt ridiculously drawn to smooth them with a finger. "What do you mean?"

"I mean we lock the door, and take care not to get rumpled."

Mary smiled. "I hate to sound crude, but have you ever even been kissed?"

Lila returned the smile as she stood. "Of course. I was the girl all the sweaty high school boys thought could be had by anybody. I wasn't one of the 'good' girls from one of the 'good' families in town, so they all tried. If I had wanted that, I would have been the town tramp by now."

Mary looked at her and tapped her ash into the huge ashtray that had once held Mr. Dubose's cigars. Finally she stubbed out her cigarette.

"I am a woman who is attracted to women in a physical way. I'm trying to be blunt without being crass. I have no idea if you are shocked by that or just curious. I don't know if you want me to stay simply because I'm the first friend you've known or what your interest in me is. I only know I don't want you trying to create a feeling you don't have to try to please me. And I know that I am very tired so I'm probably not thinking clearly."

Lila held Mary's gaze. She decided that whether Mary was or not, she herself was thinking clearly for the first time in her life.

"You are wondering, hoping, that what I feel for you is more than friendship or admiration or gratitude. It is. I want to put your mind at ease. I want to allay your doubts. Do you want me to be blunt and crass?"

Mary came around the desk. She locked the door and pulled the shades. The ceiling fan turned slowly, stirring the humid air. They clasped hands. Lila closed her eyes as they moved closer together, and she thought about fate as she shyly, tentatively brushed Mary's lips with her own. Trembling, Lila inhaled Mary's scent deeply and held it inside, as though savoring a sip of fine wine. Mary's hands came to her face, and her lips pressed firmly to Lila's, capturing them, and Lila leaned into her and responded in a way she had never imagined. Mary opened her mouth, and Lila felt the tip of her tongue, and deep inside, something changed, broke free, something Lila had not known lived within her, buried so deep she didn't know this part of herself. She parted her own lips and let her tongue touch Mary's, and the new part of her took over. Lila put her arms around Mary to keep her close, and as from a great distance she heard a small sound, unlike any she could recognize, something an animal would make. She didn't know if it came from her or from Mary.

They spent the afternoon in a curious silence and a mutual attempt to avoid each other's eyes. Mary sat and typed in stunned apprehension. That is, she tried to type, with shaking hands. She re-lived the kisses. She resisted the urge to go to Lila, to pull her out of her chair and hold her. She desperately wanted to make sure what had just happened was real, not a dream. She wanted to make it happen again. She kept her eyes on the typewriter, the letters a jumble of markings.

"Damn!" She ripped out another sheet and started over.

"What is it?" Lila asked. She had been sitting with invoices for an hour, shuffling them, sighing, with a little hitch sometimes when she exhaled. Mary forced herself not to look at Lila.

"These letters might just as well be hieroglyphics."

"Mary?"

"Yes." Mary kept her eyes on the typewriter, bracing herself for recriminations, regrets, the "I'm sorry, but I just don't think I can do that again" speech. She did not want to see Lila's reaction. "Look, Lila, it's okay. Let's not talk about this right now, all right?"

"How can you just lock it away like that? I realize this wasn't new to you, but it was for me."

With a supreme effort of will, Mary managed to keep her face blank as she forced herself to look at Lila. "What is it, then?"

"It's just that. You've had other experiences. I'm afraid that you might be disappointed—"

Mary threw her pencil on the desk. They really shouldn't discuss this now. Anyone could walk in. She got up and locked the door. Lila rose to meet her, but she gently reseated her in the chair, holding both of Lila's hands in her own. Mary knelt beside her, not caring whether it ruined her stockings.

"Sweet woman. Don't you know I've been wanting to do that for months? Can't you see how much I want to make love, right here, right now?" Mary drew a ragged breath and fought for control. "You didn't disappoint me. You gave me everything I've been craving, everything I've been dreaming about for months. My God, Lila, I can't do this right now. I can't think. Anyone could drop in. I have to lock it away. You have to put it away." Mary rose, her legs trembling, and returned to her seat. She swiveled it away from Lila. She felt tears gather. She clinched her jaws and breathed deeply. *Dear God,* she thought.

Mary had seen the look of wonder on Lila's face. Regardless of the guilt or shame Lila might feel later, Mary was relieved that for now, she clearly did not feel either. She knew they could not talk about it now, and that made her frustrated and angry. Would all their time together be stolen and rushed and incomplete like this because they could not talk now about what they had just done? Would Lila think it worth the effort?

As they got ready to leave at the end of the day, Lila put a hand on Mary's arm to make her wait.

"Why don't we hold our Thursday night bridge game at my house this week? The Sullivans have played host long enough, don't you think?"

"I suppose so. Stop by on the way home and ask them." Mary

knew it was a ploy. Lila was creating an opportunity for them to be together again. She decided that Lila would be an excellent chess player, for she had clearly thought several moves ahead in this game they had begun. Miss Louise and everyone else would grow accustomed to their visiting one another's homes.

"I was thinking we could have supper before we begin. Do you think they would come?"

"I'm sure they'll be delighted. I'll see you tomorrow."

With that, Mary tore herself away and left the office in a great hurry. She walked through the center of town, wanting to be alone with her thoughts. She wanted to flee the conventions that forced them to talk of conventional things, to engage in polite conversation as though their skin had not touched and burned. She wanted to be alone with that, since she couldn't be alone with Lila, and not have to continue the careful dance to avoid eye contact, to avoid mention of it, to avoid analyzing what had happened. It was better to be alone.

Her litany of "good evenings" on the way home was perfunctory, but Mary doubted that anyone noticed. She did not stop to speak with the old ladies gathered on front porches as she sometimes did. She did not stop at the library, though on Mondays Melissa Carpenter had got into the habit of staying a few minutes past five so that Mary could exchange books. She did not stop in the drugstore to speak to Mr. Howard Butler as she usually did. She went straight home and even managed to avoid Miss Louise. She locked her door and filled the bathtub, laying a book she totally ignored nearby. She soaked for a long time, replaying the extraordinary day as she relaxed, maybe for the first time since moving to the town. Then she deliberately recalled every touch and every minute of her time with Lila, picturing her hands and her mouth. As she had replayed it over and over again, Mary slid a hand into the water to touch and stroke herself, and found a release that was not what she wanted at all, but very much what she needed just then. That night she slept without dreaming.

That same night, Lila was restless as she had not been since first moving into the Dubose house as a bride. That word as it applied to her no longer struck her as ironic. She sat on the back porch in a daze, watching the sun set behind the trees at the back of the deep lot. The entire day ran through her head over and over again, like a movie. Lila wanted to explore this newly discovered force, this energy that was now unleashed between them. She had not known that such powerful, uncontrollable feelings existed.

Lila thought about destiny, and the role her own unknown nature had played in converging upon this point in time. She thought about God, and about old Mr. Dubose. She was grateful to both, because without their intervention, she might by now have been in a real marriage, with a real husband and even children. She gave thanks for Mary's courage, and she wondered where her own had come from, where it had been all her life. But if she had been bolder, more aware, she might have left town before Mary arrived. If Mary had been less brave, she never would have spoken as she had this morning. If either of them had been less or more than what they were, this day would not have happened.

She went to bed, and whispered Mary's name, and ran her hands over her skin. She fell asleep abruptly, like an exhausted child who had played too long and hard in the sun.

Chapter Nine

REPORT TO THE GRAND DRAGON: Seems like one of our nig-gers got hisself some money and bought a tractor. We paid him a visit, put that tractor out of commission, burned a cross. We know how to handle our niggers down here. They got to know their place.

Thursday, September 16, 1948

The Sullivans and Mary arrived at six on Thursday evening at the Dubose house and were ushered by Lila into the dining room.

"We'll eat right away, if that's all right," Lila told her company. "Tommie's leaving for the fishing cabin directly after supper. He's very excited because he gets to stay until Sunday night."

Bill Sullivan found it easy to talk to Tommie, accepting him on his level. Through dinner, they talked knowledgeably about fishing while the three women discussed the weather, the food they were eating, and recipes.

"Remind me to compliment Annie the next time I see her. Everything is just wonderful," Barbara said.

"Actually, I cooked this meal. I gave Annie some time off tonight." Lila looked at her and Mary saw that she enjoyed delivering this announcement.

"I made a blackberry cobbler for dessert," she told Barbara, and the two began to talk about baking and other sweet things that Mary didn't care for. Mary shifted in her chair and brought her napkin to her lips. She tried to avoid Lila's eyes.

"I like to cook sometimes too," Mary interrupted the two women. "I'll make a Yankee pot roast for everyone next Thursday night at my place. Miss Louise is terribly excited about having company."

"Why don't I come early and help?" Barbara offered.

Mary laughed, and tried to look grateful as she replied. "There's no need. I suppose I could let myself off early from work that day." Something in Barbara Sullivan's eyes made her uncomfortable at the prospect of being alone with her.

"I'll bring dessert," said Lila. Mary could not miss the puzzlement in the quick glance that Lila threw her.

A car horn honked and Tommie jumped up. "It's time for me to go!"

"Don't forget your bags by the door." Lila got up to follow him as he tried to round up the bags of supplies Annie was sending with him to stock the cabin. Mr. Howard Butler from the drugstore came to the door to help Tommie, smiling and nodding to everyone.

"Come on, Mr. Tommie, the fish are waitin'."

No one laughed when Tommie nearly fell through the door in his excitement. Mr. Howard Butler shook his head and gathered the rest of the supplies that Tommie had precipitously forgotten and left.

After the debarking of the fishing expedition, the four of them moved to the living room, where Annie had set up a card table. Bill dealt the first hand. Mary noticed a curious look on Bill's face as he watched Lila.

"You seem more at ease tonight," Bill Sullivan said, startling Mary by giving voice to what was on her mind. "Is it because you're playing hostess or is there something else?"

Lila looked at Bill, and again Mary felt alarm as she waited for the reply. She was certain that Lila was enjoying her tension. As the pause lengthened, Mary felt her own composure slipping away, and hoped it didn't show. What kind of game was Lila playing?

"I don't quite know. It is nice to repay your hospitality for all those months. You must think I am lacking in manners. Until now I have been too unsure of my ability to reciprocate. I wanted to, but ... anyway, now I can." Now Lila was carefully avoiding looking at Mary, but Mary completely understood the double meaning, and was certain that Lila knew exactly the effect she was having.

Barbara leaned forward and patted Lila's hand. "Don't think that way. We enjoyed your company. You needed to get out of the house, just to see that you could. You were so young when you married. It just took some time to establish your place in a new, big home, and in such difficult circumstances. You don't owe us anything."

She had gracefully stepped around the facts of Lila's marriage, and had avoided mentioning Tommie's situation, or even the role of the Duboses in the town. Mary watched the exchange, marveling how everyone in town refused to address the peculiarity of Lila Dubose's situation.

After a moment, Lila said, "Well, I do feel I owe you, and I feel I owe Mary a great deal too. She has taught me a lot that I didn't think I was capable of, and she gave me the courage to claim my place, so to speak. I feel I can never repay the kindness and patience you all have shown me. In a way tonight is a celebration for me. It's my graduation into adulthood, I think. I mean, running my own affairs at last, helping in the office, making decisions—I don't think I'd have reached this point without the encouragement from all of you."

Bill leaned over and hugged Lila, who stared at her hands and blushed, only partly because of embarrassment, Mary guessed. It was obvious to her that Lila, too, was discovering just how difficult it was for them to sit across a table from each other.

Barbara Sullivan's sharp eyes caught it all. From the slightly skeptical look on the woman's face, Mary wondered if she guessed there was more to the change in Lila than was being offered. Mary's own pulse seemed to speed up as Barbara glanced quickly at her, then away.

"Mary is so quiet," she observed to the group. Then she was gazing at Mary again. "Aren't you proud of your pupil? It seems like a complete reversal of roles for you two, with Lila speaking up and you so reserved. How did the meeting with Mr. Buchanan go?"

"Pretty well, I think." Mary suppressed a sudden impulse to excuse herself right now and go home. "Lila quite impressed him. She's done very well. I've taught her all I know."

"I doubt that." Lila looked directly at Mary, a secret challenge in her gray eyes. "You are being over-modest, Mary."

The Sullivans were watching as though entertained. "Stop all this flattery. Let's play bridge." They switched partners, which involved changing seats. Barbara brushed slightly against Mary as they switched places.

"You must think I'm very anxious to play," she said by way of apology.

"Not at all," Mary answered, with a small smile. The rest of the evening was absorbed in playing cards, though Mary noticed how frequently Barbara seemed to look at her, and for the first time realized Barbara seemed to be studying Lila as well. Her eyes held a degree of speculation that made Mary uncomfortable. She had not seen that look from another woman for a very long time, not since before she had left Houston. She had no doubts about what those kinds of looks had meant then, and she had not forgotten what returning such a look signified. For the rest of the evening, she pointedly refused to meet Barbara's gaze.

The next morning Lila went to the office early. She had not had one chance since Monday to speak privately with Mary and she intended to. She was intensely curious about how the weekend might go. Tommie wouldn't be back until Sunday night. She knew Mary had been going to the beach most weekends. She made coffee, set out some doughnuts, and waited.

She looked up when Mary came in at her usual accelerated pace. She always moved as though some purpose pulled her forward, as though trains and boats and presidents waited for her. It made everyone else seem to be wandering aimlessly in comparison. She stopped short at seeing Lila in the office before her.

"What are you doing here so early?"

"The coffee's ready and I brought homemade doughnuts. Let's sit and talk before we start work, shall we?"

Mary pulled off her gloves and put down her purse. She studied Lila for a moment, then got a cup of coffee and sat down opposite her at the desk.

"This is hardly the place for talking. Unless it has to do with the office."

"According to you, there is no appropriate place for talking privately. I think it would be better if we talk. Are you going off to the beach this weekend?"

Mary just sipped her coffee. It appeared that she was not prepared to acknowledge what had happened between them at all. They were no longer simply employer and employee, bridge partners, casual friends. Mary was being so cool. *Not like me*, Lila thought, as she studied the frown on Mary's face.

Mary released a sigh, and finally answered. "No, I haven't thought about the weekend yet. Have you? I have been going to the beach a lot, but I have nothing else to do with my time. But trying to avoid thinking about certain things is pointless; it only ensures that you will. Does it matter to you whether I do my thinking here or at the beach?"

"Of course it does. You're implying that it doesn't matter because in either place you will be alone."

"Lila—"

"Suppose I drive down with you and look it over? I've actually never been to the beach."

Lila could feel Mary marshaling her defenses. "Are you sure that's a good idea?"

"It's the best one I've had all week. Mary, for heaven's sake. You seem determined to pretend that what happened between us didn't happen. It makes me question why you ever approached me at all. Unless you propose inventing an entirely new language, I don't know any other way to have a private conversation."

Lila bit into a doughnut as Mary deliberated over her response. She was surprised to find herself almost angry. She had intended to remain as cool and logical as Mary. Mary could look very fierce when she was thinking, or not getting her way, Lila noticed. She dunked her doughnut in her coffee cup and maintained her silence.

"Okay. We can go to the beach together." Mary put her cup down and settled back in her chair. "Hell, you can buy the damn cottage if you want. We can announce to the whole world that the Dubose wife is spending weekends with the Dubose secretary, alone, *every* weekend, with no male escort in sight. What would that accomplish?"

"It might help you to stop imagining the worst. Look, Tommie likes the ocean. His father used to take him deep sea fishing. We could buy a place down there, really. Then we could all three go whenever we want. Tommie would love to come, even though we are only women and he prefers the company of men. He would be thrilled to have his own private beach, and so would I."

"Lila, there's no way that could happen. Tommie doesn't like me." The look of panic that accompanied this remark delighted Lila.

"He's still scared of you, Mary. You should get to know him better, let him see you aren't an ogre. And you can stop threatening me with

120

dire consequences. You don't scare me." To prove it, she leaned forward and put a hand on Mary's shoulder. "We've been given a gift, Mary. Something neither one of us thought was possible, and you won't allow us to enjoy it."

"It's not that simple, Lila. You surely realize what could happen."

"It *is* that simple. Now what does one wear at the beach?"

Mary sighed, then got up and went into the inner office. Lila knew that Mary was posturing, exaggerating potential danger in order to frighten her. She could see Mary pulling out her chair and sinking down wearily, as though she were carrying a heavy weight. Lila got up and went to her. She reached for Mary's hand, and felt a thrill of pleasure just from touching her. She wanted this woman.

"One wears as little as decently possible," Mary said. "One walks for miles as the sun goes down, then back watching the moon rise. Then we sit and listen to the waves crash and wonder where they originate. What giant hand puts them in motion? The same one that moved us together?"

Lila smiled smugly. Mary had failed completely at keeping the raw desire out of her voice.

Annie had made no comment when Lila went home at noon and packed an overnight bag. They made it to the beach in less than three hours. That night they sat on the sand, watching the incessant motion of the water, talking, leaning against each other in the dark, the glow from Mary's cigarette a counterpoint to the lights blinking across the bay in Mobile. Their feet were buried in sand still warm from the sun, their hair tangled and wild in the wind, their shoulders burned red. Mary brought a blanket from the cottage and they wrapped themselves up in it. Bare legs touched and rubbed unconsciously in rhythm with the waves. When they were so sleepy that their words lost all sense, they stood and reluctantly went inside.

Lila undressed and fell across the bed. Mary opened all the windows and latched the screen door. She smoked one last cigarette as she watched Lila drift into sleep, memorizing this night, the sinking sun, the rising moon, Lila's hair whipping across her face, the smell of the ocean in the air, the birds circling overhead, the sand squeaking and crunching beneath their feet. The taste of Lila's mouth in the dark.

She put out her cigarette and curled around the sleeping body in the bed. When Mary pulled away to remove the rest of her own clothes, Lila almost whimpered.

Mary kissed Lila deeply; one hand cupped a breast, squeezing her nipple gently, as the other hand moved down between them, searching for the softness, the wetness, the silky texture that she needed, wanted to feel. Her fingers slid inside Lila as she felt her tense and then open to her, the kiss changing into a counter rhythm, tongues frantically repeating the advance and slow withdrawal, the push and pull of her fingers as Lila arched and fell, urging her deeper, increasing the rhythm, until Mary pushed in as hard as she could, and Lila took it and held on; Mary kept kissing her and squeezing her nipple until she felt something begin to give way. Lila's hips rose from the bed, and all movement stopped for an indefinable length of time, a sound like moaning came from both of them, and then Lila began to relax, and Mary stayed with her as she rested; she broke away from the kiss that was simpler now, tender, soothing. She rested her head on Lila's shoulder while she tried to catch her breath. Lila's legs held her fingers firmly in place. Mary knew not to pull away too soon. She waited as Lila panted, slowing down, her breaths deeper now. She thought they would fall asleep then, but Lila eased her aside and moved down the bed.

They made love with the lights on. At times, Mary was vaguely aware of the sound of the surf outside. At other moments, the surf ran in unheeded, as they looked and felt and touched and answered unspoken questions. They fell asleep together. Lila stirred briefly when Mary turned over to shut off the lamp beside the bed. She woke again later, when Mary reached in her sleep for the hand that had been removed, placing it firmly back in its place. Mary pulled her closer, and they slept.

The next morning, Mary woke early, in a race to beat the sunrise. She made coffee and stepped outside, pulling two chairs together. Then she woke Lila.

"Wake up. Hurry. The sun is coming up. You don't want to miss it."

Lila rolled over slowly and pushed her hair out of her face. She opened her eyes to Mary's eager face and smiled.

"Kiss me."

Mary lay next to her on the bed and obeyed. She licked a shoulder and tasted salt.

"Now get up. Come on."

Lila groaned, but rose and pulled on shorts and a shirt. They padded barefoot outside where Mary had coffee already poured. She adjusted Lila's chair and sat down. Lila inhaled deeply and yawned. They sat in silence while the sun began its performance as if on cue. Lila sipped her coffee and kept her eyes on the horizon. Once she reached out a hand and Mary took it and squeezed. Neither spoke until the sun was fully above the horizon and people began appearing on the beach.

"Sammie and I used to go to the beach in Galveston. She'd swim and play in the water like a fish. She went out so far it scared me, swimming until she was completely exhausted, then staggering out of the water to collapse. She would sleep in the sun and burn until I made her turn over. She drank, you know. Everything she did, she did to excess."

Lila stood and pulled Mary out of her chair. "I don't think you are as scared of as many things as you say. And I don't think I want to hear any more memories. Come inside."

Mary was delighted with Lila's eagerness. They made love slowly and thoroughly, reveling in the open air that pushed in through the windows, the space and the time to go slowly and savor each other. As they moved and rolled together, as hands and lips sought skin, and the sound of the sea breeze and the waves accompanied their sighs and murmurs, cries of completion echoed the caws of sea birds. In the way of new lovers, they explored skin as though mapping new territory, hungrily, jealously laying claim to each other. Mary led only at the beginning, until Lila mastered her and ruled. The sound of her own cry startled Mary as it broke from her. Then they lay together watching the curtains move, feeling the perspiration dry on their skin, feeling the heat increase as the sun climbed higher.

Later that day they sat once again on the small patio and watched people on the beach.

"Do you really want to buy this place?" Mary asked.

123

"Do you think we could? Should I ask Gerald or would he think a beach cottage frivolous?"

"Buchanan would think owning an indoor bathroom is frivolous unless his own comfort is involved. Beach frontage is valuable. In twenty years this will all be developed, and worth a great deal more than it is now. You may tell 'Gerald' I said so."

"He asked me to call him by his first name. You sound as though you disapprove."

"I don't like the way he looks at you. Like he's hungry and you're his next meal." Mary thought the image very appropriate. Buchanan reminded her of a pig, with his little eyes constantly moving up and down Lila's figure.

"He just got married, for heaven's sake. He's been a perfect gentleman." Lila changed the subject. "Tommie would enjoy this. I'm not so wary of him as I was at first. He really is a child, good-hearted and cheerful, but a child. I've learned a lot from Annie about how to manage him. As long as I let him play grown-up he is quite content to do what he should. He would love the beach."

Mary knew she was being manipulated. Lila was trying to suggest there were ways they could spend time together that would not arouse suspicion. She sat in silence for a while. Mention of Lila's husband had that effect on her. Tommie had no idea of the possessiveness that most men felt for their wives. He surely had no concept that he was missing certain marital rights. He could not be jealous of something he did not know he had the right to claim. This self-serving logic did not ease Mary's guilt. She worried that the fear and respect that men had for Tommie's father would wear away, and sooner or later one of them might become brave enough to decide to educate Tommie about his duties as a husband. It bothered her that Lila seemed not to be concerned by this possibility. Of course Lila knew Tommie better, knew what he was capable of understanding and what was beyond him. But Mary refused to take comfort in the man's inability to know he was being cuckolded.

"Should we make plans to meet secretly, develop a code language?"

"You're being mean." Lila poked her. "Must you assume that we're bad, sneaking around and lying? Can't you look at it less gloomily? What we are is two people in—"

"No. We have to think of the practicalities." She didn't want to hear Lila talk about being *in love*. Perhaps in Lila's mind, love trumped everything. To Mary, it meant trouble, pain, betrayal. "How do we get time together like this without running away together every weekend? I already regret last Monday at the office. We should not have risked that." This was a line of conversation she was more comfortable with. This was being responsible and addressing the realities of their situation.

"I don't regret it at all! Would you rather have made an appointment to take my virginity? Maybe the two hours on Wednesday when Annie is gone and Tommie is asleep on the back porch? Would that have been more comfortable for either of us? There was no other place, and no other time, if I had waited for you to choose. Why did you tell me how you felt in the first place, if you believe it so dangerous as to be hopeless?"

"So we just grab these opportunities like this weekend when they fall to us?" Mary couldn't hide the condescension in her tone. It wasn't the tension or the risk, but the loss of honor that haunted her, but she couldn't put it to Lila in those terms, not now.

"Of course we do. Though I think we can be more inventive than that. Office doors aren't the only ones with locks. The beach isn't the only place where we are anonymous. Just as you said, there is no place we can go where we could be any less cautious. That's the cost of doing business, as you would put it. That's what you're trying to teach me. Everything has a price. But we're not hurting anyone. Am I being too bold or too naive?"

Mary looked out over the water. After a few minutes she spoke.

"I don't know if you are foolish to be bold, but we would have had none of this if you weren't. Whatever the real state of your marriage, the fact remains that you *are* married. I can't justify what we are doing by using Tommie's condition as an excuse." Mary sighed, and turned her gaze to meet Lila's eyes. "Even if you weren't married, we would have to lie and sneak around. I worry about us taking too many trips away together, what people might say or think about that. We have to be careful. I am afraid of being caught again, but my fear is for you."

125

Mary paused. This wasn't sounding right. "I also don't want to spoil whatever time we can steal by being too cautious. Like right now. I don't want to ruin your first trip to the beach, and our first time alone together, when all this is so new to you, but I don't want to bring trouble to you. I didn't have to tell you, you're right. We could have remained just friends. Maybe that's how most women like us handle it. But I told you. I wanted you to know. I wanted you."

Lila smiled, and took Mary's hand, but Mary was determined to continue. "I was really going to leave, to banish myself before you or the town had a chance. I imagined confessing my love and then, in a magnificent gesture of self-denial, leaving before I did more than talk about it. I'm afraid that now this is new to you, but it will get old fast. It will seem less like a problem in logistics and more like a burden, like an investment that doesn't pay a proper return."

Lila stifled a laugh. "Burden? I feel free, and light, and altogether different. Mary, I don't care about all that. I know I'm young, but my word, so are you. All my life I've wondered what it was for, and now I know. I was made for this. This is me. I have been defined. I feel wonderfully alive and capable of figuring things out. Maybe not right this minute, but as we go along. Is that enough for you? Can you live with that?"

Mary looked from the far horizon back to Lila, seeing the same horizon reflected in the depths of her eyes, brighter now than she had ever seen them, glowing with anticipation and an enthusiasm that she did not want to quash. She saw herself reflected there too, and wondered if Lila's image of her was as distorted as the one she herself saw.

"Free? I hate to sound so old and gloomy, and spoil your fun before we've had any, but I've paid the price for getting found out before, you know. It's just that this time I don't know if I want to pay it." She squeezed Lila's hand. "Come on. We should be swimming, walking, holding hands, making love, laughing. Instead we're holding a business meeting about how and what it all means, and how dangerous and exciting it is. Enough of this."

Lila stood and pulled Mary up and pressed herself against her, smoothing the frown from her face with her hands.

"Come inside. You're tired. You need to lie down. Not enough sleep last night and too much sun. After you have a nap and a shower we can start over."

They went inside, and Lila put her to bed. Mary tried to pull her down with her but Lila sat on the edge and brushed the hair back from Mary's face, a gesture so reminiscent of her dream that tears formed again in Mary's eyes.

Lila whispered, "You rest. I'm going to sit on the beach and think, like you do." Lila continued to stroke Mary's hair and face until her eyes closed.

Lila shook her head, smiling as she sat on the sand. How odd that she had never thought about the possibility of love between women, had never even heard anyone speak of it. Lila had never had a female friend. She had always felt too different, too outside herself. She had not put a name to her feelings until Mary did it for her on Monday morning. She had admired Mary, emulated her, tried to please and surprise her with each new lesson learned. There was real pleasure in simply being with Mary, even in merely listening to her talk. She delighted in teasing a smile from her. It had not occurred to her that the sum of all these feelings could be defined as love.

But that other morning on her back porch, as she'd sat and listened to this woman, something inside her had said, *yes, that's exactly right. That is what I feel.* It was as though a switch had clicked on and she had received a surge of energy that jolted her from her sleepwalk through life. Something she had been waiting for all her life had arrived. If she had discovered this about herself when she was sixteen, as Mary had, she saw that her life might then have gone the way Mary's had. Caution might have been beaten into her. Mary was right, the risks were enormous. She finally understood what it took for Mary to come to her that morning. What Mary saw as an act of weakness, Lila saw as the greatest act of courage she had ever witnessed.

As she sat and watched the waves, she understood the reluctance Mary had to fully enjoy what they had found together. It was born in the fists of her own father, in the scorn and rejection she had endured. It was sustained with the fear that this love would not be good for Lila, or enough for her. Mary thought she had selfishly exposed her to the kind of risk and danger she had already seen and did not want her to experience. Lila smiled to herself. Mary was being protective, but it was unnecessary. She did not want to be protected; she wanted to indulge herself in this new passion, explore it fully, test its limits.

Lila smelled the salty, tangy air and felt the breeze push at her face, the sun begin to burn her skin. Trouble will come, she admitted to herself. They would not go unnoticed, however careful Mary wanted them to be. She would just have to show Mary that any trouble that came would be worth it, as long as they could be together.

Around four, Lila rose and brushed the sand off her legs and feet, and walked back up to the cottage. She smiled at Mary as she sat on the edge of the bed. Lila lay down next to her, Mary fighting off sleep as she gently slid her arms around her. The sea breeze came in through the windows, fluttering the curtains. A fly buzzed lazily somewhere in the room. Mary's body felt warm and smooth, sleepy and relaxed against hers.

"You're still half asleep," Lila whispered.

This Mary was new to her, languid, stretched out full length against her, slow and careless in her movements, until they awakened a response in Lila and she realized that those sleepy movements had not been careless at all. Now they moved together on the bed.

Lila's reactions still startled her, thrilled her with alarm, though she had learned where her body was taking her. There was still the shock of urgency, the surprise of gratification, the haste and deep need to reach that point again. She should have realized that Mary never did anything without purpose. Then her mind was taken over, and all that passed through it had to do with where Mary was taking her now. "Don't stop," she whispered desperately. Like an engine pulling into a station with a hiss of steam and a squeal of brakes, metal on metal, Lila fell into place with a rush and a deep shudder, and an aftershock of quivering, shaking muscles that clasped and opened, tensed and relaxed with a will and a rhythm borrowed from the sea. Lila came back to herself to find Mary gently trying to pull her hands away. Lila used those muscles to keep Mary's hands where they were. Mary smiled and sighed.

"Don't move yet, please. I have another lesson to learn." Lila kept her eyes closed as she spoke.

Mary smiled again. "Now?"

Lila rolled closer and opened her eyes. "No, later. Let's eat and then watch the sun go down."

Lila rinsed off in the shower while Mary made iced tea and sandwiches for them both. Lila emerged, her hair sleek and wet, her feet bare. She sat down and leaned back in her chair. She sat for a while, eyes half closed, replaying their lovemaking in her head, smiling, feeling completed and satisfied, powerful and humbled by her body's abilities. She wondered if sex with a man could possibly be as fulfilling, wondered if Mary had any experience with men, but she shied away from this idea with a rush of fierce possessiveness. And she found that she had no interest in imagining what sex would be like with a man. Her physical need was for Mary alone, her passion was called up and served by Mary's hands and mouth, and she felt a frisson of raw desire burn along her skin as she remembered Mary's practiced skill in satisfying her need. Then she looked at Mary with a gleam of determination in her eyes.

"I feel glorious. I suppose the whole world knows what I've only just discovered. How and why do people keep this secret? It's wonderful!"

Mary laughed. "Certain things just aren't discussed. Have you prepared a lecture for me?"

"Not at all. Just a few admonishments. Take better care of yourself. Eat and sleep when you should. Avail yourself of the restorative capacity I've just discovered in making love whenever possible. It does wonders for my outlook. Think ahead, not behind. We are not following a predetermined pattern. Let me think a minute."

Mary smiled and Lila knew she was amused at her earnest attempt to imitate Mary's own deliberate style.

"Sorry. I got caught up thinking about predestination and free will. I know you think of me as a novice, inexperienced at all this subterfuge. I just want to say that I love what we do together in bed. I love what you've taught me, the way you look at me when you push me over the edge. I think I loved you before I knew that's what it was." She paused, caught up in the realization of exactly how Monday morning had changed her. "God. Was it only five days ago that you appeared on the back porch? It seems a lifetime."

Mary was shaking her head, but still smiling. "Think all you like.

You must know I acted out of self-interest. I simply had to speak the truth. You were literally tormenting me. Don't make me sound so noble."

Lila stood up to get a better look at some sailboats on the bay. She sat on the railing of the tiny patio and turned her face into the wind, closing her eyes. Though she was pleased with the place, already she was imagining adding a room and decorating. She sighed. Suddenly she wished they never had to leave. She fantasized about living together in the small, weathered cottage. She pictured Mary on a ladder, painting the outside walls, while she sat sewing curtains and the seagulls kept watch over them. She opened her eyes to be astounded once again at the blue sky that met the sea, with towering white clouds that reached upward forever. She turned around to face Mary with a grin of pure exuberance.

"I knew you wouldn't care to hear how I feel. I suppose you don't quite trust it. You see yourself as more experienced than I am, but let me point out that you are more experienced only in having things end badly. We are equally inexperienced in having them end well. I'm not going to let you intimidate me into thinking as cautiously as you. And I refuse to believe that what we are doing is wrong. It's the first right thing I've ever done, the first thing that's ever felt right. You think I read my Bible too much, too closely, but you read it too skeptically. Love is kind, remember? Love is patient. It 'rejoiceth in the truth.' The people in that town may force us to be careful, but they can't force me to be ashamed. If you want to scout ahead for trouble, anticipate problems, I'm sure you'll find them. But I'm not going to spoil things by worrying about what may come. Which doesn't mean I'll be careless with this great gift you've given me. Darn. I had some wonderful thoughts on the beach, things I was going to tell you."

"Look, the sun's going down. Let's go to the beach. We can build a fire." Mary clearly had heard enough.

Lila sighed and followed her inside to gather jackets and a blanket. Mary found matches and got an armload of wood. They trudged through the sand and dumped their things, then they waded out until the water hit their knees. They held hands and Mary helped her keep her balance as wave after wave came at them. Lila was scared of the water, the force of each wave pushing at her knees, the uncertain footing as the sand shifted and sucked away each time, but Mary kept a firm grip. They stood in the water and watched the sun sink, swallowed by the horizon.

They sat on the beach watching the colors reflected in the clouds over the water. Lila's short curls seemed to dance as they were parted and arranged again and again by the wind, acting as a frenetic and indecisive hair dresser. She wore pleated shorts with cuffs and a sleeveless blouse tied at her waist. Her bare legs were turning brown. Mary wore a man's white cotton dress shirt that was too large. The sleeves were rolled and pushed above her elbows, resting on her knees. The wind made the oversized shirt whip and snap like a sail. Lila wanted to tug at the buttons on that shirt herself, but there were still people out, so she watched the wind whip it around, sometimes flattening it against the lean figure staring far out to sea, revealing the outline of a small, round breast. Now the wind filled it with air until it billowed out, and Lila wanted to slide underneath it. She stared at the point where Mary's throat disappeared into the button-down collar. She couldn't help herself: even Mary's elbows, where they emerged from the bunched-up sleeves, fascinated her. Mary's forearms were crossed over her knees and her chin rested on them as she watched sailboats and shrimpers on the bay. Knowing that soon they would go inside made Lila's skin warm with anticipation. Then they would pull at buttons and cuffs and pleats. She felt a familiar hollow tension that she had only recently learned to identify as desire.

That night they moved together with the relentless wash of the waves on the beach pacing them, keeping their rhythm, carrying them forward, pulling them back, then forward, until a high point was reached and they let the waves go on without them. They slept in each other's arms and woke to the sound of seagulls and waves.

Mary drove home with all the windows down in the big Buick. She enjoyed the sensation of being close enough to touch but not touching. Here the silence was companionable, not forced.

Lila soon slumped in her seat. Then she stretched out with her head in Mary's lap. Mary drove with one hand and kept the other one against Lila's cheek. Few words had passed between them since they woke that morning. They took the back way into Myrtlewood, and Lila sat up about five miles out of town. As they turned into the driveway at the Dubose house, Tommie came out onto the porch. He had come home early.

"Lila! Where you been? Mr. Dunn got a fish hook in his thumb. We had to take him to the doctor! He got twelve stitches. He said it hurt worse than cutting the fish hook out. You have to be careful fishing. Don't get your line tangled, don't jerk it like Mr. Dunn did, that hook has a barb on it. That's why the fish can't wiggle off. Mr. Howard Butler's in the kitchen. He's been waiting for you."

Lila got her bag from the back seat. She ran up the steps and gave Tommie a quick hug, something she had never done before. He squirmed away. "I went to the beach with Miss McGhee. We had a great time. Let me say bye to her." She handed him her bag and went back down the steep steps and leaned into Mary's open window. "Take the car. I'll walk over later and drive it back. Annie's not here and I need to thank Mr. Howard Butler for looking after Tommie. I'll see you in a little while."

Mary did not want to keep the car. She did not want to park it at her house for everyone to see. She did not want Lila walking over later to get it, looking tanned, relaxed, still warm from the beach, still glowing and pleased and awed.

She backed down the driveway and drove the three short blocks to Miss Louise's in a daze. The moment she had seen Tommie standing on the porch, she'd wanted to grab Lila's arm and keep her in the car, drive away with her. She did not want to feel resentment, the flash of irritation that Tommie was home. It would have made no difference if he had still been gone. They would still have this problem of readjusting to the present, of putting away this weekend, of recreating their roles. They could not be seen giggling together on the porch or anywhere else. They should not have been seen coming home together from a trip. People were eager to imagine the worst, and sometimes slow to recognize what was right before their eyes, but in this town there was nothing else to do but talk about one another. Their trip would be noted and talked about, just as Mr. Dunn's incident would be.

Mary unloaded her things from the car and carried everything in in one trip, not wanting to come back outside for any reason. Mostly she did not want to wake Miss Louise from her afternoon nap, nor did she want to feel the neighbors' eyes watching her. The air here was thick with humidity. Compared with the salty, fresh Gulf air it was sluggish, syrupy, stale with the smells of Sunday dinners, sticky, stifling. She closed the front door, an unheard-of thing on a Sunday afternoon.

She threw her bag on the bed and watched as it fell to the floor. She left it there and sank into a chair. She saw Lila's eyes glowing in the first sunset, and burning darkly later in bed. She saw her sunburned nose, her pink toenails. Mary closed her eyes and remembered how good it felt to hold her, bare skin against bare skin.

Mary dug a cigarette out of a crumpled pack that still had beach sand in it and straightened it out, then angrily flicked her Zippo at it. She would force herself to stop the images flashing through her mind like an old silent film. She would keep away from the phone. She paced and smoked, her anger directed mostly at herself, because having satisfied her body's craving for Lila, she was humiliated to find that she felt less in control now that she was more certain of Lila. It was almost dark when she finally gave in and drove the car back to the Dubose house.

Lila was on the back porch alone. A load of washing was hung neatly on the clothesline. She was sewing a button on one of Tommie's shirts. Mary slowly and deliberately pulled her out of her chair. She held Lila's wrists, preventing her from hugging or touching or bringing their bodies into contact. She looked at Lila with such furious longing that Lila burst out laughing.

"I feel the same way. I thought it was just me. My god, what are we going to do? Look, I'm shaking."

Mary relaxed the hold on her wrists. The tension that had driven her here drained away. She understood finally that this affected them both. This desire that delighted and overwhelmed her and the responsibility for finding ways to be together were shared, and this lightened the weight for her. They would be partners in inventing stories and excuses, partners in exploring new ways to feed this passion between them, and they would share both the benefits and the burden of sustaining it. Looking into the startling gray eyes that had haunted her, Mary saw strength and resolve there, and knew she could rest now. Lila would pull her along with her innocence and instinctive ability to say and do just the right things. Mary relaxed as Lila freed her hands and drew her close for a hug.

Lila sat on the Sullivans' living-room sofa, holding a cup of tea. This was another first experience for her. She had never had tea before, sitting in someone else's living room, dressed for church on a Saturday afternoon. Taking a sip of tea, she returned her cup to its saucer. She had a suspicion about what had prompted Barbara to invite her here, but she didn't want to steer the conversation to that subject. Let Barbara lead the way.

"Is Mary working today?"

Lila smiled. Barbara would have no trouble introducing the subject she wanted to discuss, after all. "Yes, I imagine she is."

"Surely there's no real need for her to work on weekends any more, now that you're helping in the office."

"Well, I'm not sure that I am much help, as yet. I'm still learning. Miss McGhee has to stop her own work to explain things to me, so I just slow her down. It must be very frustrating for her."

Barbara set her tea cup carefully in its saucer, which she held in her hand. Lila admired the practiced skill and wished for some of that grace for herself.

"Lila, dear, you don't still call her Miss McGhee, do you? You two have become friends. There's no need for such formality between women of the same age. You make Mary sound old."

"Mary does not encourage familiarity. Sometimes she seems much older, but then everyone seems older than I." Lila was conscious of using her best grammar, and she found herself sitting straighter. Barbara had created a carefully formal setting, and Lila responded with an odd formality of her own. She imagined the two of them as diplomats negotiating terms of a treaty. Mary would be pleased if she knew I was emulating her manner with Buchanan, she thought.

"Nonsense. You've come a long way in a short time. You've achieved quite a lot since Mr. Dubose's death. Surely you know that."

Lila sighed. "I still feel like I'm playing at being a grown-up. Pretending to be a wife. I'm simply a paid companion to Tommie, almost a mother. And what I do in the office seems almost like a hindrance rather than a help to Mary. Sometimes I feel like a project

134

she's taken on." Another Mary strategy, inviting your opponent to underestimate you.

"You're still a bit in awe of her, as indeed we all are. She's smart, beautiful, elegant. Who wouldn't be?"

Indeed, thought Lila. She recognized the speculation she had seen behind Barbara's eyes, and she knew now she was not wrong about her. Pastor's wife or not, the woman was interested in Mary. Lila watched Barbara navigate the silence between them by sipping her tea, while avoiding eye contact with her. Yet there was an eagerness behind Barbara's serene expression. The genteel probing hardly disguised what they were really talking about. Were the wives of ministers bound by confidentiality? It seemed reasonable to expect that what she was about to say to this woman would never be repeated.

Lila adjusted the lay of her skirt, smoothing it over her lap. "Actually, Mary and I have grown quite close," she said slowly, willing Barbara to meet her eyes. "It's at her insistence that we maintain an employer–employee relationship for everyone. Mary has strict standards."

Barbara leaned back, clearly startled by Lila's willingness to speak honestly. Lila returned her stare. She had not been wrong, after all. She saw a slow dawning of regret and an innocuous cunning. Barbara's look became hooded, no longer direct.

"I'm really happy for you. Mary is a remarkable person."

"Yes, she is. I've learned a lot from her."

Lila kept her face carefully blank, thinking that the subterfuge and subtlety required by their new relationship really could be quite fun at times. Barbara raised her cup in a silent toast of acquiescence. Lila returned the salute; then they relaxed.

"The truth is, Lila, that bringing you two together was rather more Bill's idea than mine."

"I thought that might be the case. Still, you've been very supportive and even encouraging. That was gracious of you, and you have my thanks."

Barbara laughed. "Don't thank me. I'm not quite so magnanimous. I think that Bill and I will be moving away from here very soon. I am very happy for both of you, but I don't think you really want me waiting in the wings."

135

"Barbara, I hope that Mary is never dissatisfied in any way. But I also hope I would be as gracious as you, if she ever wanted someone else. If you don't mind my asking, how does your husband—I mean does Bill—does he know, does he accept this part of your nature?"

Barbara grinned girlishly. "He has inclinations of his own, you see. We help each other with our interests."

"You're really leaving? Mary and I both will miss you."

"Mobile is a much bigger town. More opportunities there to connect with people who are like us. I was surprised that Mary never explored her options there." She raised an eyebrow.

"No, I think Mary has found everything she wants right here."

Barbara smiled. "Well. I do believe she has. I congratulate you, Lila Dubose. I can't help but be pleased at your success. You and I must keep in touch. You are pretty remarkable yourself." Barbara leaned toward her, her eyes glittering for a moment with an inquisitive gleam that might have been flirtatious, had there not been something almost avaricious about it. "Considering the two of you, I'm not so sure I focused on the right one."

Lila sipped her tea. She would miss Barbara and Bill. She would miss the bridge games on Thursday nights, which had given her an opportunity to spend time with Mary in an acceptable social setting. She regretted how much more congenial it could have been, had the Sullivans had been more forthright from the beginning. There was so much to learn about this new life she had adopted. The necessity for circumspection was fun for her, but already she was annoyed that it had denied her and Mary more freedom to be exactly who they were with two people who understood and shared their secret.

As Lila walked home from her counsel with Barbara Sullivan, she felt like she had just joined a secret club. She had barely listened to Mary's cautionary tales, but now she felt there was more to be known than she had supposed about this society into which she had been initiated. Mary McGhee saw herself as a charter member, an authority on the entire field, and expected Lila to follow her lead. But perhaps she did not have to accept Mary's word as the rule of law. There could be other perspectives to explore. This was, after all, a whole new world. Her way of living in it might be different from Mary's.

She wondered what Mary would have to say about the Sullivans leaving town, and sighed as she engaged in another imaginary conversation with her that would never take place. Mary would have no comment, she was sure. Quiet, proper Mary would not speculate about the private business of anyone's life. She must have been aware of Barbara's interest, yet she'd never mentioned it. Lila was quite certain that Barbara's interest was not returned. She smiled to herself, feeling a certain power. She would not tell Mary anything about the Sullivans' leaving. Mary McGhee was her prize. She would defend it against any outside interests, as fiercely as a medieval lord behind castle walls. This was definitely new territory, and it was hers.

Lila walked past her front gate, and continued around the block, then took the path through the garden that led to the back door of the house. She saw Annie in the kitchen and waved, then sank into a chair on the porch. Annie came out and joined her, easing her tall frame into the porch swing. She rocked herself as she studied Lila's face. Lila didn't mind, though she knew she had that "dreamy" look again. She wasn't worried about what Annie might deduce. Right now, she didn't care what anyone thought.

"So how was your afternoon tea with the preacher's wife?"

"Just wonderful. The Sullivans are leaving soon. I suppose she wanted to say goodbye."

"Really? There's no talk downtown about them leaving." Annie sounded slightly offended that a big piece of news had escaped her detection.

"I don't think they've told anyone else yet. Annie, do you suppose it would be all right to invite Miss McGhee over for supper on Thursday nights? That was our night to play bridge with the Sullivans, you know."

"I been telling you since she came here it was all right. If you're going to be home on Thursday nights from now on, there's no need for me to be here then, is there?"

Lila looked over at Annie, and thought once again what a wise and good woman she was. "Why don't you leave making supper on Thursdays to me? You can go after dinner and have some time to yourself. Tommie and I take up too much of your time, don't we?"

"Don't you worry yourself about that. I've been seeing to the Duboses most of my life. A group of us from the church are getting together on Thursdays to make quilts, and they want me to teach the younger ones how to do it." Her black eyes pierced Lila with a look. "I suppose you and Miss McGhee can amuse yourselves after Mr. Tommie goes to bed, even without cards. I never thought Methodists approved of card playin' anyway. That pastor was a strange one."

Lila suppressed a laugh as Annie heaved herself out of the swing and went back to the kitchen. Amuse themselves, indeed! She gloried once again in the subtleties required by her new secret life. She laughed softly in the warm afternoon sun and began to invent a game that she could teach Mary, one in which she got to make the rules.

Part Two

Chapter Ten

REPORT TO THE GRAND DRAGON: *All due respect, we just don't give a damn down here about the Supreme Court ordering desegregation. Ain't never going to happen here, no matter how many uppity colored women they try to start through the University. Them boys in Mississippi, they got the right idea. Attendance was 15.*

Monday, September 19, 1955

"Anybody here?" the postman called out.

Locked in the small bathroom at the office, Lila and Mary were half undressed when the afternoon mail was delivered. Lila's stroking and kissing had dissolved Mary's awareness.

Lila, not hearing or caring, kept rubbing and fondling, pushing Mary closer to the edge. She knelt and brought her mouth to Mary, braced against the sink, her skirt pushed up, her panties and stockings in a tangle at her feet, hands gripping the sink behind her. Mary gritted her teeth and groaned softly in relief after the physical response she could not control. Aware of someone moving around in the office, Mary hurriedly rearranged her clothes, her anger rising, and stomped out, leaving Lila to wash her hands and face.

The postman was gone. Lila took her time, emerging much later from the bathroom, and refused to look at Mary as she took her place at the desk they shared. She idly sorted through papers, smiling her secret, self-satisfied smile. Mary would scold her now. But when they could next steal a few minutes alone, they would spend them again on the desire that burned without tending, without fueling, without pause.

Mary broke the silence. "That was dangerous and unnecessary. Anyone could have come in."

Lila looked at her, mimicking her serious expression. She smiled, looking insufferably calm. "We were lucky, then."

Mary had learned to hear what Lila chose not to say. She could read it on Lila's face as easily as words on a page. *Unnecessary, my hind leg!*

"Lila, this is serious. We can't do that in the office any more."

"I agree. This is very serious. Are you coming to the house later?"

"What reason would I have?"

"You don't need a reason. People have supper together. Have supper with us. Then you and Tommie and I can take a drive. He wants to show me something they fixed at the cabin."

Mary stared at her. Was she thinking clearly? The three of them on a family outing? She shook her head. "No thank you."

"Why are you avoiding Tommie? You used to take time with him when he came into the office on Thursdays."

"Tommie doesn't need to be here now. You can sign things. It makes him uncomfortable."

"It makes *you* uncomfortable. He loved coming in. He felt useful. But now—even Tommie can figure out that you don't want him here. Why?"

Mary refused to answer. She returned to her work, ignoring Lila sitting across from her. An hour ticked by with neither of them speaking. Then Lila rose and left. Mary sighed and sat back, relieved and perplexed with herself. At five o'clock she closed the office and walked home. Miss Louise was waiting for her on the front porch.

"I went ahead and made supper for us." Miss Louise rarely bothered with cooking any more, preferring a sandwich or a piece of cold chicken on the porch, where she might keep her eye on the goings on of her neighbors. "I thought you might like to have something ready for you when you got home today. It's such a nice evening."

A hoe and rake rested against the porch railing: Miss Louise's effective way of hinting for help with the yard work. Mary changed her clothes and began weeding the flower beds, some of which rose up out of circular mounds in the yard. Who on earth had decided that old car tires painted white should be used as flower pots? Miss Louise's was the only yard on the street so decorated. Mary suspected that this was an innovation Louise had made after her mother's death.

The old lady followed her about the yard, hovering uselessly. "I really need to split those bulbs and transplant some of them to the back yard, don't you think? My old bones can't manage to kneel down there long enough to do it any more."

"I'll get to it on Saturday. I talked to Henry, the boy who helps at the Dubose place sometimes. He says he can cut the grass for you once a week. He'll come by after school tomorrow."

"Now, I can't be paying him to do that."

"That's all right, I paid him. He'll get the trash out and burn it for us too."

"I'll feel just like Mrs. Dubose, with somebody doing my yard work." Miss Louise managed to sound both pleased and disapproving at the same time. "How is Miss Lila doing?"

Mary stood, straightening her back, and looked at the old lady, now perched on the porch steps, overseeing her work. "Mrs. Dubose is doing just fine. She has a real grasp of the business now."

"I just bet she does. Gerald Buchanan said she sat in the board meeting at the bank last week. Now that's getting above herself. What's she got to do with the bank?"

Why would Buchanan have bothered to talk to Louise? He considered her a cranky old woman. "Miss Louise, you know the Duboses own that bank. Mr. Buchanan cannot make some decisions without the approval of a Dubose. Would everyone rather that Mr. Tommie decided how money is loaned out?" The only reason Buchanan would stop by must be to gather information about Mary herself, Miss Louise being more than willing to tell everything she knew to anyone who gave her the time of day. Damn the prattling, thoughtless woman!

"That's all well and good, but that girl's still a Jackson. Having somebody from that bunch running around doing things like that is just as bad as Mr. Tommie."

Mary waited for the predictable reference to Lila's not being mentally capable, but Miss Louise apparently decided to hold back this time. Miss Louise was giving her a veiled and thoughtful look, as if she were considering Mary's background now, not the Duboses'. So much in the town seemed to evolve from who you were—who your people were—that Mary imagined it must drive everyone mad trying to place her without a family history to guide them. She had yet to fathom why genealogy had so much to do with every pronouncement made by Miss Louise and the rest of the town. She went inside to wash up, hoping Miss Louise hadn't burned everything again.

After a heavy supper of fried chicken and fried okra Mary was ready for her evening walk. She still walked in the evening as she did when first arriving in Myrtlewood. Over the years she had endlessly walked through the tidy neighborhoods of Myrtlewood. Eventually she walked past the point where the pavement turned to dirt roads and the houses became more ramshackle. There, the dark-skinned people stared at her silently, curiously, but no one spoke to her. Some nodded as she passed, but she was never bothered in any way. The Negroes became accustomed to seeing her after a while. They didn't seem offended that she studied their faces or examined their living quarters. She even began to smile and speak to the children who, after some initial shyness, accepted her presence and resumed their normal play when she walked each evening. Mary smelled cooking aromas that she couldn't identify, and wondered if their diet was very different from what she ate. It was on these long walks that she gradually felt her acceptance by these silent and dignified people who now sometimes smiled and nodded, even occasionally speaking a few words if she stopped to inquire about the difficulties of septic tanks or how the Negro school was advancing its plan to expand and add a new wing. Thad's daughter had told her about this, and she had sold them the lumber at cost. She had given some cash toward bricks and roofing shingles and furnishings like desks and blackboards. And books. There were never enough textbooks. They would hire two new teachers for the next school year. Then they would work on getting a central-heating system installed. No one in the Negro community expected desegregated schools to happen anytime soon, no matter what the Supreme Court said.

Janie, Thad's wife, came out on the porch and waved. "Miss McGhee! Come on up and set with me a spell."

Mary sat with Janie on the front porch of the house facing the river, and they tried to cool themselves with Jesus fans from the church as they watched dragonflies hover in the distance over the cattails along the riverbank. She looked over at the small trickle barely a foot deep that ran through the cow pasture, the same creek that supplied water for everything except drinking and cooking. Thad had dug a well for that.

"How long have you had the well?" Mary stared at the wooden structure that housed it, right at the edge of the porch, the bucket tied to a rope on a pulley sitting on the shelf that ringed the well, a tin dipper leaning inside.

"Let's see now ..." Janie tried to recall, just as Thad and Henry walked up from the field.

"I remember, because Daddy put me down in the hole and made me scoop out mud after it got so deep he couldn't work in it with a shovel. I was about six years old, I reckon. Mama yelled at him, 'Git that child out of that hole before it caves in on him!' I wadn't scared though; it was fun," Henry said.

"Hey, Thad. How goes the farming business?"

Janie went inside to light the kerosene lamps and Thad took her chair and sat next to Mary.

Thad felt it his duty to keep her updated on the state of his fields and the improvements he was making, though Mary paid little attention to projected yields and strains or varieties, or the prospect of switching from corn to sorghum, or how much hay had been baled from the upper fields, or the market prices. Henry made a payment to her every month; he would soon pay off the loan she had extended for the tractor but he never told Mary of the vandalism that happened two days after he got it. She'd learned about it from Buchanan, recalling the snide, self-satisfied tone as he had tried to remark casually about an event he evidently marked with some bit of pride. Thad went on discussing his plans to dig irrigation ditches which would also serve to drain off the water when it flooded the fields in the river bottom, effectively raising the planted rows higher than the flood plain.

"Jack, git your head out of this window right now!" Janie's voice from the kitchen interrupted Thad's narrative.

"Who's Jack?" Mary asked.

Henry laughed. "Jack's the mule. He leans over the fence that runs by the side of the house and sticks his head in the kitchen. He likes Mama's cornbread."

Mary went inside to see the spectacle for herself. Sure enough, the mule's big head was just inside the window, whose wooden shutters were thrown open to dissipate the heat from the stove, and he was calmly munching cornbread. He flapped his ears when Janie took the plate away.

Thad took two of the boys with him to feed the hogs and chickens, and Mary and Janie sat down on the porch again. Mary squinted against the setting sun; the porch was deep and wide, shaded, but the sun was bright and unstoppable.

"They said Emmett Till whistled at a white woman." Janie shook her head. "You picture Henry or any one of my boys doing somethin' that foolish? I don't care if this boy was from Chicago or the moon. They say he was tryin' to show off in front of his cousins. It just don't make sense."

"So what, Janie? What if he did? That's what fourteen-year-old boys do. It's not a crime. It may be a stupid thing, but it's not punishable by death, for God's sake."

"They came in and took him right out of his bed. Right out of his uncle's house, in the middle of the night."

Mary shared her anger over the helplessness that family must have felt. "There was nothing they could have done, Janie. The men would have been shot if they had tried to stop that bunch. You know that." As Mary herself knew that calling the sheriff would have resulted in nothing at all.

"No, they just had to stand by and take it. Like we always have to do."

Mary saw Janie's control begin to slip. "Let's talk about something else."

"How's Mr. Tommie doin'?"

"Not so good. Doc Morgan is puzzled by the way he gets sick so often."

"You tell Annie I got her some fig preserves put by. Thad'll bring them to her next time he comes."

They both knew that Mary wouldn't take them; if she did, she would have to explain where she had been. Thad's house was a refuge for Mary, and she didn't want Lila to know how much time she spent down on the river with his family. It was the only place she could breathe easier, at least for a while.

After the last man had received his pay packet and walked back to the mill, Lila opened one of the windows, and Mary put away the cash box in the safe hidden inside a closet. They pulled chairs over to the window to catch the slight breeze, and Lila took off her shoes and put her feet in Mary's lap. Mary pushed them away. Lila smiled, though with a softly disappointed look.

"What are you going to do this weekend?"

Mary frowned. "I don't know. I might go down to the beach. It should be nice weather. I don't think I can take a whole weekend with Miss Louise right now."

"Why not?"

"She prattles on and on. I need to think. That's all."

"Think about what? How we never seem to have any time alone?"

"Lila, don't, please."

"If you say this is not the time or the place one more time, I'll scream. This is the only time alone we have together, and you know it. You refuse every suggestion I make."

"Dinner with you and Tommie is hardly alone. And hardly appropriate."

"Of course it's appropriate. You mean it would be uncomfortable. What if I'm out for a walk and stop to admire Miss Louise's yard? Is that casual and appropriate enough?"

Mary was certain that Buchanan, too, was becoming a frequent customer of Myrtlewood's official purveyor of information. "She thought I was putting on airs to hire Henry to cut the grass."

Lila looked surprised. "When will he have time? When he's not in school he's helping Thad at our place."

"He needs the money. He graduates from high school next spring and he wants to save enough by then to go to college."

Lila glanced at her. "He wants to go to college?"

"Thad's making sure every single one of them graduates high school. Henry's older sister worked her way through school and became a teacher."

"Where would Henry go to college?"

"Tuskegee Institute. He wants to study agriculture."

"See, that's just like a Negro. Why spend all that money to go off from home and study something he's been doing all his life? They'd be better off if he stayed at home and helped his daddy like he's been doing. It would be a waste of money."

Mary looked out the window.

"I wish I could go with you to the beach," Lila said. "Annie's says it's time to do the canning before the garden goes to waste. We have so many tomatoes and cucumbers I don't know what we will do with them all. The squash and the pole beans have just gone crazy. Want to skip the beach and come over and help us?"

Mary watched Lila's slow grin, and she sighed. "You know I can't. I can't be here, be around you, without wanting you. It's better if I go sit on the beach. I'll be all right."

"It might be better for you, but what about me? I want to be alone with you. I don't see why we can't go to the beach together. But if I can't have that, then I want whatever I can get."

"How would we explain our taking off for a weekend together? People understand that we have supper together on Thursdays but the beach is different. We were there just a couple of months ago. It's too soon. Besides, I think Buchanan is watching me, and you obviously have things to do this weekend. I don't. I can't sit in my rooms wondering what you're up to. It's too—"

Lila reached for Mary's hands. "I know. Don't you have to go look at some timber next week in Clarke County? Couldn't I go with you? We would have the whole day."

Mary looked down at their joined hands, afraid to look at Lila, certain she would not be able to control herself if she looked into Lila's eyes.

"Buchanan is coming with me. He thinks he knows more about judging a stand of timber than I do, which is easily possible. I should take Vince Dunn, but Buchanan won't hear of that. It is just not done for a single lady to ride in a car with a mill foreman, according to him. Apparently, though, it is permissible to take a car trip with a bank president. Where are all these rules written down?"

"In the same book where it says that two ladies cannot spend a weekend at the beach together. You know that one, don't you? The book you have memorized." Lila sighed, defeated. "I hope you have a good weekend alone at the beach. I'll be here Sunday afternoon if you want to stop by. Tommie will be asleep with the radio and Annie's going to see her family."

Lila left. Mary sat for a while by the window, imagining the weekend in the kitchen: Lila's hair damp and curling from the steam, the big pots of stewing tomatoes on the stove. The chatter and laughter as Lila and Annie worked side by side. She tried inserting herself in the little domestic scene, but she could not, and it made her angry, as did the trembling of her hands that could still feel the warmth from Lila's. She hated this yearning for what she couldn't have, and detested her own body's refusal to obey her will. She began to curse silently as she gathered her things to walk home. She would stop and pick up a bottle of whiskey when she drove through Mobile on her way to the beach cottage. Maybe it would help chase these images from her mind and help her sleep. She should save some of the whiskey for after her trip with Buchanan. No doubt it would be useful in calming her homicidal urge after spending an entire day with him.

Mary sat across the desk from a man who, though about the age of thirty, looked years older. She made him wait while she sorted through some papers on her desk. He was missing a couple of teeth, whether from having had them knocked out or from poor diet, she didn't know. His face was reddened in a perpetual flush, which could have been caused by high blood pressure, or from anger or embarrassment. His eyes watered constantly. He breathed noisily through his slightly open mouth, as though his nose was blocked, probably from being broken, Mary guessed. She had some personal experience in that herself. His hands were dry, skin flaking and peeling, as though roughened by handling some caustic material. His right thumbnail was blackened, no doubt smashed by an unsteady hand wielding a hammer. She noticed he had drilled a hole in the nail in a futile effort to drain the trapped blood. He hadn't bothered to remove his wide-brimmed, dirty gray Fedora. His dungarees were streaked with grease and other dark substances Mary did not want to identify. His face was deeply creased but shaven.

He sat slumped, elbows resting comfortably on the arms of the visitor's chair, legs sprawled open, casually surveying the office. He waited quietly, staring at Mary almost, but not quite, insolently. He was there to ask for a job, after all. Mary knew from experience that had they passed on the street, even this small effort to hide his disdain would not have been made. She needlessly re-sorted papers again, trying to decide what her answer would be. She knew he needed work. The man already had four or five young children who he made haphazard attempts to support.

Finally she gave up the pretense of being busy. She would have to say yes. This wasted wreck of a man who reeked of sweat and alcohol was Lila's brother, Jimmy. She looked directly at him.

"We're running two shifts now. There's an opening on the early one. They start at five in the morning. Can you do that?"

"Hell, what's so tough about it?"

"What's so tough, apparently for you at any rate, is showing up for work on time, every day. That's why you lost your last job. I spoke to Mr. Howard Butler." She was repeating a scene she had endured with other Jacksons, and would again, she was sure.

The man grinned, his brief attempt at deference gone as the insolence, which was his instinctive response to anyone in authority, returned. She judged that with his attitude, he'd probably spent his wartime service in a Navy brig. He wagged his right leg slowly back and forth.

"You got no call to do that. I can work here if I want to. My little sister owns this whole setup."

"No, she does not, Mr. Jackson. Tommie Dubose owns this mill. I act in his behalf. Would you like to talk to him about a job?"

The sneer deepened, his upper lip curling to reveal a canine tooth, the feral gleam in his eyes adding to the wolf-like impression. She watched him as carefully as she would a rabid dog. "I ain't asking no retard for work. He don't know what day it is. Probably don't know if he's married to my sister or to you." He sniggered.

"Which is why I am here interviewing you in his stead."

"Yeah, I know all about you hirin' folks. What the hell you doin', hirin' niggers to do white men's work? Maybe I'll help you out, run some of 'em off for you." He grinned; through the gap provided by his missing teeth, she could see his tongue moving in silent mirth.

Mary refrained from snarling. She wanted to boot the man

150

out of the office. Straining for the last vestige of patience, she said, "Do you want the job or not? Are you going to show up every day?"

"Yeah, I'll be here. I need a week's advance pay. Old man Butler didn't pay me yet for my last week's work."

"Your last week's work consisted of showing up only once, at three in the afternoon, dead drunk. Do that here, and you'll get the same result."

"I need some money for groceries." His eyes challenged her to refuse.

"If you need groceries, go down to the mill store and sign a ticket to get what you need. It will be taken out of your first paycheck. Cash has a way of turning into liquid nourishment for yourself, leaving your wife and children hungry."

"You got no right to talk to me like that." The man stood up, leaning across the desk menacingly. "Maybe I'll just go talk to Lila, up at the Dubose place. She might be interested to know how you been fixin' up them nigger shacks down under the hill. It don't look right, them people livin' in better houses than us. She can get rid of you easy as snappin' her fingers."

The attempt at intimidation might have been more effective had he not been swaying, his pores oozing the odor of a longtime, steady drinker, his hands shaking not with anger but with the tremors only another drink could control.

"You can do that, and she could give you money, but you'll have no job here if you do."

Mary watched him try to decide. He surely knew better than to take her up on the dare to talk to Lila. Finally he shrugged. She knew what Jimmy Jackson was thinking. He would go down to the creek, drink some bootleg whiskey, and tell the men lies about all the ugly things he had said, right to the bitch's face. She had no illusion that he was impressed either with her position or with her friendship with Lila. Finally he nodded.

"I'll take the job. Start on Monday."

"Start tomorrow morning, at five. I'll cut you a day's pay that way. And maybe you'll enjoy your drinking this weekend a little more, knowing you got some food for your family first."

Mary doubted the man ever felt guilty about drinking up his income. She went back to her papers, as he turned and left.

Sooner or later, someone would tell Lila what she had been doing. It had started with the little boy, Mark Anthony. His daddy had been the first Negro she had hired to work at the mill. She had approached the little boy's mother, offering her husband a job as a way to finance fixing up the cabin, where they lived through the winters with blankets over broken windows. Then a couple of other women had approached her, and she had extended credit to their families as well. She had driven from Mobile with a bathroom toilet in the back seat of her car more than once, and had kept Clyde Moseley very busy on his days off from the mill, digging septic tanks, running sewer lines and installing indoor bathrooms. He didn't mind the outdoor work so much, the roofing and carpentry and painting, but he greatly disliked going inside the colored people's homes. She hired Thad and Henry for the inside work and kept looking for a Negro man who could do the work that required myriad skills, just to avoid Clyde's constant complaints about working for colored people. Still, he hadn't yet refused the extra pay.

Lila walked into the office, her smile of greeting fading as she saw Mary's tension. Mary's eyes seemed to burn into her and she was pierced by the raw need she saw, and the anger that accompanied it. She'd come in to help get the payroll ready for the next day, hoping Mary could finish work early and come to supper. Tommie wasn't feeling well and would go to bed early; they could have some time alone tonight. All those intentions left her as she returned Mary's stare.

"What is it?"

Mary didn't answer. Lila endured the harsh look as she studied the flat, ascetic planes of the face so dear to her. Mary's flaming blue eyes seemed to pin her to the floor. She could see this was not the time for teasing or trying to ease Mary past this mood. Finally, an apology began in those eyes that everyone else thought so cold. Lila turned and flipped the lock. Mary had not moved, had made no effort to greet Lila or to protest the locking of the door. Lila didn't bother to close the windows or pull the shades. She walked around the desk, pulled

Mary out of her chair, and kissed her roughly, while she slid one hand under her skirt to feel the bare skin above her stocking. She pushed Mary's skirt up high, to her hips. Mary broke away from the kiss and turned out of her arms, but not before Lila had felt her trembling.

"Buchanan's on his way over here. I just spent the whole day Tuesday driving all over the state with him."

This was the usual explanation for Mary's mood. Lila sighed. "I'll go on home then."

Mary turned to face her. "Do you have any idea what he wants this time?"

Lila feigned indifference, though she knew exactly what Buchanan wanted. "No. I play my innocent act, just like you taught me. He doesn't lower himself to discuss 'business' with me."

Mary didn't look entirely convinced. "I'll let you know what it's about at supper then."

Lila gathered her things, came closer, and kissed Mary on the cheek. "You do that. I'll be waiting," she whispered.

Mary watched Lila walk through the mill yard from her window, and then sat down again behind Mr. Dubose's desk. She couldn't think about Lila right now; her strange attitude of late had begun to signal a warning of some kind. She had to pull her wits together. She straightened the papers on her desk. Buchanan came in and stood in the outer office, as though waiting for an invitation to enter the inner sanctum. Odd behavior for him.

"Mr. Buchanan. Come on in. That was a fast walk from the bank."

He sat down across from Mary in the visitor's chair. "You look mighty comfortable on that side of the desk. I just saw Miss Lila leaving, didn't I?"

"Yes, she stopped by to invite me to supper." Mary waited.

"Did she now? That's mighty thoughtful of her, to invite a secretary into her home."

"We usually have supper together every Thursday night. As you know." As the entire town knew, Mary was sure.

Buchanan leaned back in his chair, which seemed too small to contain his bulk. "I was thinking it's time we hired a manager for the mill."

"We're doing quite well here. Vince Dunn has been an invaluable help to me. With his advice, and yours of course, the mill has been turning a nice profit."

"Douglas White wants to get ahead. His daddy is still a young man and it will be years before he lets Doug take over for him at White's sawmill. The boy wants to get some experience in being a boss before he takes over in Thomasville."

Brilliant, Mary thought. Hiring a competitor. Not on her life. "Did he come to you with this idea?"

"He stopped in the bank the other day. I mentioned how we've been running here without a proper manager since Mr. Dubose passed away."

I just bet you did, thought Mary, as she took a calming breath. She wanted to kick Buchanan's fat ass out of her office. "And have you mentioned this to Mrs. Dubose?"

"She said something about not seeing why we should pay somebody else a salary when you do the work already."

Mary grew more angry. She thought a tendon would snap, her shoulders and neck were so tense. She'd have a talk with Lila later. For now, she would retire Buchanan from the field of play.

"I've run this mill for eight years now. I straightened out this business. I've increased our contracts and our payroll and our production, and the bottom line shows that. From a business standpoint, I have to agree with Mrs. Dubose. Why should we pay someone else a salary to do what I've already been doing?"

Buchanan's eyes grew hard. "All due respect, you've done a fine job, of course. But you don't belong here. Don't you want to get back to Houston and your *friends* and Big Sam's oil business?"

That was it. He must have talked to Big Sam. "Actually, I've grown quite fond of the job and the people here."

"I can see why you would. I told Doug he could probably start in about a month."

"I don't think that will be necessary."

"Miss McGhee, you're nothing but a—" He cut himself off and paused. "It don't look right, a woman hiring and firing men. We need a man in here, somebody that knows timber and land and how to run a sawmill and boss the men. Somebody Mrs. Dubose

154

can depend on. Somebody who knows how to hire the right kind of people."

Careful of her pronouns, Mary said, "We've hired people who can do the work."

"Well, some of the men don't like working side by side with niggers. That's just a fact. And there's good people who need work and they see these Nigras taking jobs away from them, and they got families to feed. That's not how we do things here."

"The men I've hired need the work and have families to feed too." And some of them had lost their land and farms to the bank, Mary didn't bother adding.

"And another thing, while we're on this subject. There's been some talk about you putting some of those Jacksons to work. See, decisions like that show everybody you just don't know enough, coming from off somewhere like you do, about the people here and how we do things."

Mary privately agreed with Buchanan that hiring Jackson men was pointless. None of them stayed on the job longer than their first paycheck. None of them ever showed up on time, and none of them were worth anything at all when it came to getting work done. She and Vince were agreed on that.

"I can hardly refuse a job to a brother of Mrs. Dubose, can I? She is my employer, after all." Not you, she added silently.

Buchanan shifted in his chair. "May I speak bluntly? Lila is a Dubose in name only, and everybody around here knows it. She was hired, just like you were, to do a job, and that's all. You ask me, she's gettin' above herself, writing checks to the church and who knows what all, like it was her own money."

Mary said coldly, "Lila Dubose was appointed Tommie's guardian in Mr. Dubose's will, and she is the sole trustee named by Mr. Dubose. Neither you nor I have any say in what she does with the money, nor in whom she hires."

"You and her gettin' mighty friendly. Maybe too friendly, if you know what I mean."

"Yes, Mrs. Dubose has been very welcoming and kind to me. We've become friends, working so closely in the office."

Buchanan stood up. "I bet you have. Just remember, people start to talk, they start not liking some things you been doing, and they get all worked up about it. Some strange woman from up north with no family ties moves in and starts doing things that go against the grain, and you could see some trouble coming your way. I'd be careful to remember my place, was I you. You best watch your step."

He put on his hat and left, somewhat huffily, Mary thought. She lit a cigarette, trying to calm down. Buchanan's pig-headedness always infuriated her. She thought it was time he remembered his place. He himself was nothing more than a Dubose employee, when you got down to it. She'd have to talk to Lila. Should it wait until supper tonight? No, she'd call her back to the office. This was business.

A half hour later, Lila sat where Buchanan had, looking at her. Mary clenched her hands together so hard the knuckles turned white. Lila observed the tension in her face and posture, watched Mary light yet another cigarette, a sure sign that she was upset, and waited. Buchanan must have really irritated her this time. Mary drew a ragged breath and commenced a tirade.

"That son of a bitch, pig-headed bastard, narrow-minded little bigot. He wants to fire me. Doesn't think a woman ought to be hiring and firing *men*, doesn't like who I hire. Damn him to hell."

"He told you about Doug White, I gather."

"You already knew, didn't you? Why didn't you tell me? Why didn't you tell him to stick it in his ear?"

Lila grinned. "I did, Mary, dear. Maybe not in those exact words."

"Well, he didn't get the point. He seemed to think he could come in here and replace me, just like that."

"I have no intention of replacing you. You know that. I gave him the usual speech about how much I relied on your advice, what a savior you've been, how you and I have been running the office together."

"He thinks I'm just a secretary and shouldn't be making hiring decisions and purchasing decisions, or any decisions at all. He wants to put a man in here that knows the sawmill business. He wants to get rid of me."

"Calm down. That's just not going to happen. He has no say about what we do. The loans incurred after Mr. Dubose died are paid off. The sawmill is none of his business now."

"Then why do we continue to let him look over the books and why do we listen to his cockamamie ideas?"

"Because we are two helpless women who depend upon sound business advice from the president of the bank."

"I may have started that game, but it's time to put an end to it."

"That may be, but as long as we give him the illusion that we listen to his suggestions, we can keep on doing just what we want, can't we?"

"He thinks I shouldn't be hiring Negroes who take jobs away from white men who have families to feed."

Lila sat silent for a moment. How could she explain this to Mary so she would understand? "Well, that's something I've been meaning to talk to you about. Gerald may be right on this one thing. It has stirred up talk around town, you know. And some of the men who have worked here for ages don't like it." Lila watched the surprise in Mary's eyes, and saw her jaws tighten.

"So what? They need jobs just as much as anybody else."

"Yes, but you're paying them the same as the white men, and that's just not done. You're giving them the same kind of work. We've always had Negro laborers here, but not planers and edgers, not doing the same things as the other men. They usually handle the manual things like shoveling the sawdust, taking care of the waste heaps, hauling off the stuff and burning it, stacking the lumber, unloading the trucks. Not the skilled jobs that belong to the white men."

Mary's face turned red. "*Belong* to white men?"

She could see that she wasn't getting through to Mary. "Maybe we should leave this subject for another time."

Mary exploded. "Some of those men are veterans. They fought in the war, Lila, and they come home and we tell them they're not good enough to work and earn the same as everybody else?"

"This is how it's always been here. You just can't pay them the same, or give them the same jobs because it's not good for them. It makes people mad when you change things like that. It's not something you want to stir up."

The anger seemed to leave Mary's eyes then, replaced by a look Lila couldn't quite define, puzzlement mixed with confusion, but there was something else there. Whatever it was, for the first time Lila was a little scared of what she saw in Mary's face.

Chapter Eleven

REPORT TO THE GRAND DRAGON: I told everybody to stand down for the holiday. Deer season just started. We even closed down the mill for two days. Some of the boys are going up to the Dubose cabin.

Saturday, November 19, 1955

"I have no intention of inviting my family for Thanksgiving," Lila said. Previous attempts to have her family over had begun with bitter remarks about her refusing to share her good fortune with them, followed by them indulging themselves in Mr. Dubose's liquor cabinet, and ending with drunken brawls that thankfully had been confined to the back yard. "I think I made it clear enough. I gave each of them a turkey. I just can't face them and their constant squabbling. I hate how they all gang up on me when we get together. They are not subtle. 'You should take Mama in to live with you.' 'We could use some help, you know.' 'Must be nice, having that big house all to yourself, and a housekeeper to look after you.' 'Some people have to work for a living.' I hope they don't find out that Tommie's going to the cabin."

Mary found herself laughing at Lila's remarkable impersonation of the nasal, whiny accents of her relatives. "Would it really be so bad to have them over just for a meal?"

"Yes it will. They start out by trying to be polite, then they start drinking, and before I know it, they're screaming at each other and fighting, and all of it is directed at me. At least one of my sisters will take me aside to tell me how unchristian I'm being by not taking Mama in. A woman who has never been inside a church in her life will tell me Jesus is watching my every move."

Mary stared out the window, down at the lumber yard where the men moved quickly and with long-practiced skill through their duties,

158

lifting, carrying, running huge logs through the planer, the whine alternating in pitch, the sweat causing the sawdust to coat their skin until they appeared like bizarre snowmen. Mary made no comment on Lila's family. She'd had her own dealings with them. She'd had to fire Jimmy Jackson three weeks ago. All the Jackson boys had obtained jobs at the mill at various times over the years. None of them ever lasted very long, always occasioning a scene when she had to fire them. They had looked at her then as if she were somehow distasteful or unclean. She had wondered if Lila's brothers, dense as they were, suspected the truth. They made her appreciate even Buchanan's clumsy attempts at subtlety.

"Okay, I'm going to try again. I don't want my family over. Tommie and I are having Thanksgiving dinner and then he's going to the cabin with the men. I don't really think it is the best thing for Tommie with his health like it is but he's feeling good right now and Mr. Howard Butler was so insistent. I can't stand the thought of spending another Thanksgiving apart, so why not find a way we can meet at the beach? You could simply make it known that you are traveling to visit some friends, or something like that. We could drive down separately. I could say that I'm visiting my sister who moved to Georgia last year."

"Lila, everyone in town knows all your relatives are gathered out at the old place for the holiday."

"Shopping, then! Aren't rich women supposed to be consumed by it? I'll go to Atlanta for a shopping spree."

Finally, convinced not by Lila's arguments but by her own desperation and the hunger for time alone with this beautiful woman appealing so earnestly to her, Mary agreed. For four days they could talk freely. Misunderstandings could be cleared away. They could touch without fear of being seen. They could sleep together.

On Thanksgiving Day, Mary left early, much to the consternation of Miss Louise, driving down to get the cottage ready, unloading food, airing out the small, single room that had been the setting for so many of her daydreams and fantasies, and where all her imagined conversations with Lila took place. She swept and mopped the floor, which, despite her efforts, remained gritty from the beach sand that found its way inside. As she cleaned and dusted, she tried to banish

159

the rising excitement in the pit of her stomach. Stripping the bed, she remade it with clean sheets she had brought, washed the others in the sink, and hung them outside to flap in the breeze. She sat and smoked, wondering when Lila would leave Myrtlewood, when she would arrive, trying to tell herself not to take her straight to bed when she walked in the door. It would only convince Lila of her power. But then, she couldn't stop herself from imagining, in great detail, doing exactly that: meeting Lila at the door, removing her clothes, and keeping her in bed for the whole vacation.

Lila finally arrived about six that evening, after Mary's pitifully thin patience had long disappeared. Whatever hope she had of retaining her dignity fled when she saw the same hunger in Lila's eyes, accompanied by none of the teasing. Lila came into her arms with a murmur of apology. Mary barely heard what she said. They stood for a long time, simply holding each other. Lila sighed; Mary kept her face buried in the wild curls of Lila's hair, breathing in her scent. All her prepared speeches forgotten, she held Lila close to her.

Lila reached out to brush Mary's hair with her fingers, the touch Mary had felt a hundred times in her dreams. She in turn held Lila's face in both her hands, looking deep into her extraordinary eyes. They drank in details with fascination, feeling the freedom of the cottage infuse them. They did not have to lock the door. No one knew where they were. Finally, Lila looked around, her eyes now twinkling with sudden humor.

"I smell turkey!" The aroma of it, baking in the ancient oven, had permeated the cabin from the moment she arrived, but she only just now realized it, Mary knew. She smiled. They had both been distracted. Her eyes traveled to the small table by the window set for dinner.

"My gosh, I'm starving. And you've cooked for us! I was too excited to eat much with Tommie. I worried that at the last minute, you would change your mind, or something would happen so I couldn't leave."

It surprised them both: rather than falling into bed, they spent their first hours alone together over a meal, eating, talking, amazed at the calm that descended.

Finally, Mary pushed her plate away and smoked while Lila continued nibbling. The small turkey, mashed potatoes, gravy, and the canned peas she had managed to beg from Annie were all Mary could manage to prepare, but Lila ate as though it were a feast. They hadn't discussed the frustrations and interruptions and misunderstandings. Neither had delivered the planned and expected lecture. They talked instead of other Thanksgivings, Lila disguising with humor the bleakness of her family gatherings as she grew up.

Mary listened, and when she was finished, said, "My most memorable Thanksgiving—before this one—involved a woman named Claire." Lila leaned forward, forgetting her food, interested.

"Tell me, please."

"You're sure you want to hear about this?"

"Yes. Tell me everything."

Mary smiled and lit another cigarette. "I was about nineteen years old. It was in St. Louis, before the war. Claire was in her fifties, married, in fact had grown children my age. Her husband was on a selling trip to Chicago, unable to get home for the holiday, and as her married children decided to have their Thanksgiving with their families, Claire was left at a loose end. She invited me to share the holiday meal with her in a hotel."

"Not at her house?"

Mary shrugged. "She wouldn't have wanted the neighbors to know. Maybe spending the holiday in a hotel meant she could pretend she wasn't abandoned by her family. I don't know."

"So, did you? What happened then?"

"I did. I brought a bottle of wine with me. I thought that's what sophisticated people did when invited to dinner. Maybe I shouldn't have. It certainly loosened Claire's inhibitions. We ordered more wine from room service, another first for me. Then we spent a rather alcoholic weekend in bed, thoroughly enjoying each other."

Lila frowned. "I bet you did. The Mary McGhee I know would have been more cautious."

"I was nineteen years old, Lila."

"You weren't so worried then about what people would think."

"It was St. Louis, a big city, not a small southern town full of small minds—"

"That's not fair. Did you see her again?"

"I understood that it was not to be repeated. She kept saying over and over that she had never done anything like that before, that she never would again. We were supposed to go our separate ways afterward."

Lila's face revealed her skepticism. "That's not what happened, is it?"

"No. Claire forgot her own rules. She kept calling me, wanting to see me, asking to meet in the same hotel downtown. I left St. Louis soon after."

Fascinated, Lila made her go on. From this woman, Mary admitted, she had learned about how two women please each other. It had been her first experience, though she hadn't revealed that to Claire, who was obviously lying about her own lack of experience.

"Like you're the first for me," Lila said quietly. "I don't blame her at all for becoming obsessed."

"She didn't keep her word about not wanting it to happen again," Mary said, still puzzled after all the time that had passed. "It annoyed me when she kept calling. She was married, after all."

"Marriage vows are no deterrent to the feelings you inspire. I should know." Lila changed the subject. "We could add a room on to the cottage, don't you think? I mean, now that we own it we have to keep it up."

"We should definitely replace the stove and refrigerator. They're rusting away."

"I could get some material and make new curtains for the windows while we're here."

You'll have no time for sewing on this trip, Mary thought. She lit the oven and opened the door to heat the room. "We should put in a little heater."

Though it was a bit cold, they opened the window a crack so they could hear the water, feel and smell the sea breeze. Then they changed into more casual clothes, slacks and sweaters, thinking that perhaps they would walk on the beach for a while before dark. But Mary watched Lila as she changed, and finally the desire that had been held in check came flooding back.

Lila looked up from zipping her slacks and caught Mary's eyes on her. She was transfixed by the sight of raw desire, by the exposure of arousal that Mary never revealed at home. This open, honest longing tore at her heart. Sometimes Mary's distance left Lila doubting how much she really cared for the physical love between them. Mary was so good at keeping things hidden, ashamed and apologetic when she gave in to Lila's teasing, often angry afterwards. Lila worried that she was perhaps put off by Lila's own eagerness. Lila had assumed that she would eventually acquire some of the same control that Mary exhibited. Now, seeing Mary so vulnerable, all her passion and yearning laid bare, made Lila understand that her teasing had been unfair and even cruel. She came around the bed and gathered Mary to her. Marveling again at the enormous will power of this remarkably strong woman, she kissed her roughly. She wanted her to know that she regretted the teasing now. The urgency to salve that need, to make amends for playing with Mary's feelings like a child with a new toy, overwhelmed her, fueling her own desire. She wanted to give herself to Mary, to have Mary indulge and satisfy every fantasy inspired by their enforced celibacy.

Her hands moved over Mary's sweater, thrilled to find her breasts free, unencumbered by camisole or brassiere. She rubbed the scratchy wool against her nipples and Mary tensed, flinched a little.

"Did I hurt you?" She hesitated, but then Mary's hands urged her to continue.

"God, no." Mary's voice was hoarse.

Lila watched her reaction as she handled her breasts through the wool. Then Mary pulled the sweater over her head and stood naked to the waist. Lila let her eyes roam over every inch of skin, taking her time, eyes following the movement of her hands as she touched Mary. She felt goose bumps dimple the smooth flesh, saw Mary close her eyes in pleasure as she stroked her breasts, held them in her hands, luxuriating in the freedom to explore. They stood like that for a long time, Lila simply touching, Mary patiently allowing it. Lila had no thoughts at all as she matched fingertips to ribs, traced the lines of Mary's collar bones, placed her thumbs just under each ear, kissed the closed eyelids. She examined brows and nose, lips and chin, as she held in her hands the face she loved.

Lila eased Mary back until she was on the bed, and still her eyes had not opened. Lila lay beside her, raised on an elbow, fully clothed, stroking more firmly now, kneading, shaping, grasping and then letting go. Mary began to move under her hands, shifting restlessly. She pulled at Lila's clothing, trying to remove it. Mary undid the button on Lila's slacks, and slid her hand inside them. Lila lay still then, waiting. Slowly Mary pushed her hand under her panties, and Lila breathed faster. It was her punishment to submit, to allow Mary this slow savoring. She would not interrupt this because of a sudden urgent need of her own. She must allow Mary anything that she wanted. She had teased her when there was no chance for them to satisfy the teasing. Now she must permit Mary all the time she needed. It was the one thing she could give, the most precious thing: to pay out part of this time together in reassurance that she would never deny this, never refuse it. She lay still as Mary removed her clothes and brought her hand to Lila's bare breast, her nipples were already drawn hard. Mary cupped the breast and stroked it, and Lila sighed, and then her patience ran out.

She opened her eyes, and the pretense was ended. They had so little time after all, only four brief days to get their fill of each other. Mary held her away for a moment, both hands in her hair, while she searched Lila's eyes, and then they were kissing, and speaking in whispers, though there was no need to whisper.

Lila hurriedly shoved Mary's slacks down to her knees, out of her way. Mary lay on top of her, one leg between her thighs. Lila wrapped her arms around her tightly and rubbed herself on Mary's leg. She strained against her.

Lila knew what came next. She trembled. The haste she felt, the urgency, left her unable to signal what she needed, but Mary knew. She felt briefly bereft, until Mary's hands moved her legs open and she settled herself between them. Lila couldn't think, couldn't talk, could only wait until Mary's mouth found her.

Lila woke to the sound of the shower drumming behind the wall in the tiny bathroom. She sat up, surprised to find sunlight streaming in through the windows. She was naked. In something of a daze, she waited for the shower to be turned off. Coffee had been made, she saw, and last night's dishes had been cleared away. Had she slept through all that? She pulled the sheets around her to ward off the chill in the air and waited. Mary emerged from the bathroom, properly dressed and put together. She smiled at Lila and sat on the bed to kiss her.

"Coffee?"

"Yes, please. What time is it? I didn't mean to sleep so long."

Mary laughed as she poured two cups of coffee. "It's early. You haven't missed anything. I'm afraid you'll have to wait a while for the hot water. I used it all." She handed Lila her coffee and then her clothes. "Go ahead and get dressed. You can shower later. We're on vacation."

Lila dressed, and they sat at the table. Mary lit a cigarette.

"You hardly smoke at all at home."

"I know. You seem to encourage all my vices. What shall we do today?"

The transformation in Mary was disarming. She smiled, she talked, she looked directly at Lila with a frankness that was flattering and appealing. It was nothing like being at the office, where Mary was so guarded and closed. Lila smiled back. She reached across the table for Mary's hand.

"We can do whatever you like, whatever you want. But let's walk on the beach first, after breakfast. I've missed this place. I've missed you, missed seeing you like this."

"What do you mean?"

"Relaxed. Different. Not so tense. Look, I want to apologize if I've made things more difficult for you. I just didn't understand. Until last night. I mean—I've been … careless, haven't I? About your feelings."

"Don't apologize. Don't talk about it now. Let's enjoy this, and forget everything else for now."

"Last night, I didn't, you wouldn't let me …" Even now, Lila thought, there were words she couldn't bring herself to say, words she didn't think Mary would approve of.

"I know. It's all right. We will. Later."

"I wanted to. I want to make up to you for all the dreadful flirting and teasing. I wasn't trying to … This is so difficult to put into words."

"Lila, sweetheart, it's okay. Really. You have more than satisfied the one desire I have had for all these months. I wanted you in my arms. I wanted to feel you, taste you, have you." Mary stopped, and Lila waited for her to find the words. She frowned and pressed her lips together, an expression Lila had seen many times. She seemed to be struggling with some decision. Then she took a breath, and spoke hesitantly. "Lila, I've always enjoyed making love to another more than being made love to." Mary stared at her hands.

Lila tried to comprehend, and she felt a warm flush rise, and this made her angry. She didn't want to blush and look shocked. She wanted Mary to explain, and she wanted to convey acceptance, but she wasn't sure she understood what she was hearing.

Mary went on, still staring at her hands. "Giving you pleasure, being able to do that, makes me feel everything you are feeling. Everything. Do you understand?"

Lila simply looked at Mary. She did not understand. Did Mary really mean that when she fell off the edge of the cliff, when Mary pushed her until she wanted to scream with the torture of it, and she reached that falling-off point, that Mary came with her? Was that possible? Then Mary smiled again, and it delighted Lila to see the strain and the tension gone from her face. Mary seemed so much younger.

"I'm not sure you are telling the truth. I'll have to find out for myself." Lila smiled too. "I'll have to make love to you again and again, to see if I can achieve this thing for myself."

Mary laughed. "It's never happened with anyone else. I can't seem to get enough of you. And you are so responsive."

Lila blushed again, this time uncaring. "You're not the only one who has been frustrated. Let's go for a walk. I need to get out of here for a while. Otherwise, we may spend the entire day in bed."

Mary put her cigarettes in her pocket and got a jacket. They walked along the beach, holding hands, looking at seashells, sitting sometimes to watch the water. It was chilly and windy, and there was no one else on the beach. They stopped sometimes to kiss, not even glancing around. They were completely alone and free.

A wave rolled in, unexpectedly hard and fast, nearly catching Lila unaware as she searched for sand dollars. Mary laughed as she helped her regain her balance. They turned back toward the cottage when they began to feel the cold, then decided to sit on the sand for a while, holding each other for warmth. Reluctantly, driven eventually by the cold and the need to be alone in their cottage, they turned for the walk back. They had not eaten yet, and the morning had already gone.

"I could make hash brown potatoes and pancakes for breakfast," Mary offered.

"Even though it's near noon?" Lila laughed.

Approaching the cottage from the beach side, they did not see the car parked out in front. Mary held the screen door open for Lila, and she entered first. She stopped just inside the door. There was a woman sitting on their bed.

Mary followed in and Lila saw that Mary knew this woman. Mary's face blanched, and her eyes hardened and narrowed. "Hello, Sammie. I didn't realize you'd remember the directions to this place. How have you been?" Mary said, her voice cold and deadly calm.

Lila tried to stop the dismay and the panic she felt rising. There was no time for it now.

Sammie Stewart sat on their bed, her back comfortably propped against the headboard, her ankles crossed. She was smoking, using a shot glass as an ashtray. She smiled at Mary, obviously enjoying her discomfort. Mary did not smile back. She stared at the young woman, feeling a warm flush rising from her chest to flood her face. Sammie looked disheveled, as though she had slept in her clothes, and Mary supposed that she had, and imagined her pulling her car over to the side of the road, typically disregarding her safety, and sleeping. It was very likely that she'd worn out her welcome among her legions of friends by now. She looked years older than twenty-seven. Her make-up was smudged, her blond hair tangled and dirty. Still, her loveliness shone through. With high cheekbones, more prominent now than Mary remembered, and green eyes flecked with brown, Sammie had an appeal that transcended clothes or grooming. Mary tried to hide her dismay.

"The door was open, so I came on in," Sammie said, looking at Lila. "My name is Sammie Stewart. You're Lila, aren't you? I've heard a lot about you."

Lila's mouth dropped open. "I've heard about you too."

Mary walked over to the table and put her cigarettes down, carefully, slowly, as if she were on a ship and everything might shift under her feet. Her hands were steady. She looked at Lila, then back at

Sammie. Lila might be jumping to conclusions that would require much explanation, but she did not intend to give Sammie the satisfaction of doing that now.

"What are you doing here?"

Sammie stood and deliberately looked Lila up and down, taking her time. Mary clenched a fist and gritted her teeth. Sammie's smirk was slowly replaced with a look of pure delight.

"You're a real beauty!" She shot a look at Mary. "She looks like a little doe, all startled and innocent. I have to compliment your taste, Mary."

Lila must be terrified, Mary realized. Or furious, or both. Watching Sammie leer at Lila, for all the world like the half-drunk cowboys she emulated, Mary wondered if she had told Lila just how bad Sammie could be.

"I was rambling around. Going home for Thanksgiving was not an option. I thought I'd look you up."

"Look me up? I told you the last time there's no point in that."

"Yeah, well, there was no answer at your number. I took a guess you'd be here, maybe alone, and we could talk. Like last time." She smiled sweetly at Lila, "You are very lovely. Mary said you were. She didn't exaggerate one bit." With her hands on her hips, Sammie continued to stare at Lila.

Mary felt fury outweigh apprehension, but decided she would not give Sammie the satisfaction of seeing anger or apology pass between her and Lila. She recognized too well the gleam in her eyes as she inspected Lila. Without doubt, it meant trouble. This was the sort of scene that Sammie enjoyed. If Sammie had hoped to find Mary alone, then this was better, to stir up trouble between the two of them. That was what Sammie did, when she couldn't have what she wanted.

"We were about to eat. Would you join us? Why don't I see about some food and you two can ... talk?" Lila said, sounding calm, although Mary noticed she was clasping her hands together tightly.

"Sammie, why don't we talk privately?" It was all Mary could do to restrain herself from taking Sammie by the arm and dragging her outside. She went out to the patio, holding the door open. Sammie sauntered past Lila, who stood in the center of the room as if rooted to the floor, and winked at her.

"I'll be back, after your girlfriend has had her little fit. You and I can get to know one another. We have something in common, after all."

Lila watched Sammie walk out the door. She had never been looked at so frankly in her life. In high school, boys and male teachers had stared at her, but not so blatantly, and that relieved her for reasons she only understood now. In Sammie's eyes, she recognized undisguised lust and she did not feel flattered, only exposed.

She looked over at the carefully made bed that she and Mary had left in a tangled heap when they went for their walk. This woman had made their bed! Lila sat down and tried to think calmly, but it was a wasted effort. She felt neither calm nor able to think at all. What did she know about this person, anyway? What had Mary told her? That she drank excessively. She wondered if Sammie was drinking now. Mary seemed as surprised as she had been to see her here, stretched out on their bed.

Lila tried to get herself to move. Mary must have been here with Sammie before, and hadn't told her. "Like last time," she had said. How many times had they met here? Mary had made innumerable trips to the cottage alone—had she been meeting Sammie all those weekends when she said she came here because being in Myrtlewood but unable to be with Lila was too difficult? She must have met her here. But when? How could she have done that? This was *their* hideaway—they bought it! Lila stared at the bed, lost in doubt, feeling fear and a chilling anger rise up from deep within. She sat down as she tried to decide whether she was angrier at Mary or at this stranger who was altogether too familiar with Mary and their secret place.

"What the hell do you think you're doing?" Mary asked, hoping they were out of Lila's hearing.

Sammie grinned. "Knock it off. I had no idea you'd be here with her. Congratulations, though. She is beautiful, a little doll. I never imagined you'd go for that type."

"You were not my 'type' either. Why did you come here?"

"I told you, I just took a guess that you would be alone for the holiday. I thought we might ... keep each other company. What have you told her about me, anyway?"

169

Mary closed her eyes. Sammie sounded genuine—even sincere. But that was how she operated. She was not above using both her own situation and Mary's assumed loneliness to manipulate her. "Lila knows everything about you. Except that you've been here before."

"Uh-oh. So tell, me, why did you keep it a secret, since it was perfectly innocent?" Sammie smiled. She enjoyed making people squirm.

Mary watched her expression. A shadow seemed to pass over Sammie's face and Mary saw a glimpse of the real loneliness that had compelled Sammie to seek her out. In spite of the taunting, there was something sad about her admission that she needed some company. And now here she stood, one of the most confident people Mary knew, seeming to lose her smug self-assurance. As she continued to hold Sammie's gaze, Mary also watched a flicker of something flash through her eyes—regret maybe, or apology?

"You really did hope to find me here alone, didn't you?" Mary said, sighing. How many times had she herself wanted to find some comfort, some respite?

Sammie's shoulders sagged a little. She stood with her arms crossed, her unkempt hair blowing around her face, looking out at the slate-colored waves in the distance. "I'm tired, Mary." Her voice was so low Mary barely heard. All the running, partying, and hard drinking were showing on her face.

"Are you drunk, Sammie?"

Sammie shook her head, and Mary believed her. Soon, though, she would need a drink.

Mary reached for her hand. "Why don't you stay the weekend with us? We can make up a pallet on the floor for you. Come on, it's cold out here. Let's go in. But try not to scandalize Lila too much, will you?"

Sammie looked at her, clearly startled by the offer. She shook Mary's hand in agreement. "I'll be good. There must be some fun in it, after all. Why else would so many people keep recommending it to me?" She grinned again.

Lila was sitting at the table when they returned. She'd started a new pot of coffee on the stove. Sammie took the only other chair and sank into it heavily. Lila looked up at Mary.

Mary tried a little smile. "I've invited Sammie to stay here. She could use some rest and food. Even a friend or two, right now."

"Mary's afraid I've given you a wrong impression. Maybe I should explain my first visit here—or will you, Mary?"

"Sammie, please. I'm trying to be patient with you." Mary reached to touch Lila's shoulder and looked down at her. "We met here, the weekend before I came to you and told you everything, asked you to …"

"Here—in the cottage?"

Mary could see the questions in Lila's eyes.

"Yes. Lila, everything is fine. All I did was talk about you for hours, and Sammie's the one who told me to just let you know how I felt. Sometimes you get what you want. That's what she said."

Sammie added, grinning now, "I have to tell you, I was intensely curious to meet the woman who could shatter all that self-control. You must be something."

Something of her usual smirk had returned to Sammie's face. Irritated, Mary thought that she could have done without her help. She turned to gauge Lila's reaction. Lila looked back and forth between them, then appeared to regain control of herself. She turned back to Sammie.

"What I am is a great admirer of Mary. I know she thinks very highly of you."

"Really?" Sammie looked with mock disbelief at Mary. "Either of you want to join me in a drink?" She searched her worn travel case until she found a pint of bourbon. Mary handed a glass with some ice to Sammie.

Lila shook her head no, but Mary took the bottle and found another glass, pouring some bourbon into it. The situation was moving beyond her control. She might as well join Sammie. Maybe meeting her on her level would work.

"Here, you take the one with ice, I'll have mine straight up." She switched drinks with Mary. "I never meant for her to be sent away. I came here, to the cottage, to make sure she was all right. That's good whiskey." Sammie poured more. She looked over the rim of her glass at Mary, even though she was speaking to Lila. "I take it that you two have worked things out okay."

"Yes, we have. But that doesn't explain this second visit, does it?" Lila said.

Mary looked at Lila. Her chin was up and she was staring directly into Sammie's eyes. *Oh, shit*, thought Mary. She glanced at Sammie. Far from intimidated, she seemed actually pleased to be confronted.

"Honey, you get the picture, don't you? Like I said, I was lonely ..." She took a long swallow of her drink.

"It was considerate of you to think of Mary being alone during the holiday. As you can see, she's not." Lila's eyes moved to Mary, and Mary had never seen the look in them. Gray flashed like fire on a low burn.

Mary was beginning to feel numb.

Sammie was regarding Lila with a degree of sly admiration. Mary could see that she was amused by Lila's feisty indignation. Her eyes were warm.

"Looks to me like your little kitten has some wildcat in her," Sammie said. "Wonder how sharp those claws are?"

Lila frowned. "Are you *trying* to be rude?"

Sammie laughed. "Usually I succeed. Look, I really just came around to make sure Mary's okay. Because of our past history, you know?"

"You don't sound entirely certain of your motives. Are you?"

Sammie laughed again. "No, honey, I'm never quite certain of my motives. But does it matter? If Mary had been alone, then I would have been some comfort to her. She's not, so we should celebrate, shouldn't we? You broke through the ice queen's armor. That's more than I could ever do. Have a drink, Lila. Such a sweet, old-fashioned name. Come play with us."

"No thank you, I don't drink." Lila drew back, looking uncertain again. Mary's heart fairly bled for her. She so wanted to keep this side of things from Lila, its ugliness and crudeness. She wanted Lila to be able to stay innocent, to keep the purity that seemed to invest her passion and wash some of the ugliness away from Mary herself. Now Lila's lips were almost trembling. Mary wanted to reach out, to touch her, reassure her, take her into her arms and make Sammie disappear.

"I'm going to take a bath and change," said Lila.

Mary sat in the chair she vacated. She lit a cigarette and watched Sammie pour another splash of bourbon. Lila took clothing from the closet and went into the little bathroom, pulling the door shut behind her.

"When is the last time you ate anything? You look terrible."

Sammie slumped in her chair. "I want to go home to the ranch. Why can't he let me have that much?"

"Maybe he would—" Mary started, but Sammie cut her off.

"I'm twenty-seven. He can't dictate to me. But you know Big Sam. He thinks he can force me to marry someone, and then things will be fine. I'll be fixed. Doesn't matter who—as long as it's a man. I'm so tired."

"I know. You can rest here. But sooner or later you're going to have to face him, try to reason with him. If you could do that without also berating and belittling him, you two might get somewhere. You and I both know he doesn't care about the ranch any more. Look, you're the one who said it. 'Sometimes, you really get what you want.' Remember?"

Sammie reached for Mary's hand, and Mary looked into her eyes, seeing that her tenuous composure had begun to slip.

"I can't accept sympathy right now, especially from you. Not when the kind of comfort I do want is not possible." Sammie shrugged her shoulders and freed her hand. She drained her glass and looked at the bottle. Mary took it from her and put it away.

"Give me back my bourbon. This is a holiday, a celebration, right?"

Mary got up to refill the glass. "You can drink all you like, but it won't change anything. You have to talk to Big Sam. Stop wandering all over the country. You're killing yourself."

"Such motherly concern. Save it for your little girl in there." Sammie's face was stormy now, the liquor working. First the gaiety, then the gloom. Jealousy and paranoia now had free rein. "My friends have stopped wanting anything to do with me."

"Sammie. Just go home to the ranch. Act on the advice you gave me."

"It worked out for you, didn't it? She is a sweet little thing. Got some fight in her too. What's she like in bed?"

"We're talking about you."

"You know why I came here. Are you satisfied with her? Is she enough for you?" Sammie's voice was husky, deliberately and

173

drunkenly enticing. "Aren't you a bit disappointed with all that southern-belle reticence? Remember what it was like with us? Hot and hard. I bet you miss that sometimes."

The gleam had returned to Sammie's eyes. Mary tried to look away. She did remember how it had been between them. Always a contest of wills, never the tenderness that she felt with Lila. Mary swallowed, remembering the night before. There had never been anything like that between her and Sammie. She picked up her drink and sipped, to keep from speaking. For a long while, both women sat at the table in silence, until Lila came out of the bathroom, dressed in fresh clothes and toweling her hair. Mary turned her gaze to her.

Lila was lovely, delicate. *There*, thought Mary, *there is my own heart. That is what I want, what I need.* Mary's breath caught in her throat. It broke her gaze and she turned back to Sammie and was startled by the envy and longing that lay naked in her expression. Mary berated herself silently. She had been stupid to invite Sammie to stay.

"My god, you *are* delicious, sweetheart!" Sammie said. "If Mary didn't already have her hooks in you, I'd go after you myself. Let's swap stories. Was Mary your first? We should compare notes. Is she different in bed with you? I bet she is. I bet she just eats you up."

"Sammie, that's enough."

"Damn it, Mary, can't you relax? Stop acting like this is a meeting of the Ladies' Club. This is three queers, sitting here talking. Can't we just be who we are, for once? Shit, I'm not the fucking police, and I'm not her retarded husband!"

Mary gasped, stood and put her arms around Lila. She whispered, "I'm so sorry for this." Shaking with anger, Lila pulled away, not even looking at her. She sat down opposite Sammie at the table instead.

"Yes. Let's do compare notes," she said. Her voice was foreign, controlled and bitter. "Mary, you go for a walk or something. Sammie and I will be fine. Go on, now."

It was well past noon. The day had turned cloudy and threatened rain. Mary sat on the sand, some distance from where dirty foam raced in ahead of each wave. Clumps of seaweed formed a ragged line down the beach, marking high tide. It was cold and windy. Mary smoked and

174

watched the soapy foam as it curled back on itself. She measured the clouds, trying to guess when it would begin to rain. Back in the cottage, her life was being destroyed.

She was in shock. There was no way Lila's innocence could withstand Sammie's practiced vulgarity. With a kind of numbed, sick fascination, Mary tried to imagine what the two women were saying. It wasn't possible anyway, what she wanted, what she and Lila had. Was there any point in trying to plead with Lila, to try to convince her it wasn't the way Sammie made it seem? How had she ever shown Lila that it was different, after all? Constantly nagging her about secrecy and caution, emphasizing how wrong it was, begging her to pretend and lie? It was a nasty, ugly thing they did. There was no way that Lila's goodness could survive it.

She had been sent outside to play while the grown-ups talked. If it wasn't so serious, it would be funny. Lila ordering her away, Sammie sitting there with a smirk, waiting. Mary smoked one cigarette after another, her lungs screaming for relief. She watched the seagulls squabble among themselves over bits of garbage, while inside the weathered old cabin the one lovely thing in her life was being ravaged and irretrievably lost.

Why had she allowed herself to hope that she would, with Lila, find the real beauty this kind of love could hold? How could she tell that to Lila now, after she'd been exposed to the ugly reality of it, so expertly demonstrated by Sammie? It had been the worst mistake of her life to ever tell Sammie about Lila.

"Why don't we be honest with each other? What is it you really want here, Sammie?" Lila folded her hands on the tabletop and felt a bit silly, trying to maintain her dignity with her hair still wet from her bath.

"That's more like it. Mary hates discussions about wants and needs."

"I'm not asking you about Mary. I'm talking about you."

Sammie took another sip of whiskey. "Yes, you are. But let me tell you, Mary wants the love of a woman. She *needs* it. She likes to pretend she can control it, but she certainly found you in that backwater town and turned you out fast enough. I wonder, though, if the setup with you is going to be enough for her, considering your husband—"

"You couldn't possibly understand anything about my husband," Lila said coldly. She was infuriated by Sammie's assumptions. And very angry that Mary had told her about Tommie.

"Come on—I know he doesn't know what's going on right in front of him, in his own bed—"

"Tommie is none of your business. What's going on between you and Mary is my concern."

Sammie smiled. "Nothing's going on, as you put it so delicately. I'm guessing that you just wanted to experiment, find out what's it's like. Having to sneak around and hide gets tiresome, don't you think? I know what Mary likes, and how much she likes it. I just wonder, are you going to be able to keep her satisfied?"

Lila was tired of this woman with her lewd, suggestive remarks. It was obvious that she didn't really mean half of what she was implying. In her rage, Lila couldn't think of the questions she was going to ask this slovenly, rude, drunk woman. Questions about her intentions regarding Mary, about what exactly had happened between them when they had met in the cottage. She didn't care about that now. All that mattered was that Mary belonged to her. Whatever these two had shared in the past, Mary was hers now.

"Are you offering to take her someplace where you wouldn't have to present a front for people? I've found that sometimes I quite enjoy the necessity for subterfuge and deception. It keeps a certain tension, an interest, between us. If you're referring to something more explicit, I am delighted to do whatever pleases Mary, in my bed, in hers, wherever she wants it. Am I being direct enough for you?"

Sammie laughed. "Yes, you are. All that sweetness is just a cover, isn't it? You're really a little spitfire."

"Don't forget your bourbon." Lila stood up.

Sammie leaned back in her chair. "I guess it's time I remembered my manners and apologize for interrupting your holiday. It couldn't have been easy to arrange. Look, I'm heading for Florida. It'll be warmer, and there will be women in bathing suits on the beaches." Sammie leaned forward. "I'm really not such a bad person, Lila." She grinned and winked. "If you ever need me, you can call me. Mary can be stubborn sometimes about seeing what's right in front of her. Though I doubt you'll have any trouble handling her."

From her place on the beach, Mary stared toward the window, where she could see Lila standing. Then she saw Sammie come out of the cottage, carrying her suitcase. She raised a hand and waved at Mary.

Mary waited for a few minutes, then got up and walked toward the cottage, relief and hope battling her apprehension. She hoped Lila would be good enough to tell her what had been said but when Lila held the door open for her, instead of asking questions, Mary walked into her arms, and was surprised with their strength.

Chapter 12

REPORT TO THE GRAND DRAGON: *Yes, sir, you bet we can send some men up to help out. Damn shame they wouldn't listen to reason. A little personal persuasion will have'em begging to ride the buses. Attendance: 20*
Thursday, March 15, 1956

Lila came into the office and sank into the visitor's chair across from Mary. She sighed heavily. Looking up, she caught Mary studying her critically.

"Don't say it. I look tired, I should rest and eat more. I've heard it from Annie a dozen times."

Mary pressed her lips into a thin line and suppressed the urge to agree. "I need you to sign some papers." She slid the papers over and watched Lila sign them without reading anything, then hand them back with no comment. Mary put them into a folder and leaned back in her chair.

"How is Tommie?"

"Better. Last week he had a high fever, was barely lucid, called me 'mama,' and wouldn't let me out of his sight for three days. Dr. Morgan had him under an oxygen tent. It scared him." Lila laughed sadly. "I told him he's camping out in his bed. He's up today."

Mary drew in a long breath. "I could run by, sit with him, and give you some time to rest. You and Annie both."

"He wouldn't let you. He would start fretting, and that would start him coughing again."

"I could sit with you then, while you're watching him. I could feed you some soup. Let me do something, please. You're exhausted. Let me take you to the beach this weekend."

Lila managed a weak smile. "You must be desperate to volunteer a trip to the cottage. You know I can't leave Annie alone with him right

178

now. There's too much work to do. Why don't you go down alone? You look tired too."

"Have you seen the Montgomery papers lately?" Mary asked, desperate to find anything that would take Lila's mind off Tommie.

"No. I haven't had time to read."

"The bus boycott is still going on. The Negro churches have organized cars and drivers to get their people to work."

"Why do you read all those newspapers? The Montgomery one, the Atlanta paper on Sundays, even the *New York Times* when you can get it?"

Mary patted Lila's hand, so white she could see the blue veins running under the skin.

"I like to keep up with what's going on in the wide world."

Lila sighed. "Why can't they just ride the buses like they used to do?"

"Rosa Parks had no idea that something worse than getting arrested wouldn't happen to her for refusing to give up her seat to a white person. She was incredibly brave."

Lila looked at Mary. She sat back, closing her eyes for a moment. "Mrs. Parks was probably just tired."

"Yes, and at the end of the day, why should she have to give up her seat?" Mary replied.

There was something in Lila's eyes for a minute, a flash of the ire that Mary missed seeing, not because she liked to see her get mad, but because it carried a hint of the passion she hadn't shown in a long time. Lila gathered her things.

"I have to go. There's mountains of bedclothes to wash. He was throwing up all day yesterday."

One day two months ago Mary had locked the office door and made Lila lie down on the sofa while she sat and held her hand and talked until she fell asleep. Then Mary sat unmoving, watching Lila's eyelids flutter as she slept. They had not touched since.

Pulling into the driveway up to the back porch, Lila felt drained by the heat. The day was quiet, with not even a hint of a breeze to stir the thick, muggy air, and Annie was leaving to clean the church for the Sunday morning service. Tommie, finally well enough to get out of bed, was sitting on the back porch swing watching Thad work right below him in the garden. Lila and Annie had no time for the garden anymore. All that was stopping it going to seed was Thad's coming by when he could.

"Let me drive you to the church. It's too hot and humid to walk. It won't take a minute."

Annie eyed Tommie. "Mr. Tommie, you goan be good and not move from that swing till Miss Lila gets back? Thad'll tell on you if you do." She frowned at her charge; Tommie was pale and very thin, but they thought some fresh air and sun would be good for him. Tommie nodded, his head wobbling like a ball balanced on the end of a stick. "I'll stay right here. Henry's coming soon."

"That's right. And he'll sit with you till I get back. Okay?" Lila said.

Tommie nodded again, the movement seemingly requiring great effort. His usual animated and energetic responses were a thing of memory now. Lila stood, her purse and keys already in hand. "Okay, then, let's go, Annie."

Annie sat in the back and rolled both windows all the way down. Lila did the same in the front, and started the car. "Let's see if we can catch a breeze." As she backed out of the drive, Lila noticed the gas gauge was on empty. "Looks like we need to stop at Riser's before we go anywhere."

Lila eased the car down the road, afraid of running out of gas. As they rolled up to the pumps at the service station, Bobby was attending to a black Ford while a man stood and watched. "I'm going to get Tommie a Coca Cola while we wait. You want anything, Annie? It's going to be hot in the church."

Annie fanned herself with a Jesus fan. "No thank you. I'll give it a swipe through and be done. Too hot for anything else."

"Will you call when you're through?"

Annie frowned. "Nome, why don't you just send Thad when he's done and he can fetch me home?"

Lila got out of the car and leaned into Annie's window. "All right, but don't you get too hot shut up in there. I can't take care of two sick people." She walked to the soda machine and the man watched her. He was nicely dressed even though sweat rings ran under his arms and across his back, showing his undershirt through the short-sleeved, white shirt with a button-down collar he wore with a tie, even in the heat. A grimy panama hat with a faded black band was perched cockily on his head. His arms were crossed. She avoided the man's eyes as he stared at her. Fishing two Coca Colas out of the red box, she opened one for herself, and walked back to the car.

"Mighty hot today, ain't it?" the man said.

Lila nodded her agreement. Bobby cut his eyes at her with a look almost comical in its concern. She could tell that Bobby didn't like this customer. In school he'd always shown an odd, gentlemanly sort of interest in her. She smiled at him to show she was okay. "How're you today, Bobby?"

He just nodded and kept pumping gas into the tank of the Ford.

The stranger spoke again. "I see you got your maid in the car. Where you takin' her?"

Lila looked directly at the man. "We're going to the church to clean it."

"That's nice. Lendin' your maid to clean the Lord's house. That's a Christian thing to do."

"Annie's going to clean her own church, not mine."

"And you givin' her a ride, that it?"

"Yes. It's too hot to walk."

"Now that's just what I been talkin' about. All the concern we show our niggers, the care and thoughtfulness, and yet a bunch of 'em get all stirred up and now we got a situation on our hands up in Montgomery."

Glancing at Bobby, now checking the tire pressure, she saw him roll his eyes and frown. Apparently the man had been holding forth on this subject. Lila got into the car and refused to answer. She was sick and tired of everybody going on endlessly about Montgomery and the boycott. Was there no other topic at all on people's minds?

The man leaned his arm on the open windowsill of the back seat. "Why don't you git out and walk like all your friends in Montgomery?"

Lila whipped her head around. Annie stared straight ahead, her face a mask. She sat still as a post.

"Why you driving her around? Make her walk. I'm headed up to Montgomery, and one thing we'll put a stop to is all them white people who think they're helping when they're just makin' things worse, driving their maids to work and back. This is what we get for being nice, looking after the coloreds, taking care of 'em, and this is what we get. All we do for them, and they want more. It ain't enough to let 'em ride the buses, no. Somebody gives out that they need to ride up front. I say, you can go back to walking or you can go back to ridin' a mule. Coddle somebody, and they begin to expect it. They'll start riding the bus when they need to eat. Now this nigger woman looks healthy enough to me." He leaned closer and spoke directly to Annie, his mouth close to her ear as she kept her gaze resolutely forward. "Git out of this car and walk. There's a whole lot of your kin that'll be doin' a whole lot of walkin' before this thing is settled, I can guarantee that."

Lila thought for a minute that he would open the door and try to pull Annie from the car. His voice was soft, without anger.

"Come on, don't you want to git out and walk? This nice lady's got better things to do than drive you around. Git outta the car. I'll follow along behind you, just to make sure you get where you're going."

He grinned widely, as if he was just playing with them, teasing, but the rigid set of Annie's jaw conveyed that her fear was very real. Lila was frozen, unable to start the engine, unable to think, terrified and unbelieving.

Lila looked directly at him. He stood, jingling change in his pocket, a slight smile on his face—he was enjoying their fear, and Bobby looked like he couldn't pump gas fast enough. He shoved the nozzle back on its hook on the pump, dropped the gas cap when he tried to screw it back on, wiped the dirt off, and finally got the gas tank closed. The man paid him, never taking his eyes off Lila and Annie.

"Ya'll have a nice day now. You do like we're goan do, tell this woman that's her last free ride." He laughed, like the whole thing was a huge joke, touched his hat, got in his Ford and drove away, stirring up dust that settled on Lila's hair and clothes. She sat transfixed, staring after the car.

"Miss Lila, it's all right, he's gone."

"Bobby, would you please give us some gas?" Lila said, her voice shaking. She put her hands on the wheel, glanced once into the rearview mirror at Annie, and then looked down the road. The man was on his way to Montgomery. Mary had tried to talk to her about the boycott, and she had refused to listen. Tommie was sick, and she was busy, worried, and tired. Whatever was going on, she had no time for it. She and Annie were working so hard together, frantically cleaning, cooking, doing laundry when Tommie was sleeping or resting, bathing and feeding him when he wasn't able to do it himself, trying to get him to take his medicine.

"Miss Lila, you're all set. I'll put it on your account."

She started the car and drove in silence to the church. Annie got out without a word. Lila called out to her. "Annie, what was that man so mad about?"

Annie turned and walked back to the car. "He wadn't mad. He was right. I got friends and relatives in Montgomery that's been walking to work for months now. It shames me to ride while they walk. Miss Lila, that man is just scared." Then she went inside the church to arrange flowers and clean the sanctuary.

Lila drove home. She found Tommie in bed taking a nap. She sat on the back porch in a kind of dazed wonder. She sat there for a while as the day got hotter, just thinking, replaying in her head all the discussions with Mary about the boycott, hearing again all her own dismissals of the subject. She'd been impatient with the whole thing, and angry that Mary wouldn't, couldn't, focus on what was going on right here at home.

Lila rose, went into the kitchen and began making supper. As she mixed up a bowl of cornbread and waited for the oven to heat up, she recalled the hundreds of meals she and Annie had prepared together, all of them eaten separately. Hundreds of washdays, when they ran clothes through the ringer on the Sears washing machine and hung them out on the line to dry. How many bushels of peas and butter beans had they picked and shelled and put up? She took a jar of speckled butter beans from the pantry and put them in a pot with a slice of fatback, like Annie had taught her. She rolled two pork chops in salt, pepper and flour and fried them, checked on the cornbread, made some tea, and turned to stare at the kitchen table, where Annie always sat and ate her meals, while she and Tommie sat at the table in the dining room, at places set for them by Annie. She looked around the kitchen as if she'd never seen it before, and the sick feeling she'd had in her stomach since the encounter with that man went away, replaced by anger. She was home, in her own house, standing in her kitchen, and she'd never thought of it that way before, as hers, something over which she had dominion and control. A total stranger had instructed her about how she should treat Annie. A stranger had decided that Annie shouldn't ride in her car. A man she had never seen before felt he had the right to tell her what to do.

Lila sat down in Annie's chair, and felt a huge wave roll over her. She felt like she was drowning. She didn't tell Annie to ride in the back seat; Annie just got in the back. She didn't order her to set two tables for every meal. Annie just did it. That's just the way things were done. They had their place to live, and the white people had theirs. There was a school for the colored children and a school for the whites. There was the colored church and the white people's churches. It had always seemed pretty fair to her. She believed that the coloreds wanted it this way, even that black people depended on the whites for guidance and help and—she sounded just like that man. And it made her sick. In her own home, living with a woman she admired and trusted and needed, she had perpetuated this thing. Bile rose in her throat.

Mary had questioned her about the way things were and why they had to be that way. She had dismissed her as an outsider who didn't understand. Mary would learn over time that it worked best like this, whites having their ways, the coloreds having theirs. The trouble, she had thought, came when people from outside who didn't understand this balance tried to upset it, tried to change things.

The hardest thing to face was not the tremendous help Annie had given in doing all the work over the years. It was Annie's unshakable faith in her, Annie's encouragement and advice and support when most people in Myrtlewood had talked about her like she was mentally deficient or worse. Annie standing as her champion and defending her to the gossips in town, Annie's dignity upon which her own was modeled. Annie had taught her self-respect, and Lila had lost it now.

When Annie got home an hour later, the meal was ready, and Lila stood in the kitchen and watched her walk up the back drive, climb up the steps, and open the screen door. Then Annie stopped, and took in

184

the sight before her: Lila standing with a hand on a chair, two places set on the kitchen table.

"I thought we'd eat in here. It's too much trouble to set the dining room table just for one person, and we both have to eat, and it's quicker to eat in here and just do the dishes and we don't have time for setting two tables and anyway, I want to talk to you. Will you please sit down and join me?" Lila felt awkward and embarrassed but determined.

Annie put her purse on the counter, staring at Lila with big eyes, and deliberately sat down at the place set for her. Lila slowly sank into the chair opposite and passed the bowl of butter beans, then a plate of sliced tomatoes. For a while, they ate in silence, Annie clearly bemused and confounded. Lila felt as though her heart would burst.

She let out a nervous laugh. "You think somebody's going to stomp in and tell us we can't sit at the table like this?"

Annie nodded. "I imagine some would. But what happens in your own house is your own business."

"I'm sorry, Annie, for a lot of things. I listen to all this stuff on the news, I hear people talking about it, and God knows, Mary's tried to pound into my head what's happening, but I just never thought that it had anything to do with me, with us. Not here in Myrtlewood. We all get along just fine here, I always thought. All of that turmoil and uproar had nothing to do with any of us."

Annie remained silent. Lila was frustrated, unable to say clearly what she was thinking. "That man at the gas station didn't even know us. He has no idea that you've lived in this house longer than I have, that I depend on you and that I—" Lila stopped. She loved Annie. It was as simple as that.

Annie nodded solemnly, "I know, Miss Lila. I hear what you're trying to say, even what you didn't say."

"I feel like a fool. Annie, you've been more than a friend to me. You know that. You're the one who taught me how to do my hair, who taught me how to run this house, who helped me learn how to deal with Tommie. You've stood by me and stood up for me. You're not just a maid. You're a part of this family."

Annie smiled. "Don't go gettin' worked up now."

Lila struggled to hide her tears. "I am worked up. I'm ashamed of myself. Were you scared, when that man leaned into the car?"

Annie shrugged. "I've seen and heard worse. Tell the truth, I think he was just showin' off for you and Bobby Riser. Men like that like to strut."

"I was scared. I just couldn't believe he was saying those things." She hesitated. "I'm sorry for not saying anything to him." Annie didn't respond, but there was no censure in her eyes, just a gentleness that Lila had come to expect and to need.

"Child, there's all kinds of people in this world. Some are good to the bone. Some are just twisted and ugly."

"How can you dismiss it like that?"

Annie looked at Lila with that stern, you're-missing-the-point look. "I ain't dismissin' nothing. When you're colored, you don't get to choose your battles, because you lose every one. You learn to take it, you learn to figure out who's really dangerous and who's just blowin' hot air, and most of all, you learn to keep your mouth shut."

Lila thought about that kind of submissive life, always deferring to those who thought it their right to tell you what to do, how to do it, where to live, where you could go to school and work, where you could sit on a bus. She thought about having children, and teaching them as babies that there are monsters in the world and that they must avoid provoking them. She thought about Annie, the most confident, self-contained person she knew, teaching her children to submit and obey and to step off the sidewalk when white people walked by. Lila had never been to town with Annie, but she tried to picture Annie performing that ritual, and she was horrified and humiliated for her. She had never even looked into the two rooms off the kitchen where Annie lived, and where she had raised two children. For the first time, Lila began to understand why Annie's son and daughter never visited their mother here. While serving as the Dubose cook and maid had held a certain status, living in the Dubose house surely hadn't lent much respect.

"Well, I hope you won't think it too little, too late. But we're both working ourselves to death looking after Tommie, and from now on, we'll just set one table, okay?"

Annie leaned back in her chair. "Honey child, it's all right with me.

186

You always remember, this is your house. You get to say what goes on here."

"You've been trying to teach me that for a long time. Maybe it's time I grew up a little bit."

"You're doing just fine. Don't beat yourself up. It don't matter when you get there. Just keep going."

"How can you be so patient, so accepting of all this?"

"Cause it's the way it is, but it's not the way it's always going to be. You can preach, and you can pray, and people can boycott the buses, and march in the streets, and they can appeal to the highest court in the land. It takes time to change the human heart. And folks are stubborn."

"Do you really have relatives in Montgomery? Are you worried about them?"

"I got people all over. My daddy was from here, you know, but my mama's people, they come from up in Perry County, Uniontown. Just down the road a piece from Selma, on Highway 80."

"Really? I didn't know that. I don't know what you must think of me, the way I just sat there and let that man talk to you the way he did. Now tell me, do you know people involved in the boycott? Are you involved?"

Annie narrowed her eyes. "Don't go getting worried. Our church is helping out. We send money, and we take turns going up there when we can to drive people to work. They all organized, got a whole list of cars and drivers." Annie hesitated. "Montgomery's full of hills, you know? Really steep hills. Climbing up and down them hills after workin' all day on your feet, that's hard."

Lila was silent. The boycott had been going on for over six months now. Dr. King's house had been bombed, and there had been attempts to disrupt the taxi service organized by the MIA, and there had been some violence. Mary had told her. She felt silly for thinking that sitting at the same supper table was a real step forward.

"You haven't gone up there yourself, have you?"

Annie smiled. "You know I ain't been nowhere since Mr. Tommie's been sick. We got work to do here. I ain't goan leave you alone right now. I got people keeping me up to date with what's happening. I told you, don't worry about me."

Lila felt a sense of relief, and an overwhelming surge of guilt. "I do worry about you. I wouldn't know what to do without you. But all the same, something big is happening, isn't it? And I've been stupid to think it doesn't affect us, me. You're right, things aren't always going to stay the same. I feel stupid to have come to this so late, but my word, it's so wrong, so unfair. It's just not right, is it?"

"No, it ain't fair. But it'll all work out in time."

Lila had heard enough. Annie's calm, almost unemotional declamations chilled her. "Well, now that I've come to Jesus, it's time I did something about it, don't you think?" That morning on the back porch when Mary first told her she loved her flashed into her mind. She had felt freed, like a huge burden had been lifted, as though she had been walking around in a fog and with those simple, hesitant words from Mary, she could see clearly for the first time in her life. She felt exactly the same now. The two people she loved the most had no real hope of achieving what they wanted most. But Lila saw possibility. She saw how things could be, and she would do all she could to make it happen. It was time to stand up.

"You might not want to get involved. They come down pretty hard on white people who try to help out. Some have got beat up, and had their cars smashed, headlights busted out, windows, tires slashed. They get phone calls in the middle of the night telling them to stay out of it. It's ugly."

"Yes, it is ugly, isn't it? But it's not going to get any better when people who could help don't. So, what can I do?"

Chapter Thirteen

REPORT TO THE GRAND DRAGON: *We got to be patient. We'll git 'em back on the buses. It's spread down to Tallahassee now. Should've come down harder right at the start, showed that nice nigger lady what it means to bite the hand that feeds her. Attendance: 26*

Friday, August 3, 1956

"Mary, dear, would you bring me a glass of lemonade while you're up?"

Mary smiled. It was a pleasure to look after Lila. Tommie was having a period of wellness, and so she had Lila to herself for a long weekend. She intended to feed her and make her rest. She answered through the screen door, "All right. The shrimp is ready. Want some?"

"Bring them out here. I don't want to be inside."

Lila sat on the tiny porch of the cottage, soaking in the Gulf sun, watching the shrimp boats on Mobile Bay. Mary thought there must be something in the sea air that energized and relaxed them both.

Mary came out balancing a plate of shrimp and Lila's lemonade on a tray.

"Oh boy," Lila said. She took the plate and held it on her lap, peeling the first shrimp, while Mary sat beside her and watched her eat, marveling at how Lila had turned a golden brown after one afternoon of sun. Lila generously peeled one shrimp for Mary.

"No, thank you. You eat them. You're too thin."

"You sound just like Annie." Lila sighed in satisfaction, watching the horizon as she ate. "I never get tired of seeing the sunset here. Isn't it gorgeous?"

"Yes," Mary said.

Lila turned her head. "What is it?"

"Nothing. I'm enjoying watching you eat. That's all."

189

Lila laughed and blushed. "Wait a while before you begin piercing me with those looks. Let me satisfy one appetite at a time."

Mary obediently turned her gaze to the sailboats heading in after a day on the bay. She rested her head against the back of the chair. After a moment, she turned her eyes back to Lila, observing the long fingers delicately peeling shrimp, and the way her slender neck sloped down to join shoulders that were too thin. "You need to eat more."

"Please don't start nagging. I'm fine."

"Okay, I won't. I'll just appeal to a higher authority and tell Annie you didn't eat enough while we were here."

Lila seemed to have stopped listening. Her eyes were closed. She looked tired.

After a moment, Lila said, "Do you think it would do Tommie good to come down here for a few days? Annie could come with me. I always feel so much better after a stay here."

Mary tried to keep the momentary flash of disapproval from showing. She didn't want anyone else coming to the one place that was theirs alone. She frowned but answered carefully, "Well, only if you can persuade Annie to come and help." The cottage was so small. She didn't think Lila would really want to crowd it with people, even if only for a day.

Lila poked through the shrimp which lay unfinished on the plate. "Want to go for a walk?"

"Sure. A short one. Let's go to bed early tonight."

Lila smiled. "Don't worry. We have plenty of time."

They walked for a while, bumping shoulders, catching hands together.

"What did you tell Annie this time?" Mary asked.

"Please don't start. If you think Annie doesn't know by now, you're fooling yourself. I told her I was going to the beach. She told me to have a good time and get some rest."

"I put off today's meeting with our boy Gerald until next week."

"Did you tell him you were coming down here? Do you think he went to Annie to compare notes?"

"No. But he'll know you're out of town whether anyone tells him or not. You won't be in church on Sunday."

"Mary, dear, I haven't been to church in weeks. Tommie's been sick, remember?"

"Everyone knows that Tommie is a bit better. Never mind. It's just that if Gerald ever figures this out he could make a lot of trouble."

"And won't that be fun? At least it'll be a relief. No reason to sneak around and hide any more," Lila exploded.

Mary stared at her. They stopped walking to face each other. This was silly, having a fight on the beach in their bare feet. "That would serve no purpose, and you know it."

"What will he do? He knows better than anybody that we could fire him, or pull all our business from the bank, and he knows what that would do."

"He also knows we would never really do that. We could more easily get rid of him as bank president. But then we'd have nothing to threaten him with."

"Oh, my, no means for blackmail. I see. So he keeps a job where he is more likely than anyone to catch us together, and we wait for him to threaten us with extortion before we can retaliate with more threats."

"Lila, it's not funny. Buchanan has a nasty mind and a mean streak. He resents us, at least me. He could hurt us terribly, and he would be in heaven."

"Are you sure you want this kept secret because of the weapon it would give him against our business if he found out? Is that what all your secrecy is about? The Dubose money, and keeping Buchanan from getting the upper hand?"

"He could ruin us in the eyes of the whole town. After we've fought so hard to gain the trust and respect—"

"Just listen to yourself! Do you think I care that much about what those people think? So what if they turn their backs on us in church. Not that you even go to church any more."

Mary lost her composure. They were toe-to-toe in the sand, yelling at each other now. "I don't give a *flying fuck* what anybody thinks. I care about you, you idiot! I'm trying to protect you, everything you've struggled to gain in the eyes of that town. All the money you give to the church and charity! Everyone shakes their heads about it. What do you think they'd say about it if they knew the truth about us? Do you believe even one of them would keep doing business with us if they knew?"

Lila frowned, her lips pressed tightly together. She waited a moment. "The truth is, I am what they think of me. Poor white trash from the wrong side of town, who got lucky and married the son of the richest man in three counties. Who doesn't have enough sense or background even to know how to spend all the money they think I'm stealing from a retarded man. What in heaven's name do you think you're saving me from?" She had put her hands on her hips in a combative stance that Mary had never seen before. Eyes flashing, chest heaving, she nevertheless spoke more calmly. "Stop lecturing me. I'm tired of it, Mary. Tired of all the lying and hiding."

"Why is all this coming out now?"

"Because it's the truth. Maybe I *am* exhausted, just too tired to pretend it doesn't bother me. Refreshing, isn't it, even to simply talk about it?"

Lila ran ahead of Mary, and turned, walking backwards. "Catch me." She took off running.

Mary watched Lila run away from her, and her anger faded. She ran after her. For the rest of the day, they behaved like children, chasing each other into the water, splashing each other, lying exhausted side by side in the sun.

"Look," Mary said. "I'm taking off my watch."

"I'm taking off my shirt," Lila said, and did so, devilishly slowly, provocatively, revealing her breasts, which were stark white in contrast to the rest of her tanned body.

They slept together with the windows open, the chill of the night air lending an excuse they did not need to wrap tightly together. They woke and began making love still half asleep. Afterward, they stayed in bed, tussling, wrestling, doing each other's nails. They lay and stared at the ceiling as they talked for hours, carefully avoiding the business or the town or Tommie.

"Miss McGhee, you can't divest yourself of all the land," Gerald Buchanan said in a nasal voice that barely escaped whining, and which grated on Mary's nerves. "It just doesn't make sense."

"It does. It's foolish and risky to hold mortgages on hundreds of acres that have been harvested, and won't yield more timber for another twenty years. We break them up into smaller pieces, sell them off for more than the Duboses owe on them, and we buy back the timber rights when we need them."

"Most of that land is inaccessible!" Buchanan struggled not to shout, Mary noted with amusement. "It's useless. Who would pay what you're asking?"

"Scotch Lumber Company, that's who." And maybe some Negro families who had been pushed off their land by Buchanan and the bank, she silently reminded herself.

"If you sell off all we hold to them, you might as well get out of the sawmill business altogether. They have their own mills. They've been buying out all the small mills for years now."

Buchanan fought every attempt to change the Dubose business. His persistent attempts to steer Lila toward questionable business decisions made her certain the status quo suited him just fine. If the business ever did falter, Buchanan could bolster his argument that he, not Mary, should be running it. She would like nothing more than to fire him, but it was better to keep her enemy close, and to know what he was doing. Besides, a less competent bank manager might prove just as reluctant to go along with their business ideas and Mary had to admit Buchanan, as much as she disliked him, was a very good bank president.

"Just listen to me," Mary said, leaning forward, her eyes wide and blank. "I have intimated to Scotch that we might consider selling the mill, given the right offer."

"You *what*?" Buchanan's eyes darted to Lila. "Mrs. Dubose, surely you don't want to do that. The Dubose mill provides jobs."

"I know that. And we are losing some of our best employees to Scotch, who pays better wages than we do. Isn't that right, Miss McGhee?" Lila neatly tossed the ball back to Mary, who smiled.

"That's right. I propose building a hardware supply store."

Buchanan shook his head mournfully, looking like a bulldog who had latched onto a particularly distasteful rat. "You ladies don't know what you're doing. A hardware store! That won't provide nearly enough jobs to replace the ones at the mill, and you know it. You need to think about this. Miss Lila, you don't have to take everything Miss

McGhee suggests as written in stone. Let's just consider this for a while now."

"You know as well as I do that to keep operating at a pace to compete with Scotch, we need to replace equipment and upgrade our processes. It would require a huge capital investment. Which would be pointless because eventually, Scotch is going to win this war."

Buchanan snorted. "Dubose can keep operating just as it is for the time being. There's no good reason to sell the mill just because eventually you may need to."

"Tell Gerald about the jobs, Mary," Lila said gently.

"What jobs? There won't be any jobs if you sell everything!"

"No jobs will be lost. Scotch will hire most of our men to work on the transition, tearing down, rebuilding, replacing our worn-out machinery with new. It will take at least a couple of years. And they will get more benefits, health insurance, time and a half for overtime, holidays, paid vacations. Things Dubose would never be able to afford, scrambling for contracts and accounts against Scotch, if we stayed in business."

Buchanan sat and stared, open-mouthed. "You don't know any of that for sure. You don't know how long Dubose could keep going just as it is. You don't know that Scotch would force you out of business. You don't know for sure that they will keep any Dubose employees on."

Mary smiled. "No, you're right. Not for sure. Nothing is certain. This is my best advice, based on what's been happening around the state. It's in the best interest of our employees, and the town, and the bank." The two women had already gotten up. Gerald Buchanan, Mary knew, would give in, as he always did after much protesting, when he could find a way to make it sound like it was his idea. Soon there would be talk in the barber shop and the diner about the deal, and everyone would believe that Gerald Buchanan had done it again.

Mary had never felt so angry or frustrated, or so helpless. She could help if only Lila would let her. She wanted to escape, to run away. Sometimes Lila's stubbornness drove her to crave a drink, but right now, a long drive sounded very appealing. She wanted to just get in the car and wander down back roads and get lost. She packed an overnight bag and marched through the living room where Miss Louise sat dozing with the radio blaring. Turning down the volume, Mary said, "I'll be gone for the weekend. There's leftovers in the icebox. I'll see you late Sunday afternoon, okay?"

The old lady struggled to sit up straighter. "What'd you say? Going off again? All right, then. I reckon I'll see you when I see you."

Louise's pitiful attempt not to appear disappointed tugged at Mary. She hurried, starting the car, avoiding Riser's, where Bobby's all-points inspection and curiosity about where she was going and why was beyond her ability to endure right now. She'd gas up somewhere else. Turning north on the highway, she relaxed in the seat and just drove.

A couple of hours later, she stopped in Selma, and filled up.

"How far is it to Montgomery?"

The attendant screwed the gas cap on and eyed her nervously. "It's about fifty miles. You might want to go around it. They're having some trouble up there, with that boycott, you know."

"Thanks. I just keep on this road right here, then?"

"You'll want to turn right, that takes you over the bridge, Highway 80, straight into Montgomery. You be careful, now."

A very pretty drive through rolling hills took her into the state capital. Easing the car into a parking place slanted at an angle to the street, Mary set the parking brake and walked into Chris' Hot Dogs. Apparently, the menus provided were just for fanning. She ordered a hot dog, with a side of French fries and a Coca Cola. As she ate, two men in the booth next to hers argued incessantly while they wolfed down their food.

The first man wore a white short-sleeved shirt and suspenders, with a white straw hat he hadn't bothered to remove, the kind with a short brim, turned up in back and down in front. Mary focused on the hat as the men worked their way through their food in contentious tandem, eating, disputing, slurping, never missing a beat. She guessed that they worked together.

"I told you, it ain't. It just looks like marble is all. You don't believe me, let's take a walk up the hill after we eat, and we'll ask 'em. It ain't marble, it's brick, covered over, stuccoed, they call it, with something that looks like marble."

The younger, thinner man just kept shoveling in food and shook his head. "I'm not walking anywhere in this heat. You crazy? It's hot enough to fry eggs on the sidewalk." He downed half a glass of tea in one swallow. "Bet them niggers give up walkin' to work soon. This heat's a killer."

"The heat don't bother them, you fool. And you couldn't get me to set foot in the capitol building if you paid me. We got to get back to work." He stood, threw three dollars on the table, and they left. Mary paid and followed them out. They were right about one thing, the heat was debilitating. She opened the door of the car to let the inside air equalize a little before getting in. The men stood on the sidewalk, sucking on toothpicks.

Straw Hat Man pointed at her with his toothpick. "That Ford's in good shape to be so old. 1942 model, right?"

"Yes, I think so." Bobby kept the car in pristine condition.

"What do you want for it?"

"Why do you ask?"

The man shrugged. "I could sell you something a lot newer. Take that Ford off your hands in trade. Put you in a nice Chevrolet."

Why not? She found herself following the men back to Ed's Cars, Used But Guaranteed. She climbed out of the car. Her blouse stuck to her back, and she fumbled in her purse for sunglasses. The man with the straw hat, Ed himself, approached her. "See, right here, I got a 1950 Chevrolet Deluxe, whitewall tires, the works, runs as smooth as a purring kitten. Want to take it for a drive, see how you like it?"

"I think I might, yes." Thinking of Bobby Riser, she looked at the tires.

"I put brand new tires all around."

Relieved about the only aspect of a car she knew enough to check, Mary slid behind the wheel. The interior did look almost new. "I'll drive it around a few blocks and see how it handles, if that's okay."

She headed back the way she had come, to Dexter Avenue, a broad, steeply climbing street that terminated at the capitol. On her right, she saw a small, red brick church, and recognized the white stairs that began on either end and met in the middle of the second floor. On impulse, she stopped the car and got out. She stood there, just looking at the place that had spawned and sustained the bus boycott. Curious, she went to the ground-floor entrance, under the stairs. The door opened, so she stepped inside to get out of the sun. There was a man sweeping and straightening the sanctuary. She nodded.

"Can I help you, ma'am?"

Mary sank into one of the pews. It was much cooler. "Maybe. Is this where the Montgomery Improvement Association meets?"

The man leaned on his broom. He answered slowly. "Yes ma'am, it is. What can I do for you?"

Mary realized that she was alone in a deserted building with a black man. No wonder he stayed up near the front of the church. "I think I need some help. Do you know anyone who can drive a car back here for me?"

Ed was not pleased. "I ain't goan do it. I'll take your car in trade, I'll even knock off fifty dollars on the price."

Mary said, "Thank you. That's four hundred fifty, then. I'll make out a check while you get the bill of sale and the title."

Ed looked like he wanted to take his hat and throw it at her. "That was with your Ford in trade. The price of the Chevrolet with no trade-in is eight hundred."

Mary stared him down. "Eight hundred. For a car that's five years old."

"I put new tires, a new battery, all kinds of money into it." He looked like he wanted her to just disappear. He glanced over at the black man from the church she had brought back with her. "How you gonna get both cars back home?"

"That's my problem, isn't it? Here's a check for eight hundred."

Fred Jones, the man she had met in the church, drove the Ford slowly and carefully back. Mary pulled in beside her old car. Digging in its glove box, she found the registration and the title. Signing it over to Mr. Jones, she handed the papers to him and offered her hand.

Taking her hand and holding it in both of his, he said, "We can't thank you enough. Won't you come in? I'll call Dr. King. I'm sure he would want to personally show his appreciation."

"No, thank you. I'd better start heading home. It's a long way from here." She looked up at the church. "You all be very careful, all right? And I wish you good luck."

She got back into her almost new, 1950 Chevrolet Deluxe, and felt immeasurably better than she had when she began her road trip. Bobby Riser would be the only person who would be pleased to see her new car.

Lila opened the front door to Buchanan, who stood looking around the porch his hat in his hand. "Hey. Come on in."

Buchanan followed her down the hall to the living room. "I thought I'd stop by and see how Mr. Tommie's doing."

"Not any better, really. Could I get you something to drink?"

"No thank you. Miss Lila, I wonder if you've heard some things that have been going around town about Miss McGhee?"

For God's sake, Lila thought. I don't have time for this. "I'm afraid I've been confined to the house, looking after Tommie. I don't have much time or patience for gossip."

Buchanan assumed an offended look. "This idn't gossip. There's things happening right here in our own state, right here in Myrtlewood, that people don't need to be messing with. Especially not outsiders. I'm talkin' about that mess up in Montgomery. Fact is, I had a talk with Sam Stewart, that oil man out in Texas who *recommended* Miss McGhee to you years ago. I have to believe that you yourself had no idea about this, or you never would have let that man persuade you into hiring somebody we never heard of before, sight unseen."

"Gerald, as you can probably tell, I'm very tired and very concerned about Tommie. Whatever it is, spit it out. I don't have time to get involved in disagreements between you and Miss McGhee. I don't know what I would do without her running things all on her own right now."

Buchanan looked distressed at her attempt to hurry him along. "I understand the strain you're under. This is important. I wouldn't be so worried if she didn't have such a free hand, so to speak. I've tried time and again to get you to listen to me more and not to depend on that woman so much."

"What is it?"

"It appears that Miss McGhee has quite a bit of money. Seems like Big Sam actually had to pay her off to get rid of her, to keep her quiet about something that happened, involving some woman, I believe."

"How much money?"

"Like I said, a lot. Seems she finagled it out of him, you might even say blackmailed it from him. He says he would have had her arrested for fiddling with his books, if he hadn't caught her in bed with some woman, engaged in unnatural acts. Then he ships her off to you. He must have thought that was a good joke, probably figured she'd quit or you'd fire her when you found out."

A lot of money. Why hadn't Mary ever told her? "Why are you telling me this? Why should I care if she has her own money?"

"First of all, don't it make you curious, why she would continue to work as a secretary when she's got enough to live on without working? Second, it's what she's doing with this money that's troubling. And what she's influenced you to do with Dubose money."

Lila's rein on her patience snapped. "Mary doesn't 'influence' me. She advises me, and runs that business for me."

Buchanan smiled. "Now wait a minute before you go rushing to her defense. I understand that you and her are *friends*. You might want to reconsider having that woman in your home, allowing her so much control over the business, now that you know what kind of person she is. What I mean is, she's been giving money to these people, the Nigras. She's been selling lumber from the mill at cost and she's been selling off Dubose land to niggers too. I bet you didn't know that, now did you? Outside agitators coming down here and putting ideas in people's heads is likely to get them a lot of trouble. Stirring up our own folks who used to be perfectly sensible, that's got to stop."

"I don't have time for all this right now. It's time for Tommie's bath and his medicine."

"Folks should expect bad things to happen when they stir up trouble. Askin' for it. Negroes don't give no forethought to consequences. You tell Annie she's got plenty to keep her busy right here at home. Tell her she ought to think about advising her folks up in Montgomery to mind their own business before some of 'em get hurt."

"I don't see where anyone's making trouble. I just see a lot of people trying to earn a living without being subjected to ridiculous restrictions about where they sit on a public bus after a hard day's work." Lila stood. "I'll have to ask you to leave now, Gerald. Unless you'd like to help me turn Tommie and change his sheets?"

He rose slowly. Staring at her with his opaque black eyes, he said, "I'll go. But you should do some thinking about how close you've got with that woman. We don't need her type around here. People are gonna have a bad reaction to this sort of thing, and we just don't put up with that kind of behavior, sticking her nose in where it don't belong. That kind of woman is unnatural. God knows why she wants to associate herself with colored folks. You think about what I've told you. You don't want to get smeared with the same brush."

Lila held the front door open. "I'll know just where the paint's coming from, won't I? I'm very busy."

She closed the door and leaned against it. Looking up, she saw Annie at the upstairs landing, watching her. She shook her head and began to climb the stairs.

Chapter Fourteen

REPORT TO THE GRAND DRAGON: We ain't losin' this fight. By God, I'll walk to Montgomery myself. What we might ought to do is bomb some of them courthouses with federal judges who think they can ignore what white folks want whenever some nigger in a suit comes knocking on the door. White men been forced to work side by side with these dirty blackbirds at the mill down here, and we've had enough.

Friday, October 5, 1956

Tommie grew weaker again that fall. The variety of ailments that descended on him with increasing frequency and intensity perplexed Dr. Morgan, a frequent visitor to the house now. Bronchitis. Mysteriously swelling glands. One night, a temperature of 103 degrees. Pneumonia twice. His good days were outnumbered by bad ones spent confined to his bed.

"He hates the hospital," Lila said to Dr. Morgan, in a choked voice, "but he needs to go."

"He remembers his father dying there," Dr. Morgan reminded her. No inducement, not even telling him that his father had built the hospital just for him in case he ever got sick, worked.

That morning they had moved his bed downstairs to the parlor, which had windows looking out on the front porch and the street. Tommie, a little better today but still very frail, sat out there and held court. Lila listened through the open windows as she hurriedly swept the carpets and dusted, tasks she and Annie hardly had time for when Tommie was sick.

"Hey, Mr. Tommie, man, how you doing today?" The sheriff, Paul Dunagan, stopped by with Mr. Howard Butler. "When we going

201

fishing again? It's about time, we could set out some trotlines and watch 'em."

"Well, now, Tommie, you're looking much better today," Dr. Morgan said as he left Lila and joined them on the porch.

"It's time to go fishing." Tommie said to Dr. Morgan. Lila smiled as she heard this stubborn declaration.

"Is it now? We'll see. You stay well and maybe we can go to the cabin just for the day if the weather doesn't get too cold."

Mr. Howard Butler propped his bad foot on the edge of the porch. "You heard the doctor now, Tom. We'll see about going soon. Those bass we stocked are getting big enough to eat. Remember that bream I caught last year, that was mighty good eating."

Sheriff Dunagan leaned a hip against the porch railing. He spat into the yard. He chewed tobacco, which had always impressed Tommie. "I like catfish, always have," Dunagan said. "You might not believe it, but I pulled one out of the Tombigbee almost as big as I am. No good for eating, that size. The little ones are the best eating."

"Let's go fishing at the river, then," Tommie said excitedly. His voice, even in his eagerness, was weak. "We could have us a fish fry, couldn't we?"

"Sure we could. Soon as Miss Lila says you're up to it. Don't you worry, we ain't gonna forget about our fishing buddy."

Lila kept an eye on them through the window as the talk wound through stories she knew Tommie had heard a dozen times. Listening to the men talk seemed to make him happy; their deep voices appeared to soothe and comfort him. Surrounded by the men who had visited with his father all his life, and who talked about him still, must make him happy. She knew he would eventually get too tired and need help getting back inside and the men would gather him up and half-carry, half-guide him back to bed as they continued their reminiscences. Lila knew he should rest but she didn't have the heart to send the men away. They were all Tommie had left of his father.

Lila was Mary's only concern now. Sadly, there was little hope left for Tommie. Lila wasn't eating. She was growing thinner than Tommie had become. In her devotion to Tommie's declining health, she was neglecting her own and she still refused any help from Mary.

When Lila came into the office to approve the payroll Mary could not control her fear or desperation any longer.

"For heaven's sake, Lila, what are you thinking? You're going to kill yourself. No matter what you do, you can't save him. You need to rest and eat and accept some help."

"What in Sam Hill do you think I'm doing? Lord knows I'm not much of a wife, but I'm all Tommie's got. This is all I can do for him." She was shaking and her voice quavered.

"So you exhaust yourself trying to earn redemption for a sin he doesn't even know you've committed? Lila, he wouldn't care about it if he did know! Let me help you. Look, if you're trying to appease your guilt for what we've done then I should too. If there is a way to be absolved, then we both should try."

"You can't believe that guilt is my only motivation." Lila stared at her. Then she turned and left the office without another word.

Shaken, Mary picked up the phone and called the house.

"Annie, it's Mary."

"I been hopin' you'd call."

Mary hesitated. "I'm afraid I just had an argument with Lila. Annie, she won't let me … Isn't there anything at all I can do?"

"Miss Mary, I don't reckon there's anything to do except pray. Me and Miss Lila are doing everything that can be done to keep him comfortable. Dr. Morgan says his lungs are filled with fluid now. It probably won't be long."

"Oh, no. Lila was just here, but …"

"She's just tired, is all. She goes to you when she gets like that, just to get away from all this for a while. Don't you worry too much. She'll have time to rest and get her strength back later."

On a night that was misty with rain, and the air was cool and fragrant coming through her open windows, Mary's phone rang. She rose from her bed, where she had been turning sleeplessly, and heard Annie's voice softly asking her to come. Tommie had passed, and Miss Lila needed her.

The entire town turned out for Tommie's funeral, as they had for his father's, whom he was buried next to. The men who had been his father's pallbearers now served that function for the son.

The house and yard were overrun with people after the service. Lila sat in a chair on the back porch and spoke very little. She stared across the yard and patted each hand given to her in sympathy as though she were doing the comforting. Barbara Sullivan stuck to her side, bringing her tea and handkerchiefs. Lila's silence left the mourners no outlet for their sympathy, so they talked among themselves, retelling tales of Tommie's father and grandfather, of their generosity and kindness, their shrewd business sense.

"It was Tommie's granddaddy, the one built the mill, he saved my granddaddy when he got snake bit in the woods."

"Mr. Robert Dubose gave my daddy a job after he busted his leg and couldn't work the farm no more."

"Always had that big Fourth of July picnic for the mill workers and their whole families. Every year before the war."

Their adoption of Tommie was a measure of the depth of the respect they had for his father, Mary supposed. Tommie had become a symbol of the town's goodness, his happy and sunny nature a reward for their acceptance of him and his handicap. Already that day, Mary heard at least a dozen times: "He was the spittin' image of his daddy, he just never grew up in his mind. Sweet boy, that's what he was." Perhaps they grieved because Tommie was the end of that line.

Mary wearily placed a stack of newly washed and dried plates on the kitchen counter, and heard someone say, "His daddy, now, for a well-to-do man, he sure liked his moonshine and set up and ate pot likker and cornbread just like everybody else." Was that Jimmy Jackson's voice? Suddenly he was praising the Duboses? As she worked her way through the house and yard collecting empty dishes, Mary heard the praise for the Duboses slowly change to anxiety about the future.

"Wonder what's gonna happen to the mill now? Probably sell off everything, don't you reckon?" Vince Dunn posed this query to Buchanan, and Mary watched the banker circulate from group to group like a politician working a crowd, nodding solemnly at each comment, slapping people on the back, and more than once she heard him assure someone worried for their job, "I'm not about to let the

Dubose business get run down, you know that. Nobody's going to be selling off anything."

Mary's anger seethed. Buchanan already knew the sale to Scotch had been approved. Several times she saw men clustered around the banker turn toward her and stare; she knew they were talking about her. Mary waited patiently until he had finished his latest estimate of the future of the Dubose business.

"Would you like some of Annie's pecan pie before it's gone?" she asked Buchanan before he could start again.

He glanced at her—a dark look—and exchanged his empty plate for the one with pie that Mary offered. "Thank you, Mary. You know how much I appreciate Miss Annie's cooking." She retreated to the kitchen, where she could wash dishes and keep an eye on Lila and the solicitous Barbara Sullivan at the same time.

All of Lila's brothers and sisters and their families were huddled together in the back yard. One sibling after another tried to get Lila to speak, but she wouldn't. Pale, gaunt rather than merely thin now, Lila sat in the deepening shadows on the back porch with her hands folded in her lap.

"You know anything about a will? Everything goes to Lila now, don't it?" Lila's brother Jimmy pursued Mary as she gathered trash, emptied ashtrays, stacked discarded dishes, and carried everything back to the kitchen. He reeked of shaving lotion and the home brew he and his brothers made in old washtubs over open fires. He had held a special brief for her ever since his disastrous and short-lived tenure as a mill hand.

"I'm sure you could speak to Lila's attorney," Mary told him. "Mr. Ronnie Calhoun. He has office hours on Monday." She caught Jimmy's wife Charlotte, dressed in her best, staring at them, lips pursed, arms folded, and Mary was convinced the woman had thrust her husband forward to inquire about Lila's legal standing. The family was circling, hovering like birds of prey, seeking any sign of weakness to swoop in and pick over the remains. Her disgust rose as bile in her throat.

Jimmy hitched up his pants. "Lila don't need no lawyer. I'll see to her business now. And the first thing's goan be gittin' rid of you."

Mary stared at the man's red-rimmed, unfocused eyes, and turned away. Buchanan stood across the yard with yet another plate of food, watching the encounter. She wondered if he had overheard. She felt surrounded and overwhelmed. The Jackson men had been drinking bootleg whiskey from flasks in their back pockets, having finished the jugs of homemade beer. Drying her hands on a towel, Mary found Sheriff Dunagan and invited him to walk outside with her.

"Sheriff, please just look at the Jacksons and nod your head while I'm talking to you. I want them to leave now but I don't want to make a scene and I'm hoping this will do the trick."

Sheriff Dunagan nodded as Mary requested. He adopted a stern expression and rested his hand on his gun in its holster.

The Jacksons, not given to discernment, nevertheless took note and left in a sullen silence. The sheriff was standing close enough to get a good whiff of stale whiskey as they shouldered past him.

"Believe I'll ride out a ways," he said. He nodded to Mary and ambled after the Jacksons.

People lingered and ate and talked quietly in small groups until late in the afternoon, when Miss Louise was the last to leave. Barbara and Bill Sullivan had retreated to the kitchen and were helping wash up (much to Annie's annoyance, Mary was sure).

Mary had seen no evidence that rumors about the Sullivans' political activities had spread through Myrtlewood. They seemed to have been welcomed back for the funeral. She knew that Lila had kept in touch with them over the years, but Mary herself had made no effort to do so.

Wearily, she headed back to the kitchen, wondering how she could tactfully suggest it was time for the Sullivans to go. She was irked that Barbara had spent so much time at Lila's side. She should have been there and now she just wanted a chance to be alone with Lila, to find out what she was feeling. Detouring through the living room, she armed herself with a glass of whiskey and took it with her.

Annie shot her a look. Mary knew she wanted these people out of her kitchen. Barbara was washing dishes and Bill was drying. "Where's Lila?" Mary asked Annie.

"I sent her to the study with a tray of food. She needs to eat and go to bed."

Mary smiled gratefully. "I'll go check on her." Turning her back to go, she paused and reluctantly added, "Bill, would you and Barbara like to join us for a drink?"

Lila looked up when the three of them entered the study. She smiled at Mary, whose heart lifted. "I'm so glad you stayed after the crowd left. Maybe we can talk now," Lila said to the Sullivans.

Mary sat herself next to Lila. "You haven't eaten anything."

Staring at the plate of food congealing in front of her, Lila shuddered. "Oh, God, Mary, all the times I brought food to Tommie on that tray!"

"I know. But it's over now, Lila."

Lila's eyes flashed. "Don't say that! He's gone, so I should just put it behind me, forget about him? How could you be so callous?"

Mary jerked away from Lila. "That's not what I meant at all. I just meant he's not suffering any more."

"You know Tommie is in a better place, Lila," Bill said. "Lean on your faith."

Mary turned to face him. "Platitudes aren't what she needs right now, thank you."

"Mary!" Lila shot her a look that clearly meant *mind your manners.*

"I'm sorry. I guess I'm tired. Both of you, please sit down."

"This has been a very trying period. We understand," Barbara said. Her eyes shone like copper in the late afternoon sun that streamed in through the tall windows in the study. Mary watched as Barbara's gaze flicked over Lila's neck and shoulders, somehow reminding her of a snake.

Mary sipped her whiskey, appreciating its burn and then its sudden warmth. Why Lila had remained friends with these two after that "tea party" was beyond her. Still, it was her house now. If Lila wanted to visit with the Sullivans, Mary could endure them or she could leave. She took another swallow. Easing her shoes off, she said, "So how has your church been doing?"

Bill's smile changed from uncertain to beaming. "It's small. But our members are really supportive of what we're trying to do. They believe, as we do, that real change in the racial situation will not come unless decent white people choose to stand beside the Negroes and show their support."

Barbara, sitting on the ottoman, said, "And no one has been more supportive than Lila. We could never do enough to repay her for her generosity."

What? Mary knew nothing about Lila giving money to their political efforts. Then she shrugged. It was Lila's money, after all.

Lila said eagerly, "Tell me how the boycott is going." Mary kept her mouth from dropping open in astonishment. How many times had she tried to discuss this very thing with Lila, only to be put off by her indifference?

"We organize a group to go to Montgomery every Tuesday and drive people to work. Really, we couldn't have done it without your support."

"I'm glad I could contribute something. I would have gone myself, but with Tommie so sick …"

The hell you would, Mary thought as she swallowed another sip, almost choking in disbelief. Lila, driving Negroes around while police watched? Since when had she become so sympathetic to the plight of the colored people?

"Lila, we know that. You've done more than your part. Besides, driving people to and from work up there is not work for a woman. It's dangerous." Bill stretched his legs out, crossing his ankles.

Mary suppressed a snort. It was dangerous and foolhardy. Didn't Lila realize that Buchanan knew everything about how she spent her money? Checks made out to the Sullivans would certainly explain Buchanan's new hostility. Was she naive to the danger she could bring on them with her *generosity*? Damn Lila! And damn the sanctimonious Sullivans, too. It's one thing for me to give money secretly, Mary thought. That was just a way to spite Buchanan and his racist cronies with their secret meetings and their white hoods. It was quite another to deliberately invite scorn and maybe worse. Mary stood up and left the room to get the bottle, moving briskly, making no effort to hide her agitation. When she returned, she refilled her own glass but did not offer the whiskey to the others.

"I've been so absorbed in my own life, I haven't really kept up with the news. How much longer do you think it can go on?" Lila said.

"It's already gone on longer than the one in Mobile did," Barbara answered. "Still, no one has backed down yet. Not one colored person has used the bus in Montgomery yet. Some are walking miles to work and back."

Mary nursed her drink and kept silent. Recently Lila had mentioned how "Bill and Barbara's" new church was doing. Mary herself knew that the Sullivans were involved in a group of white citizens supporting the Negro churches in their civil rights efforts. She'd never dreamed that Lila would be so thoughtless as to involve herself publicly. And all this time, she'd wasted energy feeling jealous regarding Barbara's interest in Lila. Barbara was apparently just priming the pump, playing on Lila's faith and her good nature for donations, using the distance between herself and Lila to their advantage.

"So, have you two found new bridge partners?" Mary took another sip and tried to change the subject.

"Of course. They've become dear friends. You understand," Bill said.

Mary looked at him. "Yes, I think I do. As I suppose you understand about Lila and me. Which brings to mind the question of Barbara's keeping in such close contact over the years."

Lila drew back. In her black mourning dress, she looked both prim and stern. "That's uncalled for, Mary. I'm free to have whomever I please as friends, as you're certainly free to do whatever you please. You've had too much to drink." She stood up. "I'm going to bed. Bill, Barbara, I'll talk to you later. Thank you for coming." She hugged both of them and left the room with a final, furious look at Mary.

Barbara appeared stricken. "Mary, I hope you know there was never anything like that between Lila and me. I was pleased about you two. Bill was proud that he helped maneuver you together. Though I might have had another idea in the beginning."

Mary sipped her whiskey while she watched a slow grin spread across Bill's face. "Then I've made Lila mad at me for no reason?"

"Lila has been faithful to you, Mary. She called us a few months ago, and she wanted to give what she could to help the cause. You should be proud of her," Barbara said.

Proud? She thought of all the times she had tried to engage Lila's interest in this topic, all the times Lila had put her off; she thought of the guilt she had felt over the years, keeping secret from Lila her own pursuit of some equity in the treatment of the colored people. She remembered Lila siding with Gerald Buchanan over her hiring Negroes for the mill and paying them the same wage as white men. She maintained her silence and took another drink.

"Lila needs to mourn and recover from this ordeal. I know you have patience and strength to give," Bill said.

"Why do people always use words like patience and strength when referring to me? It makes me sound dumb as an ox."

Damn it, she had got her nose broken when she was sixteen for being adventurous. That had taught her not only patience and strength, it also certainly had taught her caution. Had circumstances been otherwise, she might have learned other lessons. She might have learned to be impulsive, impetuous. Even playful and teasing, like Lila.

She stared into Barbara's open and accepting face, and felt her own anger fade. These people didn't know how much she depended on Lila's free spirit to lighten her own. They had no idea why she was afraid. She needed Lila to return to her as she had been before.

Mary stood up, set her whiskey down and went to the door to listen for a sound from upstairs. None came. Without turning, she sighed and let her shoulders relax. "Sometimes I feel that my whole life has been spent waiting for something to happen. Then, when it does, I get angry because I couldn't stop it or change it. I'm angry because the nature of our relationship prohibits me from doing all I can for Lila. I'm angry because I'm forced to wait because of what I am, who I am."

"But that shouldn't prohibit anything," Bill said from his relaxed seat in the chair.

Mary turned to face him. He seemed amused by her anger. His high, shiny forehead signaled an early baldness, replacing the boyish appearance with the more earnest, even ascetic look of a priest or a monk.

"Stop grinning at me." She moved back to her seat at the desk and reclaimed her whiskey. "Tell me what I should do. What is it Lila needs?"

Then she was embarrassed by the emotion she had displayed. She did not know how to apologize for her outburst, which she felt was provoked, if unjustified and unanswerable. Barbara stood up, sliding Bill's feet from her lap to the ottoman, and came over to where Mary sat. She put a hand gently on Mary's shoulder.

"Dear woman, everyone has the same reaction when confronted with this situation. Don't you know that? Everyone wants to help but doesn't know what to do. Maybe you're just angry to discover you're not so different from the rest of the human race, after all."

Mary bit her lip (which seemed a bit numb from the whiskey) and then found herself smiling. Suddenly she enjoyed being made to feel foolish and petulant. Her anger seemed far away, or perhaps it was dissipated by the comforting warmth of the whiskey spreading through her limbs, making Barbara's hand on her shoulder feel motherly instead of possessive. She felt truly relaxed for the first time in days. She swirled the amber liquid around in her glass, then took another sip, stretching her legs out in front of her. Her head fell back and she stared at the ceiling. When she spoke, she had forgotten the Sullivans were there.

"What a sick, twisted bastard God must be."

The alcohol had accomplished what the Sullivans could not. She felt free, and light enough to fly. She could float up to face God himself. She would not be handled or maneuvered, at least not by well-intended attempts of the Sullivans. Here they sat, presenting themselves as experts on things like faith in both God and one's fellow man to wrest basic human rights from the clutches of the narrow-minded. Yet they lived as secretly as Lila and she did. They were even more afraid than she was of someone finding out the truth about them! The very people they were trying to help would reject them if they knew. They were sanctimonious hypocrites, that's what. She would go her own way, and this momentary lapse would be merely an excuse for an apology in the morning.

Now Barbara was taking her by the arm. Mary looked up at her.

"Come on, Mary, you stubborn woman," she said. "You need to go to bed."

Mary felt patronized and she resented it. She'd like to kick Barbara Sullivan, really. Barbara pulled her up and steered her toward the stairs with an arm around her waist. "Yes," Mary said, taking each step carefully. "This is the only kind of help I need from you. Keep your redemption to yourself, and leave God out of it."

Barbara was half-carrying her up the stairs. Mary felt her eyes begin to fill with tears. "She doesn't trust me. How can she not trust me, after all our years?" Mary was crying now, out of control, somehow observing her bad behavior as though detached from it.

Then Barbara, or someone, was shushing her, peeling her dress over her head. Mary stood in her slip in the center of a carpet she only vaguely recognized as the one in Lila's room. Then she was guided to the other side of a bed, gently pushed down, and covered up. She was still crying as she turned over and felt the soft, familiar shape of Lila's back. She wrapped her arms around a body whose skin seemed stretched too tightly on a frame of fragile bones and pulled closer, crying harder now, until the lamp light went out. "It's been so long," she mumbled. Then she was drifting, falling, tumbling into sleep, and her only anchor against the spinning was the body she hadn't held in months.

Chapter Fifteen

REPORT TO THE GRAND DRAGON: *The Supreme Court is wrong again. Our boys got so pissed off they took a little ride; dragged some of these niggers out of bed, the ones we know went up there and helped out. Burned a couple out. Stomped 'em down. Talking, negotiating, bargaining, all the good citizens tried all that. You can't reason with a nigger.*

Saturday, December 15, 1956

Lila was sitting on the back porch, where she spent most of her time now. She could feel Annie's watchful eyes on her. She did not want or need to hear again Annie's constant refrain about eating, exercise, and rest. By the length of the shadows, she could tell that it was time for Mary's daily visit. She resented in equal proportion the eagerness and the trepidation with which she anticipated what had become the highlight of each day. She wanted Mary to come, but she didn't want her to leave. The visits and the leave-taking made Lila feel like an invalid. She resented the solicitousness and that added to her irritation with herself and everyone around her.

"Hi." Mary sat down next to her. "Want to go inside?"

Lila reached for Mary's hand. "No. I'm not ready to go in. How was your day today?"

"Uneventful. Buchanan is on vacation, thank God. What about you?"

Lila shrugged. "Annie stripped all the beds and washed. She made dinner, then cleaned up, then went grocery shopping. She's making our supper now. I did nothing at all."

Mary sipped her tea. "Do you feel guilty?"

"I just can't seem to get enthused about anything right now."

"I know. Why don't you come back to the office Monday? Just for the morning, maybe."

"Mary—I want you two to stop treating me like a child, but then, I can't seem to stop acting like one, can I?"

"That's all right."

"Annie doesn't think so. I never thought she'd become one of those disgruntled colored women who mutter under their breath about the crazy white people they work for."

Mary smiled. "I imagine Annie does more than mutter."

Lila let a small grin escape. "Well, yes. She's quite insistent that she knows what's best."

"And I shouldn't add my advice. All I have to say is that with Buchanan out of town, we can have a little time at the office without him or one of his spies dropping by."

"I know. I'll come in Monday, I promise."

Annie stood holding the screen door open. "Ya'll come in and set down to the table. If Miss Lila's going back to work, she needs to start eating better. I'm not cooking for myself."

She waited. Lila stood up. "You heard the drill sergeant. I'm not the only one who needs food and rest."

After supper, they lingered at the table, sharing a spoon and eating banana pudding straight from the bowl. Lila forced herself to eat; she knew it pleased and reassured Mary, whose concern for her might have been touching, if it didn't make her feel so angry. She did not want to be pitied. She wanted ... she wasn't sure what she wanted. That was the problem. The sun was down now; the breeze through the open windows had cooled. Lila lifted her eyes from the remains of the now soggy dessert to Mary.

"What?"

"Let's go sit in the back yard. It's dark now."

Annie came through with her purse on one arm. "I'm going to church." She looked at Mary. "I'll probably stay with Auntie Grace tonight. Dr. Morgan says she ain't doing too well."

"We'll clean up the kitchen. You have a good evening."

Lila waited until she left to giggle. "What an actress, I swear! If she takes to rolling her eyes, I'm going to fire her." Mary raised her eyebrows. "Why is everyone making faces at me? Let's go outside."

They sat for a long time on the circular bench that curved around the oak tree, holding hands and watching the fireflies. "This is better than being together at work." She glanced at Mary who, in profile, was looking serene and lovely, a word she wouldn't normally use to describe her. The light from the house caught silvery strands in her auburn hair that she hadn't noticed before. Mary didn't answer her comment.

Lila dropped her voice. "I want you to stay with me tonight."

Mary looked toward her. "You know I can't."

"I know you *can*. There's nothing to stop us. Annie already knows. Please, Mary. Do you think people have telescopes trained on the house just to watch us?"

"Yes, I do. Maybe not literally, but you know as well as I do that there are those who will make note of when I leave here and when I get home."

Lila touched Mary's shoulder, then ran her hand across to the back of her neck. She pulled her head closer and nuzzled Mary's neck. Her other hand came up to find the buttons on Mary's blouse and undid the first two. She slipped her hand inside to cup the shape of a breast, feeling a nipple harden under her fingers. Mary's breathing quickened and a low moan escaped.

"Please," Lila whispered, her lips touching Mary's ear as she breathed into it.

Mary shivered.

Then Mary broke away, standing and leaning her hand against the tree to steady herself. She shakily began to rebutton her blouse. "No, Lila. We can't do this here—you know we can't," she said.

Lila watched her walk away in the dark.

Mary helped Annie prepare lunch that Sunday, using the time alone in the kitchen to interrogate Annie about Lila's health and mood.

"Does she help at all around the house? What does she do all day?"

"Child, you see what she does. She sits on that back porch, brooding. If you can get her back to work, then that's more than I can do. You know as well as I do that she has not left this house since the funeral."

215

Mary turned the heat down under the peas and leaned against the counter.

"It's been two months now. She said she'd come back to work tomorrow, but I don't know—"

"Reach me that bowl from the top shelf up there. My old bones are stiff." Annie sifted flour for biscuits. "She's still grieving. I reckon she might feel guilty that she wasn't more of a real wife to him, but nothing can change what Tommie was. She did as much as anybody could have done." Mary watched as Annie took a generous spoonful of lard and began working it into the flour, added a dribble of water and using her fingers now, mixed the ingredients that were indisposed to combine naturally into a wet dough. Flouring her hands, Annie absently began shaping handfuls into portions roughly the size of a saucer, which she then placed into an iron skillet, greased and floured, ready for the oven.

"She did too much. Why hasn't she got some of her energy back?"

"She will." Annie turned to look directly at Mary. "She always did love going to the beach. Why don't you take her down there for a while? That should bring some color back to her."

Mary stared at Annie, wondering at what was being acknowledged. She shied away from the idea that Annie knew about them. It made her feel exposed. She longed to go to the cottage, but she didn't want to return to the beach until things were back on track between them. "You know, Lila hasn't had a new wardrobe since Mr. Dubose bought clothes for her when she first got married. Maybe she'd like to go to Atlanta shopping. Do you think she'd go?"

Annie shoved the biscuits in the stove and cleaned her hands. "You think she won't? Go ask her." She shook her head, no doubt pondering the stupidity of white women once again.

Mary turned the wheel of the big Buick and they eased onto Peachtree. They had left by late afternoon, driving half the distance and staying overnight in a motel so that they entered the city early on Monday morning, fresh from a night's sleep blessedly alone.

"That's it!" Lila spotted their hotel before Mary, who was concentrating on the traffic and the cross streets. Mary slowed to inspect it. Thick, mature azaleas lined the walk to the entrance, trimmed into an orderly hedge, and others, allowed to grow larger, almost the size of trees, softened the building's stucco exterior. Tall, heavily curtained windows with beveled glass shone behind elaborate wrought-iron railings, giving it a New Orleans feel. Mary turned into the circular drive that would deposit them at the front door, while Lila looked this way and that, enthralled and trying to take in everything at once, her face turned away from Mary, as it had been since they entered Atlanta. Mary smiled; she didn't have to see Lila's face to know how wide her eyes were. This was Lila's first venture into a big city.

"This is the same place Mr. Dubose stayed whenever he came to Atlanta."

"Did he?" Mary said. For a moment, she felt a twinge of worry that maybe everyone from Myrtlewood chose this hotel, and hoped that they wouldn't run into someone they knew. Maybe she shouldn't have taken Dr. Morgan's recommendation. Then she relaxed. Lila was smiling more than Mary had seen her do in months. She had settled back against her seat as Mary pulled the car up to the curb where a uniformed bellboy stood ready to welcome them. Lila looked back at Mary and grinned as he opened the passenger door and helped her from the car. Mary smiled again as she opened her own door to join them.

It was incumbent upon them that they actually shop and spend money, since that was ostensibly their purpose. Mary let herself be led from store to store, writing checks from Lila's account for everything that Lila chose, from the new sheets and kitchen curtains requested by Annie to a silk business suit Lila admired but (Mary knew) would never wear. In one morning's expedition, she had managed to purchase all this, as well as three pairs of pumps with thin high heels that made Mary wince, envisioning blisters and sprained ankles.

"Mary, please buy something for yourself!" Lila was becoming insistent.

"My salary doesn't stretch to these prices, I'm afraid."

A strange look passed over Lila's face momentarily. "That's ridiculous. You never spend any money, do you?" Mary was puzzled by the look and the skeptical tone.

They were standing in the dressing room of a newly opened branch

217

of a posh New York department store. Lila was trying on a slip, a black lacy thing she was modeling just for fun, but Mary secretly hoped she would buy it. Watching her change, Mary had to look away for a minute.

Mary luxuriated in their anonymity in this city whose rapid change from sleepy rail hub to a more cosmopolitan character was beginning to attract more and more wealthy shoppers just like them. Mary also appreciated the hushed, discreet atmosphere of these shops that catered to the rich, even though she had little use for their absurdly feminine wares geared more toward wives and daughters of the country club set. She was more inclined to the finer business suits and sensible (though not unstylish) pumps.

She laughed. "I suppose I could ask you for a raise."

Again she saw that puzzling look as Lila said, "And I would give it to you." Then Lila stretched over to kiss her.

The curtain to the fitting room was closed and the saleswoman, Mary reasoned, was not coming back, assured that they were there to spend an inordinate amount of money. She slid her hands under the scalloped lace of Lila's slip and up her legs to her hips as she responded to the kiss. Lila leaned into her and opened her mouth. The kiss quickly turned passionate. *This is crazy*, Mary thought, *we're in a department store*. But her hands had already eased under the waistband of Lila's underwear to fondle her buttocks.

The curtain moved and the saleswoman stuck her head inside. Mary jerked away from Lila and saw the woman's mouth formed a silent O as she hastily withdrew and slid the curtain closed again.

"Oh, my gosh!" Lila was grabbing at her clothes, fumbling to pull on her skirt. "She saw us, didn't she?"

Mary drew a deep breath and composed herself. "She'll forget when we pay for all these things, I bet. Come on." She helped Lila zip her skirt.

By afternoon, Lila had forgotten her momentary fear, and was trying to get Mary to see the humor in it. "I bet it's not the first time she saw something like that."

They were having a very late lunch in a small café where a number of matronly looking women were also enjoying an after-shopping break. Mary glanced around, her face, Lila thought, still showing traces of shock and worry over the incident.

"That was stupid," she said in a low voice. "I never should have ..."

"Shouldn't have what? Felt me up?"

"Lower your voice, please. Where did you get that expression, anyway?"

Lila had gleaned the phrase from a paperback novel she had found in a drawer at the roadside motel outside Atlanta on their first night. Intrigued by the lurid cover, she was shocked to find such flagrantly sexual scenes in a book. She knew it was wrong to enjoy Mary's misery, but really, no one on earth knew them in this huge place. Who cared what the salesclerk said about them to her coworkers?

Mary was looking at her curiously. "You look wonderful. Why is it that you are all right now, but not at all yourself at home?"

Lila looked at Mary's serious face and decided to give her a serious answer. "I'm not myself anywhere unless you're there."

"That can't be true."

"Yes, it is. I feel so disconnected from my life right now. All my life, I never was anything. In school, I didn't like boys, so I had nothing in common with the girls. And as soon as I got out of school, Mr. Dubose and my daddy hatched this bizarre scheme and I got married to Tommie."

Lila picked at her salad. Mary's silence prompted her to go on. "Daddy acted like it was some sort of great opportunity, or something the Duboses owed him." Lila glanced at Mary and continued, her gaze wandering around the café, watching the other patrons. "I try to assign the best intentions to everyone, you know, but since Tommie's gone, I find that harder to do. My own father acted like I was a bargaining chip to extort money out of the Duboses. Even Mr. Dubose, nice as he was, apparently saw me as someone so unsure and unformed that I would be no threat to his son or his fortune. I'm just trying to see myself through everyone else's eyes. But nobody really saw me, just someone they could use. Even you."

Lila brought her eyes back to Mary and watched her flinch as though struck. "You don't mean that."

Lila looked away. "Admit it. I was a pawn in your never-ending battle with Buchanan for control of the Dubose business."

Mary's jaw tightened; her outrage was apparent. "How can you say that?" Her voice sounded strangled.

"I'm just trying to see me as you must have done at the beginning—a young, innocent girl who was overwhelmed, ready to be molded into what you thought I should be: a sharp business-woman who could be manipulated into your fight with Buchanan. Someone who needed to be educated about the meanness in the world and protected from it."

"You know that's not true."

Lila faced her, staring into Mary's eyes. "Do you realize that the only time you've ever said you love me is that morning when you told me everything?"

"Lower your voice. This is a public place."

Lila shrugged, and suddenly felt very sad. "I know. I just wonder why, even when we're alone, you can't bring yourself to say the words."

Mary had retreated into her usual reaction—anger. She hissed in a low voice, "You know how I feel about you. It just seems that ever since Tommie died, you've not been yourself. Is this public display supposed to force me into forgetting everything? Is this a reaction to his death?"

Lila grew angry herself. "Why can't you see that I loved Tommie, took care of him, and I miss him? You choose to believe that I was ashamed because we cheated him. You know I never felt guilty about that. That's your problem."

Mary sat back. "Maybe it is my problem. Maybe I've been worried about how things would change between us after he was gone. I was afraid you might consider other options now that you are free."

Lila ignored that remark. "You always saw Tommie as a burden and an obligation. He was like a brother to me, or like the child I never had, never will have." Tears formed and slid down her cheeks. Lila used her napkin to wipe them away. Mary's image blurred, but even without being able to see her expression, she could tell that she felt at a complete loss. She felt mean for attacking Mary like this in a public place, where she was sure to feel constrained to respond in kind. "Sweetheart, love has too many meanings not to really exist. Can't you trust that it does, that I'm not suddenly going to pull the rug out from under you, no matter what?"

"Lila, please tell me you know I never used you or manipulated you against Buchanan."

She gave up. No one would ever wrench or force from Mary McGhee an admission of need. "All I know is that one reason you're so afraid of anyone finding out is because it would give him more ammunition. Now that Tommie's gone, I don't care who knows about us. It just doesn't matter. I want you with me all the time, and as far as I'm concerned, there's no reason why we can't have that."

"Damn it to hell. Have you lost your mind?"

Lila didn't answer right away. She didn't like dealing with Mary's anger. Across from them four women were having lunch together. Two were older, more formally dressed, even wearing hats. She'd thought that women only still did that for church.

"Isn't it odd that they keep their hats on?" she whispered to Mary, nodding toward the women. Mary frowned and glanced over at the group, then back at her.

"You haven't answered my question."

Lila kept watching the four women. "I just wish we could be more open." She saw Mary's lips tighten in response. "I want you to move into the house with me."

Now her attention was drawn back to the women again as one of them rose from her seat to leave. She was tall and imposing, the face under the outrageous hat expressive and strong rather than pretty. She was looking down at the blond woman who had been seated next to her, a young girl of about twenty. The other two women were deep in conversation, and merely waved their goodbyes. The tall woman placed a hand on the younger one's shoulder.

"Do you think they're related?" Lila whispered to Mary. "They don't look alike."

But there was something similar about them, Lila realized, as she watched the older one bend down and kiss the blond on the cheek. "I think they're lovers," she said. Lila glanced at the younger woman's breasts, speculating.

"Stop staring. Do you want dessert?" Mary had picked up her menu to block her view of the women.

Then the woman's hand dropped to the girl's waist and lingered there as they talked. Lila's eyes followed the woman's hand as it traveled across the seated girl's body in a discreet, though unmistakable, caress. *Lovers*, thought Lila, *like us.* Suddenly she knew she was right, not just about those two. People see what they want to see. Just as they would back in Myrtlewood, when Mary moved in with her. After all, what was more logical than a widow sharing a house with a spinster? This was one fight she was certain she would win.

Mary went down the hall, locked the front door, and turned on the porch light. She peered through the beveled glass of the door for a minute. These cool, dry evenings were rare. She contemplated sitting on the front porch to smoke, but decided to keep to her evening routine. She climbed the stairs to her room. Her trunk sat at the foot of the bed, with pajamas and bathrobe tossed over it. Getting undressed, she draped her dress over one arm while she pulled the cord for the bare bulb in the closet, then hung up her dress. She took off her slip and tossed it in the hamper. Sitting down at the dressing table, she began the tedious process of taking down her hair and brushing it out. Sometimes she thought about getting it cut shorter, even very short. Audrey Hepburn wore that style very well.

She smiled at her image in the mirror, as she removed her makeup with cream. She was certainly no Hepburn, Audrey or Katharine. She peered at the tiny lines around her eyes that seemed to deepen and multiply every time she looked. She put on her pajamas and bathrobe, and went into the bathroom to brush her teeth and wash her face.

Closing the bathroom door but leaving the light on, she returned to her room and got into bed, turning on the bedside lamp. She put on her half glasses and picked up the most recent Faulkner novel, which she had diligently been reading, one chapter each night before bed. She found the sometimes convoluted sentence structure distracting. Why couldn't the man tell a simple story simply? She got up and opened the window a crack. Maybe some of that chilly air would keep her alert. Climbing back in bed, she found her place and started over.

It wasn't working. All she was doing was watching the enormous alarm clock by the bed as it ticked each minute. It made a snick each time the second hand moved, and the minute hand made a louder metallic click. Staring at it wouldn't make it move any faster.

What she needed was a more engrossing book, full of action and mystery. Like a good Agatha Christie. Glancing up every few sentences to check the time, hating the suffocating silence broken only by the loudly ticking clock, she yearned for a cigarette, but she refused to break her own rule about smoking upstairs, or after she'd brushed her teeth, or before she went to bed. Maybe she should get a small radio to keep her company. Trying to concentrate on the words, she vowed never to buy another William Faulkner novel as long as she lived.

Nine forty: close enough. She got out of bed, leaving the blankets and coverlet folded back and mussed. Then she grabbed her robe, and turned off the lamp and then the overhead light. Only the dim light leaking from under the bathroom door lighted the hall. She paused at the doorway to Lila's room, their room now, seeking Lila's eyes in the dark.

A month after their trip to Atlanta, Lila and Mary sat on the back porch. "There doesn't seem to be any reaction from the town about your living here, according to Annie. I think most people are glad that your being here prevents any of my relatives from trying to move in."

Mary put aside her Agatha Christie book. She enjoyed the color that had returned to Lila's cheeks, and the brightness in her eyes. "Yes, I think they view me as a paid companion of the sort they assume rich people are accustomed, if not entitled, to. I know that's what Buchanan would like. He'd much prefer that you take over running things, while I help Annie with the shopping and cleaning. He thinks he can control you."

Lila smiled at that. "Another false impression."

Mary did not like the grimness of the tone, but she made no comment. She wasn't up to another discussion about continuing the farce. She returned to her book to forestall it. Patience, she told herself. Gerald Buchanan had made several snide remarks about her new living arrangement. She did not see any point in telling Lila.

"I know you're being patient with me. I just need to think about everything for a while. It's like I'm replaying the past year in my head. I just haven't decided yet about work."

Though Lila held a seat on the bank's board of directors in her own right, she never attended the meetings now. That forced Buchanan to come to her at home. He probably thought this an excellent opportunity to bypass Miss McGhee's influence, but Lila didn't care.

"Now, then, Miss Lila, how're you doing today? I've brought some papers for you to look over. If we can use the dining room table, so I can sit beside you and explain everything, that would work out best."

Lila followed him into the dining room.

"If you'll look here, these are the documents that move all the joint Dubose accounts into just your name." He sorted through a sheaf of papers and held them out to her. "If you'll just sign here and here."

Instead of looking through the documents, she studied Buchanan. "I don't believe I will sign today, Gerald. Why don't you drop these papers off for Miss McGhee? Let her look through them."

Buchanan shifted nervously, holding up a hand to stop her. "Now, Lila, this doesn't concern Miss McGhee."

"I haven't the energy right now to read through everything. Miss McGhee will go through it all and we'll talk about it. We'll let you know."

Buchanan reached a decision of his own. "We don't need Mary McGhee's approval." Hesitating, he added, "I've warned you about that woman."

She smiled sweetly, sick of this game. "I'm sure I don't need anyone's approval, but I pay her for her advice."

Buchanan barely controlled a sneer. "Is that all you pay her for?" He stared at her, his eyes hard, and for a moment, Lila was frightened of him. "I'll do as you say then, and drop them off at the office. I'm sure you two ladies have better things to do in the evenings than study bank papers."

Lila met his coal black eyes. Her expression remained bland, but she felt her heart pounding. There was no mistaking the man's insinuation. She stared him down and after a moment he gathered his papers and left in a huff. She smiled as she thought of the forthcoming meeting with Mary.

Mary was not smiling when Buchanan appeared a few minutes later.

"I stopped by to say hello to Miss Lila. I must say, I would have thought by now she would be ready to take an active part in the business that belongs solely to her now. But she seems distracted, strange even—"

"Strange?"

"Practically snapped at me for no reason at all. And then ordered me to give these papers to you. This is bank business, and it has nothing to do with you. You'd think she'd show more concern now that everything is all hers, to do with as she sees fit."

"Mrs. Dubose is still recovering. It's only been four months, you know."

"Then again, she recovered enough to have you move in over there."

Mary resisted the urge to slap the snide attempt at an expression of disgust and disapproval right off his face. "It's possible you misunderstand my reasons for doing so."

"I don't believe I do." Buchanan sniffed. "Maybe she isn't thinking as clearly as she should. Maybe somebody's clouding her thinking. If she's still grieving, that seems to me like she would need to depend on her banker and perhaps her lawyer, who can better advise her about the serious business decisions she needs to be making. Instead she's leaning too much on the advice of someone who's just a hired nursemaid, after all." He stared at Mary, clearly challenging her.

"We are both employees of Mrs. Dubose, as far as that goes, now aren't we, Gerald?" Mary used his first name deliberately.

Buchanan stiffened. "I simply meant that I'm concerned. Maybe Miss Lila needs to see Dr. Morgan. It would be a shame for word to get around that she isn't well enough to make decisions and that somebody is *influencing* her to do things she shouldn't."

"I think Lila is capable of making her own decisions just fine."

Buchanan dropped the manila folder of papers on the desk. "People wonder, and they'll start to talk about what two women do, shut up in that house together every day. Every night."

Mary stood in the kitchen later with Annie, both of them looking out the window at Lila sitting on the back porch. She remembered Lila's

225

accusation that she had used her in the struggle with Buchanan. Mary felt that she was the one being manipulated now. Lila could have signed those papers; instead she had sent Buchanan running to her. And it rankled that what he had said was true: she was an employee.

"Annie, I want you to take the rest of the day off. I am going to have a talk with Mrs. Dubose that I think she would prefer no one else hear."

"About time. I've talked to her myself. Used to be I had nothing to do around here, Miss Lila did so much herself. Then we worked together when Mr. Tommie was sick. Now I could set this place on fire and she wouldn't say a word. Seems like she's always got her mind off someplace else."

A moment later, Mary heard Annie on the phone, arranging for a ride to Auntie Grace's. Then the front door closed behind her as she left. Mary watched the complete stillness in which Lila sat. Lila had changed. She was not the same spontaneous, delightful tease she had been at the beginning. Sparks of that Lila came only rarely now. Her beauty, which could still take Mary's breath away, now had a translucent, ephemeral quality. When they had first met Lila had seemed delicate and fragile, but now she was just frail and thin. The steel that had been hidden underneath was gone, replaced with an edginess that Mary thought was not entirely justified by grief.

She pushed open the screen door and went out. "Hey," she said, touching Lila on the shoulder as she sat down beside her. "I took the day off. I want to talk to you. Should we go inside?"

"No, let's sit out here. I can't stand being shut inside, whispering behind closed doors."

"You haven't had much at all to say to me lately."

"I know you're worried about me." Lila refused to look at her.

"I sent Annie off."

"So we're going to have a serious talk?"

Mary hesitated. Lila's directness always had the power to both charm and annoy. "There are some things I've been meaning to say ever since we came back from Atlanta. I feel like you've been drawing away from me. You wanted me to move in and so I did. But that doesn't seem to be enough for you. I had more of you when we lived apart, when Tommie was alive, than now."

Lila looked startled. "That's not true. It's just—"

"You seem to want me—us—to throw caution to the wind. To forget about what that might do. My living here has already made things much more difficult, you know."

Lila turned her chair to face Mary more directly. They looked into each other's eyes, and those gray eyes reminded Mary of the woman she had fallen in love with. They were clear and full of strength and delight and eagerness, but there was something more reflected in them now, a maturity and wariness.

Lila said evenly, "I understand that you feel the need for caution. I just don't let it dictate my life any more. I'm not the mindless girl you first met."

"Those clear, deep eyes," Mary said. "I used to be afraid to look into them, afraid you would see how much I felt for you."

Lila smiled, and Mary wanted to reach out and touch her, but she clasped her hands together tightly to resist the urge. She wished she had taken the time to change from her work clothes. She stood and kicked off her heels and removed her stockings. Mary sat back in her chair. "You know, when you accused me of using you, I couldn't believe it. And now you've completely withdrawn from the business. Buchanan is tired of going back and forth between us."

"He could use the exercise."

"If I moved in here to gain influence, then I've certainly lost that advantage. I could be stealing you blind and you'd never know it." This wasn't what she really wanted to say at all. "I miss you. I miss working with you."

"I thought you'd enjoy the freedom to make decisions without me slowing you down." Her tone was hard, controlled, as if she were trying to blunt the sarcasm.

Mary felt lost. She closed her eyes. How had they gotten so far apart? "You know, Lila, I didn't approach you to save you or free you or convert you. It was a selfish thing I did and it complicated your life. I simply couldn't help loving you, hadn't the strength to resist telling you." She stopped, frustrated again that she wasn't saying it right. She took a deep breath. "I want to be a real partner in the business, not a secretary. I don't want to feel like an employee any more."

Lila finally turned to her, surprised. She reached out her hand and touched Mary's cheek. "I want to feel like a partner too, and not just in the business." She paused. "Why have you never told me about the money Big Sam gave you when you left Houston?"

"What?" Mary was startled. "How did you find out about that?" She thought for a moment. "Buchanan. That's what's come between us. That bastard. I never told you because it was humiliating."

"Why did he pay you off, Mary?"

Mary laughed. "Are you asking me if I stole it from him?"

Lila's eyes turned a cloudy gray. "Did you? That story about you and Sammie 'moving' his money around, is that all you did?"

Mary sat down and studied Lila's face. In spite of the heat, she felt a decided chill. "I've always wondered if some of the money that was supposed to go to the ranch wound up in Sammie's pockets. But I didn't touch a penny of it."

"How can you be so casual about it? Could he have had you arrested for embezzlement?"

"Arrested? Maybe, but not for that. It's against the law for two women to sleep together. Don't you know that?" Mary felt an urge to shake Lila.

Lila's shoulders sagged. "Might as well get everything out in the open. Have you been diverting Dubose money, using it to finance loans to Negroes to buy back some of the timber land we're selling off?"

Mary sat even straighter. She tried to stay calm. "No, Lila, I haven't been stealing from you. I've used the payoff money from Big Sam to help people who Buchanan would never in a million years extend loans to. I can't believe that you would ever consider that I would do that to you." After a moment she continued. "This isn't a game, you know."

"I don't think it's a game. I just don't believe it's as deadly serious as you seem to think. We have a life together, you know. I don't want it to always be dictated by what Buchanan may know or what he may do. And then there's you. It seems as though you have to be locked into some kind of battle with him. I spend a great deal of my time worrying about you, arguing with you about things that are inconsequential. I don't want to have to wonder if we're on the same side."

"You also spend a lot of time placating, soothing, moving me along from one emotion to the next like a traffic cop. Have I stayed too long at the petulant, angry-over-nothing corner? Is it time now to move on?"

Lila grinned in relief. "Not at all. You may sit through the next light change if you like, and be mysteriously disturbed for no discernible reason for a while. I rather like your stern, dictatorial manner now and then."

Mary felt the ache in her chest begin to ease. "Yes, I imagine it's attractive to listen to a grown woman spout off and deliver mandates." She gathered Lila to her and inhaled her scent. "It's the heat, and Buchanan, both unendingly irritating. Both just suck the energy right out of me."

Lila lifted the hair from the back of her neck. "I suppose I'm used to both, having lived here all my life. You adjust to the heat, learn to move slower."

Mary hugged her tighter. "You're suggesting I take things slower with our favorite banker."

"Adapt to the way things are here, like the heat, the way things have always been. Take it a little slower, yes. It's not that I don't agree with you, it's just that sudden changes, like selling the mill, take some getting used to. Small, subtle increments may cause less stress, attract less notice, and give people time to accept them, that's all."

"Like the tortoise and the hare, slow and steady wins the race?" Mary shrugged out of Lila's arms. "But it's not a race. There's no one running except me."

Mary stood up, gazing into the yard. "I don't know why I didn't tell you. I was ashamed, I guess, that I took the money. And I'm not really sure of my motives in investing it in the colored school. Call it what it really is, guilt, because we, you and I, can hide what we are and escape the scorn and the backlash, and Lord knows, we have lied and pretended for years to be nothing more than friends. But they can't. They can't escape the color of their skin, they don't have the option we have, so simple, so easy, to just lie."

"So why lecture me about sending checks to the NAACP and the Sullivans as if that will expose us to harm when what you're doing, have been doing behind my back since you came here, is just as risky?" Lila said.

"Buchanan might suspect, but he doesn't know for sure."

"He knows enough. He knows you have a stash of money from Big Sam, and he knows, or thinks he knows, how you got it."

"Really? Well, Texas is just a phone call away. Why don't you call Sam Stewart and ask him yourself?"

Lila's eyes lit up. "Why didn't you ever tell me? Why let Buchanan inform me, in that sneering, nasty way of his? He made it sound like embezzlement or blackmail. Why let me be ambushed by him like that?"

Mary lifted her shoulders. "Maybe I've never been certain you'd believe me. I took the payoff, after all. I kept the money. I didn't throw it back in his face."

"Spending it all in support of the Negroes is throwing it in his face, and Buchanan's too, isn't it? Are you so unsure of me that you thought I wouldn't agree with you?"

"Maybe I was. I've never felt that you really supported me in this."

Lila hesitated. "Mary, listen. I was like that, willfully blind on this subject, for a long time. I'm ashamed that I ever believed that the Negroes liked the way things are. Then something happened. Back during the summer, when Tommie was so sick, one day I took Annie to her church to clean the sanctuary. This man approached us at the gas station and said the most awful things, insulting Annie, baiting her about the boycott, ordering her out of the car." Lila fell silent. She took a deep breath. "I did nothing. I just sat there, too shocked, too scared to defend Annie. I let that man talk to her like she was less than human. When Annie got home, I apologized, and we worked things out. That's when I started writing checks, sending money where I couldn't go, trying to help."

"Annie told me. She didn't want to but when I saw you two eating together I asked her. I figured you would tell me when you were ready. No more secrets?"

"No more secrets."

Part Three

Chapter Sixteen

REPORT TO THE GRAND DRAGON: Bull Connor up in Birmingham knows how to do it. Let 'em all out of jail, too, after he showed 'em who's boss. If you hit 'em enough times, all you have to do then is show 'em the whip and the gun. Attendance: 36

Friday, May 3, 1963

Mary stood among scattered boxes, packing tape, and numerous stacks of paper and files. "What brings you here?" she said to Lila with a look of pleased surprise on her face.

Lila looked for an empty chair to sit on. "I forgot just how stuffy it is in here. Won't it be nice to move?"

Mary was finally moving her office into the new hardware and lumber supply store next door after years of transition and phasing herself out and Scotch managers in while they upgraded equipment and rebuilt to suit a much larger operation. "I still wonder if the store manager is going to feel like I'm looking over his shoulder," she mused. "I suppose I could have an office at the bank, but then I'd have to deal with Buchanan every single day."

"We could fire him. You could take over the bank presidency," Lila said, half-joking.

Mary frowned. "We would lose most of our customers, and you know it."

"Who says a woman can't be a bank president? Where is that written?"

"In the rules of practical business, my lovely woman. It would kill the bank. Besides, I've spent years working around Buchanan. I'm used to him."

There were lines in Mary's face these days. She looked very tired. Lila sighed. "Maybe we could get him to run for mayor or something."

"He would love that. But he wouldn't give up his position at the bank. Maybe we could support him for the state senate next year."

"Promoting ignorance. Is that how all politicians get into that line of work?"

"One can only assume so."

Lila became serious. "Mary, do you want me to come back to work with you? You seem so down lately. Is there something going on that you haven't told me?"

Mary answered too quickly, "There's really not enough work to justify us both being in the office all day. You enjoy staying at home, don't you?"

Lila nodded. "I'm going to the grocery store. It's just the two of us for supper."

"Won't Annie stay and eat with us?"

"Didn't I tell you? She's gone back to Atlanta again. She won't be home until Monday."

Mary stood up and kissed her. "I'll see you at supper then."

Mary watched Lila through the window. She did miss having her in the office with her. But wishing she were still working wasn't enough to override her fear that if Lila came back to work, she would soon discover just how bad things had become. Buchanan had become much bolder since Lila was no longer there to force him to hide his disdain for them behind a thin veil of civility. Which reminded her, she owed him a phone call about an outlay of capital for the new store. Bracing herself, she dialed up the bank.

"Sherry, can you put me through to Mr. Buchanan?" Mary waited the usual five minutes for him to pick up, gritting her teeth.

"Hey, Mary. How you doing today?" Buchanan had adopted a hearty style of late that grated on Mary's nerves. He was trying too hard to be accepted as a good old boy. Maybe he really was focused on running for some political office. "Looks to me like you're going to keep that new hardware store in business all by yourself, if you have to keep replacing windows under the hill."

Mary swore silently. "I agree with you. Sooner or later, the kids who are doing it will get tired of acting on the suggestions I'm sure they hear from their elders and move on to some other kind of mischief." But she knew that kids weren't the only ones breaking windows.

"I was just going to call you. What's this about an extra two thousand for air conditioning? Who ever heard of air conditioning a hardware store? You could put some of those big industrial fans in there, save a lot of money. Get yourself one of those window air conditioners for your own office. No point in you sweating like a nigger—"

"Gerald, the air conditioning is for the customers. Carpenters and contractors will appreciate a cool place to do their figuring. These people work outdoors in the heat all day." She rubbed her head. Buchanan gave her a headache.

"Well, that's a fine idea for a dress shop, which ain't what you're running. Why don't you wait until after the first of the year? If you're still in business then, you can use some of the profit for that kind of extravagance."

"I'll put some of those fans in the ceiling then, like we had in the mill. They'll have to come from Mobile."

"That's more practical. How's Miss Lila? We don't see much of her these days. She doing all right?"

"She's fine. She's got the garden coming in. She keeps pretty busy."

"You tell her I said hey. You should feel pretty good. I just saved you two thousand dollars." Then he said, "I hope you saw the television news last night. Let that be a lesson about what can happen to outsiders poking their noses in our business."

A flash of pure anger burned through her; Mary wished she could reach through the telephone and strangle the smug son of a bitch. "Yes, I saw. You'd think someone would thank Bull Connor. He showed the entire country exactly how ugly this situation is."

"He was just doing his duty, controlling a mob, and showing those people they need to get back where they came from."

"And he's about to lose his job for it. You might want to consider that, before you encourage those brothers of yours with the white hoods toward instigating that kind of ugliness around here."

"I don't believe I need a woman, an *outsider*, telling me what to do." He hung up.

"You go," Lila said, pouring more tea. The knock had come at the back door, and as she was expecting Annie back from Atlanta, Mary went to the door, wondering why she didn't just walk in as usual. Lila looked around and saw Annie smiling, with a tall white man standing behind her.

"Miss Lila, Miss McGhee, ya'll meet Mr. Ben Powell. He's a friend of mine."

Mary put out her hand. "Nice to meet you, Ben. Can I get you some iced tea?"

Ben said, "No thank you, ma'am. I see you have coffee going. I'd appreciate some, if that's not too much trouble. I've got to drive back to Atlanta tonight." A sturdy frame held the man's height easily, along with well-muscled shoulders. He had graying hair that had not yet begun thinning, a ruddy face that looked accustomed to the outdoors, and a warm, firm handshake, thought Mary. He was a nice-looking man for his age, and she saw kindness in his blue eyes. Lila rose to get a cup, glancing with puzzled eyes at Mary.

Annie helped herself to some tea, moving in the kitchen with the familiarity of years, and joined them at the table. Ben jumped up to hold her chair. Mary smiled. That's how it was, then.

"Mr. Powell used to attend my son-in-law's A.M.E. church. That's how we got to know each other."

Ben interrupted. "Maybe I should explain. My wife, who passed away ten years ago, was a Negro. We weren't encouraged to attend my own church, so we became members of hers. It was less troublesome that way. I just kept going there after she passed. The Baptists weren't that forgiving of my marrying a colored woman, even after she was gone."

"I can't imagine that they would be," Mary said.

"Anyway, as it happens, I own a nightclub in Atlanta, and I heard Miss Annie saying how she'd like to hear some of the music like her son plays. I offered to take her. That's how we became ... friends."

"He even gets Sonny and his band to come down and play in his club sometimes. That's the only time I ever get to see my boy do his thing."

Mary thought Annie would just beam with pride, but she seemed subdued. "I know how proud you are of him. If he ever comes back, I'd like to hear him play myself," she said.

Mary noticed Mr. Powell and Lila eyeing each other. Lila seemed tense and even angry. She hadn't said a word.

"Lila and I've never known you to run from a fight, or care what other people think, Annie, so I don't know why you've kept Ben a secret from us. We're delighted for you—"

Lila stood up abruptly and went out the back door. Mary sighed. She and Annie shared a look. Mr. Powell cleared his throat.

"I believe I'll step out for minute and smoke, if you ladies don't mind."

Amazed, Mary watched him get up and follow Lila outside. She turned back to Annie and smiled.

"Oh, she'll be all right," declared Annie. "Let them be for a while. Ben has a way of charming people around to his way of seein' things. She'll come around. She's got a good heart." She clucked her tongue. "I declare, the two of you."

Mary laughed. "What about you? Ben's the secret of the century!" Then she grew serious. "So tell me, you're not going to marry this man and move to Atlanta, are you?"

Her smile faded as she saw the serious look on Annie's face. "He's been awful nice to me, and mighty patient, for years now. Ever since Mr. Tommie died, and you folks started going to the beach every weekend, he's been looking after me every time I went to Atlanta. Stood by me when my own daughter threw me out of her house, and that piss-ant son-in-law preached at me. You know yourself we could never live together here."

"It would be more than a couple of bricks through the window, wouldn't it?"

"You know it would. That decent man would be lynched, and me along with him. Baptists being so unforgiving and all."

Mary gave an unladylike snort. "Baptists? The men in white hoods, you mean. Though maybe some of them are one and the same."

"Hush up. Ben'll hear you and come rushing in, sayin' we ought to get married. He'd like nothing better than to have you on his side."

"I guess if you did get married and move, we could visit you there whenever we want. It's not that much further than driving to the beach."

"If we did, Miss Mary, ya'll would be just as welcome to relax at my house as you are in your own."

Mary nodded at Annie. Although she knew Annie had guessed about them, this was as close as she had ever come to admitting it out loud.

"Are you sure you and Ben won't get bricks through your windows in Atlanta?" She hesitated. "Just how involved are you and Ben in the civil rights movement, Annie?" Mary couldn't conceal how worried she was, or the fear she had felt like cold seeping into her bones.

She heard footsteps on the back porch, and Lila's voice. Apparently she and Ben were engaged in a fairly pleasant conversation, because she heard him laugh softly. The screen door squeaked as they came in.

"I can't be sure of anything, truth to tell. But folks have got used to him being more a part of our community than the white world, back in Atlanta. Ben's a mighty understandin' man, Miss Mary. He campaigned for Kennedy, you know. He's real involved in politics." Annie looked proud and even triumphant.

Of course, thought Mary. Lila and Ben sat down again as Annie continued her litany of praise. "He donated money, just like you did, back during the bus boycott. He even met Dr. King once and talked to him."

Ben managed to look both embarrassed and pleased to hear Annie brag about him. Mary grinned.

"Did you *see* what happened in Birmingham?" Mary regretted ever getting a television. She would never get the ugly images out of her head.

"We certainly did. I reckon the whole world sees now the kind of people we're up against," Ben answered.

Lila and Annie began their own conversation, about whether the peas and butterbeans would need to be replanted, while Mary and Ben, instantly comfortable with each other, continued to discuss the news.

The pleasant evening came to an end, and Annie went to her room after seeing Ben off for the return drive to Atlanta. Mary and Lila went upstairs to bed.

Lila's only comment after Mary joined her in bed was startling. "You know, I don't really like feeling as though you and Annie are shielding me, while you all man the front lines against the rudeness of our neighbors." Mary thought that it was much more than rude behavior, and much more than her neighbors involved, but she refrained from replying, instead folding Lila into their usual snuggling position as they drifted off to sleep.

Bobby Riser came out of the service bay wiping his hands on a rag. This was the third time that year Mary had taken her car to his service station. There was a grinding noise, again. Mary waited by the car, but he seemed disinclined to come closer. Behind him, she could see a couple of mechanics bending over the open hood of a truck.

"It's making the same noise as last time. Apparently whatever you did just made the problem worse."

"Women drivers is what it is. You just ride the brakes." Bobby stood there, in his neat striped coveralls, staring insolently, working a plug of chewing tobacco around in his cheek.

"Just fix it this time, all right?"

"Don't know as I'll be able to get to it right now." He grinned at her.

Mary stared pointedly at the empty bays. "I can see how busy you are."

Now Bobby crossed his arms. "I got to say, ya'll stickin' your noses in the school board business is mighty curious, seein' how neither one of you has any young 'uns."

So that was it. "We pay taxes, just like everybody else."

"Ain't no child of mine going to school with niggers. My girls ain't ridin' a bus with niggers. And this ain't none of your business." He took a step closer. Mary stood her ground. "Why don't you just go back up north where you come from? We don't have no use for people like you around here, you know? You don't belong."

Now he was even closer. She could smell his body odor, a mixture of motor oil, cheap shaving lotion, and sweat. Mary looked him in the eye. "If you don't want to work on the car, I'll take it to Thomasville or Mobile."

Bobby turned red in the face. "You think you something, running the Dubose business, telling Lila Dubose what to do, and she just does it like a trained dog. Givin' half that money away to niggers. Ya'll

239

do whatever you want, shut up in that house together. This is my property, and you ain't got no say about what I do. You just take your fancy car and go on to Mobile. Like I said, we don't need your kind around here."

He spat and the spittle landed on her shoe. Mary looked down at the brown glob. She looked up at him and saw a wild edginess in his eyes, like he was about to lose the remainder of his self-control. She slowly opened the car door and backed up, never taking her eyes off him. One of the other mechanics came to stand beside him as she pulled away, holding a lug wrench in his hand. As she drove away, she irrelevantly wondered why he thought her thirteen-year-old Chevrolet "fancy."

"For the tenth time, it's my money, isn't it?" Lila appeared ready to explode.

"It most certainly is your money, all of it." Mary refrained from cursing, which she thought demonstrated remarkable self-control.

"And I can spend it as I see fit." Lila's eyes were dark with anger. Mary'd never met anyone whose eyes changed as much as Lila's. Of course, Lila was rarely this angry. "The county claims they can't comply with the court order to bus the black students to the high school because they don't have enough buses. I'm simply solving that problem for them," she went on in an incredulous tone.

There's nothing simple about it, thought Mary. "The board says that they don't have enough buses because they refuse to put black and white students on the same bus. I thought they solved that issue in Montgomery."

"Mary, I know that's what they're doing. They also claim they can't find a driver who's willing to go down under the hill and pick up the black students."

Myrtlewood, and the county, was digging in its heels at desegregation, its hour come round at last, thought Mary, using a line from her favorite poem. "Your pointing out to them that they could hire the drivers who worked for the black school district for years did not go far in soothing tempers either."

Lila began to pace back and forth, something Mary had never seen her do. She lost the will to argue with Lila, fascinated by the fire and the agitation and the passion Lila displayed. In the public meeting, Lila had worn the silk suit she had purchased in Atlanta and had been sweet reason itself, offering solutions to every objection, real or blatantly obstructive, that the board and several incensed citizens had made. What really offended Lila was that Buchanan had publicly gone toe to toe with her. His deliberate insolence, after years of feigned respect, had shocked her, Mary knew. She herself was not surprised. Buchanan was positioning himself for a run for office in '64. He had to distance himself from the two of them, whose reputation as liberal agitators would not help him.

"Maybe we should calm down," suggested Mary. "However much they refused you in public, the board has never been stupid enough to turn down your money." She sighed.

Lila stopped pacing and faced Mary. "What would happen if I pulled all my money and used a bank in Mobile?"

Mary considered her answer. "You'd be a lot happier and so would I. But this bank would fail."

"And would that be so bad? How long have the Duboses kept this town running?"

It would be disastrous for Lila to withdraw from the bank, but the idea of Buchanan no longer knowing their every financial move so appealed to her that she wondered what would happen if she withdrew just a portion of their cash on deposit and banked it in Mobile, like she had done with her private funds for years. He wouldn't be looking over her shoulder any more. They would be free of him. They could do whatever they wanted.

"Mary, what do you think?"

"I think you know you can't do that with all your money. But we can with some of it." If they opened an account in Mobile, Lila could funnel the money she used for charity and political donations through that account. It could work, and it might get Buchanan out of their hair. "You know how the car's been acting up," Mary went on, changing the subject. "I think I might take it to Mobile and trade it for a new one."

Lila sat down. "What's wrong with it this time?"

"I really don't know. 'Could be this, could be that,' according to

Bobby Riser. I swear I believe that man is sabotaging the car, making things go wrong with it."

Lila looked shocked. "You don't seriously think that?"

Mary shrugged. "I do. He's a redneck, and he owes the bank from when he bought his daddy out of the business. He listens to all the men who wear suits and ties spouting the same racist rhetoric down at the diner every morning and he thinks he's gaining approval for any trouble he causes the two unnatural, trouble-making 'nigger lovers.'" Mary wished for nothing more than a good, strong drink. "Hell, they're probably all members of the Klan, Lila. Buchanan is probably their Grand Wizard, or whatever the hell they call it."

"But I've known Bobby Riser all my life."

Mary just looked at her. "So? He used to take care of our cars with the devotion of a zealot. I guess he just found another cause to embrace more fervently than car engines. The last time I went down there, he refused my business. He said he wasn't going to have any 'young 'un' of his going to school with black children, only he didn't say it that way. He actually spat on me."

"What?"

Mary smiled wearily. "The next time I read the phrase 'spewing venom' I'll know exactly what the writer means."

"I can't believe it. What's happening to this town? Has everyone gone mad?"

Lila's shocked tone of mild disapproval was wearing on her nerves. "It's the same thing that's happening everywhere, Lila. It's a fine thing to give money to causes you believe in, but on a personal level, people get angry and they take revenge, however petty and mean-spirited that sounds. I've tried to tell you that for years."

Chapter 17

REPORT TO THE GRAND DRAGON: Now we got a true Southerner in the White House. Maybe he'll behave better than that Roman Catholic rich boy. That little squirrel that killed him ain't one of us, he's some kind of commie. That was quite a shot he made though. Got to admire that.

Monday, November 25, 1963

Mary didn't feel much like celebrating the holiday; there was very little she could find to be thankful for. Lila had convinced her to come to the beach, perhaps hoping they could recapture some of the old sense of fun and escape for the holiday week, but they heard the awful news on the radio on the drive down. On Saturday Mary drove into Mobile to buy a television so that they could watch the president's funeral.

The screen door squeaked and scraped as Mary pushed it open. She sat down in the chair next to Lila. "I've got to fix that door or replace it," she said.

"You're not going to start on one of your repair frenzies, are you? I thought we were just going to rest on this trip."

Mary lit a cigarette. "I need something to do. I just can't get over his little boy saluting when the casket passed by."

"I prayed for the first lady and her children. Why do you think they did this?"

Mary looked at Lila. "Because some people are just mean. They do mean things. They hated what he was trying to do."

"He was so young. You don't think of someone so young dying."

Mary's anger boiled over. "He didn't die, he was shot and killed. Somebody murdered the president, because they disagreed with what he was doing. Don't you understand yet that sometimes people aren't nice, they don't mind their manners, they act on mean and nasty impulses?"

Lila stared at Mary. "Of course I do. You won't focus on the human loss of a father and a husband, because you'd rather think about political implications and plots and evil and how it's impossible to defeat it. It's not impossible, Mary, and every time you refuse to confront it, they win without a fight."

Mary just shook her head. Lila sighed and continued,"This has nothing to do with us and what's happening to us. You know that."

"No, I don't. You know that ever since Martin Luther King's speech in Washington, things have gotten worse for us. It got the rednecks all stirred up again."

"I know that. It's a small town. Staying at home doesn't mean I'm cut off from what goes on. Miss Louise knows more than anybody about what's happening and she never leaves her front porch."

Mary grabbed her cigarettes and went back outside.

Lila took her sweater from the back of her chair and shrugged into it. She set off for a walk. She didn't want to hear anything more about rules and giving in to fear, nor any more of Mary McGhee's anger. After about a mile, well out of sight of the cottage, she sat down on the sand. She remembered a time when she had thought Mary was the bravest person she had ever known. If someone broke your window, you simply fixed it, and you kept on. She supposed some people might move, or put bars on their windows, or get a gun. To her mind, that was only escalating the situation. She didn't want to live that way. Besides, a gun wouldn't have helped Mrs. Evers. All the guns in the world hadn't helped Jacqueline Kennedy.

She knew that Mary kept her from going back to work because things had gotten so ugly. She could no longer walk to and from work without risk of confrontation. But Lila had taken real inspiration from Dr. King's speech in August. Parts of it still rang in her head. She wanted to be judged by the content of her character too. She believed that the hope talked about in his speech included people like her and Mary. Sometimes, it just took one person willing to stand up and speak. Mary seemed to think that what one person did was ineffective against a group mentality.

The sun went behind the clouds, and for a moment she felt a chill. She glanced up, and saw that it was later in the day than she had thought. The Gulf water was sluggish today, a dull, almost muddy color. Though it grew cloudy, the waves didn't have that energy that suggested a storm. Instead of angry whitecaps there were syrupy sloshes that sucked rather than slapped at the beach. The sky and the sea seemed to have taken on Mary's mood, a sullen, angry, dissatisfied feeling that affected everything around it. She smiled at the thought of the weather mirroring Mary McGhee's moods.

Lila walked back to the cottage, where Mary was sitting outside waiting for her, the ashtray next to her filled. Silently Mary followed Lila inside. She closed the door behind them, and watched Lila pull her sweater over her head and turn down the bedspread. Mary pulled down the shades, turning as Lila began to unzip her pants. She gathered Lila to her, inhaling her scent, burying her face in her hair, letting tension drain away as Lila's hands moved over her back.

She stood very still as Lila ministered to her, with eyes closed, and felt familiar hands easing her into that place where only this could take her, where her mind turned off and she became something else. Something more than clothing was shed every time their skin met; everything was reduced to feeling and the smooth sliding of skin against skin, hands, lips, tongues. She molded Lila to her, suddenly frantic to get to that place, kissing her deeply, pushing her back toward the bed. Certain they would not get there in time, she knelt, and Lila's hand came to the back of her head, and now the anticipation of that taste in her mouth made her salivate with the need for it.

She couldn't hear the sounds that Lila made, couldn't hear her own moans and whimpers, as she sought and found the place where her tongue felt rough against velvet, where her fingers found a perfect fit, a place of wetness and heat, where there was nothing but smell and taste and feel and blood rising, heart pounding, no words, no thoughts except one. It was orchestrated and followed its own arc, rising up and up, and the heat and wetness increased. Perspiration formed and rolled down her back, and muscles tensed and strained against some benevolent force, and Lila's fingers gripped her hair, and everything stilled; there was a pause, as if they had reached the top of a long climb, and then everything began to fall. Shuddering with the uncontrolled downhill slide, Mary became conscious of gasping for breath, and felt tremors in her legs, in Lila's hands that refused to loosen their grip on her hair. The pounding in her ears subsided and she heard Lila now, sighing, moaning a soothing sound. Mary turned her face and rested her cheek on Lila's thigh. Lila released her hair, and Mary put out a hand to help her keep her balance. Lila squeezed it, using it for support as she took a step backward and collapsed on the bed. Mary sat on the floor and leaned against the bed, breathing heavily. They remained like that for a long time.

A week later, they had a new car, another Buick, this time a Roadmaster. It seemed as indestructible as a tank and Lila loved it. Mary had a meeting with Buchanan at the bank. She walked over, carrying her papers and notes. As expected, the car was his first topic.

"I saw the new automobile. That's a mighty fine car. Nicer than my old Ford. Too big for a single woman, idn't it?"

"I like it."

"I bet you do. I was a little hurt when you didn't get the financing from us. How'd you convince Lila to trade her car along with yours? That leaves her without a vehicle."

"Actually, the new car is hers. I walk as often as I can, you know. It's my only exercise."

"Still, I almost took offense that you didn't go through the bank."

"I paid cash."

"I know you did. Well, you've got a lot of money sitting in that savings account of yours. No matter what you did to earn it, you can do what you want with it, but it would have been smarter to take a loan on the car."

Enough about the car, thought Mary. "Well, if we decide we need another car, maybe you can talk Lila into taking out a loan for it."

"How's she doing? I never see her any more, seems like. Hope she didn't get her feelings hurt at the school board meeting. Miss Lila ought to know not to poke her nose in public affairs like that."

"Lila didn't 'get her feelings hurt,' as you put it. She was angry at the blind determination to try to avoid complying with a federal court order."

246

"I just thought she might be a little embarrassed, trying to get involved in the situation with integration and all that. Seems like she never leaves the house any more. People start to wonder, you know."

"No, I really don't know. Lila is free to do what she wants, to come and go as she pleases, just like everyone else."

"Don't get your dander up. I didn't mean to get you all riled up. People just might start thinking there's something wrong, with her never leaving the house. She doesn't even go to church any more."

"Lila didn't appreciate some comments made from the pulpit about her giving money to the A.M.E. church."

"Everybody knows those churches are raising money for the NAACP. Maybe it would help if I paid her a visit, talked to her about how charity begins at home. People get the wrong idea, with her giving money to colored folks like she does."

And people wouldn't know nearly as much about what Lila does or does not do with her money if it weren't for you. Mary barely kept a polite expression on her face.

"Lila has never made a show of how she spends her money, and you know it."

"You should listen to me. I'm trying to help you here."

"You're trying to warn me. Perhaps you should speak to Lila. I don't really have any say in how she spends her money. It's none of my business. I suggest that it's none of yours, either."

Buchanan sneered. "We both know that woman don't make a move without you telling her what to do. She won't spend a dime unless you agree to it. You say jump, she asks how high."

Chapter Eighteen

REPORT TO THE GRAND DRAGON: *The whole world's gone crazy. I can't believe they gave that black pansy the Nobel Prize. We shoulda taken care of him while Bull Connor had him locked up. Tell you one thing, we are going to get our own back. We'll start right here at home. Attendance: 30*

Tuesday, January 26, 1965

Mary and Lila sat almost dozing in the comfortable chairs on the back porch, the recently installed ceiling fans motionless overhead. Mary was the first to startle fully awake when the phone rang.

Lila stirred and rose. "I'll get it. I'm falling asleep out here anyway." She was gone only a minute, and came back looking concerned. "It's for you."

Mary went inside, the central hallway cool and dark until her eyes adjusted from the bright sunlight.

"Mary, dear, Miss Louise appears to have had a stroke," Dr. Morgan said.

Mary pressed a hand to her chest. "Oh, no. I'll be right there." She hung up the phone and hurried back to the porch.

"I have to go. It's Miss Louise. She's had a stroke or something. Does she have any family at all? I've never heard her speak of any."

"None that I know of. That poor old lady! Call me if there's anything I can do."

Mary posed the same question to the doctor, who looked up as she came into the old woman's bedroom. The once-talkative busybody lay silent in the darkened bedroom, shades pulled against the afternoon sun. Her face was slack. A line of drool was drying even as it slid down her cheek toward her ear. The doctor gently wiped it away with his handkerchief. She had died before Mary got there.

248

"I'm certain there was no one," Dr. Morgan said. "She was an only child, and a strange old bird. Her life was keeping up with everybody in town. Our official town crier. Knew everything about everybody. Told me my wife was pregnant before I could get home to hear it from her myself." Dr. Morgan smiled at the memory.

Mary found herself smiling through tears as she gazed down at the face deeply creased with wrinkles, most prominent around the eyes that had shone so bright with interest. Those inquisitive eyes were closed now. "Yes. She always stopped me on my way in, wanting to hear everything about my day at work. She thought I couldn't hire or fire anyone unless she gave me a complete dossier on them, including family background to the third generation, though I never understood how that determined whether a man could do the work."

"Sometimes she'd feed me dinner. It was just like my mama used to make," Dr. Morgan said, as he peered at Mary. "Until I met Miss Louise, I thought my mama was the worst cook in the world."

Mary tried to laugh, but it ended in a choked sob. "She was, you know. If I didn't cook the meal, or bring her a plate from the Duboses, I'd find her eating Saltine crackers and sardines in front of the radio. Maybe that's why she never married."

Dr. Morgan gave Mary a strange look. "Her parents kept her at home."

Mary turned from the frail figure in the bed to the doctor. "You don't mean—locked up in her own home?"

"Yes, I do mean just that. Everybody knew. She was only permitted to go as far as the front porch, so there she sat, indulging the only passion she could—knowing everybody's business. I almost fell out when I saw her at Mr. Tommie's funeral." Dr. Morgan studied Mary for a minute. "The way I heard it, apparently Miss Louise had a 'special friend' when she was young. You're a keen judge of character, I should think you'd have guessed that about her."

"I don't know what you mean." Mary avoided his eyes. She knew exactly what he meant.

Dr. Morgan sat down in the only chair in the room. "Sometimes people like to talk to their doctors about personal matters more than to their ministers or lawyers. Miss Louise asked my advice some time ago about her will. I witnessed it for her. I believe it's in the dresser drawer over there. She left her house to you."

Mary flinched as if she'd been struck. "She didn't do that."

"Miss Louise has known for some time that her health was deteriorating. She appreciated your companionship." Now the doctor was studying Mary frankly. "She admired you, always bragging to everyone who would listen about what a whiz you are at business."

"I had no idea. When I lived here, most of the time I tried to avoid her. She ran on so much. I can't accept this from her."

Dr. Morgan patted her hand. "I'm afraid you'll have to. She was a very lonely old woman, my dear. You were one of the few people who still stopped by to visit. I suspect you gave her something she longed for all her life."

Mary felt stunned, and ashamed. She needed to talk to Lila about this. She turned to regard the doctor. He had implied that he understood about her and Lila. In a way, it was a relief that he knew. Dr. Morgan was more astute than most.

She returned the doctor's open stare, for the first time really seeing him. His hair was as white as cotton, and his cheeks as pink with glowing health as a child's. He was dressed in his usual seersucker suit and bow tie, and his small hands and feet also called up an image of a cherub, or a Puck, she thought absurdly. He peered at her over his half glasses, as though waiting for her to say something.

"What about her funeral? Who is there to see to that?"

"I believe that falls to you. I'll speak to Wayne Latham—he handled Mr. Tommie's funeral—and get him to send the hearse." He paused. "Miss Louise loved gospel music. You might want to include the church choir in your plans."

"It's a God damn Buick Roadmaster. The damn thing is like a Sherman tank! It's practically new. There couldn't be anything wrong with it." Mary stood with the sun beating down on her, the sunglasses she wore doing little to relieve her eyes of the glare, nor to disguise her anger.

"Ma'am, I'm just telling you, if you drive that car like it is, you'll have a wreck. The brake lines are leaking. It's jerkin' and pullin' real hard to the right. You sure you ain't bounced over some curbs or somethin' like that?"

"Of course I haven't. I can drive." Mary watched the greasy young mechanic nervously wiped his hands on a dirty red rag. She took a deep breath. It wasn't his fault. "Do you know how this happened?"

"I don't rightly know. You got less than two thousand miles on her. Maybe Mr. McGhee has been runnin' it on some rough roads, like out in the woods? There's a hole in your oil pan."

"There is no Mr. McGhee. You mean someone has been doing something to the car, don't you?"

"Well, now, I didn't say that."

Mary stared at the man. "Never mind. Can you fix everything today?"

"Should be able to."

"I'll be back in a couple of hours to see if you're done." She hesitated, then said, "Save all the parts you replace, all right? I want to have a look at them."

Mary bought a *Mobile Register* and sat in a diner, trying to read. She should feel reassured that the new president was trying to continue Kennedy's ideas, but she didn't. Johnson made her feel uneasy, as though he was always thinking of something other than what he was actually saying. Buchanan always gave her that same feeling. She folded the paper and left it on the counter.

These were the same problems she had had with the old car. She'd thought that using a garage in Mobile would put an end to the mysterious problems. This was deliberate and Mary blamed Bobby Riser. Battery cables had been loosened. Air let out of a tire. The distributor cap had been cracked. A puncture in the sidewall of a tire. A hole in a radiator hose. She talked to Sheriff Dunagan about it, but he couldn't keep an eye on their vehicle twenty-four hours a day. Mary had been sneaking out of the house early on shopping days to check it and make sure everything was okay before Lila drove to the grocery store across town.

The car wasn't the only target. Their outside garbage can had its contents emptied and strewn all over the yard. Windows in the car shed were smashed. Anything left outside mysteriously disappeared— rakes, lawn chairs, even the lawn mower. Mary had bought a padlock for the car shed, boarded up the windows, and locked everything inside. As she drove home, she composed a story to convince Lila this latest trip to the garage had been simply a product of the anxious pride of new ownership.

Mary came out of the study with the bank statement in her hand. Lila looked up from the *Life* magazine she was reading, saw what was about to happen, and smiled, hoping to distract Mary from her monthly lecture on entering every check in the register.

"Hey. Want some tea? We could go sit on the back porch."

Mary sat down and said, "No, Lila, your checking account is a mess."

"Why don't you leave the statement to me? I'll enter all the checks I've written and balance it. You shouldn't have to deal with it."

"It'll go faster if we do it together. I'll call out the check number and the amount, you can enter it in the register in your checkbook, and then we'll have a true balance to reconcile with your statement."

Lila got her tea glass and stood up. "I'm going to get some more tea. Sure you don't want some?"

"We need to get this done. If you would just enter each check when you write it, at the end of the month we wouldn't have this to deal with."

Lila sat down, tea glass forgotten. "Mary, it's my statement, my checking account. You don't need to do this. Really." She tried to keep from gritting her teeth and forcing the words out.

"I'm just trying to show you how much simpler and easier it is if you would—"

"I know how to fill out the check register, and I know how to balance my bank statement. You taught me, remember?"

Mary looked surprised. "Then why don't you do it? All it takes is a few minutes, not even that long, to just enter each check as you write it and deduct it from your balance."

Lila resisted the impulse to pour her melted ice and tea over Mary's head. "I said, it's my checkbook and my statement, and I'll take care of it, okay?"

Mary looked confused. "Why are you getting angry? I'm just trying to help get it straightened out. I know you know how to do this. Maybe you just got behind, but if I help you, it will be caught up."

"I really don't need any help balancing my bank statement. Really, sweetheart. Just put it on the desk and I'll do all by myself, like a big girl."

Mary's expression changed from surprised to shocked. "I didn't mean to imply that you couldn't do this yourself. I know you can. But the fact remains, it hasn't been done. So let's just roll up our sleeves for a few minutes and get it tidied up."

Something inside Lila just gave way, like a leak in a damn that had finally worn a hole, through which roared a great rush of water, forcing the crack wider and wider. "You don't seem to be hearing me. I asked you to set it aside and go on to something else. Why don't you go help someone who really needs it? I can handle a simple bank statement."

Mary stood up. "Lila, you're being unreasonable. I'll leave this for you on the desk, then. Just don't let it go too long."

"I'll do it when I please. Or maybe not at all. I'm not overdrawn, am I? And just what would happen if I were? Don't you think Gerald would cover the overdraft? I'm betting he would."

"I know he would. *Gerald* would do anything for you. And then he'd call me to gloat and to crow about how I allowed this to happen, and maybe I'm not doing such a good job after all."

"That's typical of you. Everything is a potential excuse for a battle with Buchanan, your favorite sport. You are so controlling and arrogant. Why can't you accept that I'm perfectly capable of handling my own account? And that I'll do it in my own way, whenever I feel like it?"

"You're blowing this all out of proportion. Please calm down."

"I'm blowing this out of—I can't believe you said that. Mary, you're the world champion at exaggerating the danger in the most innocuous things. And you have the most infuriating habit of not listening to me. Do you really think I'm so stupid I can't balance my checking account? Why do you go behind my back and check it each month? Gerald's knowing my every expenditure doesn't bother me half as much as your going through my statements as though you have a right to do so."

Mary's voice was icy and quiet. "I didn't know you thought of it as an invasion of your privacy. I thought it fell within the scope of my *job* duties."

"As if this was actually just a job for you. It's a crusade. And I'm sick and tired of being treated as though I constantly need rescuing, or protecting."

"What are you talking about?" Mary seemed genuinely puzzled.

"Mary, it's time we changed the way we do business. You're not my teacher any more. I'm not your student. I am your lover, and we are equal partners in this relationship. We live together, honey. You're not here to look after me, to oversee my every move and approve my every decision. You're here because I love you and I want to live with you."

"I do not treat you like an apprentice."

"I've seen you sneak out early in the morning to check the car before I get behind the wheel. You think I don't have the sense to do that myself? I realize these are dangerous times and we need to be cautious. I can take care of myself. I don't need you to hide things from me."

"Lila, sweetheart, you don't know how ugly things can get. You just don't see it."

"And that's another thing. I'm constantly hearing 'Lila, you're just too innocent, too delicate, for the harsh realities of the situation.' That's just hogwash. I grew up here. I know exactly how these people are and what they are capable of. I'm not the innocent, naive girl you met in 1948. I grew up. I learned, Mary. And it's time for you to stop treating me like a child."

"You are too innocent for your own good. If I weren't so cautious, the Klan would have long since dropped by here." Mary was angry.

"Really? Your vigilance is the only thing holding off the angry hordes? How arrogant! The great Mary McGhee stands alone in the face of evil and holds it at bay."

Mary shot her a look of pure fire, her blue eyes snapping with anger. She left the room without another word. Lila sank down into her chair. Well, that certainly cleared the air, she thought. Lila already regretted half of what she said, and she knew that when Mary came back, they would apologize and make up and things would stay the same. Mary was incapable of seeing what she was doing, incapable of changing. Lila picked up the phone.

Mary thought, as they sat on the little porch at the cottage, that maybe they were getting too old to sit on the beach like they once did. She looked at Lila. Her flawless complexion, her clear gray eyes, hair wildly out of control: she still looked the same, not a day older than when they had first met. She smiled.

"Why are you staring?"

"I was just thinking, I'm getting wrinkles, and you still look the same."

Lila laughed. "You're joking. Love is blind, so they say."

Mary shook her head. "No, you really do look just like you did when I first met you."

Lila shook her head and returned to her study of the bay. It was a cloudless day, the endless blue of the sky merging with the horizon, seabirds circling overhead, and rolling waves coming in with mesmerizing efficiency. Mary sighed in contentment, recalling how she had once fantasized about living at the cottage permanently.

"You know, we could tear down this little place and build a real house here."

Lila looked shocked. "Don't you dare. There's too many memories here. We can add on, if you want, but I'll never tear it down. Someday we'll put up a plaque on the door, commemorating the place and time I lost my virginity."

Mary burst out laughing. "It wasn't lost."

Chapter Nineteen

REPORT TO THE GRAND DRAGON: Yes sir, they're all stirred up down here too, ever since that nigger boy gut shot by a state trooper in Marion died. Some kind of gathering is being planned, with white folks helping niggers. We're watching. Attendance: 32

Saturday, March 6, 1965

Opening the front door, Mary almost squealed. "Sammie Stewart! I can't believe it." She hugged her old friend to her tightly. "My God, it's been years. What are you doing here?"

Sammie's familiar husky laugh sounded in her ear. "Just passing through. You know me, I just jump in the car on a whim and see where I end up."

Mary couldn't let go of her. "It's really you." She inhaled deeply, the scent of perfume, fresh air, and something indefinably Sammie. Finally she let go and stepped back, holding Sammie's hands, and inspected her. Sammie's blond hair was shot through with silver strands, her deeply tanned face suggested lots of time spent outdoors, and tiny wrinkles around her eyes made her seem perpetually amused. She was dressed in a brown twill Eisenhower-style jacket over a white blouse, with tan slacks and expensive but scuffed brown loafers. Her figure was still whipcord thin. Mary pulled on Sammie's hand.

"Come inside and sit down. We have so much to catch up on." Leading Sammie into the study, the room in which Mary was most at home, she sat beside her on the old sofa from the mill office. "Now, start talking. How are you?"

Sammie laughed again. "Still bossy. Same old Mary. I'm fine, in fact, I'm great. I took the advice of a dear friend and went home to the ranch. I've been there a few years now."

Mary smiled. "And everything's working out for you?"

"Well, Big Sam didn't kill me or lock me up, if that's what you mean. He's actually a little afraid of me, I think, always wondering if I'm going to take off again. He just doesn't know what to expect from me, I guess."

"No one ever does with you." But Mary could feel something entirely new with Sammie. She seemed to parody her old self, as though mocking it, or as if she couldn't quite let go of the rowdy, wild girl she had been. What a nice thing, she thought, to stay on friendly terms with the person one used to be.

Sammie leaned back and crossed one ankle over her knee. "He sold the oil business, you know. Big Sam's not as robust as he was." She looked at Mary. "He's old now. He had a stroke. That shocked me. He sits on the porch at the ranch, while Red and I run around busy as all get out. He's just this frail old man now."

Mary could not quite imagine Sam Stewart as anything other than large, gruff and abysmally clueless, operating on full speed and little things like forethought and planning and consideration be damned. She couldn't picture him quietly letting life go by.

Finally she spoke, realizing that a silence that had fallen while they both thought about the man who had caused each of them such grief. "It must be hard for you to see him like that."

"I don't know. Sometimes I sit there with him, and just talk. We had some fine arguments in the beginning. Now, it's like he doesn't have the energy for it."

Mary could not foresee a time when arguing with Lila would seem pointless, not worth the effort. "Let's talk about you. I've truly never seen you looking better."

"Thank you. You look pretty good to me too. All harried and overworked, stressed, distracted, as if you had the whole world to save and not enough time."

"Sometimes it feels just like that. I can't even save my small part of the world from going crazy. So you're running the ranch? And what did you do with all the money from the sale of the business?"

"See what I mean? You really haven't changed a bit, have you? All business, nothing personal. I bought a little company that makes an electrical thing for the space program. I was on my way to Huntsville to see about it. Just swung by here on a whim to see you."

"An electrical thing for NASA?"

"Yes, I should know more about it. It has to do with the guidance systems on the rockets they're building. That's all I know. That's why I thought I'd drop in on them, try to educate myself. See, I did learn a little from you."

"But you can stay the night, at least? We have a lot of talking to do."

"No, I have to be in Huntsville first thing in the morning. How have you been? I guessed that you'd be here, in the Dubose house. I bet that really got tongues wagging."

"I moved in after Tommie died. You got the letter, right?" Sammie nodded. "Lila insisted."

"I just bet she did. And how is the lovely Lila these days?"

"Still lovely, feisty, stubborn as hell. She's out right now, some-where in the car with Annie." Mary tried to keep the anger out of her voice, but Sammie caught it.

"So who is Annie and why do you think they shouldn't be going 'somewhere' together?"

"Annie is our maid, she's worked for the Duboses for a long time, and Lila has taken leave of all her senses. She's decided to give Annie my old house on Main Street, right in the middle of town, and they're off buying paint and curtains." Mary clenched her jaw muscles.

"Don't hurt yourself. I'm sure they can choose paint colors without your help and advice."

Mary got up, impatient with herself and with Sammie's lack of understanding. "Come on. Let's go for a ride. I'll show you around town."

"Okay. Slow down." Sammie trailed behind as Mary gathered cigarettes and a lighter, stuffed them into her purse, and headed for the door. She needed some fresh air.

Standing beside Sammie's Thunderbird, Mary said, "Can I drive? There's some things I'd like to show you."

"Sure." Sammie tossed her the keys and Mary slid behind the wheel, the heavy door closing with a satisfying thunk.

Easing through town, Mary slowed and stopped beside Dubose

Hardware. "This is all that's really left of the old Dubose Lumber Company where the mill office was. I worked there for a long time." The wood-framed building that had housed her office had in fact been torn down. They were simply staring at the spot where it once stood. In its place was the new hardware supply store. Mary pulled away and drove on.

"This is the bank." The monstrosity of granite and marble sat in the middle of town.

Mary felt unsettled and uncertain just what she was doing. Sammie didn't care about a tour of the town. She turned down the street where the pavement ended at the beginning of the colored settlement, slowing for the bump, and drove slowly down a dirt road to under the hill.

Despite her slow investment over the years, buying one shack at a time and repairing it virtually from the ground up, it was a singularly depressing sight that reminded Mary of coal miners in the hollows of West Virginia. The few houses that were painted usually sported garish shades of pink or green, even purple, in a vain effort to supply some lifting of the pervasive atmosphere of poverty that began almost immediately once one began the descent down the hill.

Only the church showed signs of careful upkeep. Mary stopped the car. "Walk with me."

"Okay." Sammie followed Mary on her way through the cemetery next to the church.

"An old Negro man who claims to have been born into slavery made most of the unique headstones himself and carefully tends the graveyard. Sammie, look at this one here." A mother, she supposed, with a small child under each of her outstretched arms. Some of the graves were outlined with pieces of broken colored glass.

"Someone took a lot of care with all this. Are they just effigies or are some of these actually death masks? Look at the expressions."

"I really don't know. The attention to detail is amazing though, isn't it?" She looked around. It was so quiet. "I like it here. I always stop when I come through and walk around. Listen, I've got someone I want you to meet." Mary went back to the car. Sammie took her time, obviously moved by the loving care demonstrated by the neatly maintained plots. Huge oaks draped in moss lined the churchyard and cemetery, lending an eerie, almost ominous atmosphere to the place.

Mary drove back up the hill, back onto the paved road, and headed across the river bridge. The top was down on the convertible, and their hair blew wildly in the air, but Mary didn't mind the chill. Just past the end of the guard rail after the bridge, she turned left onto another dirt road. She turned off the engine after she pulled into Thad's yard. She sat for a minute, trying to see as Sammie would the neat cabin with its board-and-batten siding, painted white, the wooden shutters open over the windows that now had real paned glass in them, the well in the side yard; the "swept" yard lined with yellow jonquils already blooming along with cannas and irises. The mule leaned his weight against the fence, and nodded and snorted a greeting.

She and Sammie got out and stood, not saying anything. If Mary had been alone, she would have gone up the steps and knocked on the open door, but with a stranger in tow, she waited until someone came to see who they were.

Janie came bustling out, drying her hands on her apron. "Miss Mary! Ya'll come on up. We ain't seen you in a while now. Have a seat." Janie shooed a cat and a chicken off the porch and indicated chairs.

Mary went first, leading the way onto the porch with its railings made from bare saplings, worn smooth and polished by many hands. She leaned against one and said, "Janie, this is a close friend of mine, Sammie Stewart from Texas."

Janie's ever-present smile grew wider in welcome. "Pleased to meet you. Ya'll got a nice day for a drive, but that car's gonna get full of road dust with the top down like that."

"That's all right. It'll wash off. This sure is a pretty place you have here. I bet you can hear the fish jumping," Sammie said.

Janie laughed. "Not with the eternal racket when I'm watching my grandbabies."

"I suppose they're all gone, since it's so quiet right now," Mary said.

"They all gone looking for plums and blackberries. I told 'em it was too early, but they got the rambles."

Sammie sat down in a rocking chair. "I guess that's what we're doing too. Mary's showing me the sights."

"Didn't know we had any around here. Could I get you ladies something cold to drink?"

"No thank you. This sure is a beautiful part of the country."

Mary felt tears trying to form. "Yes, it is, isn't it?" Sammie glanced at her, but showed no alarm.

"Miss Janie, I have a strange urge to pull up a bucket of water from your well. May I?"

Janie got up. "You sure can. Come on."

They left Mary sitting there, fighting tears, and walked over to the well. Janie stood and watched while Sammie let the bucket down, stopping its progress to peer into the well, trying to see the water level. Finally she began hauling on the rope and pulled up a dripping, half-filled pail. Janie took it and guided it to sit on the well. She produced a tin dipper and Sammie tasted the water, grinning. Then she carried it inside for Janie, as naturally as if she had been in their house a thousand times. Mary heard their voices from the kitchen.

She shouldn't be surprised. Sammie made herself at home wherever she was. As for herself, she couldn't find a purpose in what she was doing, taking a tour around Myrtlewood to all the places that meant something to her, couldn't begin to understand why she felt a compulsion to do this. Maybe it was a factor of aging, this inexplicable rush of undefined feelings that washed through her. She tried to compose herself, to regain control, but it felt like something was spinning out of her reach. She should get up and join them, her two friends, but something kept her frozen where she was, looking out across the sleepy, wide river with watery eyes.

Sammie emerged with a jar of strawberry and fig preserves in her hand, and she and Janie were laughing.

"Mary, Janie said you could make biscuits as well as she can to go with these figs."

Mary stood, the spell somehow broken. "Maybe not quite as good as Janie's, but she taught me. She cooks on a wood stove. That makes the difference, I think." She turned to their hostess. "Thank you for letting us interrupt your day. I imagine you don't get many quiet times like this. We'll let you get back to what you were doing."

"Wasn't no interruption. Ya'll stop by any time. You always welcome, Miss Mary."

Janie stood on the porch and waved as they turned around and headed back to the highway. Sammie was trying to open the jar of preserves. "Damn, this lid is really sealed good." She gave up.

"Are you hungry? We could go back to the house and fix dinner."

"No, let's keep going. What else do you have to show me?"

Mary kept driving, enjoying the way the Thunderbird handled, even enjoying her hair whipping into her face. They wound up at Bladon Springs, the smelly sulphur water keeping them leaning against the car, as they both lit up cigarettes.

Sammie grinned. "This has been fun, but you haven't really talked about much."

Mary shrugged. "You know the important points. Tommie's gone, we sold the mill, I'm living in the house. That's about all our story."

"You've barely mentioned Lila's name. Are you two getting along all right?"

Mary looked at Sammie, meeting her eyes. "Of course we are. You know, I brought Lila here once, or rather, she brought me, when I was teaching her how to drive." She recalled that day, Lila's hair blowing the wind, her grinning face, eager and delighted.

"I bet she caught on really quick."

Mary smiled. "Yes, like everything else. Lila's smart, a fast learner."

Sammie took a deep breath. "What's it really like, living together?"

Mary studied Sammie's face. "Why are you so curious?"

"Because I've gone and got myself a girlfriend. I just don't know what the next step is. Never tried this dance."

Mary smiled and hugged Sammie. "What do you know? Sammie Stewart, settling down. I knew you could do it."

Sammie held up her hands. "Hold your horses. We haven't really talked about it yet. I don't know how in the world it will work out."

Mary had never seen Sammie so unsure and hesitant. "Who is she? How long have you known her?"

The smile on Sammie's face was a wonderful thing to see. "Her name is Gail, and she's an attorney in Houston, and we met—that's another story. Have you heard of Alcoholics Anonymous?" Mary shook

262

her head. "Neither had I, but Gail had. I met her in a bar, of course. She was there to celebrate winning a case. I was doing what I always do, drinking, checking out the women."

Sammie stopped talking and looked up into the pines. "We had fun that first night, Gail was pretty drunk. I went home with her. But after that, she straightened me out. She's dedicated to her career, very serious about her work, like you. And she talked to me. She said she liked me a lot, and fun is fun, but that my drinking was going to keep us apart. She absolutely put her foot down. She found out all about AA, gave me the brochures, took me to the first meeting, and then she left me. She said I could have her, or I could keep on drinking, but I couldn't have both."

"Sammie, I always knew you could and would stop when something came along that was worth it."

"Yeah, well, it was more than that. I went to a lot of meetings and faced up to some pretty awful things I did. I have to believe it was more than just winning a woman." She cleared her throat. "Anyway, one of the steps is to make amends where you can, apologies where you can't. That's one of the reasons I came to see you."

She turned to Mary, eyes glistening. "I'm sorry for all the stupid pranks I pulled. Sorry I cost you your job. You and I, we could have had something, if I hadn't been so wild."

Mary took Sammie's hand. "You don't owe me any apologies. I'm just happy for you."

Sammie shook off her emotion. "I do owe you something though. An ass-kicking, maybe. Why don't you talk to me about Lila? Remember when I met you at the beach, and you couldn't stop talking about her, how much you wanted her, how impossible it was? Every time I bring up her name, you change the subject. That tells me you've done something wrong, if you can't see that you have everything you always thought you'd never have."

Mary exploded. "God damn it, why does every conversation I have always come back to this? 'Mary's too hard, Mary needs to show more emotion, Mary needs help with her homework on acting like a human being.'"

Sammie put up her hands. "Slow down. I didn't say any of those things. I guess somebody did, though."

"Lila is always poking and prodding and trying to get me to go where I don't want to go. She says I'm too cautious, too protective, too controlling and bossy, no, 'dictatorial.' That's what she calls me."

Sammie laughed, that throaty low laugh Mary remembered so well. "Hell, honey, she's right. You are bossy and controlling. You think you're always right about everything. Most of the time, you *are* right. That doesn't mean people like to be told what to do. Take it from an expert at rebellion, that's the best way to lose someone."

Mary was livid. "Didn't you hear what she's trying to do? Move Annie into a house right smack in the middle of town. Doesn't she know what that will do? I declare, ever since Tommie died, Lila has been on a mission to see how much trouble she can cause. Donating gobs of money to the NAACP, to the Southern Christian Leadership Conference, all very publicly, by the way. She's just daring those rabid idiots in white sheets to come after us."

"Looks like she learned everything you taught her too well. Thinking for herself, making decisions, backing up what she thinks with cold cash. You're a very good teacher, Mary. It's too late now to wish she wasn't so smart."

Mary was yelling now. "I certainly didn't teach her this! Lila has no idea, none at all, about how ugly and dangerous these people can be. She's too—"

"Too what? Too good? Too simple? You've always idealized her, like some fairy princess. She's a grown woman with a mind of her own, a damn good one, and you treat her just like a child." Sammie lit another cigarette, as calmly as if they were discussing the weather. "You know who you sound like? Big Sam, that's who. Always dictating to me exactly what I was to do, what I was to wear, whom I should be seeing, every little thing, until I couldn't take it any more."

"Don't you dare compare me with that man! I'm not trying to control Lila, I'm trying to save her neck. Lila is too innocent to fully understand the violence, the ugliness. She believes that the people she grew up with, the people she's known all her life, would never turn on her. She believes all that non-violent, passive hogwash, that marching and confronting your oppressors will win."

Mary sobbed and reached out a hand to warn Sammie not to touch her. "I know what acting on feelings and impulse can cost. I—" she was too choked to continue. Her tears fell, huge drops, making tiny warm splashes on her hands.

"It's okay, honey. Let it out. You've been walking around scared to death for so long." Brushing aside Mary's attempt to pull away, Sammie wrapped her arms around her and held on while Mary cried.

And Mary couldn't stop. It came pouring out, in huge great sobs, in shudders and sounds that keened in her own ears like a wounded animal, all of her fear, the worry and strain, it came in streams of tears that seemed never-ending, as she tried to catch her breath, tried to stop, and then started again, when some new thing pushed into her head. Mary cried for things she hadn't known she wanted, things she wished she didn't want, all the things she had never once allowed herself to cry about. Sammie held her.

Every time she tried to speak, her voice came out in broken hitches. "They beat people up. It doesn't make sense. Why do they do that?"

Mary saw again the picture she would never forget, the one of Emmett Till lying in his casket, his face misshapen and unrecognizable. She felt her nose crunch when her father had beaten her, heard again those sounds, the horrible sounds of that day. "He was just a boy! And I was only sixteen years old. They broke my ribs, they broke me." And she leaned over, unable to stand up any longer. Sammie held onto her while she heaved.

Sammie gave her a handkerchief. Mary took it and tried to wipe her face. "They won't let them go to school, or live where they want. They come with burning crosses and torches and they drag them out in the night."

"Shh, it's okay. It's all right. Nobody's coming after you. You're safe, Mary."

Mary straightened up, still holding the handkerchief to her eyes. "No, we're not safe, don't you get it? All these violent things don't just happen to other people, they can happen to us. To Lila. And there's nothing I can do. Nothing will stop them."

"So it's safe to slap some paint on a shack and hold the mortgage for them, as long as you don't let them out of that cage, that *settlement* under the hill? Nobody crosses any lines, and we'll all be safe?"

Mary opened her eyes and looked at Sammie. "How did you know about that? Who told you I've been buying the property under the hill?"

Sammie said nothing, just looked at her.

"Lila called you. Didn't she? To talk some sense into me."

"You're close to ruining the best thing in your life. Lila's had enough of being treated like a little china doll. It's time you realized she is what you made her, a woman who thinks for herself."

Mary said coldly, "These people use dynamite and billy clubs and ropes and guns. They don't make any distinction between men and women and children. Anybody who steps across the line is in for that kind of trouble. They drug a fourteen-year-old boy out of his bed in the middle of the night, and his mother only had pieces of him to bury. You want something like that to happen to Lila?"

"Maybe Lila just wants Annie to be treated with the respect she's earned. She wants her to have her own place to live, a home. Not a room in somebody else's house."

"You and Lila had quite a talk."

"Yes, we did. She can't understand why it's all right for you to get involved and do the things you're doing, selling them land and houses, supporting the school, when all she wants is to help someone she knows and cares about to have something she never thought she could have. Kind of like you never believing you could have someone like Lila."

Sammie patted Mary on the back. "Lila thinks she needs to be involved. She doesn't see the distinction between all your efforts and what she wants to do. In for a penny, in for a pound. Oh, and whither thou goest. That's what Lila thinks."

Mary smiled. "She always has read her Bible rather literally. That just proves my point. You can't take that kind of blind faith in the goodness of people into this fight, because it will get destroyed. I don't want that for her. I'd rather she just go on believing in good and right and all the things I never have."

"Go on, light up. Maybe it will help you calm down." Sammie waited while Mary finally managed to light her cigarette with shaking hands. Staring up into the trees, she felt a shiver at the thought of Lila out there, openly supporting the marches and the sit-ins and pouring money into the groups that the FBI was watching.

"You can't chain her in the attic, you know. The only real way to protect her is to stand right beside her, every step of the way."

Mary carefully snuffed out her cigarette and put the butt in her pocket. She looked at Sammie. "You think I'm strong enough for that?"

"I think you're the strongest person I know."

"Let's go see what's for dinner."

Chapter Twenty

REPORT TO THE GRAND DRAGON: Sent some men to Selma. We know how to handle our own business down here. Our niggers don't act up. It's them white women tryin' to run things that's got to be stopped. Attendance: 34

Sunday, March 7, 1965

The phone ringing downstairs woke Mary. She looked at the clock. Two a.m. She slid out of bed just as Lila stirred. "What is it?"

"Nothing. Go back to sleep," she whispered.

Mary answered the phone in the hall, her heart racing. "Hello?"

"Miss Mary, there's some cars outside, just parked on the street," Annie said.

Oh my God. "Are they doing anything, or just sitting in the cars?"

"Nome, just sitting there right now. One of 'em must have thrown something against the side of the house, that's what woke me up. I didn't go outside to see."

"No, don't do that. I'll call the sheriff. Just make sure all the doors are locked."

"They just watching me."

"I'll be right there." Heart pounding in her chest, Mary hung up without giving Annie a chance to protest. After a hurried and whispered call to the sheriff, she slipped into her clothes in the dark—slacks and a shirt rummaged from the dirty clothes hamper in the bathroom. She put on penny loafers, not wasting time searching for socks, and ran on tiptoe down the hall. She stopped half-way down the stairs. Turning, she went back into the bedroom.

"Lila, it's Annie. Come on, hurry."

"Oh, no! Mary—"

"Just hurry, I already called the sheriff." Lila pulled on a sweater over her nightgown and followed Mary down the stairs. Flinging open the front door, they ran the three blocks, Lila outdistancing her even in her bare feet. Mary's heart pounded as she tried to catch up. The streets were eerily silent and deserted in the middle of the night.

"Lila, wait!"

There were four cars parked on the street with muddy fenders and sidewalls.

Lila pounded her fist on the trunk of the first car, startling the occupants, who sat upright and glanced behind them. One man stepped out of the passenger side. He was tall, unshaven, slightly swaying, dressed in brogans, khakis, and a dark felt hat that had seen better days.

"Well, now, what we got here? Late for one of your walks, ain't it? You come to see about your nigger woman?"

Mary moved toward the man, anger and disgust melting the ball of fear in her stomach, and spoke slowly. "What the hell do you think you're doing here, disturbing an old lady's sleep? Someone you don't even know?"

"Looks like we ain't doin' nothing but minding our own business. Maybe you ought to do the same, 'stead of setting up this colored woman *friend* of yours in town like she was good as anybody else."

Mary stood looking the man right in the eyes, her height matching his. She put her hands on her hips. "She's much better than the examples I see right now. This is my property. That woman is my friend. And if you don't get out of here, I'll have a warrant sworn out on you and your friends. Does it really take this many grown men to terrorize one woman, sound asleep in her bed?"

"You men ought to be ashamed of yourselves, harassing a person you don't even know. You are disgusting. And none of you are from around here. Why don't you go back home and leave her alone?" Lila said.

Paul Dunagan pulled up in his truck. He hung his arm out the window casually. "Hey, Miss McGhee, Lila. Nice night. Hey, Barry. You pretty far afield, looks like. These men bothering you?" The sheriff's hair was mussed, as if he had just crawled out of bed.

"Yes, these men *are* bothering me and Annie. They threw something against the house and woke her up. I'd like to see them

269

arrested for disturbing the peace," Mary said, trying to hide the relief she felt.

The stranger sneered. "You the only one disturbin' things, putting that nigger woman in a house right here on Main Street, hiring niggers to do white men's work, layin' up in that house with this little woman."

Lila's face changed into something horrible to see. She almost spit at the man, and as she took a step closer, Mary grabbed her arm. Lila, her voice deadly serious, said, "That woman is a better person and a better Christian than all of you sorry specimens of humanity. You ought to be locked up until you sober up."

Dunagan eased out of his truck, leaving the door open. He stepped up very close to the man, in the process using his bulk to shoulder Mary and Lila out of the way. "It might be best if you and your bunch just head on back across the river where you came from. Folks in Myrtlewood can handle their own business without any help from ya'll. Miss Mary's got her own ways, and she don't bother nobody else. Miss Annie, the lady that's inside this house, came and helped my wife when she had the twins. I don't know what we'd have done without her. She's helped just about everybody else in this town, and we think pretty highly of her around here." He rested his hand on his gun belt, hastily flung on over his pajama top. "Fact is, we all kind of look out for her, a widow woman all alone like she is. You might come by sometime, throwin' stuff at her, yellin' them ugly remarks, and I could be settin' up in there myself, havin' tea." He spat on the ground. "I think it's best you just take your buddies and move along." His gaze on the man was pitiless.

Tires squealed as they all pulled away. Mary watched them go, still holding Lila's arm, but for reassurance now instead of restraint. They looked at each other. When she turned to offer her thanks, she found she was shaking. The sheriff just grinned.

"We best move along, too. I reckon Annie's gettin' tired of holding that shotgun by now."

Mary turned to look at the dark house. "Annie has a gun?"

"Yep. I imagine she's had us covered the whole time."

Mary laughed, a shaky, nervous laugh, incredulous, but at least she wasn't blubbering with fear. "What if they had done something more, tried to break in, set the place on fire?"

Lila said shakily, "Don't even suggest something like that." She peered at the dark windows.

"I don't think that crowd would go quite that far. The ones around here know better. They'd have to get an okay."

"You mean from the Klan?"

Paul shrugged. "If this was a Klan thing, they'd have come all dressed up in their outfits, hoods and all. This was just a few boys out too late drinking who couldn't think up anything better to do."

Mary looked up at Dunagan's kind face, still wrinkled from sleep. "Thank you. You think this was a bad idea too, don't you? Moving Annie in here."

"It's done. People got a right to sleep in peace at night. You go on home now."

They walked home in silence, side by side. Mary eased the front door closed, and they went upstairs, undressing in the dark, and slid into bed to cling together.

Lila and Annie made it sound so easy. But Mary saw the ugly, twisted faces that stared at her from the television and the newspapers melt into the faces of the men who had calmly set out to destroy Annie's simple, basic dream. She shivered and hugged Lila closer. Lila rubbed her back like she was soothing a child from a bad dream.

"Ten pounds of shrimp and four slabs of ribs is a lot of meat for two single ladies. What ya'll goan do with all that food?" The grocery store cashier was someone Mary didn't know.

"We're having a barbecue for some friends."

"I heard about that." The girl worked the cash register, a knowing smirk on her face, refusing to meet Mary's eyes. She was a newcomer to town who had probably heard all the rumors about her and Lila and Annie, no doubt in greatly exaggerated form.

"Well, you have a nice day now." Mary waved off the assistance from the bag boy, Clyde Moseley's youngest. "I can load the car all right, Johnny. How's your daddy doing?"

"He's doin' fine."

"You and he still do some building on the side, don't you?"

271

The skinny, freckled boy shrugged nervously. "Yes'm, when we can."

She looked at him for a moment. "The back porch at Miss Louise's house is rotting on its foundation. Would you and your daddy be interested in replacing the porch and screening it in for me?"

The boy rubbed sweaty palms against his jeans, leaving marks. "Yes, ma'am, I'll ask him tonight."

"I'd want to make the new porch bigger. Run it the entire length of the house. Could you do that? And the house needs a new roof."

Johnny looked even more nervous. "That's a big job. You'd have to talk to my daddy yourself about all of that."

"I'll do that. We're having a barbecue at the house this evening. Why don't all of you drop by and get something to eat? Then we could tell your daddy in more detail about what we want done to the place. And we could walk over and look at it, after you eat."

"Yes ma'am, I'll tell him that. Maybe you should call my mama though."

"I will, as soon as I get home. Bye now."

As she loaded the bags into the trunk of the Buick, she glanced through the plate glass window of the Piggly Wiggly, saw the cashier talking to Johnny, and smiled to herself. There would be no need to call Doris Moseley. Before she got home, it would be all over town that she had invited the Moseleys to a party for the black woman who was their maid and now lived in town. She knew they wouldn't come, but there was a chance that Clyde Moseley wouldn't refuse the work she had offered. Clyde needed the work.

That afternoon, Lila was relaxed, mostly because Sheriff Dunagan had decided to drop by and say hello to Annie and have a plate of food. He said it was because of Annie's biscuits. The town was strangely quiet. No one drove by, as Mary had suspected they would. Lila was happier than she had been in a long time. Mary sat with Sonny and Ben, talking to them about music. Dr. Morgan sat at the table, never one to miss a free meal. Henry was there with his new wife. Thad and Janie had ensconced themselves next to the barbecue grills. Both were remarkable in their energy, which belied their age. Lila sat beside Annie, the guest of honor. Even her daughter Susie had come from Atlanta. She sat apart with her husband and their children, who were wide-eyed at all the food and the number of white people intermingled with them. Lila nodded toward them.

"Have they eaten yet? Should I go offer to help the kids fix their plates?"

Annie raised her voice. "Susie, you gonna feed them children? You goan fix their plates or you want me to?"

Susie reluctantly got up and took her little girl by the hand, leading her to the table, which was loaded with baskets of corn on the cob, piles of boiled shrimp, baked beans, ribs, mounds of Lila's famous potato salad, coleslaw, fried catfish (Annie's favorite), pans of corn-bread and biscuits, big bowls of peas and butter beans, pitchers of tea and lemonade, and three cakes. For the grown-ups, there was Schlitz and Pabst Blue Ribbon iced down in a big washtub.

You think I should go help her?" Lila asked.

"Better you than me, I guess."

Lila noted the hurt in Annie's voice. She walked over and got another Chinette plate and asked the boy clinging to his mother's skirt, "What do you like best, ribs or shrimp, or some of your grand-mama's catfish?"

He looked up at her. Silently he pointed to the shrimp. She obligingly piled some on the plate and asked, "You want corn on the cob?" A nod. "Baked beans? How about a big piece of this chocolate cake before it's gone?" The nods became more vigorous. "All right. Now, you want tea or lemonade?"

"Lemonade, please." She handed him the overloaded plate and said, "I'll carry your drink until you find a place to sit. How about on that bench under the tree?" He headed that way and she followed. She rejoined Annie just as Mary walked over.

Annie patted the chair on her other side. "Did Sonny convince you to visit him in Chicago? He really wants Miss Lila to see him play at his own club up there."

"He almost did. It would be fun."

Lila looked at her skeptically. "We'd go all the way to Chicago? I can't believe you'd agree to be gone that long from home."

Mary looked around at the crowd of people in their back yard before she answered, and Lila followed her gaze. Ben was now talking

273

to the sheriff, who was nodding as he chewed. Sonny was showing his nephew how to peel shrimp, under Susie's disapproving eye. Dr. Morgan was still at the buffet table and constantly refilled his plate. There was a cool breeze, and the mosquitoes had taken a vacation.

"A road trip might be fun. We could stop whenever we wanted and take our time. I grew up in a little town in northwestern Illinois, but I've never been to Chicago. Sonny says they have the best music and the best food in the world."

Lila looked at her in amazement and was about to reply when she heard the phone ring. Annie started to get up.

"You sit down, Annie. I'll get it." Lila skipped up the porch steps and returned quickly. "Ben, it's for you. There's some trouble in Selma."

"I been worried about Selma. I was thankful this party was today so Ben couldn't be there," Annie said.

Ben walked slowly down the steps. "It sounds pretty bad. They had billy clubs, tear gas, and they just started beating everyone. No one knows how many are hurt yet. Sounds like Dr. King is going to come down and lead another march. They didn't know when—"

Ben was cut off by a loud crash of breaking glass from the front of the house. Mary ran, right on Sheriff Dunagan's heels. He still had his plate of food in one hand, the other on the gun on his hip. Lila followed with Ben and Sonny right behind her. She came to an abrupt halt when she turned the corner of the house. Mary and the sheriff stood facing a crowd of eight or ten men in hooded white robes. A cross about six feet tall was burning on the front lawn. The grass next to the porch was on fire. The sheriff's plate of food was splattered all over the ground where he had dropped it. Mary was screaming.

"I know every one of you morons! You're a bunch of cowards, hiding underneath bed sheets. You can tell Gerald Buchanan that he can meet me face-to-face. He doesn't need to send a posse. Why any of you would listen to a pig-headed idiot like him is beyond me, but you tell him to come see me. That self-righteous, self-important bigot can go fuck himself! Now get off this property right now!"

"This ain't your property, now is it?" one of the hooded men answered.

Sheriff Dunagan put a restraining hand on Mary's arm, which she angrily shook off. She took a step nearer the Klansmen. "It's for damn sure not your property. And who we invite to eat with us is no one's business, certainly not yours. Now get out of here. Every one of you knows Annie Parnell. She's brought food to your homes when there was sickness and attended when your wives had their babies! You know her!"

Lila watched in frozen horror as Mary advanced yet again, her lean form rigid with anger, her voice shrill with it. "I probably sold you the two by fours for that cross, you damn fools! Now get the hell away from here before I set some of those robes on fire."

At this pronouncement, the sheriff put an arm around Mary's waist and lifted her off the ground.

"You men go on about your business now. You've done what you came for. Get out of here before I start arresting you. You'll all sit in jail for a while if I do. The judge has gone on vacation. Now move along before I take down license plate numbers and call out some deputies."

But no one seemed to be paying attention to him. "I've had all I can take from you people. You're all a bunch of ignorant hypocrites and cowards! What the hell are you so afraid of?" Mary screamed.

The men turned and headed for their vehicles that lined the street. From a safe distance, one of them turned and pointed. "The white men of the South will handle their own problems in their own way. Outside agitators will be punished and sent back where they came from. Those that try to upset the natural order will suffer consequences. This is a white nation, built by white men—"

"Oh, get in your truck, Vince Dunn, and shut up." Sheriff Dunagan took a step toward the man, dragging Mary with him. The cars started up one by one and pulled away, and everyone watched them go. After they turned the corner, Paul started stomping out the fire in the grass. Sonny turned on the water hose curled by the porch and sprayed everything down. When he was satisfied that the fire was out, he kicked down the blackened cross. Slowly the others turned and headed back around the house.

"Come on, Mary, it's over now." The sheriff spoke quietly as she stood trembling, soaked to the knees from the spray of the hose, her slacks splotched with wet ashes.

"Mary, come on now. It's okay," Lila said. Mary turned to her, but couldn't comprehend. Vince Dunn, the man she had leaned on, depended on, trusted, the man who had taught her about the mill and worked so hard with her to make it a success—what was he doing with those cretins? Staring open-mouthed at Lila, she saw tears in her eyes.

"Honey, let's go now." Lila touched Mary's arm, but Mary shook her off and stepped away, bending over. Waves of nausea rolled through her, but nothing came up. She felt Lila's hand on her back.

Hands on her hips, still bent over, Mary silently shook her head. Lila turned away. She had to get back to their guests. Mary couldn't focus. Vince Dunn had been Mary's right-hand man at the mill. How had he fooled them into trusting him?

When Mary returned to the back yard, everyone was silent and subdued. Dr. Morgan still sat at the picnic table, but had stopped eating. Lila's face was white with strain. She looked calm, though shaken. Everyone else was frozen while they waited. Mary felt out of breath and spooked, like a wild horse, nervous and unsettled, ready to run at the slightest noise.

Lila made a general pronouncement. "They threw a Coke bottle filled with gas at the porch, but it shattered against the steps. Sonny got the fire put out. The sheriff took off in his truck after them."

"Clyde Moseley's boy was driving one of the cars," Mary said.

Lila sat down abruptly. "You mean Johnny?"

"Yes, little Johnny, who used to come to the back door and beg cookies from you and Annie."

Mary's eyes blazed with anger, and she was trembling with rage. Susie was dumping plates into the fifty-five-gallon drum used for garbage and calling her children to get in the car, parked in the back driveway. They left without turning on their headlights. Everyone watched them go. Susie's frightened face was grim with an I-told-you-so anger. Dr. Morgan got up and stood beside Mary.

"You need to sit down," he pronounced. Gently pushing her into a chair, he pulled a bottle out of his hip pocket and poured some whiskey into his lemonade. "Here, drink this. It won't help, but it won't hurt you any." He handed the drink to Mary.

Ben stood next to Annie, and he nodded at Sonny to come over. "I

276

think we should leave, don't you?" he asked Sonny in a lowered voice.

Annie looked up. "Leave and go where?" Her chin quivered.

"There's no need to go anywhere. You haven't finished eating yet," said Lila.

Mary took a sip of the doctor's drink and handed it back to him. When would Lila wake up and see that her neighbors and friends weren't safe, that some of them weren't to be trusted, and that they were in danger? She got up and went into the house without a word.

Lila watched Mary climb the steps, resisting the urge to follow.

Ben nervously cleared his throat. "I think it might be best if Sonny and Annie went back to Atlanta with me. I'd worry if I left them alone in that house tonight, I really would."

Lila looked at him. "I don't like having you chased off by a bunch of drunks hiding their faces and—doing what they did. I'll talk to Johnny myself. He's not that kind of boy."

"Maybe he's not, but whoever was with him was. That kind is what we got around here. Maybe it would be best if we left now," Annie said.

Lila hugged Annie and watched as everyone except Dr. Morgan departed. They walked inside together to begin the enormous task of cleaning up. "Is there anything I can do? Will Mary be all right?"

Lila shrugged. "I don't know. She barely sleeps any more, always on guard, waiting for something like this to happen. They could have burned this house down. Funny, but I hadn't realized that for a long time now I've thought of this place as our home, no longer the Dubose house. They attacked our home."

Dr. Morgan patted her awkwardly on the back. "Maybe some time away from here would do you both good. Why not take Sonny up on his offer? Why not go for a visit and get away from all this for a while?"

The house shook from an enormous blast. "What was that?"

"It sounded like a shotgun to me," said Dr. Morgan.

Mary came running down the stairs, the gun clutched to her chest. "It's Miss Louise's, Annie's house. I shot at them from the upstairs porch. Come on!"

As she flung open the front door and headed down the street at a run, Lila called after her, "Wait! What's happening?" She turned to the doctor. "You better stay here, call the sheriff's office. Tell him—tell him Mary's got a gun and she's mad."

Then she ran after her. As soon as she left the front porch, Lila could see it—an orange blaze that lit up the sky. Miss Louise's house was on fire. She ran toward Mary's figure in the distance.

Lila caught up to her on the sidewalk, clutching her arm as Mary shakily tried to extract the spent shell and reload. "Mary, what are you doing? Who are you shooting at?"

"Them, the bastards in white sheets! I saw them from the upstairs window. They were throwing gasoline in the windows. That fucking traitor, Vince Dunn. They did this."

She pulled the gun from Mary's grasp. "Let me do that. You're shaking. Probably couldn't hit the side of a barn anyway. Where did you get a gun, for heaven's sake?"

"Annie gave it to me."

Lila inserted the shell and closed the weapon, holding it over her arm like she was going hunting. "Well, you couldn't hit anything from three blocks away with this thing, thank God. You definitely scared them off, though."

Three men in smudged white robes appeared from the back yard of Miss Louise's, their conical hoods misshapen and tilted. Staying well away from the flames, they advanced on the women. Mary grabbed the gun from Lila and pointed it at them. "You stop right where you are. Don't think I won't shoot."

"The sheriff's out chasing a bunch of cars down a long dirt road. He won't be back in time to rescue you again. It's time somebody put you in your place. We've had enough of your interference around here in things that don't concern you. It's time we showed you the consequences of your meddling ways."

The roof collapsed, and a whoosh of smoke and sparks and ashes blew toward them; the Klansman who had spoken jumped, afraid of catching on fire. Mary's finger jerked on the trigger; the noise deafened them all. Mary dropped the gun and ran toward the other men, and one of them grabbed her. Terrified, Lila scooped up the gun; she watched as the man dragged Mary toward the burning house, bellowing, "I'll burn you up like a witch at the stake for being unnatural on my own kin! Let the flames eat the sins and the sinner!"

Lila screamed, "No! Stop, just stop it!" She grabbed Mary from behind, but couldn't free her from the stronger man's grasp. She held the empty gun by the barrel and struck the man over the head as hard as she could. He crumpled to the ground, out cold, and as his hood fell away, she barely registered that it was her brother Jimmy. The third man ran off, and so they stood there, Lila restraining Mary from trying to get any closer, helpless to do anything but watch the flames increase. Writhing on the ground in a tangled, dirty robe, Vince Dunn lay bleeding from the birdshot in his shoulder, the red against the dirty white of the robe creating a tableau of sickening incongruity. Mary and Lila stared, still unable to believe it was a man they had always considered a friend.

Dr. Morgan arrived with his black bag and began examining the two injured men. He made Lila apply pressure to the gunshot wound, which seemed confined to the meaty part of Vince's shoulder, while he peered into the eyes of Jimmy Jackson, still unconscious. Just as Jimmy came round, sitting up slowly, a trickle of blood running down his face from his scalp, Paul Dunagan drove up in his truck and stepped out to survey the scene, hands on his hips.

"What we got here, Doc?"

Dr. Morgan finished applying a bandage to Jimmy's head and stood, straightening his back. "We got two women in shock. Two men down, one shot with what looks like birdshot in the shoulder, one cracked on the head. He'll need some stitches. Both'll be fine. Probably deserved worse than they got."

"Who's the shooter?"

Dr. Morgan shrugged. Mary answered, "I am," sounding as though she were proud of almost killing someone.

On her knees, still pressing a bandage that was slowly becoming wet with blood, Lila said, "These men, and one other who got away, were advancing, threatening us. Mary fired in self-defense. When this man grabbed her and tried to drag her toward the burning house, I hit him with the stock of the gun." She couldn't bring herself to say their names, nor to look at either man. It just wouldn't sink in, the fact that her own brother and a man who had worked for them for so many years had—

Lila moved away and stood as Dr. Morgan knelt to take her place.

Her hands were covered with blood. Looking down at Vince's face for the first time, she registered how pale he was. He groaned and rolled onto his side to throw up.

Finally Myrtlewood's lone fire truck came screeching up under a wailing siren. They moved across the street, and watched the useless efforts of the volunteer firemen as they did what they could to contain the fire. They stood for a long time, watching Miss Louise's house burn down to ashes. Jimmy Jackson and Vince Dunn were loaded together into the ambulance and hauled away to the emergency room. Mary and Lila finally left, persuaded to follow Paul Dunagan to his office and give statements. Lila looked back one last time. Miss Louise's cannas and wisteria were destroyed, trampled or burned. The place was just gone.

It was a long night, and morning had come before they returned home to the big house, its front yard a soggy, blackened mess, the scattered remains of the abandoned party left strewn about in the back yard, though Dr. Morgan had made some headway in the kitchen. He rose silently to make coffee when they walked in. Mary hadn't spoken a word on the short drive home from the sheriff's office, and neither had Lila. They sat now, wearily leaning toward each other, soot and blood and grime on their ruined clothes proof that the night they had lived through was not a dream.

"Coffee's making. You two need a shower and some clean clothes. I'll have breakfast ready when you come down. Hop to it. Then you can go to bed and get some rest."

Mary turned haunted, uncomprehending eyes to him. The doctor just looked back at her. "Get moving."

They stood and left the kitchen like children in dread of a scolding, which they probably deserved, Mary thought, as they trudged up stairs. Lila didn't make it to the bathroom, collapsing on the bed, so Mary pulled the covers over her and let her sleep. She felt better, a little more clear-headed, after a bath. She re-entered the kitchen to find Dr. Morgan watching avidly as bacon popped and sizzled in a skillet. He had eggs going in another.

"Do you ever rest, or for that matter, do you ever go home at all?" She sank into a chair opposite him.

He just grinned. "Here's where the food is."

"How can someone so small eat so much and so often?"

His grin disappeared. "I was on Bataan. I don't think I'll ever get enough food in me to forget it."

"I didn't know that."

"It was a horrible thing, being a doctor who could help no one, not even myself. I watched lots of men die from hunger and dysentery. I imagine all of us who made it through eat like termites, anything and everything we can get our hands on."

He set plates on the table, and then sat down with his own.

"It's been a long time since I've stayed up all night," said Mary, "I forgot the kind of dreary clarity that comes over you the morning after, like a motor that can't be turned off."

"It's adrenalin, and it'll wear off. The food will make you sleepy." Dr. Morgan dug into his breakfast.

Mary raised her cup with both hands to take a sip. "I can't really begin to believe everything that's happened. It feels like a nightmare."

"Those bruises are real enough. So is the birdshot I picked out of Vince Dunn's shoulder."

Mary felt nauseated. "I still can't believe that Vince, of all people … I worked with the man, depended on his skill and judgment, considered him a friend. Why on earth would he have done this? Who was the other one?"

Dr. Morgan glanced up as Lila came stumbling in, as though sleep-walking, still in her dirty, smudged clothes with blood on them. Guiding Lila into a chair, he said, "You need to sit down and eat."

Lila spoke as if still asleep, dreaming. "Vince was the leader. I saw a cross embroidered on his robe when I was trying to stop the bleeding. Buchanan was the third one—the one who ran away."

Dr. Morgan laughed.

"What? Are you sure?" Mary couldn't believe it. "I always thought Buchanan was pulling the strings but I never thought he would get his hands dirty. That son of a bitch."

Lila said, "I never believed you about Buchanan."

Dr. Morgan reached for the blackberry jam. "He's running for office. He had to do something to show he's not spineless. He was probably just trying to win the support of the Klan."

"Is that how you gain favor with the voting public?" said Mary. "Blow up an old woman's house, burn it down?"

"It was Jimmy who tried to drag you into the fire. He must be crazy. He could have killed you. My own brother. Why?" Lila sat there, pale, as if she were dreaming, unable to wake up.

Mary erupted in anger again. "Yes, your brother, who hates me, us, whom I fired more than once, who has always made accusations and threats and who was probably subsidized by Vince Dunn all along to cause us trouble, just like Bobby Riser, who tried to spit in my face, except his aim was off. Just like last night. Vince was obviously mad at me, but instead of coming here, they burned down the only home Annie ever had."

Dr. Morgan responded. "That little bastard. He's probably peeing down his leg right now. Mary, whether you believe it or not, there's people in this town that understand what you've done for it, for us, over the years."

"And what have they ever done for me, except talk about us, spread malicious gossip, speculate about whether I'm a conniving, larcenous, homosexual cheat who stole from the Duboses, from Miss Louise, from Big Sam, about everything I ever did for God's sake? I know what they call me: a nigger-loving, woman-loving Yankee outsider who has no business here at all."

Mary pushed her chair back and stood, the smell of food nauseating to her. Lila looked up at her. "Who cares what they think?" Mary continued. "So a handful of people are grateful. I ought to burn down this town, every brick and board of it. I ought to pack my bags and leave here right now before I go on a shooting rampage and put a bullet in Vince Dunn's head." She drew a breath. "I just don't give a shit any more. Whatever my motives were for getting involved, I can't see that anything's been accomplished at all." Tears stung her eyes. She shook Lila's hand off her arm.

"Some of us understand. One person can make a real difference. One person can change things." Lila spoke softly.

Mary laughed a harsh, nasty sound. "A difference? When a man I trusted and worked with could do this to us? When your own brother could try to kill me?" She couldn't stop. "They shot Medgar

Evers down like a dog in his own driveway. They blew up a church and killed four little girls, then turned dogs and hoses on the people who took to the streets in outrage." Mary choked back the bile that rose in her throat. "They burned down a house without knowing or caring whether Annie was inside. I watched them from upstairs. They didn't even check. These people will never change, never learn." She wiped tears from her face.

"Some people have sense enough to understand that what you were doing would help all of us," Lila told her. "It's not what I did with Dubose money, it's what you're doing with your hard work. One house at a time, one person at a time, you're effecting real change in this town you hate so much. I am changed, myself. All of us have been. Henry graduated from college. Look at what you did for Miss Louise, and for Annie. Just look around this town. When the schools do get integrated, those children will have a better chance because of all you did for them."

Mary hunched her shoulders; she was outraged to hear years of hard work listed as achievements, when it felt like wasted effort. She thought back to 1955, when the death of a young boy in Mississippi had caused her to sit on a porch by the river and contemplate leaving. Then 1956, that long year of the bus boycott and Tommie's dying, and all the arguments with Lila. The horrible events of 1963, when the murder of children and even the president seemed to prove that hatred had won.

And now, the next march to Montgomery surely meant more violence, more ugliness, another step backward. She had lost any real hope for permanent change. She had been marking time, waiting for the next awful thing, and now it had come.

"Go shoot somebody, burn this place down, take all your money and leave," Lila went on. "It won't change what you've done here. But there's plenty of people in this town who would help you continue what you've started."

Her hand gripped Mary's sleeve, and suddenly it reminded Mary of that morning so long ago when she had confessed her feelings to Lila. She turned toward the back porch, as if she could see their younger images there still. It had been hot then, so early in the morning, even as it was now. The inescapable heat of this place had once appealed to her. She caught the lingering smell of the burned house drifting in through the screen door.

"I don't see the point of continuing. All I've done is bring trouble."

Dr. Morgan, who had remained silent, now intervened. "So you just let the bigots win? Things got ugly, so you quit?"

"It's not that simple. It could be this house next time. Next time, they could be the ones with guns."

"I believe Paul will have most of them in jail by noon. He doesn't mess around. He's quite fond of you and Lila, in case you weren't aware."

"Really? Is he going to throw Gerald Buchanan in jail?" Mary asked.

"Maybe not, but Vince Dunn is already sitting in a cell," Lila said quietly.

"What jury of his peers would convict him of arson and attempted murder, when most people believe the stupid, interfering bitch had it coming to her?" Mary drew a ragged breath.

Dr. Morgan spoke again. "Some of them might prefer to see you in jail instead. You shot the man, after all. And some folks'll vote for Buchanan and some won't."

"He's the next mayor." Mary turned to the sink. "I just don't think I can stay here and watch him be rewarded like that for what he did."

Lila smiled. "I imagine there'll be finger-pointing, all right, and another round of lurid rumors, and whispered comments. Just like old times, right, Mary?"

Mary stared at her lover, who must have lost her mind. "Did you hear what I said?"

Lila raised an eyebrow. "Yes, I did. You always exaggerate the worst possibilities. I never listened to you before. If I had, we wouldn't be together now, would we? If you want to cut your losses and run, I'll go with you."

Mary stared at Lila. She looked into gray eyes she had no reason to believe could still show the spark that had drawn her in almost twenty years ago now. She saw again the same acceptance, the same challenge, the same appeal to her better nature, felt the same tug against her will, felt her resistance drain away, as it always had, and her anger slipped away too. This woman would always intrigue her, she knew. Nothing else really mattered. She couldn't walk away, couldn't destroy what they'd built. She took Lila into her arms.

"Cut our losses? We could do that. Go live at the beach year round and rail at everything we read in the papers about what's happening to other people. Or I suppose we could stay here and fight it out along this line, if it takes all summer."

As they stood, arms around each other, looking out the window over the back yard, Thad and Henry pulled up in the old truck, the trailer behind loaded with rakes and lawn mowers. They began cleaning up the mess from the night before. Dr. Morgan slipped out the back door to join them.

Clyde Moseley turned his truck into the driveway, his boy Johnny beside him, slumped down. Mary watched as his father dragged him by his arm toward the steep back steps, the forced apology about to be delivered making their faces solemn with determination.

Down the street, two cars full of black people from Annie's church pulled up at Miss Louise's house and began picking through the rubble that still smoldered.

Watching friends she hadn't realized she had, Mary said, "Maybe we should call Annie and Ben, see if they want to ride to Selma with us."

Bett Norris

Bett Norris was born and grew up in Alabama, a place that calls her back on occasion. She graduated from the University of Alabama with a degree in history, has taught school, worked in government, and now lives in Florida with her partner. She does indeed rise at 3 am every single day to write. She has no other skills or hobbies.

Bywater Books

DANCE IN THE KEY OF LOVE

Marianne K. Martin

"Marianne Martin is a wonderful storyteller and a graceful writer with a light, witty touch ..."
—Ann Bannon, author of the Beebo Brinker series

Paige Flemming is on the run. From the police, from her history, and from love itself. After sixteen years looking over her shoulder, she realizes it's time to run again. But when she pauses in her headlong flight to catch her breath with old friends, she crashes straight into another ghost from her past. And this time, it's not one she can easily escape.

In this long-awaited sequel to the best-selling lesbian romance *Dawn of the Dance*, Lambda Literary Award finalist Marianne K. Martin reminds us that there's no footwork fancy enough to dance out of the shadow of the past.

Paperback Original ◆ ISBN 1-932859-17-9 ◆ $13.95

Available at your local bookstore
or call toll-free 866-390-7426
or order online at www.bywaterbooks.com

Bywater Books

UNDER THE WITNESS TREE
Marianne K. Martin

"*Under the Witness Tree* is a multi-dimensional love story woven with rich themes of family and the search for roots. This is a novel of discovery that reaches into the deeply personal and well beyond—into our community and its emerging history. Marianne Martin achieves new heights with this lovingly researched and intelligent novel."

—*Katherine V. Forrest*

An aunt she didn't know existed leaves Dhari Weston with a plantation she knows she doesn't want.

Dhari's life is complicated enough without an antebellum albatross around her neck. Complicated enough without the beautiful Erin Hughes and her passion for historical houses, without Nessie Tinker, whose family breathed the smoke of General Sherman's march and who knows the secrets hidden in the ancient walls—secrets that could pull Dhari into their sway and into Erin's arms.

But Dhari's complicated life already includes a girlfriend she wants to commit to, a family who needs her to calm the chaos of her mother's turbulent moods and a job that takes the rest of her time.

The last thing she needs are Civil War secrets that won't lie easy and a woman with secrets of her own ...

Paperback Original ◆ ISBN 1-932859-00-4 ◆ $12.95

Available at your local bookstore
or to order call toll-free 866-390-7426
or order online at www.bywaterbooks.com

Bywater Books

HOSTAGE TO MURDER
A Lindsay Gordon Mystery

V. L. McDermid

"One of my favorite authors, Val McDermid is an important writer—witty, never sentimental, taking us through mean streets with the dexterity of a Chandler."   Sara Paretsky

Lindsay Gordon—investigative journalist, tenacious sleuth and unashamed lesbian—is facing a midlife crisis. Back in her native Scotland after a long absence, she has no job, no friends, and no desire to even think about her girlfriend's worrying preoccupations. A chance encounter with free-lance reporter Rory McLaren offers her an irresistible invitation to open a new chapter in her life. From there it is just a short step to political corruption and other juicy stories— all welcome distractions from Lindsay's problems at home. But when a local car dealer's stepson is kidnapped, Lindsay and Rory trade journalism for detection. The trail leads them to St. Petersburg and a dangerous snatch-back opera- tion that will test Lindsay to her absolute limits in every area of her life.

Paperback Original ◆ ISBN 1-932859-02-0 ◆ $12.95

Available at your local bookstore
or call toll-free 866-390-7426
or order online at www.bywaterbooks.com

Bywater Books

GREETINGS FROM JAMAICA, WISH YOU WERE QUEER

Mari SanGiovanni

*Warning: This book may make you
laugh out loud in public.*

Marie Santora has always known her Italian family is a little
crazy, but when she inherits her grandmother's estate, they
now have a million more reasons to act nuts.

Marie plans her escape. She'll give her family a parting
gift and then move to Hollywood to chase her dream of
writing film scripts. But with millions at stake, it will take
more than a free vacation to Jamaica to get the erratic
Santora family to toe the line. And the timing couldn't be
worse when her hot pursuit changes from screenplay to
foreplay.

Climb aboard this hilarious rollercoaster ride where
Marie is left wishing "out" was the new "in," and where
every lounge chair is a hot seat when the Santora family
ventures this close to the equator. The island of Jamaica
just may not be big enough …

Greetings from Jamaica *is a runner-up for the
first annual Bywater Prize for Fiction.*

Paperback Original ◆ ISBN 978-1-932859-30-0 ◆ $12.95

Available at your local bookstore
or call toll-free 866-390-7426
or order online at www.bywaterbooks.com